Neither Bond Nor Free

Other Books by the Author

Suffering and the Nature of Healing

Touch and the Healing of the World

Neither Bond Nor Free

A Novel

Daniel B. Hinshaw

RESOURCE *Publications* · Eugene, Oregon

NEITHER BOND NOR FREE
A Novel

Resource Publications
An Imprint of Wipf and Stock Publishers
199 W. 8th Ave., Suite 3
Eugene, OR 97401

www.wipfandstock.com

PAPERBACK ISBN: 978-1-5326-9992-4
HARDCOVER ISBN: 978-1-5326-9993-1
EBOOK ISBN: 978-1-5326-9994-8

Manufactured in the U.S.A. 11/14/19

With sincere hope for reconciliation and healing that will transcend the many estrangements that afflict our troubled nation, this book is dedicated to the memory of those extraordinary persons who, rising above every barrier imposed by race and prejudice in antebellum America, struggled in the cause of human dignity and freedom—the enslaved who courageously seized their liberty and those who assisted them, including my ancestors from among the Society of Friends. In remembering and honoring their fellowship of suffering, may we overcome our divisions and be united in the discovery of our common humanity.

... Woe to him who crushes the soul with chain and rod,
And herds with lower natures the awful form of God!

—John Greenleaf Whittier from *The Branded Hand*

For in a warm climate, no man will labour for himself who can make another labour for him. This is so true, that of the proprietors of slaves a very small proportion indeed are ever seen to labor. And can the liberties of a nation be thought secure when we have removed their only firm basis, a conviction in the minds of the people that these liberties are the gift of God? That they are not to be violated but with his wrath? Indeed, I tremble for my country when I reflect that God is just: that his justice cannot sleep forever ...

—Thomas Jefferson from *Notes on the State of Virginia*, Query XVIII

Knowledge unfits a child to be a slave.

—Frederick Douglass, *Life and Times of Frederick Douglass.*

The past is never dead. It's not even past.

—From *Requiem for a Nun*, Act I, Scene III, by William Faulkner

A few words must be offered by way of explanation to the modern reader for the story recounted here. The struggles and suffering of the antebellum period of American history continue to echo down the more than 150 years since the events described in this narrative to our own day, and in many ways still define us as Americans. It is important to note that the mind and spirit of antebellum America had a very different orientation from that of our current culture. Americans living in the first half of the nineteenth century were overwhelmingly a religious people and that religion was predominantly expressed in various forms of Protestant Christianity. High infant mortality rates coupled with frequent deaths due to epidemic illnesses made death an ever-present reality, especially for those struggling with the challenges and uncertainties of life in a frontier setting. Suffering and death were encountered and understood within this religious ethos.

Because the heart of the story related here involves the fate of enslaved Americans of African descent, it has been necessary to use colloquial expressions of the period that reflect the attitudes and common usage of the time that are recognized as degrading and unacceptable in our own time (e.g., the "N" word). It is not my intention to offend the modern reader but rather to as accurately as possible recreate the atmosphere, including the derogatory verbal environment that enslaved persons endured.

Finally, although the specific elements and several of the primary characters of this narrative are fictional, the background events setting the stage for their adventures and many of the supporting characters were real. For the interested reader, and for those who may doubt some of the more startling aspects of the narrative, I have provided some chapter notes at the end of the book that may provide additional references to those interested in delving deeper into the lives and times of the many heroes and heroines, both black and white, who suffered and often risked their lives for freedom.

Acknowledgments

In contemplating the origins of this book, I would like to express my deep gratitude and acknowledge my indebtedness to several individuals and institutions. Michael and Donna Kehoe were early readers of the manuscript who gave excellent feedback and much needed encouragement and direction to the project. Deborah Meadows of the African American Cultural and Historical Museum of Washtenaw County provided great inspiration through her fascinating tours of sites important to the activities of the Underground Railroad in Ann Arbor and Ypsilanti, Michigan. The passionate enthusiasm of the docents and staff of the Levi Coffin House in Fountain City, Indiana for the exciting roles played by antebellum citizens of Indiana in the Underground Railroad was infectious and served as an additional impetus to share the remarkable story of this community with modern readers. I am grateful for the knowledgeable assistance of the staff of the Bentley Historical Museum of the University of Michigan in making the antebellum University of Michigan Medical School doctoral theses stored on microfilm available for my review. Perhaps, the most compelling force catalyzing this project has been the opportunity to witness and learn from the deep spirituality manifested by so many of the African American patients that my wife Jane and I have had the privilege to know and serve during our medical careers. The profound character, wisdom, and authenticity that can be seen in the spirituality of many contemporary African Americans have retained the indelible marks of the patient endurance born out of the suffering of their enslaved ancestors. Finally, I am grateful for the patient encouragement and careful editorial eye of my wife Jane.

Part One

This peculiar institution is one for which there is no remedy, and so, as wise men we must all acquiesce. When we formed this country, we accepted each other for better or worse. The northern states adopted us with our slaves, and we adopted them with their Quakers.

—Henry Lee, a native Virginian

Silence filled the Quaker meeting house. It was a warm stillness that caressed like the touch of a mother's hand. A fly buzzed lazily back and forth between the boy and the window near his seat. A shaft of light penetrated the window and the shadows of leaves from a tree danced on the floor beside him. Something else partially obscured the vision of the dancing leaves. A fine lacy pattern was faintly superimposed on the motion of the leaf shadows. His eye was drawn to the window, and in one corner, attached to the windowsill, was a spider web that glistened as the light pierced it. The warmth of the sun flooding the room called him to a dreamy bliss.

Suddenly, an intense buzzing coming from the window broke the spell. The fly had become caught in the web and was struggling to free itself. As it flailed, the creator of the web appeared at the end opposite the fly. Isaac Burgess, whose silent meditation had been interrupted by the distress signal of the captive fly, now watched with horrified fascination as the spider approached its victim. With the embrace of the spider, the buzzing of the fly ceased, and the stillness of the place was restored. For one brief moment, the light coming through the window seemed to focus all its brilliance on illuminating the death throes of the small creature.

Isaac's attention was drawn away from this vision as an elderly man sitting near him struggled slowly to his feet. After removing his hat with a shaking hand, he brushed aside wisps from a long, snow-white beard that partially obscured his mouth and began to speak with a profound intensity.

"Friends," the man began, "'the light shineth in darkness; and the darkness comprehended it not.'"

After solemnly pronouncing these words, the old man surveyed the entire assembly with a deep, penetrating gaze as if to search out any darkness that might be present, and then with a pained expression on his face cautiously resumed his seat. The stillness of the silent meeting quickly returned and was audible, almost palpable, in the form of the slow, heavy breathing of some of his elders whose silent meditation might have taken on the form and appearance of sleep to the casual observer.

After what seemed to Isaac to be some significant portion of eternity, a dignified, middle-aged woman sitting on the front bench facing the meeting coughed, cleared her throat, and rose to speak. She was taller than average, thin, and with her excellent posture created an imposing appearance, not only for those attending meeting on that spring day in 1847 but especially for her students, including the nine-year-old Isaac. She was the teacher at the Friends School adjacent to the meetinghouse. Hannah Way was also one of the elders of the Newport Antislavery Friends' Meeting and had served in this capacity for several years. She was honored among Friends as a "Mother in Israel" for both her wisdom and calm, inspirational leadership that were manifested through her word and presence. She consciously strived to be a healing force in all her encounters and hoped her ministry would serve to complement the work of her husband, Henry Way, the local physician. Streaks of gray highlighted the blond hair that was exposed when she removed her bonnet to speak and faint wrinkles in her cheeks served to augment the smile that developed from her lips.

She cast a slow, thoughtful glance over her audience with her deep blue eyes that radiated warmth and said, "Dear Friends, with your permission I want to add to the reflection that has been emerging out of our silence this First Day regarding the light that shineth in the darkness. What can be said of this darkness in which the light shineth? Darkness takes many forms, but the ultimate effects of evil in this world come as suffering and death. We are surrounded by reminders of this harsh reality in our daily lives, especially as we witness the wounds inflicted by suffering in the faces and bodies of those seeking freedom from the oppression of slavery.

"But what is this light that the darkness comprehended not? John, the beloved disciple of our Lord, identified the light with life, specifically the life of Jesus Christ, the Word of God. In his first epistle, John clarifies the nature of this struggle between light and darkness: 'He that loveth his brother abideth in the light, and there is none occasion of stumbling in him. But he that hateth his brother is in darkness, and walketh in darkness, and knoweth not whither he goeth, because that darkness hath blinded his eyes.' To live in the light that is such a central doctrine of our Society means to have the Lord within us, guiding our thoughts, speech, and actions.

"Later, in this same epistle, the Beloved Disciple says this about the Lord within us: 'God is love; and he that dwelleth in love dwelleth in God, and God in him.' Friends, the light that the darkness cannot comprehend is love. We must be that love which shines forth in this world of suffering and death."

"Sam, dost thou think that flies can suffer?" Isaac asked.

"Isaac Burgess, whatever possessed you to ponder such a thing?" Samuel Johnson looked over at his friend with a mixture of curiosity and amusement as they lay side by side in the grass. Sam, a free negro, Isaac's best friend, and a classmate of Isaac's in the Friends school, lived on the farm opposite the Burgess farm. "You come up with some of the strangest notions at times."

"During silent meeting this morning I watched a fly get caught in a spider web," Isaac explained. "The poor creature struggled and struggled but could not escape the spider's grasp. Mrs. Way spoke about how we should be light in the world, helping to relieve the suffering of others. It's hard for me to see the light of God's love in the spider killing that fly."

Sam laughed and said, "Isaac, you forgot to look at it from the spider's perspective. Just think how grateful to God that spider was to have a nice meal sent his way."

"Well thou hast me there. I would never have thought of it in that light."

It was one of those perfect spring days. The chill of winter had finally departed while the humidity of summer had not yet arrived. Wild flowers were spread in profusion throughout the tall grass by the creek that flowed behind the Johnsons' farm. Fresh leaves emerging from the branches of overlying trees in their newborn innocence and intense verdure cast their shade over the boys as they lounged in the grass beneath. The light that filtered through the canopy of trees seemed to dance with joy on the water that flowed slowly over stones in the creek bed. The mingled voices of the soft murmur of flowing water and leaves rustling in the trees seemed to form a choir of praise and thanksgiving that ascended back to the Source of such magnificence.

Both boys were reticent to leave this moment behind them but finally got up and stood at the edge of the creek for a while, skipping small stones on the water. Their concentration on obtaining the ideal trajectory for the flight of their stones was suddenly interrupted by a discordant sound nearby.

"Did you hear that?" Sam asked.

"It sounded like someone cried out over there in those bushes," Isaac replied.

The boys crept softly in the direction of the sound that had come from some bushes about fifty feet away. At the edge of the thicket they paused and listened intently, but neither boy could hear any sound beyond that coming from the flowing creek, the wind in the trees, and the intermittent pecking of a woodpecker.

"Sam, were we just hearin' things?" Isaac whispered anxiously.

"No, I'm certain someone is in these bushes," Sam whispered in reply. "Are you afraid to look in the bushes?"

"Not, if thou aren't."

As they circled the thicket looking for a point of entrance, Sam noticed a small cleft in the wall of brambles and undergrowth. Isaac followed him through the cleft and both boys paused as they heard the unmistakable sounds of soft moaning mixed with labored breathing. They pressed forward in the dimly lit interior of the thicket and nearly tripped over a body lying on the ground.

"Whoa!" Sam cried.

The figure merely continued to breathe rapidly and emit intermittent moans in response.

Once their eyes became accustomed to the shadows which surrounded the prone figure, a young man of greater-than-average height with a muscular build was revealed to them. By complexion he appeared to be a mulatto, and by the state of the tattered rags that partially covered his body, the boys had no difficulty concluding he must be a runaway slave. The runaway's face was clearly that of a young man, no older than twenty years of age, and yet, etched into it were lines of pain and suffering that could fill a lifetime.

As Isaac and Sam were staring with great curiosity at the unconscious runaway, his handsome face contorted in pain and he uttered another deeper, more intense groan that sent a shiver down Isaac's back.

"Sam, he must be in great pain," Isaac whispered.

"I think there is more than pain in that groan," Sam replied. "But, what's this? It looks like he's got a nasty wound here on his shoulder!" Sam pointed to dried blood that had soaked the runaway's tattered shirtsleeve over his left shoulder. "Isaac, go get Doc Way as quick as you can. I'll stay with him."

Without further dialogue, Isaac extricated himself from the thicket and set off at a run across the fields toward town in search of Dr. Way.

By the time Isaac caught up with him, Henry Way had already had a long and difficult night. He had been called out at two in the morning to see a sick child who had developed the croup. The character of the little girl's cough had changed to a hoarse bark over the previous few hours. When he saw the child, he prepared for a long vigil at her bedside.

When her parents asked him what they should expect, he said, "I am afraid she has the croup. In its more severe form, what French physicians call diphtheria, it could take her life. Sometimes warm, moist air helps. Please heat up some water in your kettle so that we can produce some steam near her. If her fever and cough get no worse through the night, the crisis may pass." He paused briefly, then added, "I would keep the other children away from her, if possible."

Mrs. Way had directed Isaac to her husband's place of vigil, and when he arrived he cautiously knocked at the door of the small farmhouse. "Good afternoon, Mrs. Clarkson. I've come to fetch Doctor Way on an urgent call."

"Please come in, Isaac, thou lookest very out of breath," Mrs. Clarkson said, motioning for him to enter. "Doctor Way has been up much of the night with my Alice."

As Isaac's eyes became accustomed to the dimly lit interior, he recognized Dr. Way sitting by the bedside of little Alice Clarkson, a playmate of his seven-year-old sister, Rebecca. She was sitting up and taking a small amount of broth while Dr. Way gazed at her with a weary smile and stroked her forehead. Isaac drank in the whole scene and marveled at how Dr. Way could have the strength and patience to do his work so cheerfully after a sleepless night.

"Ah, is that thou, Isaac Burgess? Don't come too close. Well, here is another miracle of God's mercy. I hope and pray that young Alice is over the worst of her illness." At this, Henry Way gave a big yawn and said, "I sure could use a nice nap about now."

"I am so sorry to bother thee, Doctor Way, after such a long night," Isaac apologized, "but there is another person in desperate need of thy help. Sam and I were playing by the creek behind his farm and heard moaning in some bushes and found a wounded runaway! Sam is waiting with him as we speak. He is very sick and did not wake up when we found him. It looked like he had a wound on his left shoulder."

Henry Way sighed, stroked Alice's forehead one more time, and said, "Isaac, we'll need help to carry thy new friend to the Johnsons' farm. Couldst thou go on ahead and find Mr. Johnson or thy father to help me carry him? I'll meet thee by the creek as soon as possible. Anna, would thou be so kind as to pour me another cup of thy excellent coffee? Thanks to both of you."

As Isaac hurried off in search of his father and Mr. Johnson, he couldn't help but ponder over what he had seen at the Clarksons' home. From the expression on Dr. Way's face, it was clear to Isaac that the physician had not been so optimistic about Alice's chances of recovery when he had first settled in for his long, late-night vigil. *I wonder how many times he has kept vigil when the result has not been so happy*, thought Isaac.

Unable to find his father, he quickly told his mother about the situation. Priscilla told Isaac that she would meet him and the others at the Johnson farm and that he should go look for Benjamin Johnson out in his fields since his wife Mary had told her earlier that he would be working there today. So, Isaac again set off at a run, this time in the direction of the well-cultivated fields of the Johnsons' neighboring farm.

Benjamin Johnson bent down, sifted some dirt in his hands, and smiled. There was no other way to put it: he truly loved the soil. He felt an indescribable bond with the land. His love for his wife, Mary, was deep, steady, and intermittently punctuated with passionate desire. His devotion and commitment to his children were unquestioned. But there was something different about his feelings for the land. He had helped his father clear this land many years before. Over the years he labored to bring forth crops that eventually became the envy of his neighbors. He seemed to have developed an uncanny sense for reading the weather as well as identifying which crops to plant at the right time. Seeing the first green shoots of fresh life emerging from the ground that would someday give life to others continued to produce a profound thrill every time he witnessed it. Although Mary would sometimes worry out loud about his apparent lack of enthusiasm for formal religious services, he would respond, "Don't worry about me, Mary. When I am out in the fields working, I feel closer to God than I could anywhere else. I feel His pleasure when I help Him grow things."

As he straightened up, he noticed Isaac Burgess running toward him. "Mr. Johnson, Sam and I found a wounded runaway down by the creek. Dr. Way will be here soon. He told me to come and ask for thy help."

On hearing this news, Ben's brow furrowed a bit but then he grinned and told Isaac, "Let's go meet a new friend."

"Ben, I'll take his head, if thou canst take his feet. I want to guard his left shoulder as much as possible while we are moving him," Henry Way said as they maneuvered the runaway out of the thicket. Once they had moved him out of the thicket, Henry said, "Let's lay him down briefly here on the grass so I can assess him quickly before we move him to thy home. He has a strong pulse, but its rapid character suggests a fever. I hope there is no putrefaction in the wound."

As Henry was making these remarks, the runaway stirred, opened his eyes, and looked with terror at the white man staring down at him and tried to get up but grimaced in pain and fell back to the ground.

"Don't be frightened, young man. Thou art among friends."

Ben smiled at Henry's unintended pun, but it seemed to be lost on the young runaway. However, when he saw Ben's dark face smiling down at him, he seemed to calm down a bit. Ben now spoke to the young man.

"I am Benjamin Johnson, a free person of color. This is Doctor Way, who is truly a friend. You'll be staying with my family while you recover." Then turning to Henry, he asked, "Shall we go ahead and move him?"

"Yes, I think we can move him now. Isaac and Samuel, could you please help us by supporting his arms at his sides while we carry him?" The young man looked around helplessly and periodically grimaced and groaned in pain when any tension was placed on his left shoulder during his transfer to the Johnson home. Mary Johnson, their eldest child Eliza, and Priscilla Burgess were waiting for them at the door of the farmhouse.

"Ben let's put him in the parlor for the present," Mary said. "Priscilla, Eliza, and I have set up a bed for him there."

Mary was quite comfortable taking command when encountering the unexpected, especially on the domestic front. Since the Johnsons had been quite active in assisting fugitives from slavery, this was not an infrequent experience. Isaac and Sam helped position the runaway on the improvised bed in the parlor and then stepped back to watch the women take charge. Rebecca Burgess and the two younger Johnson daughters had been peering around the corner trying to catch a glimpse of the action. Mary and Priscilla dismissed the others briefly while they stripped as much of the runaway's rags off him as possible and then proceeded to bathe him in bed, leaving the injured shoulder for Dr. Way's closer inspection and attention after they were finished.

"Mary, I will need some clean rags, lint, and water to clean and dress the wound," Henry requested in preparation for his exploration of the injured shoulder.

"I have them right here," Mary replied as she pointed to the supplies at the base of the makeshift bed.

"Thank thee, Mary. Thou art the most efficient of the Lord's soldiers, and here they are, right under my nose!"

At this point, Isaac's curiosity (plus a strong dare from Sam) got the better of him and he came up to Henry and asked timidly, "Doctor Way, may I assist thee with the care of his wound?"

Henry looked closely at Isaac and smiled. "Thou seemest to be quite interested in the healing art, young master Burgess. I must warn thee that it may distress thee. However, if thy mother has no objections, I would welcome thy assistance."

Priscilla turned to Henry and said, "Isaac seems to have a growing interest in the care of the sick. Perhaps, this will be a good test of his interest and commitment. Isaac, thou hast my blessing to assist Doctor Way."

"Ben, please help me reposition the bed so we can catch more light from the window."

Henry was always in search of more and better lighting. He was fond of saying, "Darkness is the bane of medicine." With better lighting and a rolled blanket placed under the runaway's left side, the patient was now positioned for a more thorough examination of his left shoulder.

"Doctor Way, here is a bucket for you to put any of the dirty things from your work," Eliza said as she placed the bucket as close as possible to the patient.

"Thank thee, Eliza. We'll have need of that. Now, Isaac, do not be afraid. Come up close so that thou canst see and help me."

As Isaac edged closer to the site of interest, he became aware of some slight movement in the rags that were still attached to the runaway's injured shoulder. Henry also noticed the movement and smiled at Isaac. "My young friend, thou mayest be surprised momentarily. I must warn thee that appearances may truly be deceiving. What thou art about to see is not so bad as it will seem to thee." As Henry slowly and gently peeled back the dried, bloodstained cloth from the runaway's shoulder, the cause of the movement was revealed to Isaac.

"Doctor Way, there are worms crawling in his wound!" Isaac shuddered, felt nauseous, and turned away.

"Isaac, those are maggots. In a short time, they will mature into flies. At the moment they are doing a valuable if not entirely pleasant service for our patient," Henry explained.

Isaac's vision was drawn inexorably, as if by a magnet, back to the revolting sight. He could not help but stare with morbid fascination at the sea of wriggling forms in the wound.

"These humble maggots are keeping this wound clean," Henry explained. "For all their loathsome qualities, they are not the source of this young man's fever and delirium. There are two wounds in his shoulder: one larger one in the front now occupied by our little friends, and another smaller wound in the back which worries me more."

As Ben helped Henry prop the wounded runaway up more on his right side, they were able to have a better view of the smaller wound in the back of the left shoulder. Any gentle pressure in this area elicited groans of pain from the runaway.

"I am afraid that putrefaction has developed in this wound and that this is the cause of his fever and delirium. It is quite inflamed but is occluded and has no means of drainage. There are no friendly maggots assisting at this site, unfortunately," Henry said with some irony. "It appears that he was shot several days ago. The ball entered through this smaller wound in the posterior aspect or backside of his shoulder, and exited through the anterior aspect or front side," Henry apologized for using anatomical language. "I will need to open the posterior wound so that the purulent material can escape as it normally would during the healing process." He then addressed his patient, "I hope thou canst understand me. I need to cut away some dead tissue and drain some pus. Thou mayest feel some pain. I will give thee some laudanum before I begin my work to help alleviate the pain."

The runaway opened his eyes and met Henry's gaze with an equally intense look and said, to Henry's surprise, "I understand, and I trust you. Please go ahead with your operation."

Henry proceeded to give the runaway some laudanum while marveling at his grammatically correct speech. After waiting several minutes for the laudanum to take effect, Henry reached into his medical bag and took out his scalpel.

"Ben, please steady him as I make my incision. Isaac, have some rags ready to soak up the blood and pus."

Isaac steeled himself for this next experience. He was familiar with bleeding, having helped his mother with killing and preparing chickens for supper on several occasions, but he had never seen a knife used on another human before. Henry carefully and quickly incised the entrance wound with his scalpel, opening it to three times its original diameter. Dead, necrotic tissue present at the entrance to the wound was also quickly removed with some additional dissection. He then probed the wound with a wire probe and about two ounces of pus mixed with blood came out. The runaway initially flinched with the touch of the scalpel but did not cry out. Isaac passed the cloth rags to Henry so he could mop up the pus and blood. Henry then asked Isaac to wet a rag, which he also used to clean the wound. As Henry was dressing the wound after the procedure, Isaac, who had been so preoccupied to that point with helping during the procedure, looked at the good doctor with admiration, felt strangely lightheaded, and awoke later to find himself lying on the floor of the Johnsons' parlor.

"It appears we have two patients to attend to here," Henry said as he peered down at the groggy Isaac with a smile.

When Isaac came to himself, he was initially embarrassed, flushed a deep crimson and began to apologize for passing out. "I'm sorry, Doctor Way, for being so weak."

"Isaac, thou needst not apologize at all," Henry replied with a smile. "Thou hast been very brave indeed. I expect I would have passed out sooner than thou didst, if I had been in thy place. The surgical act is not natural to man. In the medical profession we are sometimes called to perform violent actions that cause pain in order to aid the process of healing. We should never make light of such actions, but recognize that a sacred and intimate bond has formed between doctor and patient in the process of such a drastic but necessary act. I hope that the memory of thy experience today will stay with thee even though thou becomest more comfortable in the future with the sight of scalpels, bleeding, and pus."

Sam came up to Isaac and exclaimed, "I didn't think you could do it, Isaac! Maybe you really are meant to be a doctor someday."

Rebecca had rushed forward as soon as Isaac fainted, and remained kneeling at his side, stroking his hand while wearing a worried look. Although Isaac secretly appreciated her comforting presence and touch, he felt sheepish that his young sister should be making such a fuss over him.

"Thank thee, Rebecca, but I'm just fine," he said gruffly as he tried to get up.

After the pain and stress of the procedure, the runaway slept soundly, leaving his rescuers perplexed about his identity. As Ben helped Henry, Eliza, and Mary clean up the mess created by the operation, he commented, "I don't believe I have met very many runaways who speak like this young man."

"I was struck by the character of his speech as well," Henry replied with a nod.

"Father, what could it possibly mean?" asked Eliza, who had taken a special interest in the mysterious stranger.

Mary, who had been observing her eldest daughter's intense interest in the handsome runaway, said, "I suspect that there is quite a story to be told here. Eliza, it is essential that we all respect his privacy. He may not feel he can safely reveal more of his history to us. Do not press him for more information about himself than is absolutely necessary to assist him. Our responsibility is to keep him safe while he recovers from his wound and guide him on his way to freedom."

Although Sam heard his mother's words, he could not repress saying, "But Ma, Isaac and I found him. He owes us a good story!"

Henry laughed.

"Mary, thy son hast a point. However, our young friend will likely be in no shape to tell a good story for a while. Sam, thy mother's advice is very sensible. Put thyself in the place of this runaway. None of us can begin to imagine what he has experienced and whether he has much reason to trust other members of the human race. I suspect that he will reveal quite a story to all of you, but it may take some time before he fully answers the mystery of his excellent use of the English language.

"In the meantime, he will require close observation. My hope is that this procedure will address the putrefaction in his wound. The next day or two should tell its own story. His condition may become worse before it gets better. Please call for me, if there are any major changes."

Eliza looked intently at the runaway and then at Henry. "Doctor Way, what should we look for as signs of his condition worsening?"

"He may become more feverish and delirious. The boys said they found him because he cried out. Be prepared to witness, either tonight or during the next day or so, some portion of this young man's sufferings that may be revealed by the delirium."

Isaac looked with admiration at his uncle, Levi Coffin. His mother's brother had been a source of inspiration not only for Isaac but for many in the anti-slavery Quaker communities of eastern Indiana. Levi was a man of average height, approaching his fiftieth year, with graying black hair and even features. The most notable aspect of his appearance only became apparent when he was about to speak, frequently after some period of thoughtful deliberation. For more often than not Levi could not help having either the smallest twinkle in his eye or the slightest smile on his lips even in what otherwise might be quite tense circumstances. And with just such a flicker of a smile, Levi spoke to the family members gathered in the Coffin dining room.

"It is truly with mixed feelings that Catherine and I will be moving in a few days to Cincinnati," he announced. "For twenty years, we have fought the good fight here in Newport, helping many refugees make their escape north to freedom from the evils of human bondage. I might add that during that time we have assisted, on average, one hundred souls each year in their journey toward liberty, much to the annoyance of our Southern brethren, who have bestowed upon me the honorific title of President of the Underground Railroad. Although I revel in the honor they have bestowed upon me, it would be truly immodest of me to receive the plaudits for an effort made by many dedicated and mostly unnamed individuals, who have risked much to serve those in need. Whereas many of us in the North who have been engaged with supporting the activities of this so-called underground railroad are actuated by principle, there are many in the Southern states who, perhaps due to pecuniary interests, have been driven to provide no less essential support in the transportation of freedom seekers. We are grateful that God works out his merciful will regardless of the motives of his human instruments.

"As you know, the Anti-Slavery Friends' Yearly Meeting has urged me to assist in the development of free-labor merchandising, so that, to the greatest extent possible, Friends and other foes of slavery will not have to provide material support to the slaveholder or reap personal benefit from the unrequited labor of the bondsman. We will be moving in a few days to Cincinnati to take up this new work, but it is our sincere hope that we may return again to this community, which is our dear home, once the task is completed.

"Priscilla and John, we are grateful that you have kindly offered to take over the responsibilities of our business here in Newport and will also assume conducting duties at the Coffin Depot of the Underground Railroad."

Then, surveying his sister, brother-in-law, and their two children with a grin, he added, "I promise that I will send you plenty of southern cargo via Cincinnati that will require safe transport and delivery to Canada."

After finishing the last bites of a piece of warm apple pie, John Burgess could not help saying, "Kitty, thou hast outdone thyself! Thou hast exceeded thine already remarkable reputation with this meal. We will all miss the frequent opportunities to share fellowship with Levi and thee over such excellent cooking."

Catherine Coffin was quick to respond, "John, it is always a joy to share the fellowship of a meal with thy family. I very much appreciate thy enthusiastic endorsement of my cooking, but I must also confess that in today's feast we have all benefitted greatly from the expertise of one of our southern guests. Friend Olivia, please come and receive the credit due thee."

A slight, middle-aged black woman wearing a brightly colored headscarf came up the stairs from the kitchen below and quietly entered the small dining room. Rebecca, full of curiosity, came up the stairs right behind her from the kitchen where she and Isaac had been eating an early supper with the colored woman and her son.

"Olivia has for many years been the cook on a large plantation in northern Tennessee," Catherine explained. "She and her son Toby have been on a difficult and dangerous journey coming north and have been guests here at the Coffin Depot of the Underground Railroad for the past two days. During their stay with us, she has been so kind to teach me some of the extraordinary secrets of her cooking."

"Missus, yo be'n ex'lent cook. I cain't teach yo nuttin yo don't a'redy knows," Olivia insisted with modesty.

Catherine gave her a big hug and replied, "Olivia, the art of fine cooking is only a small portion of the wisdom thou hast shared with us in the short time thou hast been with us. Olivia made the decision to flee to the north about two weeks ago when she overheard her master discussing the sale of Toby, her only remaining child, to a slave trader for transport to the Deep South. Toby has had the misfortune of growing up into a tall, strong young man of fourteen years, which has increased his value for sale tremendously. Olivia has already lost four other children to the slave trade, as well as her husband, all of whom were sold and transported south during the past five to six years."

At this point, Olivia interjected, "I cain't bear no mo' chillun o' mine bein' sol' away fum me! I jes' had to steal mah boy away fum massa."

Catherine resumed, "It is a strange and painful thing that parents would have to steal their own children. From reports Levi has received earlier this morning, it appears that slave catchers may be coming in pursuit and are not too far from Richmond."

Toby cried out in fear, "Mammy, what's we gwine do?"

Levi calmly rose from the dining table and gently approached the boy and his mother. "You will both be safely in Canada in less than two weeks. Do not be afraid. It will be necessary to take the precaution of moving you on to the next station, though. John, I think you may need to take them by wagon later tonight."

John exchanged glances with Priscilla, as if to say, "We both knew that our lives would be changing rapidly once we moved into thy brother's home, but we never realized how quickly." Although John and Priscilla were staunch abolitionists, they had only been peripherally involved in the work of Priscilla's brother Levi in prior years. This would be the first time that John Burgess would take primary responsibility for sheltering and transporting fugitive slaves on the roads of Indiana. Prior to this, John and Priscilla had helped under less-risky circumstances. They had justified their indirect involvement in the activities of the Underground Railroad by citing the demands of running their farm and more recently with the advent of their two small children after many childless years of marriage. They had both come to acknowledge that fear had always been a major force in the background keeping them from taking a more direct and active role in the work. When Priscilla's brother announced his plan to move to Cincinnati, their consciences would not let them hold back anymore. While recognizing the dangers associated with the work, they had also become firmly convinced that this experience must be a central element in the spiritual formation of their children.

While not at all as confident as his brother-in-law in the inherent safety of his charges, John turned to Toby and his mother and addressed them in as reassuring tones as possible, "Friends, I will do all in my power with the help of God to safely direct you both toward freedom in Canada."

After Olivia and Toby returned to the kitchen, Levi spoke again in lower tones to John and Priscilla, "I want to quickly review some of the more unique features of this house with both of you before John takes charge of his passengers. Kitty, could thou please help our guests prepare for their journey?"

As his wife, Catherine, was preparing food and water for the fugitives, Levi took John and Priscilla to the upstairs bedrooms. A large bed and dresser occupied the first bedroom. Another large bed and a built-in closet with shelves and drawers, a unique innovation that Levi had seen during his travels and had introduced for the first time in Newport, occupied a second bedroom located across the landing. This room connected with another room toward the back of the second floor. Two bedsteads occupied much of the living space in the third upstairs bedroom. Levi approached one of the beds and first pulled and then pushed it aside. As he displaced the bed, a small low door in the wall behind the headboard was revealed. He opened the door and invited John to crawl through the opening in the wall. At first John could see nothing, but as his eyes became more accustomed to the dark he began to realize that a chamber of some significant size had been opened before him. It was narrow and deep but would not allow an adult to stand erect within it.

Levi looked in on him and said, "I have accommodated more than ten guests in this space at one time, although I must say it was a bit crowded."

Priscilla peered into the dark space into which her husband had disappeared and said admiringly, "Levi, thou art a very creative and clever man."

While John and Priscilla were exploring the hidden chamber, Catherine came breathlessly up the stairs with the two fugitives. She anxiously spoke in a low tone, "Levi, it is a good thing that thou hast been showing this chamber to John and Priscilla, for we have need of it now! Henry Way just came to warn us that slave catchers are already in Newport, inquiring about two runaways from Tennessee and the location of Levi Coffin's house."

Levi turned to the frightened fugitives who had followed his wife upstairs.

"Please climb into this room with my brother-in-law and remain very quiet," he instructed. "I will take care of these slave catchers. We may have to adjust our plan slightly. Do not be afraid, but trust in the God who brought you both here safely."

A loud rapping was heard at the door. Levi quickly addressed John.

"Please stay with them while I address our visitors."

Levi then closed the small door in the wall and replaced the bed in its original position, effectively hiding the presence of the chamber and imprisoning the two terrified fugitive slaves with John in total darkness. The rapping downstairs grew louder and was now accompanied by foul language. Levi urged Priscilla and Catherine to keep Isaac and Rebecca down in the kitchen while he dealt with the slave catchers.

By the time he had descended the stairs, Levi was quite surprised to find the front door open and Rebecca speaking with two men. The two men from the south were equally surprised to encounter the young Quakeress. Both men appeared the worse for wear, having accumulated several days' or possibly weeks' worth of dirt and grime, which clung to every exposed surface of their bodies and provided an additional layer of insulation protecting their clothing and flesh from soap and water. One of the men was quite a bit taller and thinner than the other, but due to poor posture was stooped, which made him look like a somewhat bedraggled buzzard. This, combined with a hungry look, added to his charms.

He pushed several greasy strands of hair away from his eyes and peered down at Rebecca and then turned to his partner and drawled, "D'ya spose, Jed, that this young 'un is one of them danj'rous abolitionists?"

Jed, a short, overnourished, balding man with a bad squint replied, "Why she's too purty to be one, but she's dressed like 'em. She might be jes' the one to help us find who we's lookin'fer. They sez these Quakers cain't tell lies. That cud be mighty convenient fer us."

Rebecca looked innocently up at the men and asked how she could help them. "What's yer name missy?" asked Jed.

"My name is Rebecca. What is thy name?" she replied.

"What'd I tell 'e Joe. She e'en talks funny like 'em! Well, missy, my name is Jed, and this ere's my pardner, Joe. We collect stolen property. You wouldn't be havin' some nigger slaves hidin' 'ere would ye, missy?"

At this moment, Levi had arrived at the front door and promptly interposed himself between the two slave catchers and his niece.

"Thank thee, Rebecca for greeting these gentlemen," Levi said. "Thou canst go to the kitchen now to help thy mother and aunt with the dishes. I will answer their questions."

As Levi was taking the measure of his foes, a crowd had been gathering in the street and had effectively surrounded the Southern visitors. Dr. Way had not only warned Catherine, but had gone on to quietly rouse the community in support of Levi and his family.

"I heard that you have been looking for Levi Coffin," Levi replied, addressing the slave catchers. "I am he. What business do you have here in Newport, Indiana?"

Jed responded, "We bin trackin' a couple o' runaways all the way from Tennessee, a mother and son. We knows yer a noterious an' danj'rous Quaker abolitionist. Y'all Quakers aint s'posed to tell lies. Deny in front o' these 'ere witnesses that ye have run'way slave niggers in the house!"

Levi calmly surveyed his accusers and began to speak, "Friends, I have never denied my opposition to the institution of slavery, an unjust and cruel institution that I believe should be abolished as soon as possible. I guess that may qualify me as one having abolitionist sentiments. I have always tried to follow the precepts of Our Lord in which He enjoined all Christians to feed the hungry, clothe the naked, visit those in prison, and care for the sick. Nowhere in the Good Book does it say that this ministry of mercy should be exclusively administered to one race of men. All those who come to me in need will be offered succor, including those with dark skins.

"As for allegations that I harbor fugitive slaves, how am I to understand such accusations? What can be their basis? The Southern legal system has always dictated that a slave's testimony is unreliable and thus inadmissible in a court of law. In the light and wisdom of southern jurisprudence how am I to interpret statements that poor, starving, colored persons may make about their personal history when they come to me in need? Clearly, all I can do is care for the wounded person in front of me as I would do for you gentlemen or any other person in acute need or distress.

"Finally, are you gentlemen aware of the laws against trespass in Indiana? Do you possess an appropriate writ, obtained from a judge in this state to search my home? If not, and it is clear from your faces that you don't have one, you should proceed with your business elsewhere."

A strong murmur of support rose from the crowd gathered outside the Coffin home and Jed and Joe felt the necessity to beat a hasty retreat.

While Levi was entertaining his uninvited guests at the front door, John Burgess, Olivia, and Toby were trying to adjust to their new environment. In a hushed whisper, John tried to calm the fears of the fugitives and cautioned them to remain silent. After his eyes had acclimated to the darkness, John could barely make out the forms of his fellow prisoners. As he sat there in the darkness, he realized how little he knew of the kinds of trials through which Olivia, Toby, and other fugitive slaves had come, not just since their escape from slavery, but during their whole existence as slaves. In listening to their rapid, heavy panting, he was struck by the similarity of the fugitives' plight to that of hunted animals, except that these hunted were fully able to reflect in terror on their situation and calculate their prospects for ultimate success or failure. He felt shame that he had held back so long from more actively helping fugitives and marveled at how quickly he had been transformed from being a passive witness to an active participant in the work of the Underground Railroad. He also wondered at the providence of God that now connected him so intimately with the safety and hopes of these strangers.

O Lord, he prayed silently, *help me to bring these Thy children to safety. May I not prove a stumbling block to them. Guide and guard them on their journey to freedom.*

Rebecca was sitting at the dining table with Isaac, Priscilla, and Catherine. "Aunt Kitty? Were those men looking for Olivia and Toby?" Rebecca asked.

Isaac, who had gone outside through the side door and talked to several friends in the crowd outside the Coffins' home, interjected, "Rebecca, thou art too trusting. Those are bad men who would have taken Olivia and Toby back into slavery."

Rebecca began to cry and asked, "Why would they want to do that?"

Priscilla took her on her lap and held her close. "O Rebecca, what a precious treasure thou art! Isaac is correct in saying that they want to take Olivia and Toby back to slavery, but he is wrong to say they are bad men. We cannot, we must not judge these men. Only God knows their hearts and only He can judge. They are being tempted to do an evil thing for money and we must pray for them so that they would repent and change their ways."

Catherine added, "Dear Rebecca, when thy parents have guests like Olivia and Toby staying here in the future, it will be best for thee to not tell anyone about the guests. Let thy parents speak to strangers when they come and ask questions. We must be as wise as serpents and gentle as doves."

Isaac laughed and smirked at his sister, "Rebecca thou art gentle as a dove but not so wise as a serpent!"

Priscilla smiled and said, "Isaac, thy sister possesses a rare wisdom of the heart that has made her gentle as a dove. All too soon she will gain the worldly wisdom of which thou speakest. May God protect both of you as we embark on this new path together!"

Levi popped his head into the dining room and said, "They are gone for the present, but we will need to move Olivia and Toby soon. Jed and Joe will be waiting for them near Cabin Creek. Before they came to our door, they had been asking which direction runaways typically take when passing through this area on their way to Canada, and several of our citizens obligingly told them the truth that many pass through Cabin Creek to the north on their journey to freedom since it is a large community of free colored people in which they may find shelter and protection.

"Rather than send Olivia and Toby on this route via Detroit to Canada, they will take a detour south and east, retracing some of their journey and then travel to Sandusky, where they will gain passage across Lake Erie to Canada on a vessel friendly to our cause. Levi went upstairs and released everyone from the secret chamber, and explained the plan to John, who will transport Olivia and Toby east about ten miles to the next depot across the state line for transfer to an Ohio branch of the Underground Railroad.

"John," Levi began, "neither of the slave catchers has seen thee here. I propose that thou takest a load of wood and hay in the wagon with thee in addition to thine other cargo on the journey. Let us go load and organize the wagon."

Levi and John walked back to the Coffins' barn and examined the family wagon. At first glance, it seemed like any other buckboard wagon but after Levi opened the back end and brushed away some hay and other debris, it became apparent that the wagon had a false bottom. After providing Olivia and Toby with some provisions for the journey, Levi invited them to climb into the crawl space under the false bottom after explaining that there would be plenty of breathing space available and that they would need to be silent during the journey. The two men then stacked some wood on top of the false bottom and piled hay in the back to obscure any sign of the entrance to the crawl space underneath.

After they had hitched two horses to the wagon, Levi then shook John's hand and said, "Thou art having quite an initiation into this business today. I am not too concerned about pursuit. Neither Jed nor Joe seemed particularly endowed with intellectual gifts. Before thou departest on thy journey, I want to give thee and thy family a special sign and memento of this work thou hast embraced."

Levi and John walked back into the dining room and Levi called the rest of the family together. He then opened a drawer in a cupboard and pulled out a small round object. Turning to Isaac, he handed the object to him and asked, "Isaac, what dost thou see?"

Isaac held the round medallion cautiously in his hands and described the image.

"Uncle Levi, there is a negro slave kneeling in chains. He is holding his hands up and looks like he is pleading."

"What is written in the inscription around the edge of the medallion?"

"*Am I not a man and a brother?*"

"Well done, my young scholar nephew. This medallion, which was produced by the great English abolitionist Josiah Wedgwood, has been a continuous source of inspiration for Kitty and me over the years as we have worked on the Underground Railroad. May it continue to be a source of inspiration for the Burgess family as they take up this blessed vocation!"

Priscilla hugged and kissed her brother. "Thank thee, Levi, for sharing this powerful memorial of the commitment Kitty and thou have given to this cause. We are deeply honored to receive it. It will be placed on the mantel over the fireplace as a continual reminder for us of the commitment we have also made on behalf of those suffering in bondage."

Out in the yard, as John was taking his leave, Levi said, "Godspeed thee in thy journey."

Before John could take his seat at the front of the wagon, Priscilla rushed up and hugged him tightly. "John Burgess, come back safely to thy family!"

Later that evening, as Priscilla was helping Isaac and Rebecca prepare for bed, she knelt with the children in an initial period of silent prayer, which was their custom as Quakers. After a deep quiet had enfolded them, Rebecca prayed, "Please, dear Jesus, shine Thy light into the souls of Jed and Joe so that they will want to help the colored people."

Isaac added, "O Lord, in case Jed and Joe don't repent right away, please keep them confused so they aren't able to harm father and Olivia and Toby."

After giving Rebecca a goodnight kiss, Priscilla leaned down over her son to give him a kiss, but Isaac interrupted the process by looking intently into his mother's dark eyes and saying, "Mother, thank thee for allowing me to help Doctor Way care for the wounded runaway. During meeting this morning, I saw a spider catch and kill a fly for his meal. Then later I saw maggots, which will become flies, feeding off the decay in the runaway's wound, cleaning it as they fed themselves. Do animals go to heaven? Dost thou think it possible that even flies could go to heaven, considering the many good things they do? Does God love even flies?"

Priscilla's long, graying hair framed a face showing a mixture of surprise, mild humor, and awe inspired by her son's questions. "Dear Isaac, I can only quote the Lord who said that even the hairs of our heads are numbered. I am certain that nothing happens in this world without His permission, whether we perceive it as good or bad. The death of that fly and its nourishment of the spider and the work of the maggots in the runaway's wound have not happened outside the will of God."

Isaac again gave his mother an intent look and said, "I hope that with all the flies, maggots, and spiders, God will have enough time to spare so that He can also keep an eye on father tonight."

Chapter Three

Eliza looked down at her charge with a mixture of intense curiosity and other emotions she could not clearly identify. She had insisted on taking the first watch during the all-night vigil at the bedside of the young fugitive. Eliza had taken an active interest in her parents' and the community's support of fugitive slaves for as long as she could remember, but there was something different about this fugitive that captured her imagination. For one thing, he could not be too much older than her. When she had helped earlier with removing his tattered clothing, she was horrified to see the deep scars on his back that were evidence of prior whippings. She shuddered involuntarily at the thought that her own black skin would also condemn her to similar suffering but for the papers indicating her status as a free person of color. How did this young man acquire speech free of the slave dialect? Surely he must also be literate, but how, since in slave states it was illegal to teach slaves to read and write?

Transcending the many thoughts that circled in her head, as she looked into his face she was struck again by how handsome he was. It appeared that the fugitive's suffering had not marred his features; rather an imprint of sorrow had been left that ennobled his youthful face, while at the same time bringing a maturity to it that spoke of a life experience rich beyond his years. As she pondered these things, he began to stir, and his facial muscles became contorted by an intense grimace of pain. Eliza gently grasped his left hand with both of her hands and began to steadily stroke it. Her patient slowly opened his eyes and initially looked around with fear. When he saw the source of the human contact his expression relaxed, and he smiled as he examined Eliza intently with his gaze.

"I'm sorry to wake you," Eliza replied. "You were grimacing. I was trying to bring some comfort to you. I hope I didn't make it worse."

"Thank you. It helped me greatly. Forgive me for staring at you so intently just now. Your face is so beautiful and kind. I haven't seen or felt anything so comforting in a very long time," the stranger said as he admired Eliza's delicate features and perfect complexion. Eliza felt heat rushing to her face, a not-altogether-unpleasant sensation, as she began to fully absorb the compliment.

"I'm just glad that I can be of help. Doctor Way left some laudanum to help relieve your pain. Would you like for me to give you some now?" Eliza inquired as she tried to move their conversation into safer territory.

"I probably could benefit from some medicine for pain. At times, my left shoulder feels like it is on fire; but I must know the name of the angel who has been so kindly watching over me," replied the runaway, who would not be deflected from the earlier theme of their conversation.

Eliza again felt the heat rise in her cheeks and replied with a smile, "I'm not sure that I'm the person to introduce you to your guardian angel but I would gladly tell you *my* name on one condition: that you tell me yours."

"That does indeed seem a fair bargain," replied the runaway. "I promise that I will tell you my name after I hear yours."

"My proper name is Elizabeth Johnson, but my friends and family call me Eliza."

Eliza now looked at the stranger with great interest as she awaited the revelation of his name. He smiled at her and said, "Eliza, I hope you won't laugh when you hear my name. Slaves typically acquire the surname of their owner. For my own safety and that of you and your family, the less you know about my owner the better. My master gave me the name Tiberius. You may prefer to call me Tib, which is my nickname."

Eliza valiantly repressed a giggle and asked, "Why did your master pick such an unusual name?"

"My master had been something of a Latin scholar in his youth and thought it would be great sport to name his slaves after notable Roman patricians and rulers," he replied. "Thus, in addition to the emperor Tiberius, his plantation was also graced by the presence of many other Roman emperors, including Augustus, Caligula, Claudius, Nero, Titus, Trajan, Hadrian, et cetera. I must add that none of us enjoyed quite the imperial splendor that our names imply." At this point, Tib smiled weakly and yawned. "I think the laudanum is having its effect."

"Tib, you must rest now. My mother will be very upset with me if I've exhausted you." Eliza tried to assume the commanding air that her mother could so effectively employ.

"Eliza, you have not exhausted me. Rather, you have given me hope that will sustain me through my troubles."

Tiberius quickly reentered his restless slumber and Eliza resumed her bedside vigil. As the evening progressed, Eliza found herself drifting off into visions of black Roman emperors working side by side in their togas, tending the crops on a certain Southern plantation. In the midst of this somewhat incongruous vision, she heard cries coming from the direction of the slave quarters.

How can this be? she thought.

The emperors in the field seemed quite content, ignoring the cries as they worked steadily, while trying at the same time not to soil their togas. Yet, the cries from the quarters would not be silenced. Someone (could it be another emperor?) was crying out, "Have mercy! Please stop!"

The cries became louder.

As she turned around to see the source of the cries, she saw a handsome young emperor whose toga had been stripped from his back. A pale barbarian, who with others of his kind had invaded the peace of the imperial plantation, was flogging him. As she approached to get a better view, the wounded emperor looked directly into her eyes and cried, "Eliza!"

Waking suddenly from her dream she saw that her patient was quite feverish, sweating profusely, and continued to cry out for mercy while also crying for her by name. She moistened a cloth rag and began to mop his forehead while trying to comfort him with soft words.

"Tib, Eliza is here. You'll be fine. No one will whip you anymore."

Her mother, who had been awakened by the cries, joined Eliza. "Eliza, you should have come for me earlier. You have been with him longer than we had agreed."

"Mother, I fell asleep and only now awakened when he cried for me by name."

"Yes, I noticed that even in his delirium he is on a first-name basis with you. So, in the morning I want to hear more about your conversation with him. You'd better get some sleep now, though."

"I'm not sure I should leave him since he's been calling for me by name."

"Eliza, he's delirious. Get some rest so that you can be of some real help to him tomorrow."

Eliza reluctantly yielded to her mother's wisdom and authority. As she settled into bed, the excitement and associated fatigue of the past several hours combined to dispatch her swiftly back to the realm of dreams in which even negro slaves could be emperors.

As she mopped the sweat from his forehead, Mary Johnson looked down at Tib with fresh curiosity. "You are a real puzzle, young man," she said softly as she continued her ministrations. "You've definitely caught the attention of my Eliza, and maybe more than just her attention. But, what kind of a man are you? How many scars do you carry besides those we can see?"

When Doctor Way came the next day to check on his patient, he was met by an excited Sam.

"Doctor Way, his name is Tib," Sam said. "That's short for Tiberius. He told Eliza his name last night. From what he told her, there's a whole bunch of Roman emperors on his plantation." Sam smiled with an air of triumph at being able to divulge this important information.

"Thank thee, Sam, for this interesting news. I have heard of some peculiar ways of naming slaves that are popular among the Southern slave owners. This is certainly a creative if not ironic approach to take," Henry replied as he reflected over his patient's condition.

"Ma said he was real feverish last night," Sam added as his mother entered the parlor.

"It appears that his fever has broken," Henry said as he turned toward Mary.

"I hope so. He was restless and sweating most of the night, but by dawn he settled into a much more peaceful sleep," Mary confirmed. Isaac, who was also present for the doctor's visit, asked, "Doctor Way, wilt thou change the dressing to his wound today?"

"What dost thou think we should do Isaac, my young apprentice? What is thy opinion?"

"I think it should be changed so that we can see what has happened since thy operation yesterday," replied Isaac, who was beaming at his promotion.

"I agree with thee, my young colleague. Let us proceed, assuming thou art prepared to see the wounds again."

As Isaac was about to affirm his fearlessness in the face of potentially more blood, pus, and maggots, Mary interjected, "Henry, I'm glad that you are preparing Isaac for another encounter with ugly wounds, but have you forgotten some other necessary preparations?"

"Please forgive me, Mary. Of course, we will need to have dressing supplies, a bucket of water, and another bucket for refuse. Isaac, couldst thou go and fetch a bucket of water?" Looking up, Henry noticed that Eliza had entered the room. "Sam, couldst thou help thy sister collect some dressing materials for Tiberius's wound and a bucket for refuse?" Then Henry sat close to Tib and spoke gently as he leaned over and touched his forehead with a wet rag. "Tiberius? I am here to check thy wound. It's Doctor Way."

As Tib slowly came to consciousness, he opened his eyes to see Henry, Mary, Eliza, Sam, and Isaac looking down at him. Rebecca and Eliza's younger sisters were also hovering in the background. He gave an awkward smile and said, "I didn't know that I should merit such interest from so many kind people. Thank you, doctor, for your care. I wish I had some means of repaying you all for your kindness to me. I am afraid that I'm a burden to this kind family and community. I should probably move on north and not impose on you further." Tib tried to sit up but the pain in his left shoulder and lightheadedness again arrested his motion.

"Why art thou in such a hurry to leave?" Henry remonstrated. "Art thou afraid of pursuit? We have many means at our disposal to protect thee. Besides, thou hast a long period of recovery ahead of thee before thou canst continue thy journey north."

"Tib, you are not leaving here until you are completely mended," Mary stated emphatically. "And besides, I think there may be some ways you can help us on the farm while you are recovering." The look in Eliza's eyes spoke volumes to Tib that transcended her mother's words.

Tib answered slowly, "Actually, I think the risk of pursuit is low. I was being pursued vigorously by the time I reached the Ohio River. When I stole a skiff to cross over to the Indiana side, I am quite certain that its owner recognized me as a wanted fugitive because I fit the description on several handbills that were circulating in the community along the river. I happened to see one of the handbills and it indicated a substantial reward for me—*dead or alive.* As I was rowing out into the river, he shouted at me to return to the Kentucky side or he would shoot me down like a dog.

"I kept rowing, heard the crack of his musket, and felt a searing pain in my left shoulder and dropped my left oar into the river. As I reached over the side of the skiff to recover it, I lost balance and fell into the river. I remember hearing an angry shout from the Kentucky shore, 'Damnation! I jes' lost my reward!' What he didn't realize was that I could swim, a rare talent among slaves.

"By this time, I was closer to the Indiana shore and drifted for a while, clinging to the side of the skiff as it headed toward the Indiana side. The thought came to me while I was clinging to the side of the boat that if I could survive my wound, it might help me secure my freedom since my pursuers would assume I had been killed by the owner of the skiff. My hope expanded as I thought that their pursuit would likely end here at the Ohio River. Even though my shoulder hurt quite a bit, I could leave the skiff to drift further downriver and swim directly the remaining distance to the Indiana shore. My fears of pursuit changed to fears of discovery as I moved north. I was afraid that there might be many pro-slavery men in southern Indiana. What would they make of a wounded mulatto dressed in rags? I can only express again my deep thanks to all of you."

After giving his account, Tib looked around him meeting the gaze of all those in the parlor.

When he met Mary's gaze, she said, "Tib, I hope we now have an understanding. Don't you dare mention leaving again until I say you are ready!"

"Yes Ma'am," Tib replied somewhat sheepishly while stealing a glance at Eliza, who quickly averted her eyes as she again felt a sudden warmth rise in her cheeks.

"Ah, this is definitely encouraging. There is still some purulence, but there is no more necrotic tissue," Henry stated with satisfaction as he surveyed Tib's wound. "Isaac, it looks as though our patient may be on the road to recovery. I don't think I will need to do anymore debridement of the wound and I am pleased to see it draining well."

Henry then directed his attention back to Tib.

"It will likely take many weeks for thy wound to heal completely and for thee to regain thy health. From thy account of the adventure crossing the Ohio, I agree that thy risk of further pursuit is low. However, no fugitive slave is completely safe until he stands on Canadian soil. As thou spendest the next few months with us, I would recommend exercising due caution in thy encounters, especially with white people. The county seat of Richmond is just a few miles south of our town of Newport. Although there are many in Richmond who are friends of those seeking freedom, there are also many with strong pro-slavery sentiments." After giving this cautionary advice, Henry turned to Mary and declared with a big smile, "My prescription for this young man is plenty of rest combined with thy excellent cooking. In two or three days, I think he should be able to get up and do some walking."

Chapter Four

Mrs. Way sighed, stood up, and, with what looked to Isaac like relief on her face, announced with the ringing of the bell on her desk that school was out that Friday afternoon in mid-June 1847. As Isaac and Rebecca walked back into town from the schoolhouse with Sam and his sisters, thirteen-year-old Hattie and six-year-old Louisa (seventeen-year-old Eliza had finished her studies at the Quaker school the preceding year), the conversation shifted from exultation at the end of the school year to the latest news of fugitive slaves. The Burgess family was currently hosting six runaways who had arrived the day before. As promised, once Isaac and Rebecca's Uncle Levi and Aunt Catherine had established themselves in Cincinnati, they sent a steady stream of refugees from slavery on their way north via Newport. Priscilla and John Burgess, in addition to managing the general store in town and helping John's brother William with the family farms, spent the majority of their time practicing hospitality for fugitives.

"Why don't you and Rebecca come over this afternoon and play with us?" Sam suggested to Isaac. Louisa seconded this notion enthusiastically.

"I can't," Isaac replied. "I've got lots of chores to do to help prepare for this evening's meal. We have six more mouths to feed. Rebecca can go with you, though. I'll come for thee later, Rebecca."

"Oh, thank thee, Isaac. I'll work very hard to help thee later," Rebecca promised as she squeezed Louisa's hand and began to skip with her friend down the road. As the rest of the group went on to the Johnson farm, Isaac turned toward his uncle's old home, looked in quickly to tell his mother about Rebecca, and walked toward the barn where he began to chop wood.

"I bet Eliza's makin' eyes at Tib again," Hattie, who would have been thrilled if Tib looked at her the way he did at Eliza, said with a smirk.

"So, what of it? You're just jealous of Eliza," Sam pointed out with the annoyingly lucid insight of a younger brother.

"Well, what if I am?"

"I s'pose you'd be crazy not to be. He's so smart and strong," said Hattie (*And handsome*, she thought). "He sure has recovered fast over the past two months. He's a real hard worker, and like Pa, he knows a thing or two about farming. I think Pa really likes him."

"I hope he doesn't leave soon. Last week, Doc Way told him that he's almost fully recovered. He may feel like he should move on," Hattie said dolefully.

"I don't think he'll leave before fall, if he ever leaves," Sam surmised. "I heard him offer to work for Pa through the summer because he wants to pay us back for helping him so much. But I think the reason you're jealous of Eliza also has somethin' to do with it."

"Well, I just hope he can recognize that Eliza is not the only pretty Johnson daughter," Hattie said with renewed hope that Tib might notice her womanly charms sometime soon.

"Hattie, don't you worry 'bout that. Tib told me this morning before we went to school that I looked very pretty," Louisa said reassuringly.

"Oh Louisa Johnson! You can be such a pest sometimes," growled Hattie as she entered the front door of the farmhouse.

"What did I say wrong? Why is she so cross at me? Louisa asked.

Sam laughed. "Louisa, don't worry about Hattie. There's pretty and then there's *pretty*. She wants to be a different kind of pretty than you are right now."

After entering the farmhouse, Rebecca, who had been listening quietly to the debate among the Johnson children, came up to Hattie, grasped her hand, and looked into her face and solemnly declared, "Hattie, a smile will give thee great beauty that is all thine own."

What started out as a sarcastic smirk melted into a smile that revealed the prophesied beauty. "Oh Rebecca, how can I resist you?" Hattie exclaimed as she hugged her.

Coming in from the fields, Ben and Tib entered the kitchen through the back door. Smelling the food cooking over the fire, Ben exclaimed, "Mary, these are heavenly smells! When can we eat? I believe Tib and I may starve to death if we wait much longer."

Mary looking up at her husband with mild humor said with mock pity, "Tib, please escort this starving wretch to some soap and water. I want him to be clean before we bury him."

"Yes, Ma'am!" Tib replied with a slight smile before glancing in Eliza's direction.

"Tib's certainly a serious one," Mary remarked to Eliza as they were putting the finishing touches on the meal.

"Yes, mother, he doesn't joke much, although I have seen him enjoy the humor of others," Eliza replied. "Thank God I haven't heard him cry out in his sleep for the past two weeks. His past must contain many painful memories, which continue to haunt him. Oh, that I could bring healing to him!"

Rebecca, who had joined in the early supper at the Johnsons' farm, was helping Louisa clear the table.

"Isaac hasn't come to fetch you yet, Becky. Maybe you can stay longer and sing with us," Louisa speculated hopefully.

"Oh, Louisa, I would like that very much. But maybe I'd better head home before it gets dark," Rebecca said as she remembered with some regret that Friends didn't usually encourage such activities, being very sober about all aspects of life.

"Isaac told you that he'd come for you. Don't you think you should wait for him? While you're waitin' you can at least listen to us sing," Louisa pointed out.

This line of reasoning was difficult for Rebecca to resist as she had found herself from her earliest memories drawn to song and music like a moth to a candle flame. She especially enjoyed being present when the Johnsons would sing slave spirituals in their home. Some of the older members of the local Friends' meeting had spoken out strongly during meeting about the spiritual dangers of singing, how the powerful emotions that could be aroused would divert the faithful from the beauty and purity of silence. Indeed, a pleasing melody or rhythm could take root in the soul and before one would know it, one's feet might be keeping time to the beat and the whole person might even be tempted to start dancing.

Another difficulty for Rebecca was that the Johnsons, who were serious Baptists, also expressed grave concerns about the spiritual dangers of dancing. And yet, when she would see them sing, especially the slave spirituals, they would invariably start clapping their hands, swaying back and forth, and eventually stomping their feet, keeping time to the rhythm. Mary once tried explaining it to Rebecca.

"When we start singing to God," she began, "His Spirit grabs us, and we just can't help but sing praises to Him with our whole body. But Rebecca, you must understand that's not dancing. No, dancing's dangerous because we might forget God and do it just for the pleasure of it."

Rebecca, wondering why Friends couldn't be moved by the Spirit the same way that the Johnsons were, asked her mother about it. Priscilla had tried to explain that it just wasn't the way Friends praised God, but emphasized to Rebecca that God blessed both forms of worship: one suited to people like the Johnsons, and another that suited members of the Society of Friends. Rebecca accepted her mother's explanation, but remained perplexed. As a conscientious young Quaker girl, how could she enjoy and be drawn to both forms of worship? After that conversation, she always felt a certain guilty pleasure when she witnessed the exuberant musical joy expressed in the praise of her neighbors.

> Wade in the water
> Wade in the water, children
> Wade in the water
> God's gonna trouble the water;
> Who's that yonder dressed in red?

> Wade in the water
> Must be the children that Moses led
> And God's gonna trouble the water . . .

As the sound of the song began to reverberate within the Johnsons' parlor, there was a noticeable effect on the singers. They began to sway back and forth after the initial stanza. With additional stanzas, clapping and foot-tapping to the rhythm ensued, and finally they could not be repressed any longer. They were soon up on their feet swaying, clapping, and stomping out the rhythm.

Eliza looked across at Tib who remained seated but whose eyes glistened as the song progressed. She had secretly worried over him. He had consistently been respectful, gentle, and kind in all his interactions throughout his time with the Johnsons but had been very reticent to attend the local Baptist church with the family on Sundays. When she had urged him to join the family at the worship services, he politely declined the invitation.

"Eliza, God and I have our differences," he replied. "You go ahead. Please sing a hymn for me. I'll work on some jobs around the farm while you are gone."

> . . . Who's that yonder dressed in blue?
> Wade in the water
> Must be the children that's coming through
> God's gonna trouble the water, yeah . . .

As the chorus swelled to "Wade in the water, wade in the water, children. . ." another voice was added, a sweet and poignantly beautiful soprano that burst the bonds of propriety. Rebecca found herself joining in the full experience as she jumped to her feet and began to add clapping and stomping to her joyful vocal expression.

But all the other singers paused except for Rebecca, who was now in raptures, when a deep, mellifluous baritone took up the next stanza joining her in duet,

> You don't believe that I've been redeemed
> Wade in the water
> Just see the Holy Ghost looking for me
> God's gonna trouble the water,
> Wade in the water,
> Wade in the water, children
> Wade in the water
> God's gonna trouble the water!

Tib looked meaningfully into Eliza's astonished eyes as he sang the chorus with a fierce joy she had never witnessed before. As the rest of the Johnson family exchanged surprised glances at hearing such a beautiful duet from their guest and young Quaker neighbor, Tib jumped up from his seat and rushed over to Rebecca lifted her up in his arms and twirling around, repeated the stanza, "'Just see the Holy Ghost looking for me, God's gonna trouble the water!' What an amazing thing! God could make harmony come from the mouths of an unhappy runaway and a somber young Quaker!" Turning to the others, Tib said with fervor, "I can't thank you enough for the kindness and love you have shown me. You can't begin to know how much healing there is in this home." Looking down at Rebecca, he said, "I hope I didn't frighten you just now."

Rebecca whose face was shining exclaimed, "Oh no, Tib, thou didst not scare me; thou and I got caught by the Spirit and I don't think He's let go of us yet," and she giggled as he hugged her once more.

Isaac, who had quietly slipped into the Johnsons' parlor and witnessed the climax of the singing, came up behind Rebecca and said, "Rebecca, thou hast a beautiful voice. I like to hear thee sing. I am not sure what mother and father would say, though. We had better go home now."

Rebecca blushed and felt a twinge of guilt but also a thrill of pleasure after hearing her brother's compliment. She whispered back, "Isaac, please don't tell mother and father that I was singing."

"I promise I won't tell them," Isaac reassured her.

As they walked back toward town in the gathering darkness, Rebecca couldn't repress singing a few more lines of the spiritual.

> Wade in the water,
> Wade in the water, children
> Wade in the water
> God's gonna trouble the water . . .

"Isaac, am I a bad Friend? I feel the Spirit move me sometimes when I am at meeting, but I also felt Him real strong just now when I was singing with the Johnsons. Mother said that there is one kind of worship for Friends and another kind for Baptists like Louisa and Sam's family. If both kinds of worship are blessed by God, why would it be wicked for a Friend to like to sing?"

Isaac looked at his sister and struggled for an answer to this profound theological question. "Well, maybe God has allowed the slaves and their descendants the consolation of music and singin' since they've suffered so much," he suggested.

"But doesn't the Bible talk about singin' and dancin' before the Lord? Didn't King David do that? I don't think he was a slave and I'm pretty certain he wasn't a Friend either."

"Well, I don't know what to tell thee," he replied. "I'd be careful about asking mother and father these questions. Thou mightst upset them. Maybe thou couldst ask Mrs. Way some day. After all she's a *Mother in Israel,* a real wise elder among Friends. She might have an answer for thee. Be careful though. What if she gavest thee an answer thou didst not want to hear? There is something else we should consider. Perhaps, thou art part Friend and part Baptist. That might explain why the Spirit can speak to thee through both kinds of worship."

Rebecca had never considered such a possibility. It did fit with her mother's explanation and her own experience. "Isaac, I wonder how much of me is Baptist and how much is Friend."

"Well, I think it's pretty safe to say that thy singing organ is completely Baptist."

After the singing had ended, Tib invited Eliza out for a walk to enjoy the last remaining vestiges of daylight.

"Tiberius, you surprised me."

"I surprised myself," he replied. "When I saw the power within that spiritual reach out and produce such a beautiful response from a young Quaker girl, I felt I could resist no longer. I have always loved to sing."

"You also have a beautiful voice. It was awe-inspiring to hear you sing with Rebecca. The Burgesses are some of our dearest and closest friends."

"That's just it," Tib replied. "I had come to the conclusion that it was impossible for white people and negroes to live together as equals, let alone as dear friends, and yet here you are living that reality. In spite of my lack of enthusiasm for attending church with you, I do know something of the Scriptures. I'm pretty sure that spiritual we just sang refers to a gospel passage in which Jesus approaches a man who had been paralyzed for thirty-eight years. The paralyzed man and others with him waited by a pool of water hoping that an angel of God would come down and trouble the water so that the one who got into the water first after the angel acted would be healed. The amazing part of the story is when Jesus asks the paralyzed man, 'Do you want to be well?' I always used to think when I heard this passage read in the past, What a strange thing to ask a man who has been suffering for almost forty years.

"But tonight, a revelation came to me when I heard all of you, but especially young Rebecca, sing together so joyfully. When I realized that the next stanza would be 'You don't believe that I've been redeemed / Wade in the water / Just see the Holy Ghost looking for me / God's gonna trouble the water,' like a flash of light I realized that the spiritual was speaking directly to me. Then I remembered Jesus' question to the paralyzed man and understood that I have been that man for some time now, paralyzed by hate. When I looked into your eyes, dear Eliza, I saw Him asking that question, 'Do you want to be made well?' I could no longer prevent the answer from rising within me, 'I do Lord, I do!'"

Tib hugged Eliza close.

"Please be patient with me. You'll hear my full story someday, but for now it's too painful and embarrassing for me to share it with you. I hope that you can trust and love the man you know as Tib in the realization that he has many wounds and scars that are healing slowly. Please understand that none of us has the opportunity of choosing the ones who bring us into this world. If I had ever had the privilege of choosing my parents, there are none better than Mary and Ben Johnson!"

"Tib, here you are only nineteen years old and such a man of mystery and wisdom! In my seventeen years I've seen so little of the sorrow in this world, but I know that whatever lies in your past, I love you through it all. I have loved you from that first delirious day you came into our lives nearly eight weeks ago."

"I know, Eliza. I only hope that I can be worthy of you, because if I stay here much longer, I must ask your father's permission to marry you. But what shall I do? I have nothing to offer you other than my painful past and an uncertain future. Eliza Johnson, I love you and pledge myself to you, if you will have me. First, I must prove myself worthy to ask for your hand."

"Tib, you are so serious that I almost want to shake you," Eliza said as she firmly grasped his arms with both her hands and laughed. "You don't need to prove anything to me, nor I doubt to my parents."

"But, my dear Eliza, I have to prove this to that same self who but a few minutes ago told the Lord that he did want to be healed."

The warm sunshine seemed to reach out and embrace Isaac as he sat by his father on their buckboard wagon. In trees nearby, birds were engaged in romantic conversations, expressing their joy on this early spring day in April 1848. As he contemplated the antiphonal splendor of the birdsong that nearly surrounded them while they traveled along the wooded lane, he almost forgot why they were there.

"Father, the trees look like they are growing a fuzzy green coat," Isaac said. "It is so exciting to see life come back when spring returns."

"Yes, even some of the leaves as they unfurl go through a full reversal of the process of dying they underwent last autumn. The earliest shoots of some of the leaves take on the reds and yellows of fall before they are drowned by the brilliant and pure green of spring. It is a marvelous thing to behold, Isaac," John Burgess exclaimed, having been caught up in his son's enthusiasm.

"It's a shame that our cargo can't enjoy what we are seeing right now," whispered Isaac as he referred to the four fugitive slaves hidden in the bottom of their wagon.

John looked warily behind them and said, "The less we speak of our cargo the better. It appears there are some horsemen overtaking us. Please let me do all the speaking, if they want to talk to us."

Although John Burgess's career on the Underground Railroad had been fairly busy in the past several months, he still did not have the level of confidence sometimes approaching bravado that his brother-in-law Levi Coffin exuded in the work. His actions were driven more from a steely determination borne out of moral commitment which was heavily seasoned with fear. Levi seemed to enjoy the sheer adventure of the work while John could only breathe a deep sigh of relief when each delivery was safely accomplished. The incredible stories of the fugitives' suffering ultimately fueled John and Priscilla's commitment to continue the work in spite of their fears.

He and Isaac had been transporting four fugitives from a station near the Ohio line to their home in Newport with plans to transport them further north via the Cabin Creek settlement of free negroes. Their passengers were a husband and wife in their late thirties with two teenage sons. They had fled their plantation when the wife who was cook there had heard her mistress speak to a friend about selling the cook's husband and sons for transport to the deep south to settle some recent family debts.

John's misgivings increased as the horsemen quickly overtook them, and he thought about Isaac's safety. This was the first time that he had taken Isaac on an actual trip on the Railroad. Isaac had begged for the opportunity, and as it was a Saturday, John thought he could take Isaac along. He really had had no major problems in his clandestine transportation services since the Coffins had left Newport. In fact, he had had no direct encounters with slave catchers, although he had narrowly escaped a few by the aid of Providence or luck depending on one's perspective. But now he wondered whether he was putting his son at too much risk by including him on this trip. The last stationmaster had warned John that he had heard a report that slave catchers were in pursuit of this family.

Initially, the family had gained a head start in the chase. Once they arrived on the north side of the Ohio River, some kindly abolitionists had fed their master and his posse of three other men misinformation about the direction of their flight north. They crossed at the small town of Ripley, Ohio, east of Cincinnati. A typical and more direct path to freedom would be to head north to Sandusky, following the Ohio canal for much of the distance and then take passage on a steamer across Lake Erie to Canada. The Reverend John Rankin and his sons, who were formidable abolitionist foes of slave catchers, lived above the town on a bluff that overlooked the river. A light burning at night in one of the front windows of their home served as a beacon for many fugitives, including those hiding in the Burgess wagon.

On the morning after the slaves's escape across the Ohio, Mrs. Rankin happened to be visiting some friends on the waterfront when the owner of the fugitives arrived by ferry with his posse. When he began to make inquiries of the small group of local citizens regarding his missing property, he was met with hostile stares and silence. His temper rose as he began to speak excitedly in louder tones.

"Do none of you have respect for private property?" the man had shouted, exasperated. "Certainly, one of you must have seen or heard the movements made by a family of four slaves that crossed the Ohio last night. I am certain they crossed last night, and this is the most likely spot. There is a house up there on the bluff that keeps a lantern lit to guide fugitives at night. It is common knowledge on the Kentucky side that a so-called Reverend Rankin and his sons help many fugitives to escape north. I just can't understand how someone who claims to be a man of God can be so wicked as to be an accessory to such crimes!"

Mrs. Rankin anonymously stepped out of the growing throng of people, attracted by the noise and vehemence of the slaveowner's speech, and approached him. "Sir, I am sorry that you are so discomfited by the loss of your property. I think you can begin to appreciate from the lack of response to your inquiries that many of the citizens here do not share your perspective. Although I have not seen or heard any suspicious activities overnight, I can tell you that I have personally witnessed the transit of many fugitives through this community over the past several years. You are correct to be concerned about the Rankins. Their objections to slavery are so strong, they can even be violent at times. Their favorite route to transport slave property north lies along the Ohio canal."

The slave owner looked at Mrs. Rankin with a mixture of gratitude and suspicion. "So many of your fellow townspeople seem hostile to my cause. Why are you being so helpful?"

"I believe it is my Christian duty to reduce conflict in this world, sir. Although I am in no great sympathy with your cause, I can appreciate how conflict over slavery is tearing at the heart of our country. I would hate to see violence done to you or your friends by the Rankins. I think you could go north, bypassing the Rankins and then intercept your slave property in a community where the risks of violence would be much less."

Another woman stepped out of the throng of citizens and angrily shouted at Mrs. Rankin, "You traitor, Sarah! Why are you telling these men such information? Now you will endanger the lives of the runaways." She advanced toward Mrs. Rankin, gave her a shove and began to upbraid the slave owner. "You must leave our community. You are not welcome, coming here and creating trouble by appealing to weaker constitutions with your lies!"

The slave owner and his posse mounted their horses and, turning, he tipped his hat to Mrs. Rankin and then proceeded north in the direction of the Ohio canal. As the horsemen disappeared out of sight, the people in the throng came up and congratulated Mrs. Rankin.

"That was a performance truly worthy of the stage, Mrs. Rankin and Mrs. Bradley," said one admirer.

"Our fugitives are well on their way to Levi Coffin in Cincinnati. Hopefully, this ruse will give them more of a head start. I don't like the look of that slave owner or his posse. He clearly is not going to lose that much valuable property without a fight," exclaimed Mrs. Rankin.

As John was still pondering the risks to which he had exposed Isaac, four horsemen who had been riding hard slowed their pace as they approached the wagon from the rear. Looking at the father and son wearing broad-brimmed hats typical for Quaker men, the leader of the group of horsemen slowed his horse to a walk alongside the wagon and exchanged greetings with John.

"It's a mighty fine morning."

"Yes, indeed it is. Have thee and thy friends been traveling long?"

The stranger smiled when he heard the plain Quaker speech. "Why yes, we've been travelin' for more than a week. This is new territory for us. Are we still in Ohio?"

"No, thou hast been in Indiana for the past five miles or so."

Again, the leader smiled. "Are there many Quaker settlements in this area?"

"Yes, many Quaker families from North Carolina have settled in various communities in this part of Indiana. Art thou looking for a particular family or dost thou have a relative here?" John asked hoping for a benign answer to his question.

The stranger looked at John with amusement and then at the other horsemen who all began to laugh with him. Then acquiring a stern and intense appearance, the leader of the horsemen said, "It is my understanding that Quakers don't respect the property rights of Southerners. Indeed, I have been told that many runaway slaves receive encouragement in their efforts to flee from their masters by the support and protection they receive from Quakers and free niggers in the North."

As the stranger continued his speech, John and Isaac could almost feel the intense anxiety being experienced by those hidden in the back of the wagon. John interrupted, "Friend, there are many poor souls, both of dark and light complexion, who come through this part of Indiana in need of succor and aid due to their poverty or fatigue from long journeys. Members of the Society of Friends are enjoined to show hospitality to the stranger and person in need. It is not our custom to ask a lot of questions about a person's past—"

"Well let me get to the point," interrupted the stranger. "My companions and I are Kentuckians. Almost two weeks ago, a nigger family—husband, wife, and two sons—ran away from my plantation. We tracked 'em across the Ohio but lost the scent for a couple of days. I believe we were intentionally misled, but we got back on the scent after realizing that the damn abolitionists who were helping them escape had sent them through Cincinnati where there's one of the most scurrilous of all abolitionists, a man named Levi Coffin, a Quaker like you folks. We have reason to believe that Coffin sent them this direction on the so-called Underground Railroad. Have you seen any runaways in the last day or so, or do you know where the different stops on the Underground Railroad are in this region? I am anxious to recover my property peacefully and then return home to Kentucky."

It was very difficult for John to maintain composure as he thought anxiously of how to respond to the slave owner. As John was about to tell his first lie, Isaac said, "My father and I have been on this road all morning and haven't seen anybody." The stranger now focused his intense gaze on Isaac.

John piped in, "That's right. We went to collect some wood early this morning about five miles back in the direction from which thou hast come, and are now on our return journey home."

John discovered that telling lies was rather easy.

"If thou art looking for information about runaways," he continued, "thou mayest find more assistance in Richmond, our county seat. There are many who are sympathetic to thy views living there. The road to Richmond will fork to the left in about a mile."

The slave owner looked suspiciously at John and Isaac and then surveying the wagon, which was indeed loaded with wood, he smiled furtively and said, "Thank ye kindly for your help. I am embarrassed to say I forgot my manners. Please let me introduce myself. My name is Henry Chalmers. My friends here are three brothers: Tom, Tim, and Titus Sharpe. They specialize in recovering slaves who have lost their way."

Forgetting his newly found skill at lying, John said politely, "I am John Burgess, and this is my son Isaac."

The rather tall and handsome Henry Chalmers straightened up in his saddle, bowed slightly, and motioned for his companions to ride off at a gallop.

When the horsemen were out of sight, John spoke to the passengers hidden in the false bottom of the wagon. "You must be quite frightened. They are gone for the moment. Isaac and I will do everything possible to keep all of you safe."

A quavering female voice spoke up, "Dat wuz our massa. He gotta big debt to pay. He wanna sel' my man an' boys ta pay de debt. He mitey clevuh. He ain't done wid us yet. Please save us!"

"We'll do our best to save you, but this is the time to pray with all your strength," John responded.

"O Lawd hab mercy! We's prayin' real hard."

Henry Chalmers and the Sharpe trio quickly disappeared around the next bend. As they passed out of sight of the Burgesses, Henry came up alongside Titus Sharpe and gave him an order, "Stay out of view of the Quakers in the wagon back there, but follow 'em and watch where they go and what they do with their load of wood. When you are done, join us in Richmond. We'll be in the largest saloon in town gathering more information."

Chapter Six

Isaac turned to his father, "I'm sorry to have spoken to those men. I know thou didst not want me to speak but I wanted to keep thee from lying. I know how painful that is for thee."

"I always feared the day I would have to lie to save another person," John said. "Thank thee for trying to protect me but I should be protecting thee."

"But everything we have done today has been a lie even before the slave owner came," Isaac whispered.

"Thou speakest the truth. The lives of our passengers depend on how successfully we deceive others."

"Dost thou thinkest that Henry Chalmers believed us?" Isaac asked anxiously in a low whisper.

"I don't think we have seen the last of Mr. Chalmers. I wish I had lied about our names," John reflected. "We must be vigilant during the remainder of our journey and give no observer a reason to be suspicious of our actions."

Isaac and his father were silent and reflective during the last few miles of their trip. As they were entering Newport in the early afternoon, John whispered to Isaac, "I haven't seen anyone following us, but I still feel uneasy. Let's quickly unload our cargo in the barn and then transfer the more precious portion to the house as rapidly and quietly as possible."

Titus Sharpe had been traveling under cover of the trees alongside the road at a safe distance that allowed him to follow the Burgesses without detection. As they entered Newport, he dropped back further as he joined the road that passed through town. He was able to see the Burgess wagon turn right out of sight just beyond a red brick house. Making mental note of its location, he dismounted, tied up his horse, and cautiously advanced on foot toward the Burgess home. Before arriving at the house, he quietly turned to the right down an alley that passed on the other side of the house. He could see a barn in the back and recognized the now-familiar figure of John Burgess helping

Isaac direct the wagon into the barn. Titus was pleased that he had managed to come into town without meeting anyone and now tried to blend with the shadows under awnings as he approached the barn as quietly as he could. The alley passed between the Burgess home on the left and another house on the right, which miraculously for Titus appeared to be unoccupied on this particular Saturday afternoon. To his left, Titus noticed a small vegetable patch and flower garden that filled the intervening space between the house and the outhouse. Hearing the voices of Isaac and John more distinctly, he positioned himself behind a large bush that was located between the outhouse and the barn. He had a good view of the back of the Burgess property while at the same time being able to hear the voices of the Burgesses in the barn.

"Isaac, please hand me the harness," Titus could hear distinctly from his position behind the bush.

After some minutes of patient listening, Titus's efforts were further rewarded. His heart began to beat faster when he heard John Burgess say, "Isaac, please escort our cargo into the house. It seems it is a bit damaged from the long journey. I think thou shouldst enter through the back."

As Titus watched quietly from his hiding place, he could clearly see Isaac, who was now in the backyard, looking in the direction of the barn and motioning for someone to come with him. Silently and quickly, four negroes followed him as he led them into the house. Titus could see that they matched the description Mr. Chalmers had given of his slaves to the Sharpe brothers. As silently and unobtrusively as he had entered Newport, Titus left the town and then galloped off toward Richmond, Indiana to find his employer.

Titus rode the ten miles to Richmond, quite pleased with himself. At 27, he was the oldest of the Sharpe brothers. Tom and Tim were 25 and 22 years of age, respectively. He felt he had a real gift for this kind of work. Almost everything else he had put his hand to had been a dismal failure. He hated farming, he wasn't much of a scholar, and he just wouldn't stick with various apprenticeships, including blacksmithing and cobbling. Such trades were a lot of work, and besides which, they weren't very exciting.

He began to seriously consider slave-catching as a profession after an incident during his last attempt at regular work on a neighbor's farm back in Kentucky. All able-bodied white males were expected to serve on slave patrols in their community. A lot of his friends complained about having to help the rich plantation owners keep an eye on their slaves, but Titus enjoyed his patrol duty. His family had always been too poor to own slaves, but it had always been his father's aspiration to become a real man of property someday and that meant owning a plantation, even a small one, with several slaves.

Titus inherited his father's dream. Even if he didn't yet own a slave, patrol duty gave him the opportunity to really feel like he could be a master someday. For Titus, it also reaffirmed that even if he were dirt poor, as a white man, he would always be better than any negro. He loved to reminisce about how one evening while on patrol duty, he was able to first challenge and then help track down six runaways as they initially overpowered him and ran off. He was able to alert their owner, and even though he had been pretty badly bruised by the runaways, he insisted on helping the plantation's owner and overseer track them down by the next morning. The owner was so pleased with his help that he gave Titus a handsome reward for his efforts and offered Titus the opportunity to discipline one of the runaways, a young buck who had given him most of his bruises. Titus could still recall the intense thrill and pleasure he felt as he held the whip in his hand—what power! And then to hear the slave beg for mercy after he had given him twenty lashes, it was almost as if he owned him. He realized with some careful stewardship and hard work that the rewards for finding and returning runaways could help set him up financially to eventually become a real man of property. Since slave owners were often not very willing to pay if he came back empty handed, he negotiated his fees based on success or failure, in writing, and in advance, always adding a generous expense account.

In his experience over the past two years in his new profession, most slave owners were happy to delegate the responsibility of the actual pursuit and capture to the slave-catcher. To Titus, Henry Chalmers was clearly very desperate to personally participate in the attempt to regain such valuable property, which must be due to the pressure of his indebtedness. Titus recognized in Mr. Chalmers's dilemma an opportunity to introduce his younger brothers to the profession since they also had not shown a strong inclination for more conventional forms of manual labor.

Chapter Seven

As the light of the setting sun filtered through the windows of the saloon, which was a short walk from the county courthouse, Titus lit a cigar and grinned triumphantly at his brothers and Henry Chalmers.

"Well, Titus, what do you have to report?" Henry asked impatiently.

"I have some information that you'll find mighty interestin' Mr. Chalmers," Titus gloated.

"Come on, out with it then! What did you see?"

"Oh, I saw plenty, plennty! You'll be amazed."

"Not unless you tell me, damn you! Do you think I have all evening? Spit it out!"

"Well, where shall I begin?"

"Did you see my niggers, you fool?"

"Now, Mr. Chalmers is that the way you'd treat a star witness if you were goin' to court?"

"Okay, okay, I'm sorry," Henry finally capitulated. "Please tell me your story."

"Now, where was I? Oh, yes, I was about to tell you what I saw."

Titus proceeded in meandering fashion to tell about his adventure spying on the Quakers and the resultant discovery of Chalmers's slaves as they were entering the Burgess's home.

"Are you prepared to swear under oath before a judge to the truth of what you saw?" Henry asked anxiously.

"I know what I saw, and I saw four niggers that looked just like you said they would enter that house. Those damn Quakers lied to us," he swore to emphasize his indignation.

"Are you sure they didn't see you or suspect they were being followed?

"I'm pretty certain they didn't see me, but they seemed awful anxious to get them niggers into the house."

"Well, this all fits with the information that some of the folks here in Richmond were willing to share this afternoon. When we asked about John Burgess, several people said that he had taken over the business of his brother-in-law who had moved to Cincinnati a year ago. His brother-in-law just happens to be that abolitionist scoundrel Levi Coffin," Henry said with grim satisfaction. "We have no time to lose. If that rascally woman and her men were hidden in that wagon and heard my voice, they won't be staying there long. We must get a proper writ from a judge to search that house tonight!" Henry exclaimed with determination. "Tim, go ask the bartender where the local judge lives so that we can get a writ from him tonight."

When Tim asked the bartender the whereabouts of the local judge, he smirked and pointed to a table in the corner of the saloon. "There's yer judge. He might be a bit likkered up by now, though," he laughed.

"Please, Lucy, calm thyself," John Burgess tried to reason with the distraught runaway after supper. "We didn't see anyone following us. I think that all of you are safe for the moment. Clearly, you are all quite fatigued from much travail during your desperate journey north. I would advise you to rest tonight. We can certainly move you out of Newport first thing in the morning but now rest is in order."

"But you don' know Massa Chalmers. I cud hear de 'spishun in his voice when you wuz talkin' wid 'im on de road," Lucy said with conviction. She then came up close to John and Priscilla and whispered, "Y'all don' know dis man likes I do. When he want sumthin', he expect to hav'it. You see ma boys ober dere? One o' dem look kind a yeller an' t'other real dark. Dat yeller one, he be de son of Massa Chalmers. He willin' to sell his own flesh an' blud, dat he wud," she said bitterly. "If'n you keeps us here t'night, pleaz hide us. I jus' knows he's a cummin fer us t'night."

John and Priscilla were frightened by the intensity of the poor runaway's pleading. John responded to Lucy, "Priscilla and I need to make some preparations upstairs. We'll be back soon to help you get ready for your night's rest. Please stay here in the kitchen with our children Isaac and Rebecca until we return."

"John, what a terrible thing that slaveowner has done!" Priscilla exclaimed when they were upstairs.

"Thing?" John repeated bitterly. "His violation of Lucy belongs to a whole pattern of behavior born of the institution of slavery. It certainly explains the fear and loathing that poor woman feels for him. I suspect she may be right about him. He's probably very much accustomed to having his way and may stop at nothing to assure he has it in this instance. Perhaps, we should pay heed to Lucy's intuition and lodge them tonight in the secret hiding place. They seem so afraid that I don't think they'll mind the discomfort or inconvenience."

For the third time, Henry Chalmers shook Judge Adams by the shoulders to arouse him. "Judge, do you understand me? I am here to recover my slave property. Here is my proof of ownership, an affidavit signed by the judge in our county in Kentucky, and here is the witness who will swear under oath, if necessary, that he has personally seen my slaves enter the house of John Burgess in Newport, Indiana, this afternoon. Before the slaves try to escape further north, I need a writ under your authority to search the house for my property, and I need it now, not tomorrow! Tomorrow will likely be too late. My houseslave Lucy is a crafty one, who certainly recognized my voice. I am concerned she may be afraid that I do know where she is and will act quickly to escape."

"Huh?" the judge responded. This evening he was not demonstrating his full intellectual vigor, such as it was, due to a fondness for liquid comfort.

"Titus, bring him more coffee," Henry ordered.

My only recourse is to draft the writ for the old drunk and get him to sign it, thought Henry. He asked for paper and pen and began to write carefully in a clear hand.

As he looked over at the intoxicated judge, Henry told the Sharpe brothers, "I clerked for a while with a lawyer when I was younger and have drafted many legal documents. I think I can assemble a writ that will serve our needs tonight. But we do need the old fool's signature."

Titus and his brothers worked on Judge Adams while Henry finished drafting the writ authorizing the search of the Burgess home. "Whad you do wimmy whiskey?" Judge Adams complained in a slurred voice.

"Here; have some more coffee, Judge. You gotta sober up now so's you can help us."

"But I want my likker right now."

"Soon as you sign this here writ, Judge, we'll buy you another bottle of whiskey. Don't that sound like a fair trade?" Titus drawled soothingly.

"Sounds plenty fair t'me," the judge replied with a thirsty look in his glassy eyes.

"Then sign right here," Henry said impatiently. With the precious and still recognizable signature in his possession, Henry said, "Give the good judge another bottle of whiskey. He certainly has earned it."

With the delay necessitated by obtaining Judge Adams's signature, Henry Chalmers and the Sharpe brothers finally left Richmond at 10 pm. As they entered the outskirts of Newport nearly an hour later, Henry turned to Titus and said, "You and I'll confront Burgess at his front door. Tom will cover the back. Tim will watch the north side of the house. I hope we aren't too late."

Isaac just couldn't understand why the neighbors were hammering away on their house next door on First Day. Everyone knew to not work on the day of worship. But they just kept at it and started to shout even. Suddenly, as he came to consciousness, he realized that it was night, and the hammering was someone pounding on their front door and not construction at the neighbors' house. He also heard a familiar voice.

"Open the door, Burgess! I know you have my slaves in there. I have a signed writ from Judge Adams in Richmond authorizing me under the Fugitive Slave Statute of 1793 to search your premises immediately for my property."

Isaac then heard his father respond in a loud voice, "I hear thee. I am coming, please wait a moment."

By this time, Isaac, who slept in the room that included the entrance to the secret chamber, also heard a frightened female voice from within the chamber exclaim, "Massa Chalmers has cum fer us, jus' like I feared!"

Isaac quickly responded in hushed tones through the wall, "Please don't make a sound. I think they'll search the house. Keep thy courage! I will let thee know when thou canst speak again."

"If you don't hurry up, Burgess, I may have to break your door down, you damn Quaker abolitionist!" Henry Chalmers swore vehemently as he became more excited by the perceived delay.

With the noise created by the pounding and Chalmers's excited speech, other citizens of Newport were awakening and lights were lit in several neighbors' homes.

John lit a lamp and, with Priscilla following close behind, descended the staircase. He hesitated, gave Priscilla an anxious look, said a silent prayer, and opened the door.

"Well, it's about time, Quaker liar!" Chalmers sneered triumphantly.

"What is the meaning of all this noise, creating such a disturbance at this hour?" John demanded while trying to maintain composure in all the excitement.

"I think you know very well what this is all about, you damned abolitionist! Titus, here, followed you back to Newport and saw my four slaves enter your house this afternoon. Try to lie your way out of that mischief, Quaker scoundrel!"

"So, all the evidence thou hast is the report of thy hired man," John responded skeptically.

"It was good enough evidence to obtain a signed writ from Judge Adams under the 1793 Fugitive Slave Statute authorizing me and my hired men to search your home, you damned rascal!"

By this time, Dr. Way walked up to the front porch and said, "Friend, I am Doctor Way, the physician here in Newport, please let me examine the document with Mr. Burgess."

The two Henrys eyed each other warily and finally Chalmers reluctantly handed it to Dr. Way. Henry Way drew John aside, looked anxiously into his eyes, and then scanned the document with him.

After reading it carefully and reviewing the signature, Henry whispered, "John, it looks authentic. I know Judge Adams's signature, although by the look of it, I suspect he was intoxicated when he signed it. Nevertheless, it will be the word of their witness against thy word. The judge will honor a document that he has put his signature to, even though I suspect he won't remember having signed it."

"Thou mayst call me a liar, if thou wish," John said, turning to Henry Chalmers, "but I spoke truly when I said that members of the Society of Friends are enjoined to care for the poor and afflicted in their need regardless of complexion. Thou mayst enter our home but please do not further disturb the peace of this house with thy oaths."

When Henry Chalmers saw Priscilla in the background, he smiled and said in his triumph, "I certainly don't wish to cause offense to the lady of the house. I will try to be more circumspect in my speech. Please lead on with the tour of your home."

"Priscilla, please light another lamp so that there will be sufficient light for the inspection."

"Titus," Henry Chalmers said, "watch the entrance here while I follow them on the tour. I don't want anyone to slip by us while we are inspecting the place."

"Yes sir."

John and Priscilla took Henry Chalmers on a tour, first of the downstairs kitchen and then to higher levels of the house. As they explored the kitchen, Henry pointed out a door in one wall. "Show me where that goes."

As Priscilla opened the door, she said, "This is our pantry where we keep various foodstuffs and cooking supplies."

As Chalmers surveyed the room, which had two levels connected by a short spiral staircase, he said, "Looks like you have a lot of space to store supplies. There must be some prodigious appetites here to need all this space," he commented with sarcasm. John looked at Priscilla but kept his silence.

"Here is where we dine," Priscilla said as she continued the guided tour. Henry looked at the dining table, chairs, and cupboards closely and then moved on to the parlor on the first level.

"Who's the man in this picture?" Henry asked as he pointed to a portrait on the wall.

"That's a portrait of my brother, Levi Coffin," Priscilla answered.

"So that's what the scoundrel looks like, the President of the Underground Railroad," Henry sneered. Shifting his attention to the mantel over the fireplace, Chalmers exclaimed, "What's this? Well, I'll be! A medallion inscribed with an abolitionist slogan: 'Am I not a man and a brother?' You people are so deluded. Negroes do not share equality with the white man. They are incapable of making independent decisions. It is a kindness for us to protect and guide their lives."

Priscilla couldn't help remarking, "It appears that when thy slaves ran away, they made at least one independent decision."

"That's because abolitionist agitators come down south and fill their feeble minds with all sorts of dangerous ideas that only lead to their suffering. Even though you don't believe me, truly the Southern slaveowner has the welfare of his slaves as his central concern. They would starve and perish quickly without our benevolent care."

"Shall we go upstairs now?" Priscilla tried to change the subject of conversation.

"Yes, I'm ready to search the next floor," Chalmers said, but he wasn't quite ready to leave his harangue. "You Quakers are peace-loving people. I just don't understand why you insist on stirring up conflict with your Southern brethren by assisting fugitive slaves. It can only end in war someday."

"There are two issues here," Priscilla responded. "John and I are Southerners. We were born and raised in North Carolina. Our ancestors owned slaves. As Christians, the Society of Friends realized the error of slaveholding and committed to the manumission of all their slave property in the last century. Our ancestors' former slaves and their descendants live quite successfully as free persons of color without any dependence on white people other than that which is shared by neighbors and friends. It is our fervent hope that we can convince our Southern brethren to peacefully do the same for their slaves as our ancestors did for theirs.

"The other issue comes directly from Scripture. Christ commands us to feed the hungry, clothe the naked, care for the sick, and visit the prisoner. Nowhere in the Bible does it speak of doing this for white people only."

"Well, I can see you are convinced in your beliefs and very determined," Henry responded. "However, you haven't convinced me; I'd like to see the upstairs now."

"Our daughter is sleeping here in this room, please try not to wake her," Priscilla requested as she pointed to a room just to the left of the landing on the upper floor. Rebecca was a sound sleeper, but as Chalmers and her parents entered the room, she was awakened by his voice and the tread of his boots on the wood floor.

"Who art thou? Mother, who is this stranger?" Rebecca asked with surprise as she saw her parents following him into the room.

"Rebecca, it's all right. He's visiting us briefly. Don't be afraid."

Chalmers took the lamp Priscilla was holding and peered around the room and then approached Rebecca's bed and shined the lamp down on her with mild interest. "I'm just enjoying some of your fine Quaker hospitality," he said with a peculiar grin as he stared at the frightened Rebecca.

"I'm sorry that thou camest so late sir. If thou hadst come earlier, I could have helped to feed thee something," Rebecca replied.

Priscilla quickly interjected, "Rebecca, I don't think our guest is hungry."

"That's very kind of you missy to offer your hospitality when I've come and awakened you so late," Chalmers replied. "I'll have to take you up on your offer another time." He then turned to Priscilla, "I'm very impressed at how well you teach your children fine manners. Shall we go on to the next room?"

As they crossed the landing before entering the next room, Chalmers noticed what appeared to be a small door to his right.

"Open it!" he commanded.

As he peered into the open door, by the light of his lamp he could see very steep built-in steps leading up into a small attic overhead.

"Aha!" he exclaimed triumphantly. "So, who do ye have hidden up there?"

"Watch thy head as thou climbest!" John Burgess warned Chalmers.

But the advice came too late and Chalmers emitted another oath as he hit his head entering the low attic above. After a careful search identified no hidden slaves, he uttered another oath in frustration as he began his descent to the landing. John and Priscilla then showed him their room.

"What's this over here?" Chalmers asked suspiciously as he noticed what appeared to be a built-in cupboard, which Priscilla's brother had added as a new innovation to the usual freestanding wardrobe that most people owned.

"It is a cabinet for clothing that my brother built into the room. It is quite an innovation in domestic design; we use it instead of a wardrobe," Priscilla said with some pride in her brother's cleverness.

"Open it for me," Chalmers ordered.

"It's just a wardrobe."

"Open it!" Chalmers raised his voice, as he became more suspicious.

"Certainly, please don't upset thyself," John said as he went over and slowly opened the doors of the built-in wardrobe. Chalmers shone the lamp on the contents and said, "Remove everything from inside."

"Art thou certain that thou desirest to do this?" Priscilla asked with some evident hesitation in her voice. "It will slow down thy search."

"I think you have something to hide here," the slaveowner exclaimed with suspicion. Priscilla helped John empty the folded clothing and other contents of the closet onto their bed so Chalmers could carefully examine the entire interior of the built-in wardrobe. Besides the shelves located on both sides of the interior there was a central panel of wood, which Henry examined first with the lamp and then tapped on with his fingers, hoping to discover a hollow area indicative of a hidden chamber. He was eventually disappointed in his search, even after tapping out the wooden base of the interior of the wardrobe.

"There must be a hidden chamber here. I just can't find an entrance," he expressed with great frustration.

"Wouldst thou like to visit the last room upstairs and complete thy inspection?" Priscilla asked.

Chalmers turned toward Priscilla and John who were watching him anxiously, lifted the lamp while peering into their faces, and said, "There is something about this room. I know I am missing something! I can just feel it, looking at you two. I think you know by this time that you won't be able to fool Henry Chalmers."

He rooted around with the lamp, going to each corner of the room and peering intently. After a prolonged search and sighing with deep frustration, he pointed to another door in the back of the room and growled, "Where does that go?"

"That's an entrance to the last upstairs bedroom. There's a door from our bedroom as well as from the landing into the room," John answered. "Our son is sleeping there. Again, please be as quiet as possible."

Isaac had long since ceased to be in a state of slumber after the racket made by Henry Chalmers and his crew had awakened him. He listened intently to the voices of his parents and Chalmers in the next room. When he heard his father say that he was asleep, he pretended to be asleep and prayed that the hidden runaways would be silent.

"Why are there two beds in this room?" Chalmers asked in a loud whisper as he thrust the lamp in the direction of the beds, the closer of which was occupied by the apparently sleeping form of Isaac.

"As we told thee earlier, we try to provide hospitality to those in need as well as to visiting friends and family members," Priscilla answered. "Thou mayest wish to examine the bed more closely. There is no one hiding there."

Chalmers proceeded to tear off the sheets and blanket from the unoccupied bed. Finding no one, he exclaimed, "Lucy, I will find you yet, you witch! I'm not done searching for you, by any means."

Isaac, feigning being awakened by the angry slaveowner's exclamation, sat bolt upright in bed and cried out, "Who's there?"

"Isaac, this is Mr. Chalmers, whom we met earlier today. He is here looking for his runaway slaves."

"I don't understand, Mr. Chalmers. We told thee we didn't see anybody on the road today," Isaac said with perplexity.

"Well, young man, one of my men followed you and is certain that he saw my slaves enter your house this afternoon. That's why I'm here."

"Art thou sure thou canst trust him?" Isaac asked innocently.

"I'm not sure I can trust anyone right now," Chalmers muttered under his breath. "Oh Lucy, Lucy! You must be here, but where?" he cried as he left the room and re-entered the landing, now more frustrated than ever. "Titus Sharpe, come up here right quick!"

Chalmers shouted down from the landing, forgetting all requests for restrained speech from John and Priscilla. As Rebecca and Isaac both emerged from their bedrooms onto the landing in response to the shouted command, Chalmers met Titus halfway down the staircase and began to whisper to him in heated tones while pushing him down to the first floor and out of hearing of the Burgess family.

"Titus, have you played me for the fool? I made a thorough search and can't find 'em!"

"Mr. Chalmers, I know what I saw. I bet they're still here hidden somewhere in the building."

"Look at the crowd of people outside. They'll be pressing us to leave soon, since we've been allowed to make a good search of the house. The writ doesn't authorize more than that and their doctor friend'll know it. I'm afraid that wily slave Lucy and her family may have gotten away. In case they are still hidden somewhere here, either in the house or neighborhood, two of us should stay here a few days and watch the house closely while the other two head north to track 'em, in case they've left already."

When no slaves emerged from the Burgess home, Henry Way quietly approached one of the younger neighbors who had assembled in the crowd outside, gave him the description of the slave property as it was written in the writ, and said, "Thomas, wouldst thou please inform our friends in the Cabin Creek community that this family just passed through their community headed north toward Michigan?"

"Doctor Way, it would be my pleasure to confuse our Southern friends," Thomas said with a big grin.

Thomas was off by horseback headed north within five minutes. Meanwhile, Dr. Way approached Henry Chalmers who was now standing in the doorway of the Burgess home. "Mr. Chalmers, thou hast had the opportunity to search the Burgess home in compliance with the writ signed by Judge Adams. May I suggest that thou leave this family in peace, so that they may get some rest during the remainder of the night?"

"I appreciate your compliance with Judge Adams's writ and I'm sorry for the inconvenience," Chalmers said insincerely but with due consideration of the crowd assembled outside the Burgess home. He then motioned to Titus to collect his brothers and leave.

"Oh, how I love thee, my brave wife!" John exclaimed as he hugged Priscilla once Chalmers and the Sharpe brothers had retreated.

Henry Way smiled and said, "We should confer with your guests about the next steps to be taken."

"Yes, Henry, we have much to be thankful for this night," John replied. "Clearly, our adversaries know that Lucy and her family heard and recognized her owner's voice and would likely be anxious to keep moving north. I think that we were able to sow additional seeds of doubt in Mr. Chalmers's mind during his search. Hopefully, he will be anxious to pursue them in a northerly direction away from Newport."

"How art thou, Lucy?" Priscilla asked as she helped Lucy and her family climb out of the hiding place behind the head of Isaac's bed. Lucy, who was still trembling with fright, exclaimed in a whisper, "Thank de Lawd! Massa Chalmers' awful mad. I expec' he gonna watch dis house fo' a spell."

"I agree with Lucy. Her master is still very suspicious and will likely divide his forces, sending some north while also leaving some in this vicinity to watch the activities at this house," Henry said.

"I was hopin' to hab de pleasure o'sendin' him a letter fum Canada, tellin' him dat we's arrive dere safely," Lucy laughed grimly.

"There is no reason, Lucy, that thou shouldst not have that pleasure," said Priscilla. "I think that there are the seeds of a very good plan in thy desire to write to Mr. Chalmers of thy safe arrival in Canada. Does he know that thou canst write?"

"His chillin learned me to read an' write a bit, fo' their fun. Dat's how'd I copy de pass he write so's we cud escape. He shud be mighty angry wid dem," Lucy laughed again.

"Henry, dost thou think it possible that Lucy could write a letter to her master and then have one of our agents on the Underground Railroad post it from Canada?" Priscilla asked. "If his family receives it in about two weeks, I think, he would be fully convinced that he has lost his slaves to the safety and freedom of Canada. Meanwhile, if necessary, they can remain here with us until he receives the news and ceases his pursuit."

"Priscilla, that is, indeed, a very clever plan," John said with admiration. "Thou hast some of the same sagacity that thy brother possesses. What dost thou think, Henry and Lucy?"

Both Henry and Lucy agreed with her family that it seemed the best plan for the moment, realizing that they would have to watch the action of the slavecatchers very closely over the next several days.

"Is there anything, Lucy, that thou canst add in thy letter to thy master to make him certain that it is coming from thee?" Priscilla asked a short while later as she watched Lucy slowly draft her letter.

"Missus Burjis, dat be a good idea!" Lucy responded enthusiastically. "Missus Chalmers won' like it, but she know'd dat I know'd intimate tings 'bout Massa Chalmers. Dat'll shore make it clear dat de letter be fum me."

Priscilla blushed and said, "Lucy, I didn't mean for thee to use such information."

"Don't you worries now, Missus Burjis. Dat's de bes' info'mashun I gots."

"Lucy, I would recommend that thou mention in thy letter that thou and thy family escaped north through Toledo, Ohio, and crossed into Windsor, Ontario in Canada from Detroit, Michigan. Mr. Chalmers and his associates will be expecting thee to be traveling through Indiana northward to Adrian, Michigan and on to Detroit via Ann Arbor, Michigan. He will need to learn that we have several routes open to us on the Underground Railroad," Henry Way explained.

"I am thankful that Mr. Chalmers didn't notice the fact that we have a spring feeding an indoor well in the base of the pantry," Priscilla said as she reviewed the details of the search with Henry Way and her husband. "We should be able to minimize any evidence of more than four occupants in the house with our access to this hidden source of water."

"Priscilla, I think we will be having dinner guests quite frequently during Mr. Chalmers's siege. That should also confuse him about the amount of food entering our home," John suggested. "Henry, wouldst thou and Hannah like to be our first dinner guests?"

"Yes, of course. Hannah and I would be very pleased to dine with the Burgess family at anytime," Henry laughed, and soon John and Priscilla were laughing as well.

Chapter Nine

"I know those damn slaves are in that house," Titus complained to his brother Tim as they rode toward Cabin Creek, a small community of free negroes about ten to fifteen miles north of Newport. "I wish Mr. Chalmers had let me do the search. He musta missed somethin' obvious."

"Titus, he could be right about them leavin' the Quakers right quick, especially since they'd heard his voice when they were in the wagon," Tim observed.

"Well I 'spose it's possible, but damn it all, if they got away, we're gonna be out of a real nice reward. Besides, I'm mighty tired and not enjoyin' traveling in the dark in hostile darkie country. How can Chalmers expect us to get any cooperation from free niggers in the north?"

"Money can make mos' folks mighty helpful," Tim reflected.

"Well, I guess that's where our expense account will come in handy."

As the first rays of the rising sun began to peek over the fields of the farms surrounding the small village of Cabin Creek, Indiana, the two weary southern travelers approached the first farm on the outskirts of town. Pounding on the door of the farmhouse, Titus received a response from within.

"Who are you and what do you want at this hour?"

"We're mighty sorry to disturb you so early but we need to ask you some questions," Titus replied. After some time, the door opened slightly, and the muzzle of a shotgun was pointed out at them. In the early morning light, they could barely make out the features of the owner of the weapon, a stocky middle-aged negro male.

"We're looking for some people who—"

"You mean you're slavecatchers," the owner of the shotgun cut Titus's introductory speech short. "Why in hell would you think I would want to help you scum?" growled the negro as he leveled his shotgun at Titus.

"Whoa, now! We mean you no harm," Titus tried to reassure him. "We are willin' to pay fer any information you might be able to share with us 'bout comin's and goin's in the last day or so.

"So, you think I would betray one of my own race for money. Go to hell!" and the negro slammed the door in Titus's face.

As Titus and Tim were licking their wounds on the front porch, they heard a female voice inside ask, "Why were you so unkind to the strangers, Frank?"

"Jessie, they're some wretched slavecatchers askin' questions about recent travelers comin' through our community. They even offered me a bribe."

"I hope they don't go to our neighbors," Jessie replied. "They're desperate enough with all their debt that they might tell 'em somethin' for some money."

Frank looked out the window and saw the slavecatchers wink at one another as they walked back to their horses. He whispered to Jessie as a big smile illuminated his face. "It's a good thing that our voices carry easily through the walls of this house."

"Well those fools told us a lot of helpful information, which didn't cost us a penny," Titus laughed as they rode on to the next farm.

Another quarter mile up the road, Titus and Tim turned in at the next farm and repeated the procedure of knocking on the front door. A suspicious voice within called out, "What do you want at this hour?"

"We've been travelin' a long while and are looking fer some folks. Do you think you could help provide us with some information? We'd be happy to pay you fer your trouble," Titus said as ingratiatingly as possible.

The door opened slightly, and an elderly negro poked his head out to survey the strangers. "Why you ain't local white folks is you? You look like you fum de South, maybe Kaintuck?"

"Yes indeed, Kentucky's our home."

"I be fum Kaintuck. I shore do miss it sometimes," the old man said wistfully. "My massa he done free me when he die many years ago. Some of my bes' memories are fum workin' fo' him. It'd be a hard life here in de North for us free niggers."

Titus began to warm to his subject on hearing the old man's story. "We're lookin' fer a family of negroes that might've come through here overnight headin' north."

The old man eyed Titus and Tim with suspicion and said, "Is you tryin' to catch those po' niggers? Ah better not talk no mo' wid you," and he began to shut the door.

"Wait, please wait, old man!" cried Titus. "You said how much you miss Kentucky. We just want to bring them home so they won't have to suffer like you have up here in the North. Besides, we appreciate your talkin' so much with us that we'd like to pay you fer your trouble."

The door opened a bit more. "How much yo' willin' to pay?"

"Two whole dollars!"

The door pulled shut.

"Three dollars!"

"Come on, old man, we just want to help these poor people return to their rightful home in Kentucky. Okay, four dollars."

The door opened again, and the old man looked furtively about him and in a whisper asked, "What duz yo' wants to know?"

Titus smiled at his brother and then turning to the old negro asked, "Have a woman named Lucy, her man, and two sons, big strappin' bucks, passed through here in the last twelve hours or so?

"Well, dey's been some folks dat meets dat description cum thru here 'bout ten hours ago. Dey's in a mitey big hurry."

"Which way did they go?"

"H'm I got's to think 'bout dat a bit," he said as he eyed the empty palm of his hand. Titus finally caught the hint and started to count out four one-dollar coins into the palm of the old negro's hand.

"Oh, now's I remembers," he said with conviction. "Dey's gone north to Mishigun thru Indeeana. Dey means to gets to Canada thru Adrian an' Detroit, Mishigun. Dey be long gone by now, I expec," he said with a somber expression.

"That's very helpful old man, but where are they headed in the next day or so?" Titus continued his interrogation.

"Dey wuz talkin' 'bout goin' to Smithfield ober dere in Del'ware County," the old man pointed vaguely in a northwesterly direction.

"How can I get directions to Smithfield?" Titus asked impatiently.

"Well, I's not so sure 'bout dat. Yo' needs to go up de road pas' de town fo' 'bout two, maybe three mile an' ask fo' a man, Jones by name. He can tell you how to git dere."

Titus felt he had got about as much meaningful information as he could out of the old man. He told his brother as they walked back to their horses, "It sounds like the niggers got ahead of us after all. We need to find someone who will carry a message back to Mr. Chalmers to let him know what we've learned and that we are back on the trail of the niggers."

While Titus was writing a note to Chalmers, the old negro was relating his encounter with the slavecatchers to his son and daughter-in-law.

"Pa, you sure are a master of slave speech," his son said with admiration.

"Well don't forget, I was a slave many years ago," he replied. "These slavecatchers love to hear 'bout de po' niggers who wish dey still wuz on de massa's plantation. They are so gullible! Equal doses of greed and ignorance blind them. I must say, though, that their investment of four dollars was well spent, at least from my perspective," and he and his family laughed until their sides hurt.

As Henry Chalmers settled in for a long siege, he became a familiar sight on the streets of Newport. He found the lack of saloons in the dry community a real trial. Although it wasn't much compensation for the lack of ardent spirits, in their own way the citizens tried to make him feel welcome. After all, the Quaker commitment to hospitality must extend even to enemies.

Being an occasionally enthusiastic Baptist, he wasn't sure how to respond to repeated invitations to attend silent worship at the Newport Antislavery Friends meeting. His only other option was to worship with the free negro community in their Baptist church. He thought it might be useful and a little fun to show up and frighten the colored people with his presence. Beyond the mere pleasure of intimidating the local negro community, the possibility of hearing some news about his fugitive slaves from one of the worshipers was also an attractive prospect. He still wasn't fully convinced that Lucy and her family had escaped. It was as if he could somehow feel her presence close to him there in Newport, in spite of all the evidence to the contrary. He was also just plain tired and needed a rest from the hunt. Anyhow, there was nothing but angry creditors waiting for him back home in Kentucky. A multiplicity of similar thoughts created eddies as they flowed through the turbulent regions of his mind while he sat in the small dining room of the only hotel in Newport. No, he would stay here and wait it out while the two Sharpe brothers pursued the trail of the fugitives to the north. The Quakers may have hidden the fugitives better than he thought. The possibility that they could still be in the Burgess home waiting patiently for him to give up the pursuit tormented him.

"Tom, you keep an eye on the Burgess place this mornin'. I'm going to worship at the nigger church."

"Mr. Chalmers, I didn't know you liked to worship with niggers!" Tom exclaimed with some surprise.

"Tom, it's the Lord's day. Why shouldn't I worship with them? Would you have me worship with those Quaker abolitionist fanatics? Just because they're ordained to be slaves in this life, doesn't mean they haven't got immortal souls. God is merciful. The curse of Canaan won't extend to the next life. If they've been faithful servants in this life, who are we to begrudge the poor wretches a small piece of heaven in the next?" Henry Chalmers reasoned. "Besides, maybe I can learn something about my slaves from one of them who might have a loose tongue."

"I can't hear you! Now where's your faith? Are you gonna hide it under a bushel or let it shine out for all to see!"

"Glory, hallelujah!"

"Amen, brother! Amen!"

Ebenezer Jones, the pastor of the Baptist church of the free negro community in Newport surveyed his congregation with pride. He was just getting warmed up. "What did the good Lord say 'bout lovin' one another? What did He say? I can't hear you!"

"I think he said, 'Love one another as I have loved you,'" Sam responded tentatively.

"Why Samuel Johnson, you got up your courage and gave a very good answer," Pastor Jones beamed with pleasure. "Well, brothers and sisters, is young Sam right; does he know his Gospel?"

"Yes, he's right. Praise the Lord! Amen!" Members of the congregation shouted out in confirmation.

"Now here's the hard part. What did the good Lord mean when he said, 'as *I* have loved you?'" Pastor Jones looked out over his flock with his penetrating gaze, waiting for an answer. "What happened to the good Lord, who gave this commandment to his disciples? Come on, help me now."

As the pastor looked out over his congregation for someone to answer his rhetorical question, he could see that Sam was ready with another answer. Ignoring Sam, who was now trying to catch his attention, he asked, "Can no one help me find an answer to this most vital question?"

"I think I can, Pastor," Sam spoke out with more confidence this time.

"Well out of the mouths of babes and infants. . .why is everyone so tongue-tied today, except for this young man? Okay, Sam, please tell us what happened to the good Lord who gave us this commandment to love one another as *he* loved us."

"Pastor, the Lord was whipped like a slave and killed on a cross!" Sam exclaimed triumphantly.

"Amen, brother Samuel. Amen! I couldn't have said it more clearly. Young man, you may have the preacher's calling in you. What can we say to these words of truth spoken by such a young member of our congregation?"

"Amen," "Glory hallelujah," "The Lord be praised," and other expressions of joy erupted from Pastor Jones's flock. At this point, beads of sweat began to appear on his bald head as he began to pace back and forth, casting sidelong glances toward various members as he paced faster and faster.

"Brothers and sisters, didn't I tell you that the *hard part* was comin'? The Lord's tellin' us to love each other the same way he has loved us. And how has he loved us? No less than by allowin' himself to be whipped, tortured, and crucified by his enemies!" He had been pacing so fast during this part of his sermon that many in the congregation were a bit dizzy from following his movements as he spoke with his eyes largely cast down. His voice rose as he said these last words, and then, looking up to fully face the congregation, he almost shouted, "Isn't that so?"

"Yes, amen, that's so!" jumped out of the mouth of a newcomer before anyone else could respond. Pastor Jones was utterly speechless as he met the gaze of the enthusiastic Henry Chalmers, who had quietly slipped into the back of the church at an earlier point during the service.

A profound silence that might have been the envy of many a Quaker meeting settled briefly over the congregation as negro pastor and white visitor eyed each other. The pastor's temporary paralysis was cured by Henry Chalmers, who grinned and said with persistent enthusiasm, "That's a mighty fine message, pastor; a real inspiration. I hope you won't mind if I share it with my people back home in Kentucky."

"I think it's time for some singin'," Pastor Jones replied. He felt that there was safety in numbers and began to lead the congregation in song.

"Amazing grace how sweet the sound. . ."

Chalmers, who was a fine bass, joined in singing the popular hymn with passionate conviction. He seemed blissfully unaware of any initial awkwardness as his voice merged with that of the congregation.

The slaveowner shook Pastor Jones's hand at the end of the service and in a loud voice repeated his compliments on the quality of the sermon. "You have a fine congregation here, pastor. I don't s'pose you know why I'm here in Newport."

"We know exactly why you're here," Pastor Jones responded.

"Well I s'pose you might not be real excited 'bout my reason for being here," Chalmers said raising his voice, "but if you or any of your congregation could provide me with information about my runaways, I'd be mighty obliged and would be happy to pay you for your trouble."

"I won't be able to help you, Mister. . ."

"Chalmers, Henry Chalmers."

"May God help you to find your way," Ebenezer offered his cryptic benediction as Henry Chalmers left the church.

"I feel invigorated in spirit," enthused Henry later on as he described his morning's experience to Tom Sharpe. "I wish I could have that nigger preacher give sermons to my slaves like the one he gave today. He'd have them ready to accept their whippings just like Jesus, submissively with love. It was an inspired message!"

"Did you find out any more about the runaways?"

"After I made a request for help at the end of the service, one of the church members approached me on the sly as I was coming back here and offered me some information for a dollar."

"What'd he tell you?"

"He said pretty much the same thing that Titus heard from the free niggers north of here. There was a family that passed through here quickly on Saturday eight days ago and didn't stay the night they were so scared of being caught," Henry related with some fatigue and frustration. "That seems the most logical explanation, but I still feel there's somethin' not quite right about it. It's just too simple and my Lucy's too clever. Besides, the last news from Titus sounded like the trail was growing cold up north. What if they're still hiding in that damned abolitionist's house even while we speak? I guess that's what keeps me here waiting and watching."

Priscilla Burgess, who was carrying a tray of food, knocked softly on the door and heard, "Cum in pleaz," in response.

As she opened the door to Isaac's room, she saw the now-familiar faces of Lucy, her husband Joe, and her two sons, Bill and Abe. During the long siege, the runaways had stayed in this upstairs room in case they should require immediate refuge in the hidden chamber. Other than time spent in the hidden chamber, the four walls of this bedroom had circumscribed their sojourn in Newport, Indiana. To add to the gloom and inherent boredom of their situation, the curtains of the windows were drawn to prevent their detection. They were now well into the second week of being under siege in the Burgess home. Of necessity, they had learned to be patient and quiet during their experience as fugitives; but even so, they were all feeling restive, especially Bill and Abe. "When dis all gonna end?" Bill, the younger mulatto son asked anxiously, looking first to his mother and then to Priscilla.

"One of our friends from the free negro community told Isaac yesterday that Mr. Chalmers attended their church on First Day, that is Sunday last. Apparently, your master enjoys worship services for he was very active in the service," Priscilla smiled as she related this bit of news.

"Yes'm, massa always enjoy de preachin' and de singin'," Lucy confirmed. "In fac' he like nigger preachin' de bes'. It nebber kept 'im from whippin' his people when he cum back fum de church, though."

"Mr. Chalmers asked for information about you all from the congregation," Periscilla said. "One of the folks in the church told him that he had seen you leave quickly headed north on the Saturday you came to us."

"But, yo' sees how he be. He still here watchin' de house. He don't gib up so fast," Lucy intoned mournfully.

"Let us all be patient," Priscilla advised. "It could take two to three weeks for your letter to reach his home in Kentucky and then for a message to arrive here. Meanwhile, we must minimize any remaining suspicions that Mr. Chalmers has about you still being here. Please continue to be very quiet, stay in this room, and don't give them a chance to see you at the window. We are committed to helping all of you pass through this danger unharmed. Beware of boredom that might lead to carelessness."

As Isaac and Rebecca were walking home from school that afternoon, they heard a familiar voice say, "Good afternoon, my young Quaker friends."

Looking up first, Rebecca's eyes met those of Henry Chalmers and without any hesitation, she responded with a smile and said, "Thank thee, Mr. Chalmers, and good afternoon to thee, also."

"How are your guests today?" Henry asked as innocently as he could, directing his attention to Rebecca.

"I'm not sure what thou meanest, sir. Many guests visit our home. Almost every day friends and neighbors come to share a meal with us," Rebecca answered, her cheeks reddening slightly.

"I'm thinking of four negroes that have been staying with you for almost two weeks now," Chalmers said as mildly as he could.

Looking directly into his face with her dark brown, innocent eyes, Rebecca said in steady, measured tones, "Sir, thou must be mistaken. We don't have any negro guests staying with us. Our friends the Johnsons, who are negroes, come frequently to visit and have dinner with us. Wouldst thou like to meet them?"

"No, thank you." Chalmers tipped his hat to Rebecca and marched off with a grim expression on his face.

Isaac and Rebecca quickened their pace after parting ways with Henry Chalmers. As they entered the side door of the Burgess home, Isaac quickly closed the door behind them, and Rebecca burst into tears.

"Oh mother, I am so wicked! I told my first lie today," Rebecca said with a quavering voice as she buried her tear-stained face in her mother's apron.

Isaac broke in, excitedly, "Mother, Rebecca was real brave just now. The slavecatcher was trying to trick her into saying that we have negro guests staying here, but she kept the secret and told him that we don't have any negroes staying with us." Isaac looked at Rebecca with admiration and said, "Thou didst very well, Rebecca. I am very proud to be thy brother!"

In between sobs, Rebecca replied, "But I lied. Friends never lie. Oh, I feel so horrible. Will God forgive me, mother? I just couldn't let that slaveowner catch Lucy and her family."

"Oh, my darling child, thou hast received the wounds of love today," Priscilla supported Rebecca's chin so that their eyes could meet. "Thou chose the better part and thou hast saved the lives of this family. When we follow God's law of love, we may have to sometimes break lesser laws, including the prohibition against lying. Thou hast done a noble and righteous deed today and yet thou also lied. Rebecca, thou canst praise God in thanksgiving that He showed thee thy path in that very difficult moment, but also ask His forgiveness and pray that the duty to lie may not be imposed upon thee again. The apostle Paul himself tells how God blessed the lie of the Canaanite woman Rahab when she hid the spies of Israel and saved their lives."

Isaac turned to his sister and said, "Remember how Aunt Kitty told thee that thou must be wise as a serpent and gentle as a dove? Well, I think thou hast gained some of the wisdom of the serpent today."

Rebecca looked toward Isaac and then into Priscilla's eyes and said tearfully, "But, why should becoming wise be so painful?"

Chapter Eleven

Henry Chalmers was not having a good day. He had been in Newport almost three weeks and was beginning to feel like a fool for being so reliant on a mere intuition. After all, Titus and Tim Sharpe had reported traces of his slaves' flight north for quite some distance beyond the environs of Newport. All the evidence pointed to a successful escape on the part of his slaves and yet he could only ruminate on how close he had been to capturing them while they were hidden in the Quakers' wagon.

Everything about Newport was beginning to irritate him beyond toleration. His visit to the Baptist church this past Sunday was not as uplifting to his spirits as the first had been. The placid and impassive faces of the Quaker inhabitants were at times maddening to him. They clearly were watching him in their own quiet way as much as he was trying to spy on them. This realization was almost unnerving at times.

Finally, he was becoming quite concerned about the fate of his plantation back in Kentucky. He had a modest plantation with twenty slaves, including Lucy and her family. As he had tried to expand in recent years he had taken on significant debt, which was coming due during his time away. The debt would largely be paid by the sale of Lucy's husband and boys. Henry had written his wife Amy from Richmond asking her to try and reassure his creditors that he would be able to discharge the debt soon but to please give him an extension while he recovered his property. He had sent the letter on the same day, earlier in the afternoon, just prior to his search of the Burgess home when he felt he could almost taste the victory of a successful quest. But that had been nearly three weeks ago and in the interim, five days previously, he had received an anxious letter from Amy stating that the creditors were not willing to give him more than another two weeks to raise the money or they would seek legal redress in the form of an auction of property of equivalent value to cover his debts. For Henry, this clearly meant loss of other prime field hands, which he could ill afford to lose. His actual work force on the plantation was at best two-thirds of the number of slaves he owned since the other third was comprised of house servants and elderly slaves who could no longer provide meaningful labor in the fields. If he lost anymore slaves in addition to Lucy's men, he could not maintain the plantation at its present level of productivity. Not only would his dreams of increased prosperity be dashed, but also the plantation would enter an inevitable death spiral. He would effectively be ruined. Additionally, the two Sharpe brothers had returned from the north, and with their brother Tom had made rude references to the apparent failure of the pursuit and their desire to be paid for their labor.

These anxious thoughts whirled in his head as he sat down in the hotel lobby to open another letter that had just arrived from his wife. As he scanned the contents of the letter, his face flushed, and without being aware of his surroundings swore loudly, "That damn woman has ruined me! Damn her to hell!"

Absalom Penrose, the hotel's proprietor and the meekest of Quakers, approached Henry with some trepidation and said, "Sir, please calm thyself! Thou art disturbing the other guests of the hotel."

This was indeed true for every eye in the lobby was fixed on the source of profanity, residing in Henry Chalmers's body. Henry looked up with an angry, distracted look and said, "Oh yes, I'm sorry. I need to settle my bill with you immediately."

He rushed upstairs to collect his things before shaking the dust off his boots and departing from Newport. As he ran up the stairs, some guests could hear him speaking to himself, "The wretched woman! Not only does she gloat from her safety in Canada, but she also reveals her intimate knowledge of my anatomy to Amy. How ungrateful and cruel she is! I'm ruined, I'm ruined!"

As Henry swung into his saddle, Titus Sharpe and his brothers approached on their horses. "Mr. Chalmers, you appear to be in a mighty big hurry to leave. Have you got some bad news from home?"

Henry, who would have been relieved to quietly slip away from his companions, realized the need for some honesty as the three Sharpe brothers effectively blocked his path. "Yes, I just got word that my slave Lucy sent a letter from Canada to my home to gloat over the fact that she gave us the slip! I need to get back to Kentucky to settle some debts as soon as possible."

"Mr. Chalmers, we'd be delighted to accompany you as you return home, but first we'd like to settle our accounts with you, if you don't mind," Titus drawled.

"I understand your desire to settle accounts, boys, but don't you think it could wait until we get back to my plantation?"

"No, we'd feel a lot better, if you'd pay us right now."

"I'm not sure I have enough with me to pay all that I owe you," Henry admitted helplessly.

"We'll be happy to take what you got now with a receipt for the rest which we'll collect when we get back to your plantation."

"How will I pay for lodging and food on the journey back?"

"Don't worry Mr. Chalmers, we'll take care of it and add it to the debt you owe us. Why don't we head on down the road a spell? I'm gettin' mighty tired of Quaker towns. A saloon would be a welcome sight right now," Titus said with a laugh.

A grim looked passed across Henry's features.

"Now Mr. Chalmers, don't you fret," Titus continued. "As soon as we get to a town with a saloon, I promise to buy you a drink," and then silently to himself, *And I'll add that to your debt, you fool!*

A half hour after Henry Chalmers checked out of his hotel, Absalom Penrose, having checked to make sure that all the Kentuckians had left Newport together, walked quickly up the street and knocked at the front door of the Burgess home. When Priscilla opened the door, she could see that Absalom was not in his usual state of composure.

"Mrs. Burgess, may I come in?" he asked breathlessly.

"Of course, Absalom, please come in and sit down. It appears that thou hast had a violent shock. It is not like thee to be so flushed and anxious. Please tell me what has happened to thee."

The timid Absalom looked up at Priscilla over the rim of his glasses and in agitated tones proceeded to describe the untoward behavior of Henry Chalmers in the lobby of his hotel. He also quoted Henry's despairing comments, deleting the oaths but including the references to the contents of the letter that were especially disturbing to his former guest.

"Absalom, thank thee for thy report. It appears that our guests from Kentucky have left Newport for good," Priscilla said with relief.

"Lucy, I think that thou hast been rewarded amply for thy patience," John said with a smile the next day as he, Priscilla, Rebecca, and Isaac exchanged parting hugs with the fugitives. "May God protect thee and thy family as you all finish your journey to freedom in Canada! Thy master is now reaping what he has sowed. Please send us a note confirming your *actual* arrival."

Chapter Twelve

Benjamin Johnson looked over at Tib and pointing to the rows upon rows of thriving corn said, "Isn't this just about the prettiest sight you ever saw?"

Tib smiled and replied, "Sir, there's no question that with its healthy green color and exceptional growth this field of corn is a wonder of nature. But I don't know if I would use the word "pretty" to describe it. That word seems more suited to a certain person I know."

Ben laughed. "You've got a bad case of Eliza Johnson on the brain, don't you?"

"And in my heart! I'm afraid it's incurable," Tib said laughing at himself. "I have to sometimes stop and check myself to make sure I'm not trapped in the middle of a dream. I don't ever remember such happiness or peace as I have experienced these past fifteen months with your family. Eliza sometimes seems more an angel than human to me. I've rarely ever seen great physical beauty combined with such loving kindness and good sense in the same person. I still can't believe she will be my wife in a few weeks—"

"And you will fully be a part of this family," Ben finished the thought as he gave Tib a hearty handshake. "I only worry about your safety here, Tib. It does seem likely that your owner has given you up for dead, but the risk of discovery and capture is still there, even if it's small. You should seriously consider taking Eliza with you to Canada. I know she'd go with you to the ends of the earth, if it would ensure your safety."

"Mr. Johnson, I don't think it will be necessary. I feel very safe right here in Newport." Tib also thought to himself, *I could never take Eliza away from her family. Never!* Changing the subject, Tib said, "I guess it is only just that a farmer who can raise up such a beautiful daughter can also raise up the finest crops in Indiana!"

Ben beamed at the compliment and proceeded to regale Tib with a long but pleasant monologue on the virtues of generous manuring.

The wedding was scheduled for the sixth of August, only three weeks away. Mary Johnson, whose prodigious talents included being an excellent seamstress, was doing additional measurements and adjustments for Eliza's wedding dress, while Hattie, Louisa, and Rebecca were watching with fascination.

"Eliza, are you sure that Tib doesn't have a younger brother who wants to escape north?" Hattie asked again.

"I told you he still isn't comfortable talking much about his family back in Kentucky," Eliza replied. "The only family he's talked about at all is his mother and sister. They were sold down the river. I know he grieves for both of them. He's afraid he'll never see them again."

"I just like to imagine what Tib's younger brother would be like, if he did exist," Hattie said wistfully.

"Well, I'm certain that the poor fellow would immediately fall in love with you, Hattie Johnson, whether he liked it or not," Louisa interrupted with only a small hint of sarcasm before she burst into laughter which spread throughout the room.

Hattie glowered at Louisa. "Louisa Johnson you just wait. I'm saving up some powerful teasing for you when the right time comes."

Louisa furtively stuck out her tongue at Hattie, which escaped Hattie's notice but not that of her mother.

"Louisa, you can be a saucy, clever and very funny child at times, but you also need to learn your limits before you hurt other people."

"Yes, Ma'am. I'm sorry, Hattie. I'd be pretty happy too, if there were more Tibs to share around here."

Rebecca drew closer to look at the white fabric of Eliza's partially completed wedding dress. "Mrs. Johnson, this is so beautiful. I've never seen such a dress before."

"Oh child, it's a pretty standard type of wedding dress but with a few flourishes of my own added," Mary said modestly.

"In Friends meetings, when people get married the bride just wears the regular clothing that she normally would wear for First Day meeting. The bride and groom stand up before the whole meeting and say they want to be husband and wife and if they are blessed by the elders and all those attending the meeting, they are married," Rebecca explained.

Mary and her daughters paused to absorb Rebecca's revelation about the simplicity of Quaker marriage and weren't quite certain how to respond.

"Because it happens so quickly, if I'm not paying close attention, it feels like it didn't happen at all," Rebecca added.

"Rebecca, thank you for sharing that interesting information about weddings in the Society of Friends," Mary replied, at a loss for what else to say.

"But, Mrs. Johnson that's what's so different between Friends and Baptists," Rebecca continued. "We don't really have a wedding. Friends just get married and that's that. Eliza told me that when Baptists get married there's a separate, special ceremony, a wedding, and when you get married, there's no struggle figuring out when and if it happened. I'm really looking forward to thy wedding, Eliza."

"So am I," Eliza said, turning with a radiant smile.

"Don't move, young lady, while I'm working on your dress or you might end up having a Quaker wedding after all!" Mary growled.

"Sorry mother. I keep forgetting the dress and everything else."

"Oh, young love! The fire's burning bright right now but just remember that as the first blaze settles down, you'll need to be constantly blowing on the embers to keep it going."

"Mother, that's not very romantic."

"Eliza, I'm actually quite romantic in my own way and I don't want to spoil your joy, not at all. But, my dear child, marriage is hard work. It may be some of the hardest work you'll ever do. You must be prepared for some challenges, perhaps even sorrows as well as the joy. Why, you must prepare yourself for the possibility that he may snore!"

Mary looked somberly at Eliza and then they both burst into laughter.

August 6, 1848 dawned like so many other summer days in eastern Indiana, with a lingering hint of the evening coolness, which was rapidly chased away by the sultry humidity that settled over the region. Neither Eliza nor Tib were especially aware of the weather that particular morning, however. Indeed, a winter blizzard would only represent a momentary distraction to the young lovers as they arose from restless slumbers to make the final preparations for their wedding. Tib had been encouraged in no uncertain terms by the ladies of the Johnson household to make himself invisible until the wedding ceremony.

"It's tradition darling," Eliza had explained. "It just won't do for you to see me in my wedding dress until the actual ceremony," she added as she gave him a tender smile followed by a passionate farewell kiss to compensate for his temporary banishment. Isaac was excited to host the bridegroom that night in his room at the Burgess home.

"How dost thou feel this special morning?" Isaac asked as he woke up to see Tib standing and looking out the window.

"It's hard for me to describe all my feelings right now. Part of me feels so happy that I think I could explode, while at the same time I also am afraid and a little sad."

"Afraid of what?"

"I'm not sure, though I'm certainly not afraid of marrying Eliza. Finding her and my new family has been the best thing that could ever happen to me. I think it's a crazy fear at the back of my mind that I will wake up and find that it all has been a wonderful dream. I guess I can't help but wonder of my mother's and sister's fate at a time like this. I wish so much that they were here and could know Eliza and her family. That makes me sad."

"I sure hope that thou canst be reunited with thy mother and sister someday."

"Thank you for your kind sentiments. I wonder how that could ever happen. I don't even know if they are still alive, let alone where they are," Tib mused sadly.

Pastor Ebenezer Jones looked at the beautiful bride and handsome bridegroom and smiled. Weddings were his favorite service. Rarely were they unhappy occasions, although he had officiated over a few that were not the happiest, like the time he had united a very pregnant bride with a rather sullen bridegroom. No, even those memories couldn't mar the joy of such an occasion as today's wedding. The unhappy ones were the exception, not the rule, as far as Pastor Jones was concerned. He could look at a couple like Tib and Eliza in all the fresh beauty and vigor of youth and see it all, his whole ministry right there. He could see their love mature, ripen, and bear fruit in the form of children he would someday baptize. He could also perceive the sorrows, maybe even the losses that would have to be carried within that love. The suffering and the joy of life, here they were fully embodied in this couple standing together before him.

"The apostle Paul has some mighty fine things to say about the holy state of matrimony. I don't think any of us married folk can ever hear it enough. 'Wives submit yourselves unto your own husbands, as unto the Lord. For the husband is the head of the wife; even as Christ is the head of the Church. . .Husbands, love your wives, even as Christ also loved the Church and gave himself for it. . .so ought men to love their wives as their own bodies. He that loveth his wife loveth himself.'" Ebenezer looked up from reading at this point and slowly surveyed the congregation. "If you love your wife as your own body, you'll never be tempted to hurt her, either with words or with blows. Am I right? What do you think, brothers?"

"Yes, brother Ebenezer, you're right. Amen!" came the shouted response.

"Now what about you, wives? Why does he say, 'Wives submit yourselves unto your own husbands. . .?' Now I know from careful observation and personal experience that wives are most often smarter than their husbands. Hold on a minute, brothers, before you protest. You know deep down inside that I'm right. What does the apostle say to wives? He says, 'submit yourselves. . .as unto the Lord.' He says that so as to keep you humble, wives. Even if your old Joe or whoever he may be isn't the smartest man you ever met, he's there for you to practice being humble 'as unto the Lord,' and the Lord, when he sees how a smart wife humbles herself, will bless her and her husband. Isn't that so, ladies? Let me hear what you have to say."

"Yes, that's so. Praise the Lord! Hallelujah!"

After his homily, Ebenezer turned to Eliza and Tib and said with great solemnity, "Eliza and Tiberius will now exchange their vows. Tiberius has chosen to take the Johnson family name as his own. Will you Tiberius Johnson, have Eliza Johnson to be your wife? Will you love her, comfort and keep her, and forsaking all others remain true to her as long as you both shall live?"

"I, Tiberius Johnson, take thee, Eliza Johnson, to be my wife, and before God and these witnesses I promise to be a faithful and true husband," Tib stated with emotion as tears came to his eyes.

"Now Eliza, it is your turn," Ebenezer said again with solemnity. Will you, Eliza Johnson, have Tiberius Johnson to be your husband? Will you love him, comfort and keep him, and forsaking all others remain faithful to him as long as you both shall live?"

With her eyes glistening, Eliza said, "I, Eliza Johnson, take thee, Tiberius Johnson, to be my husband . . ."

When she had finished reciting her vows, Pastor Jones said, "It is with great pleasure that with the authority vested in me as a minister of the Baptist Church, I now declare you, husband and wife!" Pausing for dramatic effect, he then added, "Well what are you waiting for, Tiberius? You may now kiss the bride," and then Pastor Jones laughed, with the whole congregation joining him.

After the laughter and the rather long kiss had finished, Ebenezer spoke again, "Before we end the service, Tiberius had requested of me earlier that we all sing a song at the end of the service, which has for him signified his healing and rebirth in this community."

Ebenezer slowly began to sing, and soon the congregation joined in. The Burgesses, Ways, and a few other Quaker families who were friends of the Johnsons and Tib and who had been present for the service, were the only ones in attendance who had not taken up the song.

> Wade in the water
> Wade in the water, children
> Wade in the water
> God's gonna trouble the water;
> Who's that yonder dressed in red?
> Wade in the water
> Must be the children that Moses led
> And God's gonna trouble the water . . .

As the congregation warmed to the song, there was a movement, first swaying back and forth, followed by stamping of feet and finally Pastor Ebenezer's flock were up on their feet keeping time to the music of the spiritual. Rebecca Burgess, who had been quietly watching the service with great fascination up to this point, found herself fidgeting in her seat beside her mother as she again heard the words which had so powerfully moved Tib—and her as well—that night many months before. When the next passage was coming, Rebecca felt her eyes being drawn almost magnetically to make contact with Tib, who smiled at her knowingly, and then, as if on cue, she was up on her feet, stamping out the rhythm and singing with Tib, who had joined the chorus, to the astonishment of Priscilla and John Burgess.

> You don't believe that I've been redeemed
> Wade in the water
> Just see the Holy Ghost looking for me

> God's gonna trouble the water,
> Wade in the water,
> Wade in the water, children
> Wade in the water
> God's gonna trouble the water!

When the spiritual was finished, Rebecca ran up to Tiberius and he grabbed her up in his arms and hugged her. Bringing her back to Priscilla and John, he said, "Please forgive me. I tempted your daughter more than she could bear. Many months ago, the Johnson family was singing that very song after dinner one evening. Your daughter, who to my knowledge had never sung that song or any other negro spiritual before, began to join in with the most beautiful soprano voice. Seeing a white child sing that song with so much love poured into it melted my heart and brought great healing to me that night. Rebecca has a wonderful gift that has truly blessed me. I know that Quakers usually don't sing, but I hope you can make an exception for Rebecca."

"I am not certain what to say Tib, other than to congratulate both you and Eliza," Priscilla said as she was trying to absorb what she had seen and heard her daughter just do.

Hannah Way came up and observed, "Rebecca, thou hast a beautiful voice. I am glad that thou couldst bring joy to Tiberius and Eliza on their wedding day."

Rebecca looked up gratefully at her teacher and said, "Thank thee, Mrs. Way. I love to sing, but I know that Friends don't sing as part of our silent worship. I was afraid that I might be part Baptist and part Friend."

Smiling at Priscilla, who was feeling some relief hearing a Quaker elder say such things, Hannah said, "God clearly has given thee a gift, which has already helped to bring healing to one suffering soul. Far be it from me to speak against the grace of God."

John and Priscilla both exchanged glances of relief. Henry Way came up and, leaning down, gave Rebecca a hug and whispered in her ear, "I hope that thou wouldst sing like that for me sometime."

Part Two

"Am I not a man and a brother?"

—Inscription on Wedgwood antislavery medallion

"Margaret, what a beautiful day it is! There's nary a cloud in the sky, the birds are singing, the bees are buzzing, the flowers are blooming, and there ain't another soul on this here road to spoil it. I cain't tell you how much these intimate times together mean to me. You're just about the most perfect companion a feller could have. Where can I begin to describe your most excellent qualities? You're very patient. You're always a good listener and even if you don't have much to say, you always let me know your thoughts in your own way."

Silvanus Beecham sighed and continued, "Now, if only my wife Lavinia could learn from you what a man really needs and wants from a woman. Lavinia is always asking questions, raising objections, generally complaining about the sorry state of the world and about how I should improve myself. But you, Margaret, why, you never, well hardly ever, complain, and when you do, you don't preach a sermon like Lavinia. It's getting to be so's a feller can hardly stand upright fer all the words flying at him. No, Margaret, you've never talked back to me, never judged me, and as long as I feed and water you. . . oh, and of course, scratch between your ears we have an understanding between us.

"Why Margaret without you and the law I'd be lost. The law is a real comfort to me. As a United States marshal these past eleven years, my duty has always been clear. I must execute the letter of the law, not interpret it. It's just plain black and white—a solid rock upon which a feller can set his feet. Poor Lavinia's tormented by shades of gray. She's always complaining about laws being unjust. Well, what if they are? After all, who made the laws? Politicians. That's right Margaret—damned politicians. Politics and politicians: they're not my cup o' tea. I've always said, if you don't like the law, change it, and that usually means getting rid of the politicians who made the law and startin' over. But thank the Almighty that ain't my job. My *job* is to enforce the laws, warts and all.

"Take fer example this new fugitive slave law. Lavinia says it's unjust. And she may well be right. She cain't bear the thought of those poor devils being forced back into slavery. But fer me the law's real clear. U.S. marshals are required to assist in the recovery of slave property, and I'm a U.S. marshal. My duty is clear as long as I follow the letter of the law. I will have the law be my guide, looking neither to the left nor to the right. No fanatic abolitionist or slavehunting scoundrel will make me deviate from my course as directed by the law."

Silvanus had been traveling north from Madison, Indiana for the past two days in response to a message from the federal commissioner in Richmond, Indiana, requesting assistance from a U.S. marshal in the recovery of a fugitive who was to be returned to Louisville. Whenever he had some problem or other to work through, he was always grateful to have Margaret's sympathetic ear. "Lavinia was mighty upset with me fer accepting this job. When she found out I was goin' on fugitive slave business, she really gave me a talkin' to," Silvanus said before proceeding to share the painful memory with Margaret.

"'No good'll come of this, Silvanus,'" she told me.

'But, Vinnie darlin', what would you have me do? This is part of my job as a U.S. marshal,' I explained.

'Maybe you should quit and find some other kind of work. It's just not right. Negroes are human beings, not animals to be bought and sold.'

'But the current law of the land says they can be property to be bought and sold. What other work could I do? This is what I know, And, I might add, I'm good at it.'

'Silvanus Beecham, you are so frustrating at times. I know you're an honest man and I love you for it, but cain't you see that this is a wicked law? Don't you remember two years ago right after the fugitive slave act became law the three white folk who were almost dragged into slavery by a scoundrel who claimed them as his property? Any wretch can come into our state and claim before one of those federal commissioners that "so and so" is his property. The burden then lies on the poor "so and so" to prove that he ain't someone's property. Those rascally commissioners get ten dollars for agreeing with the scoundrel and only five dollars if they protect the rights of the poor soul who is being threatened with slavery.'

'Vinnie, please be reasonable. You know that I don't take bribes and that I pride myself on being fair in all my actions. I won't be party to any tomfoolery that is outside the law. If I continue to serve as a marshal, I will do my best to protect those in my charge from harm. Ain't that worth something?'

'Of course, it's worth a lot. But don't you see that when you enforce the federal law, the poor negroes have no right to defend themselves even though they would under Indiana law?'

'Vinnie, my dear, who's been filling your head with all these legal notions? Have you been listening to those abolitionist rascals? They're only stirring up conflict that'll tear this country apart. The Fugitive Slave Act of 1850 was designed to correct problems with enforcement in the original one of 1793. All peace-loving citizens who want to preserve the union of the states should give it a chance to work.'

'Silvanus, it's been two years and you know as well as I do that all we've seen from that law is mischief! As for the abolitionists, I'm getting closer every day to seeing the truth of what they say.'

"You see, Margaret," he continued, returning to the present, "married life is challenging. Lavinia is very dear to me and I s'pose she must be a kind of saint to put up with me. But I think my head would burst if I tried to keep all the conflicting thoughts in it that she does in hers. Until a better law comes along, I have to enforce what we've got."

The ground was still damp from the brief thunderstorm of the preceding day. A slight breeze brought some relief from the humidity of late morning on June 10, 1852. Tib had been weeding in the vegetable patch behind the cottage that he and Eliza shared on the Johnson farm. After their wedding nearly four years earlier, the local community quickly came together and helped them build the cottage. As he paused and straightened his aching back, he smiled as he thought about the many pleasant memories he had already shared with Eliza in their new home together.

"Papa!"

Tib's reverie was suddenly interrupted by the arrival of his son, Bennie, who had just turned three a week earlier. Bennie's grandfather, Ben Johnson was quietly very pleased and honored to have his first grandchild named for him, although he had protested at the time of his birth, "Surely, you have a better name to give him than Benjamin."

Tib, who was especially emphatic in insisting on honoring his father-in-law in this manner, replied with a laugh, "He's just going to have to tolerate the fact that he hasn't been named for a Roman emperor."

Bennie toddled up to his father, stood on his left boot while grabbing onto his left leg, and holding on as if for dear life, cried, "Papa, give Bennie a ride. Please Papa!"

"Okay, Bennie, hold on tight."

Tib danced around on his right foot while giving Bennie a horsie ride on his left leg. As he slowly twirled, he waved at Sam and his father-in-law who were working side-by-side several hundred yards away on another part of the farm. Next, he saw Eliza, who was big with their second child, flash him a radiant smile as she ambled slowly toward him from the back of her parents' farmhouse. The next sight almost made him lose his balance and he abruptly stopped twirling.

"Papa, more please!"

"I'm sorry Bennie, I can't right now," Tib said as a shadow of fear crossed his face.

Seeing his change of expression, Eliza looked in the same direction as Tib and then with intense anxiety in her eyes screamed, "Run!"

But it was too late. U.S. marshal Silvanus Beecham was a methodical planner who hated messy arrests. He had deputized ten men from Richmond to serve as a posse in Tib's capture and transport south, all of whom were on horseback. They had already blocked any avenues of escape and were now closing in on their prey. As Bennie looked curiously at his father, Eliza came running as fast as she could in her seventh month of pregnancy while Sam and Ben also came running up. Ben turned to Sam and said, "Run and rouse the neighbors, especially see if you can find Doctor Way and the Burgess brothers. We're going to need a lot of legal help from sympathetic white folk." Sam hesitated for a moment and Ben hissed at him, "Run!"

Sam split off from his father's side and disappeared behind some luxuriant raspberry bushes close to the farmhouse to pursue his mission, undetected by the posse. As Sam ran away from the posse, a sound suddenly rent the air around him and sent shivers down his spine. It was as if the primal howl of a wounded and doomed animal had merged with the deepest and saddest of groans.

Silvanus dismounted, approached Tib who was now on his knees still shaking after uttering his cry of anguish with a weeping Eliza and bewildered Bennie at his side. Using his best official speech, Silvanus stated his business, "Under the Fugitive Slave Act of 1850, as a United States marshal, I am charged with the unpleasant duty of escorting you as the alleged fugitive slave, Tiberius, a chattel of Mrs. Malvina Newby of Kentucky, to a hearing with the federal commissioner in Richmond, Indiana. If you are confirmed to the satisfaction of the commissioner to be the escaped slave, Tiberius, my posse and I will further escort you to Louisville, Kentucky as per the instructions of Mrs. Newby."

As he placed handcuffs and leg irons on Tib, Silvanus added, "I'd appreciate it, if you wouldn't struggle."

Ben approached Silvanus and asked in as polite a voice as he could muster under the circumstances, "Sir, could we please have a few moments to say our farewells before you take him to Richmond?" Silvanus hesitated and then remembering his wife's impassioned speech said, "You may have five minutes."

At this point, Mary, Hattie, Louisa, and Rebecca Burgess, who had been playing with Louisa that morning, came running up. As tears began to flow all around, Ben told Tib in a whisper, "Sam has gone to rouse the community and to get the assistance of Dr. Way and the Burgess brothers. They have to take you before the federal commissioner in Richmond to confirm your identity. We'll do everything in our power to obtain your freedom."

"I know you will, but I don't want any of you to risk your lives or freedom for me. The penalties for obstructing this law are severe. You could be imprisoned and ruined financially by the fine," Tib said in a low monotone, which arose out of the gathering numbness and despair in his soul. "I have had the greatest joy a man can experience in the nearly five years I have been with you. I will always love all of you."

Turning to Eliza and gently placing one hand on Bennie's head and the other on Eliza's belly, he said with a voice choked with tears, "Dear Eliza, I am so sorry to have ever put your happiness at risk because of my own selfishness. I have experienced the joy of a lifetime with you. However, the knowledge that my forced separation from you will cause you grief and pain makes that happy thought dissipate like a morning mist in the noonday sun. I have awakened from my joyful dream to the nightmare that I thought I'd escaped nearly five years ago." Then clasping Eliza's hands in his own, his voice no longer quavering, he declared, "I swear before God and this company of people so dear to me that I will return. You shall see me again in this life. I will know my second child. Your father will not be separated from you. My love for you, Eliza Johnson, cannot be shackled."

"Oh Tib! I love you. My love will be with you always. It will free you," Eliza exclaimed as she began to sob.

As the others gathered around Tib to hug and kiss him, Silvanus intervened. "I'm sorry but it's been well past five minutes. We need to leave now. We'll need to help you up into the wagon, Tiberius."

As Tib was being assisted with his shackles into the wagon, Dr. Way and John Burgess came running up with a trail of other townsfolk following.

"What is the meaning of this?" Henry Way asked with considerable knowledge of what it meant but in hopes of slowing the process. Silvanus patiently repeated his charge under the Fugitive Slave Act and then added, "We really must go. I need to report back to the federal commissioner before close of business today. His hearing before the commissioner will be tomorrow at 9 am in the Wayne County courthouse in Richmond. Any interested parties have a right under the law to attend the hearing."

"Thou must delay the hearing," protested Henry. "We need time to appoint legal counsel to present evidence in his defense."

"I don't think you understand the statute very well," Silvanus interrupted. "It's a ministerial type function in which we will be engaged tomorrow, not a judicial proceeding. The function of the hearing tomorrow is for the federal commissioner to determine if the claimants for the alleged fugitive have provided credible evidence verifying his identity and the owner's claim of ownership sufficient to justify his transport back to Kentucky. Any formal legal proceeding involving a proper trial with counsel and witnesses for the fugitive would have to be initiated in the state of Kentucky. Now, we really must leave."

Henry gritted his teeth and thought to himself, *This U.S. marshal knows his business and it appears that those claiming Tiberius have been laying their plans with care.* He replied to Silvanus, "Thank thee, sir, for thy patient explanation. We look forward to the hearing tomorrow."

As the wagon with its posse of ten armed men on horseback carried the forlorn figure of Tiberius out of Newport toward Richmond, a train of weeping family members and friends followed for some distance until Silvanus insisted they go back. A grim-faced Ben took counsel with Henry and John while Sam listened intently to their discussion.

"I'm afraid this appears to have been well planned on the part of the slave-owner and her agents," Henry said sadly. "The U.S. marshal spoke correctly about the hearing. Under the federal statute, the fugitive is not afforded any legal redress in the state in which he is captured. Even so, there are very able attorneys in Indianapolis, strong abolitionists, who I am certain could at least delay the process, if we had time to engage their services."

"What good would that do, since he can't have any legal support in Indiana under the federal law?" Sam asked.

"Sometimes the process of legal action can be useful in and of itself," Henry explained. "For example, we might be able to pay for his manumission by his owner, but such efforts could definitely benefit from more time to explore sources of funding for what I'm sure would be a large sum of money."

"Oh, I understand now. It could also give us more time to plan a rescue," Sam said.

"Yes, Sam, but we must be very discreet in our speech and actions," Henry replied. "Tib made it clear that he didn't want any of us to risk injury, whether physical or financial, on his behalf," Ben added.

"Pa, do you mean you won't try to rescue him?"

"I will do everything possible to rescue him, son. Tib is also thinking of his two children and Eliza's safety and well-being. As hard as it sounds, I'm confident that he would want us to make sure their future is secure as the first priority."

"Thy father is correct, Sam. Eliza and their children's needs have to be considered, in case he is not freed. If thy father goes to prison trying to rescue Tib, the source of security for everyone whom Tib loves may be in jeopardy," John reasoned.

"Well, I'm prepared to go to prison," Sam said grimly. "I wish Isaac were here instead of with his Uncle Levi down South. We might be able to make some pretty good rescue plans together."

"I'm not sure at all where Isaac and his Uncle Levi are at present. Levi had said they might be out of contact for days to weeks at a time while they are visiting small farms looking for potential Southern partners to provide cotton and other goods that are not produced by slave labor," John replied. "They will be distraught at hearing the news of Tib's capture."

"Sam, you must allow your elders to do some planning. We will include you in any plans we make but please do not try to do something on your own," Ben admonished.

"Yes sir."

"Unfortunately," Henry replied, "the federal marshal will be able to use the Richmond county jail to house Tib, since Indiana, unlike Michigan and many of the states in the northeast, has not enacted any legislation blocking the use of state institutions to support the provisions of the new Fugitive Slave Act.

"However, there are many individuals in Richmond who are hostile to this law. Even though we may not be able to delay the hearing with the help of legal counsel, perhaps we can create sufficient confusion by the number of people attending the hearing that an opportunity for Tib to escape might arise. Let's encourage as many friends of abolition as possible to attend the hearing tomorrow in Richmond as we think of other options."

"At least it would be gratifying to force the U.S. marshal to deputize more people to serve in his posse. I think they will be fearful of trying to transport Tib overland very far in territory hostile to the Fugitive Slave Act," John speculated.

"It may force a change of direction and mode of transportation," Ben added. "The Richmond-to-Indianapolis rail line is still under construction, but the National Road will be easier for their movements and for security. My guess is that the U.S. marshal may try to transport Tib to Indianapolis so that he can use the Indianapolis-Madison railroad to transport Tib under heavy guard to the Ohio River at Madison. The more direct but smaller country roads will seem less secure to him."

"I agree," said Henry meditatively. "If our crowd tomorrow can encourage such thoughts on the part of Marshal Beecham, we might still be able to engage the help of some very able legal counsel in Indianapolis. I'll send a rider tonight to alert George Julian and John Coburn, two very excellent abolitionist lawyers who practice there, to the situation. Perhaps, they can file a countercharge of kidnapping in an Indiana court."

"Well nigger, it looks like you can't escape justice."

Tib looked up just in time to receive a sharp jab from the butt of a musket in his ribs.

"There'll be more of that in your future, boy!" exulted a member of the posse, a scrawny, ill-clad fellow who reeked of alcohol.

Hearing the last sentence spoken by this member of his posse, Silvanus saw Tib wincing in pain and rode back promptly to the wagon carrying Tib.

"Stop the wagon! Stop, all of you! Right now!" Silvanus shouted.

He rode up close to Tib's tormentor, a man named Jedediah Smithson, or simply Jed to his few friends, and looking directly into his eyes, said, "If you or any of the rest of you so much as touch this prisoner or threaten him with words again, I'll have you clapped in irons and charged with obstruction of justice! Do you understand?"

"Yes sir," came the sulky response.

Turning to Tib, Silvanus asked gently, "Are you all right?"

"Sore, but I think I'll be all right. Thank you."

Tib gave Silvanus a grateful look for his intervention as he thought about the irony of his situation. He couldn't help but marvel that the U.S. marshal, who was returning him to slavery, appeared to be a decent, even kind man. Oddly enough, the kindness of the U.S. marshal became a source of hope for Tib. Ever since his life had been torn from him in that excruciating moment when he realized the nature of the mission of the armed men approaching him at the Johnsons' farm, Tib had been thrust into deep despair. This one act of genuine kindness from his captor had opened, ever so slightly, a door through which a ray of hope shone, if only dimly. He remembered his solemn oath to his wife, family, and friends to escape and return. He also pondered Eliza's tender words, which even now enveloped and caressed his bruised and painful chest, relieving much of the pain. *Her love will free me. No matter what happens, I will remain faithful to my oath to escape and return to Eliza and our family. I must trust in her love*, he thought as the wagon jostled him on its bumpy journey to Richmond, Indiana.

Another set of thoughts began to intrude upon his ruminations. He had hoped to never hear the name, Malvina Newby again. It would take a love as pure as Eliza's to fully neutralize the hate his old mistress cherished for him. He realized that the nearly five years separating him in time from his last encounter with Mrs. Newby had not in any way diminished her malice; but, why now? He wracked his brain thinking about his activities in the past several months.

I must have been recognized recently by someone from my past life in Kentucky. I've tried to be very careful to avoid drawing notice to myself, he thought.

As he mentally reviewed his activities over the past year, he was suddenly struck so powerfully by one thought that he exclaimed out loud, "That's it!"

He looked around anxiously to see if any of his captors had noticed him speaking. The horseman closest to him only reacted with a smirk and resumed a look of indifference. He realized that he had begun to go into Richmond with Ben or John Burgess during the past six months on short business trips during the day. This had been a major change in behavior, which at the time he had minimized, explaining to himself, and then to family and friends, that surely he was dead in the mind of his owner, and besides, the risk of meeting or being recognized by someone from Kentucky should be very small. The realization came to him that tomorrow at his hearing he would likely meet the person from his past who had recognized him. Oh, how foolish, how careless he had been and how uncertain and fragile had been his happiness! As they approached the outskirts of Richmond, he resolved to be vigilant for any opportunity of escape and to watch for any cues that his family and friends from Newport might give him.

As Silvanus Beecham entered Main Street in Richmond later that afternoon with his posse and prisoner, he was dismayed to see a large crowd of people lining both sides of the street. The majority of the facial expressions were sullen or somber. *Clearly, this is not a welcoming committee of supporters of federal law*, thought Silvanus as he rode slowly up the street. He glanced ahead toward the county jail with some apprehension, remembering the distinct lack of cooperation that the local sheriff had expressed on the preceding day.

"Marshal, many people here in Richmond ain't goin' to take kindly to usin' the county jail to send some poor devil back to slavery."

The sheriff's response had annoyed but also alarmed Silvanus. What kind of disturbance might develop in reaction to housing his prisoner in the county jail? Now, as he estimated the size of the crowd, which could become a mob at any time, he realized that he would need more deputies to safely house his prisoner, maintain order at the hearing, and successfully transport him to Kentucky. He also realized he may need to think of another route. There were many places suitable for ambush along the country roads from Madison to Richmond. It was a real shame that the Richmond-Indianapolis rail line had not been finished yet. As he was entertaining these thoughts, someone from the crowd shouted, "Kidnappers!" Several stones were then thrown, many of which hit their mark causing members of the posse to cry out and respond with threats.

Suddenly, a shot rang out and Marshal Beecham, who had discharged his pistol into the air, shouted, "That's enough! I don't want to see any bloodshed here in Richmond. This crowd will now disperse. You all will have an opportunity to hear the federal commissioner's assessment and judgment tomorrow. Now, go home!"

Silvanus motioned for his posse to move on down the street to the county jail. Speaking in low tones to one of his deputies, he said, "I want you to quietly, and I mean quietly, transfer our prisoner to the county jail. You will secure the prisoner with a guard of two men inside and another two men outside at all times. Allow no one to approach or communicate with him without my expressed permission. That includes any written messages. It is my understanding that he can read and write. Do you have any questions?"

"No, sir."

"Margaret, enforcing the law can be a trying experience at times," Silvanus said as he brushed and stroked his horse in her stall in the stable across the street from the Main Street Hotel. Rather than commenting, Margaret continued to munch on the hay and oats in the trough in front of her. "The law's real clear, but sometimes I wonder if it's really doing any good. You know they talk about the devil being in the details, but the way I see it, the devil's grinning right at me in every part of this law. I'll never forget the cry our prisoner made when he realized what was happening to him. Sometimes, I wish I wasn't such a careful planner. It was as if he was a trapped animal with nowhere to go. But the fact is, and Vinnie's right, he's a human being like the rest of us. In fact, he strikes me as being a bit more human than most of the members of this posse o'mine. I was so tempted to knock that wretch out of his saddle who hit him. Brutalizing an unarmed, shackled prisoner is about the lowest sort of entertainment anyone could seek. Maybe I should've clobbered the rascal anyway."

Silvanus paused, scratched his head, and kicked the dirt floor.

Chapter Fourteen

Thaddeus Pettibone took one last admiring look at himself in the mirror and adjusted his cravat, while also working out which facial expression best suited his dignity as a federal commissioner for his duties that morning. Should he smile ever so slightly? No, that might give the wrong impression to those attending the hearing, although he desperately wanted to show the humane aspect of his important work. After all, was there any reason why the law could not take on a sympathetic aspect? He looked again, this time with a somber expression, but straining at the same time not to frown. This was made all the more challenging by the rather chubby, some might even say fat, face that peered back at him from the mirror. How could a face that normally reveled in the joy of consumption, which became ruddy and jolly after imbibing some delicious liquid refreshment, naturally assume the necessary gravitas of such an important personage as a federal commissioner?

Thaddeus was by disposition a happy man, and although he was very pleased to have been appointed federal commissioner, his law practice having been a bit thin at times, he still found the actual work rather tedious and even unpleasant. It seemed that after embracing the Fugitive Slave Act shortly after its enactment in 1850, most of the populace in Indiana and the other neighboring northern states had cooled in their enthusiasm for this carefully crafted measure to preserve the union. He was well aware of the unrest of the prior day and felt that it may have been in no small part due to the fact that many of the state's newspapers had also turned on the law with a vengeance. They were particularly angry about its denial of basic rights to those being claimed as slaves, including *habeas corpus* and a jury trial by peers in which evidence and legal counsel could be provided for the benefit of the defendant under Indiana law. Fear of legalized kidnapping of free persons of color or even some whites with no apparent negro ancestry purely on the testimony of a person claiming to be their owner had caused tremendous hostility to the law and augmented a growing sympathy for abolitionist views.

By the behavior of the crowd that had gathered on the prior afternoon, he was afraid there would be mischief today during the hearing. He felt somewhat reassured by the U.S. marshal's presence. Marshal Beecham seemed like a well-organized, no-nonsense kind of man. When Beecham had come to him last evening and stated flatly that he would need to double the size of his posse to twenty men and reroute the transport of the fugitive through Indianapolis, Thaddeus's anxiety increased. From his preliminary review of the evidence from the claimant, it seemed pretty straightforward. However, the eastern part of Indiana was a particular hotbed of abolitionist sentiments and it appeared that they were rapidly gathering their forces. It seemed that his best course would be to act as quickly as possible and then transfer the prisoner west under heavy guard along the National Road to Indianapolis and then south via the Indianapolis-Madison railroad. It galled him to think that he would be taunted for being partial to the claimant's side of the case. He didn't write the law. If it so happened that he would be paid ten dollars for a decision in favor of the claimant versus only five dollars for the defendant that was not through any fault of his own. It was simply a matter of what the law dictated. As he pondered the peculiarities of the statute, he couldn't help but think also about the very pleasant dining experiences that ten dollars would bring once all the dust settled.

The courtroom of the Wayne County courthouse was packed that morning. Quaker men and women mingled with free persons of color as well as a host of curiosity-seekers.

As the nine o'clock hour approached, Henry Way joined John and Priscilla Burgess in the back of the courtroom and whispered to them, "My agent was able to brief George Julian, the abolitionist lawyer in Indianapolis on the situation. I just received a brief telegram confirming their conversation. He says he will do what he can, but unfortunately, he is quite pessimistic of the outcome. I'm afraid that our options may be very limited. Our chances of success would be greater if we were dealing with a slavecatcher rather than a U.S. marshal. We might then be able to intervene through the Indiana judiciary on a charge of kidnapping prior to the federal commissioner's involvement. I seriously doubt that any judge in our state will intervene when a U.S. marshal and federal commissioner have already acted within the letter of the federal statute."

"What recourse do we have?" Priscilla asked anxiously.

"He has always been in God's hands," Henry responded. "We must continue to pray that God's will be accomplished. It is difficult for me to accept that deliverance won't come in some form. I hope and pray that Tib and his friends will be able to recognize the hand of Providence when it comes."

"Sometimes God helps them who help themselves."

Pastor Ebenezer Jones smiled grimly as he shared this insight. He and Ben Johnson had joined Henry and the Burgesses just prior to Henry's call for increased prayer.

"Indeed, Pastor Jones," Henry returned the sentiment. "Let me amend my statement to add that we must also pray for wisdom as we work to accomplish his will in all things."

"Amen, brother! That prayer just about covers it all," Ebenezer said as he shook Henry's hand. "I've alerted our people in Indianapolis. If the federal marshal intends to transport Tib by way of the Indianapolis-Madison Railroad, there will be some challenges placed in his path."

Thaddeus Pettibone looked up from his desk at one end of the courtroom and surveyed the crowd of people. All seats had been taken and yet more people were jostling to enter and stand at the back. To his right stood the prisoner Tiberius, still in handcuffs and leg irons, with Marshal Beecham sitting at his side, and on the commissioner's left at a small table sat two men who were facing the commissioner. One appeared to be much older, possibly in his sixties with a fringe of white hair around his balding pate, well dressed, and a look of serene dignity on his face. The other younger individual was either in his late thirties or early forties, tall, with a full head of dark hair and an overall appearance that on many accounts might be considered to be handsome if it were not marred by a nasty scowl that seemed to be permanently etched on his face.

To Tib's dismay, he immediately recognized both of his adversaries when they entered the room. The older individual was the honorable Percival Thornton, a prominent slaveowner, justice of the peace, and cousin of his mistress Malvina Newby. The younger man was none other than Thomas Blavey, the overseer at the Newby plantation who had been more than happy to comply with Mrs. Newby's orders for Tib's frequent whippings. Tib resolved to say as little as possible and to do his utmost to avoid any self-incriminating actions.

Commissioner Pettibone banged his gavel to indicate the beginning of the hearing and Marshal Beecham rose and said in a loud voice, "Order! The hearing before the honorable Thaddeus Pettibone, Federal Commissioner for southeastern Indiana, of the claim of Mrs. Malvina Newby of Shelby County, Kentucky regarding the alleged fugitive slave, named Tiberius, will now begin on this eleventh day of June 1852. Two witnesses are here on behalf of the claimant."

Thaddeus Pettibone gave Marshal Beecham an appreciative look and then struck his gavel again.

"Before we begin, it is important to remind all those in attendance that the function of this hearing is not judicial. The only purpose of this hearing is for me as federal commissioner to hear and weigh the evidence provided by the claimant regarding the identity of the person in question. The alleged fugitive cannot testify on his own behalf. However, if anyone present can present positive proof of his freedom such as papers proving his status as a free person of color, which are appropriately verifiable or other credible witnesses to that effect, I am more than happy to hear their testimony and to review the evidence they can provide.

"My task, and it is mine alone, is to determine in my best judgment whether evidence presented here is sufficiently compelling to remand this person to the authority of the state of Kentucky or not.

"It's legalized kidnapping!" a voice shouted from the back of the courtroom.

"Order!" shouted Silvanus again. "The next time I hear someone disturb the peace of this hearing, I will clear the courtroom." Silvanus looked around the courtroom and at the two exits and noted with satisfaction the presence of ten of his armed deputies, who were all alert and standing at their posts. "The first witness is the honorable Percival Thornton, a justice of the peace in Shelby County, Kentucky."

After being sworn in, Percival sat down with a complacent expression on his face awaiting Commissioner Pettibone's questions.

"Mr. Thornton, please explain your knowledge of the fugitive slave, Tiberius, and present your evidence that this person standing before you is indeed the same person."

Percival Thornton smiled and, turning toward Tib, said, "I am very familiar with this slave. I personally drew up the papers transferring ownership from his previous owner, Mr. Horton Newby of Shelby County to his wife, my cousin, Mrs. Malvina Newby, on March 23, 1844. Here is the document for your perusal. As you will note, there is a detailed description of the slave Tiberius in the document. At the time of his sale he had reached his full and considerable height of over six feet and was nearly fourteen years of age. He is described in the document as an intelligent mulatto with even features including an aquiline nose, somewhat atypical for his race, and most importantly there is a prominent round birthmark in the form of a so-called port wine stain measuring approximately two inches in diameter located on his right buttock."

"How did you become aware of his presence here in Indiana?"

"I was here in Richmond last April visiting my sister's family who had relocated to this region a few years ago from their home in Kentucky. During my visit, I happened to see this man unloading materials from a wagon in front of the general store on Main Street. I was initially quite surprised to see him as he had long ago been given up for dead, having been thought to have drowned in the Ohio River after he was shot trying to escape across to the Indiana shore by the owner of a skiff he had stolen. So, you can imagine my surprise to see him alive and apparently well almost five years after his escape."

"How can you be so certain that he is the same man who escaped several years ago?"

"I believe you can appreciate that he has a remarkable appearance being a tall mulatto with striking physical features, which would not be soon forgotten by those who were acquainted with him. From the account given by the man who shot him while he was escaping in the stolen skiff across the Ohio River, I would also predict that he has a scar on his left shoulder from a gunshot wound."

"Can I assume that you had seen him more than once and not just on the occasion of the transfer of ownership to your cousin?"

"Having neighboring plantations in Shelby County has created frequent occasions for reciprocal hospitality during which one inevitably becomes aware of the servants on each other's plantations."

Turning to the younger man, Commissioner Pettibone said, "I'd be obliged if we can hear your testimony at this time, Mr. . . ."

"Blavey, Thomas Blavey, sir."

"Marshal Beecham, please swear in the witness."

"Do you swear to tell the truth, the whole truth, and nothing but the truth, so help you God?"

"I swear. Yes, sir, it'll be my pleasure," Blavey added, licking his lips.

Yes, Massa Tom, you'll truly enjoy giving your testimony, Tib thought bitterly.

Commissioner Pettibone turned to Thomas Blavey and said, "Please give an account of your knowledge of the alleged fugitive, Tiberius."

"I've served as overseer on the Newby plantation for the past eight years. I was hired shortly before the transaction transferring ownership of the slave Tiberius from Mr. to Mrs. Newby."

"What was your relationship to the slave, Tiberius?"

"Well, your honor, among my other assigned duties, Mrs. Newby wanted me to break uppity slaves."

"How is this information relevant to your testimony?" Thaddeus asked, fearing the answer.

"You asked about my relationship to the slave, Tiberius, sir. I can prove he is the property of Mrs. Newby of Shelby County, Kentucky, if you'll let me explain."

"Proceed, Mr. Blavey, with your testimony."

"As I was sayin', one o' my tasks, was to break uppity niggers. . ." An angry murmur passed through the audience at this. "Uh, I mean, discipline disobedient servants. This here fugitive, Tiberius, was the worst of 'em that I've ever had to discipline."

"It seems you were not very successful," Commissioner Pettibone observed mildly to loud laughter in the courtroom.

Blavey whose face reddened, responded, "Your honor may be correct, but the story's not over yet. I've found it necessary to supplement the lash with branding at times. This escaped slave has brands of the letter 'N' on each buttock in addition to scars from the lash across his back. If you will allow me to show you these marks and his birthmark, documented in the bill of sale from 1844, I am certain that you will agree that this man is the escaped fugitive slave, Tiberius, whose rightful owner is Mrs. Malvina Newby of Shelby County, Kentucky."

A gasp arose from the crowd followed by angry shouts of "You can't do this!" as Blavey moved toward Tib, apparently intent on stripping him before the crowd.

"Order!" Marshal Beecham shouted. "Stand to, deputies!"

"This hearing is in recess until I fully review all the evidence," Commissioner Pettibone declared. "Clear the courtroom!"

After they had left the courtroom, Sam turned to his father and said, "Pa, it's a good thing you didn't allow Eliza to come to the hearing. My blood's boiling. I can't imagine what effect all this would have on her and the baby.

Ben, turned to Sam with tears in his eyes and said, "They've got him, son."

"Why do you say that, Pa?"

"All the physical evidence that they mentioned; it's all there."

"You mean that he has brands on his buttocks?"

"Eliza told me about them once. We can only begin to imagine the suffering he has experienced."

"That damned overseer deserves to die!"

"Watch your language son. Although I must say I share your sentiments," Ben replied, "the terrible reality is that Tib's owner has the law on her side, which in practical terms means a very capable U.S. marshal plus twenty armed deputies versus a disorganized mob. Did you notice how he has doubled his deputies overnight?"

"Yes. They're everywhere."

"Pastor Ebenezer has sent word on to the free negroes of Indianapolis to let them know that Tib will likely be transported via Indianapolis to Madison on the railroad." Then whispering, Ben said, "Perhaps a little work can be done to slow the train and create an opportunity for escape."

"What if that fails, Pa?"

"Dr. Way is looking into the possibility of buying Tib's freedom. Most runaways who are captured are sold down the river to the Deep South; since they are viewed by their owners as being at high risk for future escape attempts. Perhaps, if a generous amount of money were offered to buy his freedom, his owner would be pleased to accept the cash from a quick and relatively simple sale in exchange for his freedom."

"Pa, where are we going to get the kind of money that she is likely to demand? It could be well over a thousand dollars."

"The abolitionist societies have been growing in strength since this law was enacted. Henry Way thinks that it may be possible to raise a considerable sum of money on short notice."

"I hope he's right."

"I'm sorry to expose you to this indignity, but the commissioner must examine your body to confirm the evidence these witnesses have provided," Silvanus explained to Tib.

"Why are you so worried about the niceties, marshal? Strip the goddamn nigger!" Tom Blavey swore.

"Deputy, remove this man from the courtroom!" Silvanus ordered.

"Why are you doin' this to me? That's the prisoner over there and after all he's just a nigger."

"He is my prisoner and as long as he is my prisoner, he will be treated humanely and with the respect due to another human being! Nowhere in my reading of the Fugitive Slave Act of 1850 is physical or verbal abuse of prisoners condoned."

"You mean it ain't mentioned."

"As I said. Now remove him from the courtroom."

As Tib was slowly stripped with the help of a guard and the heavy scars from multiple severe whippings were revealed traversing his entire back, Silvanus was sickened by what he saw. Commissioner Pettibone looked on dispassionately but did make verbal note of a scar on the left shoulder that might be consistent with an old gunshot wound, "Ah, that appears to be the wound received during his crossing of the Ohio River."

The honorable Percival Thornton only smiled as he watched with pleasure.

"Now pull down his breeches," Commissioner Pettibone ordered. The port wine stain and two symmetrically placed brands with the capital letter 'N' on either buttock were revealed. "It seems the evidence is overwhelming in favor of the claimant," Thaddeus said with a yawn. "Let's get this business over with as quickly as we can."

Thaddeus pounded the gavel again. "This hearing is now reconvened."

The crowd, if anything, had grown and seemed even more restless than earlier in the morning. Silvanus had whispered his concerns to the commissioner about the security of the proceedings and that he now felt he might even need thirty deputies in the posse. Thaddeus had reassured him he would have his men.

Thaddeus again surveyed the many hostile faces in the packed courtroom, noted the presence of nearly twenty armed deputies, and finally screwed up his courage to speak.

"I have reviewed the evidence presented by the agents of the claimant, Mrs. Malvina Newby of Shelby County, Kentucky, including the deed transferring ownership of the slave Tiberius to Mrs. Newby in March of 1844, which appears to be valid in all respects. Upon careful examination of the physical evidence presented both in the documentation of ownership and by the claimant's witnesses, I am satisfied beyond any doubt that the mulatto man standing before you is the escaped slave known as Tiberius, who is claimed by his owner's agents under the Fugitive Slave Act of 1850. He will be remanded without further delay under armed guard to Louisville, per his owner's instructions."

Shouting and general pandemonium broke out in the courtroom as Thaddeus finished his pronouncement.

"Order! Stand to, deputies!" Silvanus shouted. The show of force seemed to calm the crowd somewhat. Thaddeus spoke again, "I should not have to remind those in attendance of the severe penalties, including fines and imprisonment that will come to anyone who in any way interferes with or obstructs the U.S. marshal as he fulfills his duty under this statute in the transfer of the prisoner out of the state of Indiana. This hearing is now adjourned."

"Knowing so well the sad realities of life on the Southern plantations, I felt that in purchasing and using cloth made from cotton, grown by slaves, I made use of a product which had been planted by an oppressed laborer, fanned by sighs, watered with tears, and perhaps dressed with the blood of the victim."

Levi Coffin paused, and then, turning to look at his nephew Isaac, who was standing beside him, continued.

"Isaac, I think thou canst readily see why we must at least try this experiment in purchasing cotton and other Southern products that have been produced through free labor. Otherwise, we might rail against the evils of slave labor and yet as hypocrites profit from the very evil we condemn. Also, by buying those items obtained through slave labor, we in the North continue to provide a strong incentive for the South's peculiar institution to persist."

"Uncle Levi, thou hast always said that the Southern slaveowners should be persuaded to freely choose to emancipate their slaves as the Society of Friends had chosen to do in the last century through the efforts of John Woolman and other Friends. Dost thou think it actually possible to persuade them to freely give up their wealth and power?"

"I may be very naïve, but I think of the example set by John Woolman and so am inspired to follow his path as much as I can. Any other means of universal emancipation would likely entail the use of force. One evil would then succumb to another. What then would be the outcome? Would it be possible for former slave and master to live together in peace if their prior relationship was ruptured by force? I submit that the inevitable resentments of the aggrieved former master would create unbearable hardships for the emancipated slave. If only we could persuade the South of the practicable nature of emancipation as it occurred within the Society of Friends."

"But Uncle, doesn't the work of the Underground Railroad inflame the passions of the Southern slaveowners? Can that really be said to be a peaceful form of persuasion? Many attribute the harsher nature of the new Fugitive Slave Act as a direct response of angry slaveowners to the support that abolitionists have given to runaway slaves."

"Yes, I suppose thou may'st be correct about the reasons behind the enactment of this new fugitive slave law," Levi conceded. "Many of the Southern slaveowners are angry because of our activities on behalf of fugitive slaves. It's a fine balance between different forms of persuasion. The primary reason to aid fugitive slaves has always been to follow the Lord's precept of feeding the hungry, clothing the naked, and the like, regardless of the color of their skin. Following His Law may put us directly into conflict with earthly laws. I would rather persuade gently, using reason. But sometimes one must oppose evil in more direct ways, short of physical violence."

Isaac looked out over the waters of the Ohio River as their steamboat headed south toward the mouth of the Tennessee River and wondered at his uncle's reasoning.

"Uncle, why wouldst thou stop short of violence, if thou art confronted with a great evil?"

"I can only hope that I would not succumb to the temptation to use evil means to fight evil. Is it possible that a positive good could emerge from evil means? I wonder."

Isaac and his uncle were on their second day out from Cincinnati as they entered the mouth of the Tennessee River. At fourteen years of age, Isaac had acquired considerable height, just shy of six feet, and was now a tall, slender youth whose Uncle Levi was now compelled to look up to during conversation. Isaac was quite excited as the steamboat made the turn south, and he walked quickly to the stern of the boat to give his farewell to the Ohio River and the North. His uncle followed at a more leisurely pace. As he approached the stern, the continual whoosh of the paddlewheel seemed to keep time with the rapid, almost mechanical hum of thoughts rushing through his mind. Among all his impressions as they traveled south, one thought kept intruding upon his consciousness: he was now entering a land from which so many were hoping and trying to escape.

Even on the river, the heat was intense as they headed south. Isaac was thankful for a slight cooling breeze that rose off the water, which brought some relief from the oppressively hot humid air. As he looked out toward either shore in the bright midday sunlight from under the protective shade of his broad-brimmed hat, he noticed with growing interest large gangs of slaves working on riverfront plantations. He and his uncle moved to the starboard side of the paddle wheeler to obtain a better look, as the steamboat was closer to the river's western shore. Isaac couldn't help but stare at the slaves with an almost morbid fascination. Most of them, both men and women, were dressed in tattered and filthy rags that only partially covered their sweaty bodies. As Isaac couldn't help but gawk, some of the slaves on shore noticed the tall young white man in the plain dress of the Quakers and stared back with sullen expressions. Isaac shuddered and turned away as he realized that he, the observer, was being observed.

"It appears that our friends from yonder plantation have noticed thee, Isaac."

"Yes, Uncle. I'm ashamed to admit that I was staring at them and they justly returned the favor," Isaac said ruefully. "It's almost impossible for me to reconcile in my mind the fact that my best friend, Sam Johnson, might be in a similar state of degradation if his ancestors had not been emancipated."

"How do you find our Southern plantations, gentlemen?" A portly, well-dressed, middle-aged man had joined Isaac and his uncle, interrupting Levi before he could expound further on the subject of voluntary emancipation with Isaac. "The plantation we are now passing is one of the richest cotton plantations in this area. You are seeing only a small fraction of the total number of negroes that work this plantation."

Levi and Isaac turned to look at the newcomer, and with a smile Levi said, "The land appears to be very well cultivated and quite productive, although the laborers' attire appears to suggest some neglect on their account."

"Yes. The darkies don't show much motivation to take care of the clothing that their master gives them," the stranger sighed.

"That's not quite my meaning," Levi responded.

"Oh, I can assure you that every one of these negroes receives a new set of clothing at least once a year, and I might add at considerable expense to their master. The odd thing is that most of them will be dressed very well for Sunday worship. In fact, they seem to take particular pride in their worship attire. Please allow me to introduce myself. I am Stafford Pell from Tishomingo County in the fair state of Mississippi."

As Levi shook Mr. Pell's hand he said, "I am Levi Coffin, and this is my nephew Isaac Burgess. Here is my business card."

"Hmm. What does 'commission merchant and dealer in free-labor cotton goods and groceries' mean? I see that is how you describe your business activities," Stafford Pell expressed with some curiosity.

"Thou canst see from our manner of speech and dress that we are members of the Society of Friends, or Quakers," Levi began as he was warming to his subject. "We are on our way south to purchase cotton goods and groceries produced exclusively by free labor, just as my business card indicates."

Stafford Pell's face flushed, and he became quite agitated. "Why this is outrageous, sir! Are you trying to consciously undermine our Southern economy? There is nothing at all wrong with the cotton produced by the servants on our plantations. Northern abolitionist agitators like you are threatening the very survival of the Union with your incendiary activities."

"I am certain that the cotton grown on thy Southern plantations is very fine, indeed. Quakers, as thou may or may not know, bear a testimony against slavery. No one can be a member of our society and own slaves. Many feel for those in bonds as bound with them. As a result, quite a few have concluded that they could not consistently partake of the unpaid labor of the slave. I propose to help those Southern farmers whose crops and produce are generated without slave labor find a market for their goods. The fruit of their efforts is also a part of the Southern economy, is it not?

Apart from this, thou must understand that I am a Southern man, born and raised in Guilford County, North Carolina. I have many friends and acquaintances in this region who have emigrated here from North Carolina when my family relocated to Indiana. Although I have always been opposed to slavery, it is no part of my business in the South to interfere with Southern laws or its slaves."

Mr. Pell calmed a bit after hearing Levi's speech, but then feeling it his duty to rescue a Southern brother from the abolitionist delusion, said, "Sir, I am delighted to hear that you have roots in North Carolina. My family also moved here from Randolph County, North Carolina, which practically makes us neighbors. I hope I can persuade you of the error of your thinking on this subject.

"You see, the real slaves are the poor factory workers in the North. They are often in a pitiful condition with very little care given to their most basic needs, whereas our slaves are provided for quite generously. The Northern factory worker has to rely on minimal wages to clothe, shelter, feed, and provide for all the needs of his family. On the other hand, their master, sometimes at great expense, provides all the needs of the Southern slave, such as food, shelter, clothing, and even medical care. We did not choose it, but the burden of caring for the African has fallen on us in the South. It is our duty to help them lead productive lives, which without our constant supervision would be impossible. Many eminent medical men, both from North and South, have demonstrated the unique deficiencies of intellect and will inherent to the African race. This lack of mental acuity sometimes necessitates what may appear to be harsh measures to encourage productivity and obedience on the part of the slave. But I assure you it is for their own good. After all, they bear the effects of the curse of Canaan."

By this time a crowd had gathered, looking for a diversion from the monotony of river travel. Levi smiled and, before responding, placed his left hand on Isaac's right hand in order to quell an angry eruption of speech defending the race of his best friend. "Mr. Pell, thank thee for sharing those insights with us. I have a question for thee: Dost thou remember those poorly clad slaves we saw working some minutes ago? Thou made a very interesting observation about the clothing they wear for worship services. Is it customary for their master to pay for such clothing?"

Stafford Pell hesitated, sensing a trap, and then replied, "Most masters allow their slaves to tend gardens of their own to help supplement their diets, as long as this activity does not interfere with their regular work responsibilities. If they are industrious, they may grow more than enough to meet their own needs. They will sometimes sell their produce and with the profit obtained purchase the Sunday finery of which you speak."

"Mr. Pell, can thou think of any reason why slaves might take better care of the clothing they wear for worship than their work clothes?"

"Well, they only wear such clothes once or twice a week at most, whereas they wear their work clothes the vast majority of the time."

"To be sure, sir. But isn't there something else affecting their attitude of neglect for the one and concern for preserving the other, the paradox of which you noted yourself? It seems to me that thou hast provided the answer in what thou said earlier about the means of purchasing the finery. First, their masters did not give the finery to them. Second, they earned the money to buy the clothing themselves. Canst thou see how they take much greater pride in something they have purchased themselves through their own labor that has been rewarded with monetary value?

"Yes, I suppose that may be one possible explanation," Stafford replied with suspicion.

"Although the Northern factory worker may indeed have to endure degrading working conditions, he still enjoys the *possibility* of bettering his condition through industry, unlike the industrious slave who tends his own garden with the hope of financial reward for his extra labor but who nevertheless will remain a slave. As for thy concerns about the inherent inferiority of the Negro, would any race of men not acquire a degraded aspect and demeanor, if they were held in servile bondage for more than two hundred years? Finally, I wish thou couldst see the free negro descendants of my ancestors' slaves who live peaceably in community with white persons. They are as industrious, intelligent, and law abiding as any white person."

"So, as I feared, you Quakers are advocating amalgamation of the races!" Stafford exclaimed.

"Certainly not, Mr. Pell. I have always been against amalgamation. The evils of slavery that I have witnessed from my youth in North Carolina, particularly relate to the disruptive nature of the institution on the family. When a slave marriage has no legal standing, a host of evils can follow. At any time, a husband, wife, or child may be torn from the bosom of their family and sold as property to be traded in the marketplace, never to see their loved ones again in this life. Over the years I have been requested by many slaveholders to assist them in relocating their slave mistresses and mulatto children to the free state of Ohio, when it has been their intention to emancipate them, since they would not be able to remain in their native states as free negroes. On one occasion, the same slaveowner requested help with relocating a second family of mulattoes from another of his plantations to Ohio. What kind of effect is such behavior having on the children of such alliances and the moral state of the surrounding community, not to mention the slaveowner's white family? The inherent inequality of the relationship between master and slave places almost irresistible temptations before the slaveowner when he possesses absolute power over the person of his slaves. How can this but degrade the humanity of both slave and master? It is extremely difficult to fully comprehend the attendant evils when one is compelled by financial necessity to sell his own child."

"Mr. Coffin, I share your concerns and horror regarding the deleterious effects of amalgamation on our society. Thankfully, in my experience, it is a rare phenomenon caused by a few bad apples. Unfortunately, as our laws protect the essential property rights of Southerners, thus limiting interference by the state in the management of one's property, an occasional scoundrel may take advantage of these same protections. We have had quite a healthy debate, my Quaker friend. May I offer you a libation in the saloon of this vessel?"

"Mr. Pell, thank thee very kindly for thy hospitable offer. I'm a temperance man myself and will only use ardent spirits as medicine." This response brought a round of laughter from the crowd who had been listening to the debate. "But, sir, if thou wouldst like to treat me to a glass of lemonade, I would be very pleased."

Stafford Pell grinned and replied, "You Quakers are an amazing lot. Lemonade, it shall be. We might have to agree to disagree about some things but let us celebrate our common heritage from the great state of North Carolina!"

When they returned to the privacy of their stateroom on the *Southern Belle*, Isaac nearly exploded. "Uncle Levi, I am so angry with that man!"

"That's why I placed my hand on thy hand as a signal to remain quiet."

"Yes. I understood the message, but I just don't understand how thou couldst remain so calm. It makes my blood boil to hear such slanders against negroes. When I think of the Johnsons or any other negroes in our community back in Indiana, I think of them as I would any other person, regardless of the color of their skin. 'Lack of mental acuity!' It's these Southerners who have a lack of mental acuity!"

"I share thy horror regarding the attitudes expressed by this gentleman. Unfortunately, much of what he said would not only be affirmed by his Southern brethren, but would also be echoed by a majority in the North. What thou knowest from direct experience in thy relationship with Samuel Johnson and his family, very few of our countrymen have seen or would be willing to recognize as a possibility, let alone reality. It's essential for thee to be very careful in thy speech and to avoid conflict during this journey. I wanted to bring thee to the South so that thou couldst better understand the evil against which we struggle. Violent argument will not convince the Stafford Pells of this world but will likely make them more obdurate in their opinions. We must always strive to persuade with our speech rather than bludgeon with it."

"Yes. I think I understand, and I will try hard to control my tongue. I admire thy ability to remain so calm." After a pause, Isaac then asked, "Uncle, what did thou mean when thou said that thou art opposed to amalgamation? Wouldst thou be opposed to marriage between a negro and a white person, if they truly loved each other?"

"Ah, I knew thou wouldst have a question for me about this," Levi smiled. "It's the inherent inequality in most relationships between whites and negroes, even outside of slavery, that causes me concern. If there could be full racial equality between the individuals entering such a union, I see no reason to object. As you know, even if negroes are free-born in this country, they are not treated equally under the law. More importantly, most states have made such unions illegal and the couple united with God's blessing would suffer intensely the opprobrium of society. Many hearts would need to change before such a couple could raise children safely and successfully in this country. So, Isaac, dost thou have some lovely young negro woman in mind for thy future wife, or art thou only asking such challenging questions out of theoretical interest?" Levi grinned at his nephew.

Isaac blushed crimson and replied, "I guess it was purely out of theoretical interest, although I know some who would make wonderful wives."

"By my reckoning, it's just about supper time," Levi said, changing the subject. "Shall we go discover the exciting repast awaiting us, Isaac?"

"Yes sir!"

With his recent rapid growth, Isaac had discovered that food was a source of nearly constant interest for him, although just like the many gamblers on board the *Southern Belle*, the dietary experience on the steamboat also entailed a bit of gambling for the hungry passenger. The saloon was a large centrally located room, with a vaulted ceiling that ran about two-thirds the length of the steamboat. As Isaac and his uncle entered the room they were greeted by a cacophony of sounds amidst clouds of smoke. Travelers in hope of their evening meal already occupied a number of tables. Intermingled with the serious diners were many tables that hosted a variety of individuals who reflected a wide range of social strata, some of whom appeared to have no interest in food at this time.

Levi took his nephew aside and whispered in Isaac's ear, "It appears we may be seated near some rather rough characters this evening. Be cautious, listen much, and say very little. I'm afraid many of our dining companions may be intoxicated and have very little control over their behavior."

A waiter approached and said, "Gentlemen, it looks like we will have a full dining room this evening. Would you be willing to share a table with this couple here?"

The waiter, who appeared to be harried by his duties, hastily pointed to a trim, well-dressed, middle-aged man and a young woman.

Levi responded, "We would be delighted to share a table as long as it is convenient for our fellow travelers," and bowed slightly in their direction.

"That would be most agreeable to us, sir," replied the gentleman with a distinct Southern drawl. "Please allow me to introduce myself. I am Jamison Endicott II and this is my daughter, Penelope. We are returning from a visit to my sister in Cincinnati to our home in Hardin County, Tennessee."

As Levi introduced himself and Isaac to the Endicotts, Isaac stole a furtive glance at Penelope Endicott. A short, slender figure, she appeared to be Isaac's age, with a very pretty face and deep blue eyes framed by a profusion of blond hair arranged in multiple ringlets. Isaac became aware that Penelope was also surveying him and inadvertently blushed in response to her appraising look. Penelope seemed to enjoy the power she exerted over Isaac's complexion and a subtle smile developed at the corners of her mouth.

"This way, please," the waiter said as he guided them to the table they were to share. While en route to their table, Isaac found it necessary to dodge flying spittle from various directions, as tobacco-chewing patrons ignored the concept of spittoons. While Isaac struggled to avoid near collisions with tobacco juice, he watched with admiration as the pretty young Southerner deftly negotiated the hazards of the dining room without the slightest hesitation or mishap. The closest neighbors to their table were a group of four men intently playing cards. Several empty whiskey bottles were present on their table and clouds of smoke rose from cigars planted in their mouths. Periodic oaths and threats would be uttered amongst the players and then the hostilities would seemingly settle quickly again.

"Mr. Coffin, I enjoyed hearing your discussion with Mr. Pell this afternoon," Jamison Endicott said as they settled at their table. "You have quite a reputation in Cincinnati. My sister has associated your name with the epithet, 'President of the Underground Railroad.' She is a great admirer of yours. Although my sister and I don't agree on the slavery question, I share her respect for your reputation as a man of integrity. After hearing you this afternoon, I certainly would not propose to debate you, but am very pleased to dine with you."

"Mr. Endicott, thank thee for thy kind words. What is thy sister's name?"

"Sara Phillips. She married a Methodist minister, Daniel Phillips, who took her north to Cincinnati."

"Ah, my wife Catherine and I are well acquainted with their many good works. They are very faithful laborers in the Lord's vineyard."

"And in the Underground Railroad it seems," Jamison added. "I love my sister very much but this disagreement over the property rights of Southerners has made it very difficult and painful for us. The rest of my family will not speak or write to her and have refused to see her again. I can never do that to my sister and her husband. I feel torn between my love for her and the rest of my family's affection, indeed even my loyalty to my native state and its customs. I have been anxious for my daughter to know and love her aunt as I do."

"Miss Endicott, how didst thou find Cincinnati? Didst thou have a good visit with thy aunt's family?" Isaac asked.

Penelope looked at Isaac, again making him blush slightly, and said, "Mr. Burgess, I share my father's love for my aunt, uncle, and Ohio cousins, but I must say I don't feel at home there."

"Why dost thou say that?"

"My Uncle Daniel split with the Methodist Episcopal Church South some years ago. He says it is wrong for us to own other persons who have immortal souls. Perhaps he is right. Some of the people I love the most in this life are negroes on our plantation. I pray for them every day. I can't help but feel that we would be abandoning them, if we suddenly emancipated them. Many of them are so like children; I don't think they could survive on their own. When we free them, it should be carefully planned over many years so that they can be prepared for freedom."

"What my daughter has neglected to say, is that she has faithfully for the past two years, since her twelfth birthday, been teaching Sunday School to the slaves on our plantation," Jamison added proudly. It was Penelope's turn to blush as Isaac looked at her intently in an effort to comprehend the apparent contradictions he perceived in her.

"My best friend is a free negro. He is also one of the best students in our school back home," Isaac said. "We hope to go on to study at college together."

"Are there colleges in the North that allow negroes to study together with white persons?" Penelope asked with some incredulity.

"Oberlin College in Ohio admits not only negroes and white men for study together, but it also admits women," Isaac stated triumphantly.

"Your friend must be quite remarkable to be such a good student. Most of our fieldhands struggle to grasp the most basic concepts."

"But dost thou not see, Miss Endicott, that the difference between thy fieldhands and my friend Sam is in growing up as a free person with the opportunity to learn as any other white person?"

"You make an interesting observation, Mr. Burgess, but I must comment that there are many free white persons who remain woefully ignorant in spite of the opportunity you mention," Penelope retorted.

"But the difference, is that they have the freedom to choose to be ignorant or to learn. It's a matter of freedom and motivation. I know many negroes who, when given the opportunity, are highly motivated to learn. Perhaps it would not take so long to prepare thy slaves for freedom as thou dost think."

Penelope smiled at Isaac and replied, "You have given me much food for thought, Mr. Burgess."

As Isaac was beginning to congratulate himself on a successful exchange with Miss Endicott, shouting that erupted at the table next to theirs interrupted his musings. One of the card players who was dressed as a dandy had begun to consolidate his winnings and was preparing to leave the table when one of the losers rose at the same time, spat on the floor, and shouted in a slurred voice, "You cheated me yadamn rascal! Hanover that deck o' cards so I cancheckit."

"Calm down! You're drunk and in no fit state to play cards anymore."

"I ain't so drunk that I cain't teach you a lesson or two about honesty," the unhappy loser replied as he pulled out a large Bowie knife and brandished it at the dandy. The dandy stepped back from the table and gave his former comrade at cards a contemptuous look. Before anyone could intervene, the man lunged with his Bowie knife at the dandy who was only two feet away from the table at which Isaac, his uncle, and the Endicotts were sitting. Penelope screamed as the two men briefly rolled around on the floor.

As quickly as it had started, the combat ended with the dandy in possession of the Bowie knife and the drunken loser moaning on the floor with bright red blood staining his shirt. The dandy dusted himself off, placed the Bowie knife on the table, and walked away with his winnings, leaving confusion in his wake. Upon seeing the wounded man on the floor, Isaac urged Mr. Endicott to take his daughter away to spare her further distress, jumped up, and was quickly at the side of the man examining his wound.

"Uncle Levi, please have someone inquire if there is a doctor on board and bring me some linen bandages immediately!" Isaac barked the orders without thinking how incongruous it might seem coming from a youth his age. Once the wounded man's shirt had been torn away, Isaac could see a horizontal wound approximately three inches in length in the abdomen just above and to the left of the navel. A small jet of bright red blood was emanating from the depths of the wound. As the wounded man in his drunken state struggled and strained to get up, Isaac also noted that no bowel emerged from the wound. He remembered seeing a similar abdominal wound from a farm accident earlier in the spring with Dr. Way. The good doctor was always sharing pearls of wisdom from his experience with Isaac; and now on the steamboat he could hear Henry Way speaking to him.

"Isaac, if a patient with an abdominal wound is straining and no abdominal contents emerge, it is likely that the wound is superficial to the abdominal cavity and may result in a happy outcome."

Dr. Way's pearls did not end there. Isaac also vividly recalled being told by Henry of how holding pressure over a spurting artery might at least temporarily stop the bleeding prior to application of a ligature. While waiting for the arrival of a doctor, Isaac tore a sheet of fabric from the nearest tablecloth and stuffed it directly into the wound and held tight pressure.

Levi returned with more material for bandages and said, "Good work, Isaac. Dr. Way would be proud of thee. Members of the crew are looking for a doctor."

"Uncle Levi, couldst thou please hold this man down while I hold pressure in his wound? He keeps trying to raise himself up in his confused, drunken state. I am confident that his wound is not mortal as long as we can stop the bleeding." After holding pressure for what seemed an eternity, Isaac looked up to see that the captain of the *Southern Belle* had arrived. The captain, marveling at Isaac's youth, apologized for the delay.

"I'm sorry but the one doctor on board, Doc Simmons, is indisposed at the moment and can't come to help. Unfortunately, he's more intoxicated than your patient there. How have you acquired such medical knowledge at your age, young man?"

Isaac smiled and was about to reply when Levi answered for him, "My nephew spends his free time assisting one of the best doctors I know, Dr. Henry Way of Newport, Indiana."

"I hope to go to medical school someday," Isaac added.

"Well, you've been a Godsend for this poor wretch."

"He has a bleeding artery in his wound. I don't have the means or skill to tie it off. Dr. Way has taught me that sometimes with constant pressure the bleeding from a smaller artery will stop permanently even without a ligature. There has been no fresh bleeding for several minutes. I suggest that a tight bandage be wrapped around his torso to maintain pressure on the dressing in his wound. He must not get up for several hours, otherwise he might start bleeding again."

After securing the dressing in place with the tight bandage around the wounded man's torso, Isaac offered to stay with him to keep him from moving.

The ship's captain said, "I think I have a better solution that will allow all of us to get some rest tonight. Wait here a moment." The captain disappeared quickly and returned in two minutes with a small vial. "Doc Simmons may not be of much use this evening but the laudanum from his medical supplies will be of considerable assistance."

About thirty minutes after receiving the laudanum, the wounded man was sleeping soundly, emitting an occasional snore. Isaac looked up at his uncle and the ship's captain with some satisfaction and said, "The fresh dressing and bandages that we added almost forty minutes ago are dry without any evidence of bleeding. Thank thee, captain, for all thy help. The laudanum has already been very effective. Let's move him to a more comfortable place to rest overnight and then, with thy permission, I would like to wash up and change my shirt."

"I owe a great debt to you and your uncle," the captain said after they had moved the wounded man to a cot at one end of the saloon. Observing the contrast between Isaac's calm face and his blood-spattered shirt, he added, "Young man, you clearly have a calling as a doctor. I wish you every success in your future work."

"Thank thee, sir. We are thankful that we could be of assistance. He may need another dose of laudanum later tonight. If he does well overnight, he should probably not be active for another day or so."

The clear night sky was resplendent with stars as Isaac and his uncle walked on the deck of the steamboat at ten o'clock prior to turning in for the night.

"We will disembark at Hamburg Landing first thing tomorrow morning," Isaac's uncle said. "I've arranged with the shipping company to hire some free laborers to unload the flour, cheese, and other produce we plan to sell here through a local merchant. Thou hast had quite an adventure this evening. I hope thou canst get some well-earned rest tonight."

Prior to returning to their stateroom, Isaac visited his patient once more. The wounded man was still sleeping peacefully, exhaling a strong odor of alcohol. Most importantly for Isaac, his dressing and the overlying bandage around his torso remained dry. As Isaac drifted off to sleep, the image of the beautiful young slaveowner returned to his mind. He remained perplexed by what seemed to him an irreconcilable mix of genuine compassion and goodness with the evils of the slave power of the South.

Isaac rose just before dawn and quietly dressed so he could check on the wounded man's condition. He was pleased to find that the man could be easily roused and was without evidence of further bleeding.

"Thou art fortunate that thy wound was not very deep," Isaac said as he examined him.

"I 'pologize fer anythin' unseemly I said or did las' night, and thank'e kindly fer all yer help. Yer offal young to be doctorin' ain't ye?"

"I spend my spare time with a real doctor who has taught me a lot. I hope to become a doctor someday. Thou might want to avoid strong drink and bad company in the future. He could have killed thee."

"The missus has been after me to take one o' them temperance pledges. I guess I oughter think about it."

"Please do. It may save thy life."

A short while later, Isaac stood on the deck of the *Southern Belle* and breathed in the fresh, cool morning air off the water as the sun slowly made its ascent on the eastern horizon. The *Southern Belle* was rapidly approaching a landing on the river; *too rapidly* for a safe docking in Isaac's estimation. Isaac anxiously approached one of the deck hands and asked, "Sir, aren't we coming too fast to dock safely here?"

The deck hand laughed and said, "We're not landing here. This here's Pittsburg Landing. We'll be at Hamburg Landing in just a few minutes."

"Oh, thank thee!" Isaac said with relief, but also with embarrassment because of his ignorance of their route.

In a very short time, they were docking at Hamburg Landing on the Tennessee River. Isaac watched the docking procedure with some interest and then noticed that many black stevedores were already climbing aboard to help unload the vessel. When some of them began to unload his uncle's cargo, Isaac became alarmed. Uncle Levi had told him specifically that free laborers would be handling the cargo the whole way to preserve it from the taint of slave labor. He ran up to the black stevedores and asked, "Art thou freemen?"

One of them, a muscular, well-built man in his late twenties, replied, "Why no, Massa. We's slaves."

"Thou must not unload this material here," Isaac pointed out his uncle's cargo.

"Pleaz allow uz, Massa! We be mitey careful wif de cargo."

"It's not that. . .I'm sure you would be very careful, but . . ."

"Fo' evry dollar we earns we keeps a dime. We's awful sorry we ain't freemen but how kin we becum free wifout buyin' our freedom? Pleaz, allow us to de work so's we can make money to buy oursel's."

This was a wholly different perspective on the free labor question than any Isaac had heard from his uncle.

"Please forgive me. It's my mistake. Please go ahead and unload all of this cargo as well," Isaac said reversing himself as he pointed out his uncle's goods.

Just then, an agitated Levi Coffin arrived on the scene. Isaac grabbed his uncle by the arm, pulled him away from the stevedores and explained the situation.

"Should we block their own efforts to buy their freedom? Can we buy their freedom so as to keep the taint of slave labor from thy goods? Dear Uncle, the longer I am here with thee in the South, the more I am impressed that we are confronted with moral compromises in every direction we turn. Can we really keep our efforts completely pure from the evil of slavery?"

"Isaac, I thought to bring thee on this journey for thy education. It appears we both have much to learn. I will take my own earlier advice to thee and try to hold my tongue. I am upset with the shipping company for their betrayal but perhaps this had to happen for me to appreciate the perspective of the slaves who would be denied an opportunity to better their own condition. My scruples of principle should not take precedence over the demands of my neighbor in need."

As Isaac and his uncle disembarked from the *Southern Belle*, they passed Mr. Endicott and Penelope who were already on the wharf. Isaac and his uncle bowed slightly and tipped their hats to the Endicotts who returned the gesture.

"It was a pleasure dining with both of you last evening," Levi said. "I am sorry the meal was so abruptly interrupted. Perhaps we may meet again during one of your future visits to Cincinnati."

"That would be a pleasure, sir. If your present itinerary allows, we would be honored to have you as visitors at our home. Mr. Burgess, I hear that your patient will make a full recovery," Mr. Endicott said with admiration. "You clearly know much of the healer's art and I am certain will make a very fine physician someday."

"Thank thee, Mr. Endicott, for thy kind words. I wish thee and Miss Endicott a safe and pleasant remainder to your journey home. Miss Endicott, I will pray for the continued success of thy Sunday School."

Penelope was surprised by the young Quaker's well wishes and, blushing, replied, "Thank you very kindly, Mr. Burgess. You really must come and visit us over a weekend, so that you can witness it yourselves."

Looking at his Uncle Levi, Isaac responded, "If my uncle feels we have the time, it would be a pleasure to visit your home and worship with thee."

The early morning sunlight filtered through the oak trees and warmed the small figure as it searched among the blades of grass and last year's leaves for acorns. After a careful inspection, the blue jay found its treasure and, grabbing it in its bill, flew up and perched on one of the lower branches of an oak to revel in a delightful repast. After finishing breakfast, the blue jay looked quizzically at a motionless face that was framed in the barred window of a nearby building. Even after making its raucous call, as if to say, "Look over here," the blue jay was disappointed by the lack of a response. The bird had almost decided that a closer examination was in order when the eyes imbedded within the face blinked suddenly and the mouth emitted a deep sound that to any human observer would have been recognized as a groan. Hesitating, the bird decided to once more commiserate using its own language and vociferously called again to the no-longer-motionless face. This time the face moved in response to the bird's call and for one brief moment the suffering of the one was met by the exuberant *joie de vivre* of the other.

In one flash of insight triggered by the insatiable curiosity (and was it empathy?) of the blue jay, Tib realized that circumscribed within this small creature's existence was everything that he lacked. His groan was quickly followed by a laugh, a hearty visceral laugh emerging from deep within his being, a laugh that could no longer ignore the irony of his situation.

"Oh, my little friend," Tib lamented, "if only I could borrow your wings!"

One end of the main park in downtown Richmond, Indiana was in close proximity to the rear of the county jail. The view of the park from the barred window of the prison cell was the one slight consolation offered to prisoners. As he heard footsteps approaching, Tib thirstily drank one last draught of the vision that was presented through the barred window and said, "Farewell, my feathered friend. Your kind concern and sentiments are much appreciated."

U.S. Marshal Silvanus Beecham rose early that morning with a headache. In fact, he had not slept well at all. He just couldn't stop worrying and planning for every contingency. What kinds of obstacles might be thrown in his path as he tried to transport the prisoner south? Would twenty deputies be enough? As he would work through one potential problem, another would rear its ugly head, as if to taunt him. When he finally thought he had laid all of the practical concerns to rest, another image would stand before him and deny him sleep. The quiet dignity and restraint shown by the slave Tiberius during the examination of the claimant's evidence of ownership particularly haunted him.

As he sipped his coffee and brushed Margaret's mane, he could only shake his head and say, "Margaret, I can't get over the fact that I like that slave a whole lot better'n either of those rascals who've come to claim 'im."

When the appearance of one of his deputies interrupted his chat with Margaret, assuming his official pattern of speech, Silvanus said, "Deputy, we've got nearly seventy-five miles to travel today on the National Road to Indianapolis. If we make good time, we might be able to cover the distance in twelve to thirteen hours. It's already nearly seven a.m. We should've been on the road by now. It's my hope that we can catch the night train that leaves from Indianapolis at ten p.m. for Madison on the Ohio River."

"Marshal, ain't you worried that this slave's friends might try to rescue 'im?" asked the deputy anxiously.

"Of course I'm worried. The faster we can transport him, the less time anyone has to plan a rescue. One thing in our favor is that we'll be traveling on a well-maintained section of the National Road. I was on the same stretch about a month ago and it was in an excellent state of repair. The hard-compacted gravel should make travel with the wagon a lot faster."

Tom Blavey, the Newby plantation's overseer, and the Honorable Percival Thornton were finishing breakfast at the Main Street Hotel when Silvanus approached their table.

"Are you both sure you want to travel with me as I transport the prisoner back to Madison?" Silvanus asked. "There may be some dangers along the way. Someone might try to rescue him."

"It is our duty to Mrs. Newby to see this business through to its successful conclusion," Percival remarked blandly as he finished the last bites of his bacon.

"As long as you are aware of the risks, I have no objection."

Looking up, Silvanus saw a vaguely familiar figure approach the table where he and the agents for Mrs. Newby were chatting. A middle-aged man dressed in the fashion of Quakers came up and introduced himself.

"My name is Henry Way. I practice medicine in Newport, the small town in which the slave Tiberius has resided for the past five years. I represent a group of interested parties who would like to purchase his freedom." Turning to Percival Thornton he said, "As the agent for Mrs. Newby, wouldst thou be willing to explore her interest in selling the slave Tiberius? Such a transaction might satisfactorily address many issues, including recovering Mrs. Newby's financial loss, reducing the myriad problems and expenses that are associated with transporting a fugitive slave in a potentially hostile environment, and resulting in a happy conclusion for all parties concerned in this affair."

Percival Thornton, surveying the Quaker physician with some curiosity, smiled and replied, "Your proposal may have real merit, Dr. Way. I assume you realize that Tiberius would fetch a pretty penny in the current market. Is it really possible for you to raise between one and one and a half thousand dollars in just a few days?"

"I think that it is quite possible, even in such a short time, to raise a competitive sum to purchase his freedom. With his history of being a runaway, his value on the open market may be diminished significantly. Settling upon a purchase price as soon as possible may be quite advantageous to Mrs. Newby," Henry reasoned.

"Your suggestion is worth exploring further, sir. I would be happy to send a telegram describing your offer to Mrs. Newby," Percival replied.

Silvanus interrupted the negotiation at this point. "I think it is essential that we start our journey immediately. Mr. Thornton, if you would like to send your telegram, please do so right away and have the response forwarded to Indianapolis."

"Thank thee for thy consideration of this proposal," Dr. Way said as he began to make his leave. "I will make sure that either my agent or I personally will meet thee at the telegraph office in Indianapolis."

On his way out of the hotel lobby, he was surprised to find the U.S. marshal at his side, who then whispered in his ear, "Dr. Way, if you are successful in negotiating a purchase price with Mrs. Newby, I would like to offer a small sum in support of buying your friend's freedom. I'll wait to hear more from you in Indianapolis."

Before the startled physician could reply, Silvanus had disappeared in the direction of the jail.

"The legal agent for Mrs. Newby seemed genuinely interested in negotiating a purchase price for Tib's freedom," Henry reported. Ben and Sam Johnson and John Burgess were listening to Henry's account of his meeting with the Kentuckians with great interest.

"That's the most hopeful news we've heard since the beginning of this nightmare. What a strange business; that federal marshal, of all people, being so sympathetic to Tib!" Ben exclaimed.

"However, don't for a moment assume that he will break or even bend the law that he is sworn to uphold," Henry replied. "I believe he is a good man caught in a terrible dilemma."

"Let's go on ahead to Indianapolis," suggested Ben. "Henry, you and John can work on the financial issues. Sam and I will work with some of Pastor Ebenezer's contacts in the negro community there to develop a rescue strategy if for any reason we lose the option of buying his freedom."

"I have sent out telegrams to all of our contacts in Ohio, Michigan, and Indiana alerting them to the situation and that we are attempting to purchase Tib's freedom," John replied. "Many of our abolitionist friends have set aside modest sums of money for just such an occasion. I hope we will be able to quickly raise the required sum, once Henry has been able to negotiate a purchase price. Ben and Sam, I would recommend concentrating your efforts on developing a rescue plan for the Indianapolis-to-Madison portion of Tib's transport. I hope and pray that we can avoid any bloodshed."

"My guess is that Marshal Beecham is hoping to catch the ten p.m. train from Indianapolis to Madison. If he misses that train, he will have to house Tib in the county jail in Indianapolis overnight. As long as there is no reason to raise the marshal's suspicions through overt action, but only a distressing delay due to bad road conditions, buying more time could be very useful," Henry reasoned.

"We'll see what we can do to make the journey to Indianapolis more inconvenient for the good marshal," Ben laughed.

The cool morning air gave way to a smoldering heat containing a heavy admixture of humidity. Tib could not avoid breaking out into a sweat as he sat shackled and fully exposed to the sun's rays in the open wagon. Initially, the journey progressed at a good pace for the first two to three hours. Silvanus felt more confident of keeping to his self-imposed schedule as he watched the steady progress of the wagon with its human cargo and escort of twenty deputies. The level, relatively smooth surface of the National Road made the ride much more tolerable for Tib than had been the short ride between Newport and Richmond two days earlier. He was able to prop his back against the side of the wagon, which helped reduce his discomfort.

As they proceeded toward Indianapolis, he noticed that the volume of traffic increased on the road. The width of the road that could accommodate traffic was twenty feet. On their way out of Richmond, they had passed some slower travelers heading west, but now they began to encounter increasing amounts of eastbound traffic in addition to overtaking more westbound traffic. Silvanus approached one grizzled old farmer heading west who had a scattered train of farm animals languidly following his wagon, apparently headed for market in Indianapolis.

"Sir, I'm a U.S. marshal taking a prisoner to Indianapolis. Can you please collect your animals so that we can pass by? You are slowing our progress."

The old man stopped his horses, slowly turned his head, meditatively spat some tobacco juice after looking at Tib, grinned and said, "I don't expect yer prisoner is in any hurry to git to Indianapolis."

"Well, that may be so, old man, but I am!" Silvanus was becoming exasperated.

"Now hold yer horses, Marshal. My animals can be mighty stubborn."

The old man slowly got down from his wagon and started in a meandering fashion to collect his animals and pull them over to the side of the road.

"Deputy, help him with his animals," Silvanus ordered.

"I wouldn't recommend that, Marshal. I told ye my animals can be real stubborn. In fact, they can even be onry, when they don't wanna do sumpin."

Unfortunately for the deputy, the warning came too late and the old man's mule gave the deputy a sound kick in the chest, knocking him flat in the dust of the road.

Silvanus came running up and shouted, "Are you all right?"

The dazed deputy gasped a reply, "I'm awful sore, Marshal, and I'm not breathin' so well."

"Do you think you can remount your horse?"

"I'm not sure." When he tried to stand, he winced, cried out in pain, started gasping for air, and collapsed. Silvanus ordered two of the other members of the posse to pick up the wounded man and place him in the wagon with Tib, saying, "Be gentle with him now." Turning to the old farmer, Silvanus asked with mounting frustration, "How close is the next town with a doctor?"

"Oh, it's about three miles west o' here." The old farmer gave the wagon a mournful look, spat some more tobacco juice and said, "Sorry about yer deputy, Marshal!"

Another fifteen minutes passed before the onry animals were finally corralled to one side of the road, allowing the wagon and posse to resume the westward journey.

Tib looked over at his companion and noted that he was breathing rapidly and almost continually wincing in pain. After fifteen minutes, Silvanus circled back to the wagon to check on his wounded deputy.

Tib looked up at him and said, "Marshal, he's not doing well. His breathing has become more rapid and shallow. If there is anything you would like for me to do to help him, I give you my word that I won't try to escape, if you unshackle me."

"Thanks for your offer. I believe you'd keep your word, but I'm not sure there's much either of us can do for him but to try and find a doctor as quick as possible." Turning to another member of the posse, Silvanus said, "Ride ahead as fast as you can and fetch a doctor."

Silvanus then climbed up into the wagon, knelt down beside his deputy, and opened the wounded man's shirt. He was startled by what he saw. Besides the abrasions acquired from the mule's hooves over the left side of his chest, there was uneven swelling of the skin in the same area. When Silvanus touched the area, he felt a crackling, popping sensation just under the skin.

"How do you feel, Jim?"

"Marshal, it's real hard to breathe and the pain in my chest is somethin' fierce," the deputy said between gasps.

"I wish I had some medicine to relieve your pain."

"Am I gonna di. . .die?" Jim uttered with a look of terror in his eyes.

With glistening eyes, Silvanus met the young man's gaze and said, "Son, are you a praying kind of man?"

Jim responded with a look of panic in his eyes and between gasps whispered, "My ma was always urgin' me to git saved. She told me the devil might come to take me at any time. Oh Marshal, I'm a goin' to hell fer sure!"

"No you're not! Now I want you to pay real close attention and pray with me. "Our father who art in heaven. . .""

Tib watched the two figures pray, one out of sheer panic and the other with sincere fervor, and marveled. He couldn't help but be moved deeply by the scene before him while at the same time being struck by the horrendous irony of the situation. If he had never gone into Richmond to deliver the produce on that fateful day several months ago, he would not now be in chains on his way back to bondage. Neither would the poor wretch lying in the wagon beside him be dying.

How closely intertwined are the lives and fate of men! Tib thought as he involuntarily shuddered.

"Stay with me, son!" Silvanus exhorted the wounded deputy who seemed to no longer be listening. The look of panic and terror was fading rapidly, being replaced by bluish discoloration of the lips and a vacant expression in the dying man's eyes. As sudden and irrevocable as the kick of the mule, his rapid, shallow breathing ceased.

"Oh Lord, he's dead!" Silvanus exclaimed in disbelief. "What will I tell his mother?"

"You will tell her that his last words were the Lord's Prayer."

Silvanus gave Tib a grateful look. "Thank you. Of course that's what I'll tell her. You're a good man, Tiberius. I wish my duty lay elsewhere. You've got many friends who are hoping to buy your freedom. There's a doctor by the name of Henry Way who is organizing the effort. I hope they succeed."

This revelation should not have surprised Tib, but nonetheless it was like a drink of cold water to a thirsty man. "Thank you, Marshal, for sharing that information, and for your sentiments. I do have many wonderful friends; more than I deserve."

At this a clatter of hooves interrupted Tib's conversation with the marshal. The doctor had arrived. After hearing the marshal's account of the incident and examining the dead man, he turned to Silvanus and said, "Most unfortunate. I'm quite certain from my examination that he sustained several rib fractures from the kick of the mule. At least one of these penetrated his left lung and produced what the French have called a *pneumothorax*. What you felt in the skin of his chest is air that has escaped from the damaged lung. If the air leak is progressive and cannot escape from the chest cavity, it will cause collapse of the lung and then compromise the function of the other lung and the heart as well. I am sorry that I was not able to arrive in time."

"What could you have possibly done to save him?"

"Marshal, there have been reports of successfully treating such patients by placing a hollow metal tube called a trocar in the chest to evacuate the air before it causes full respiratory collapse."

"So, he might have been saved, if we had found you earlier."

"In situations like this, time is of the essence. Marshal, don't blame yourself. You could not have known how precarious the situation was for your deputy."

"Thank you, Doctor. . ."

"Doctor Davis, Jonathan Davis, at your service."

"How can I recompense you for your time and effort, sir?"

"Nothing is necessary, Marshal. It is not my custom to charge for services rendered to the dead. I only hope you have an uneventful remainder of your journey."

After Silvanus sent a telegram to Richmond explaining the circumstances of the young man's death and conveying his condolences to his mother, he hired a local wagoner with the doctor's assistance to take the dead man back to his family. As he rode out ahead of the prisoner escort, he spoke in low tones to his horse, "Margaret, I think my wife Vinnie was right. Nothing good will come out of this law. A freak accident takes the life of a young man who had the misfortune of being deputized by me to enforce a law that requires placing another man in chains and dragging him back to slavery! What can I do? I'm sworn to uphold this law. How much more evil will come before we're finished with this task? Oh, how I hope the abolitionists can buy his freedom!"

Looking at his pocket watch, Silvanus realized that it would be very challenging to catch the train for Madison from Indianapolis. They had lost at least two hours of precious time.

"Margaret, with yer blessin', I think we still ought to try to catch that train tonight. There's a chance we might make good time, if the traffic ain't too heavy."

"Marshal Beecham, do you think we can still catch the ten p.m. train?" Percival Thornton asked after he and Tom Blavey rode up to join the marshal.

"I hope so. We'll have to make up some lost time."

"The death of your deputy was most inconvenient," Percival blandly commented.

"Yes, indeed it was, especially for him!" Silvanus replied with equal parts sarcasm and anger.

As they resumed their journey, Tib reflected on the news he had heard from Silvanus. He hadn't fully appreciated how isolated and abandoned he had felt since his capture, until the news came to him of the efforts being made on his behalf by his family and friends.

I've been so preoccupied with my fears and grief that I had almost forgotten all the love and concern that is directed toward me, he thought with some chagrin.

Initially, the thought of the efforts to buy his freedom brought considerable comfort. But, the more he thought about it, the more he became convinced it was a much-too-rational solution to the problem. Reluctantly, he had to admit to himself that Malvina Newby's concerns were not limited to merely recovering her property.

As his thoughts wandered, he also became convinced that other contingency plans must also be in the process of development. Although his Quaker friends eschewed violence, he knew that Ben and Sam, as well as others from the free negro community, were likely planning some form of rescue attempt that could easily turn violent. He dreaded the possibility that his loved ones might risk serious injury, imprisonment, financial ruin, and even death for him. How would Eliza and his children cope with not only the loss of their husband and father, but possibly of other family members? He pondered two potential rescue scenarios: the first involved rescue while he was in transit to Indianapolis on the National Road, and the second involved the journey by rail to Madison from Indianapolis. Either scenario would require the element of surprise, such as creating a diversion that could facilitate quick action in the midst of chaos. He was certain that Marshal Beecham would be aware of such possibilities.

His ruminations were interrupted by the sound of thunder coming from the direction of their destination. With all the distracting thoughts he had failed to notice that thunderheads had been gathering on the western horizon. A third possibility became evident as he heard another distant rumble. Marshal Beecham had been quite anxious to keep to a schedule that morning. Clearly, they had lost considerable time with the tragic accident. Was it possible that they might miss the train connection in Indianapolis, necessitating an overnight stay in the jail there? Such a scenario would give his would-be rescuers more time for planning as well as increase the possibility of a rescue in the city. Perhaps nature was conspiring against the slave power. His hopes rose with the realization that the advent of a sudden and violent thunderstorm during the latter part of the day's journey might be most opportune.

"The Lord has provided very nicely for us this day," Pastor Ebenezer Jones said with a smile as he looked up at the angry thunderheads.

"Some of our friends among the local abolitionist farmers have also felt the need to drive their livestock toward Richmond along the National Road this afternoon which may create some traffic problems," Ben added drily. "Hopefully, Marshal Beecham and his posse won't quite make the ten p.m. train to Madison, which should give us more time to plan for a little disruption along the rail line tomorrow, if needed."

Sam and Ben Johnson had ridden ahead of the marshal's escort with Pastor Jones to meet with the local negro and abolitionist community to explore potential rescue plans.

Intense flashes of lightning and loud peals of thunder were now coming at increasingly shorter intervals as the company traveled further west along the National Road. Silvanus was also distressed to see that the traffic, rather than abating with the advent of the storm, seemed to be increasing in volume. At regular intervals they were encountering farmers driving cattle or other domesticated animals along the road in the west bound direction. Although polite, many of the farmers, who were dressed in the manner of Quakers, seemed rather languid in their attempts to get out of the marshal's way.

"Margaret, it's as if the human race and nature are both conspiring to prevent us from catching that train!" Margaret threw her head back, shook her mane, and whinnied in response. "You're telling me Vinnie has been right all along, ain't ye, old friend?"

As large drops of rain began to fall, Silvanus shook his head and sighed as he stared at the dark wetness ahead that would soon envelop them. If they had to stay overnight in Indianapolis, the next day being Sunday would create some additional challenges for the secure transport of his prisoner. The daily morning train to Madison would be delayed until early afternoon out of respect for the day of worship, giving plenty of time for free negroes and abolitionists to create mischief. A bright flash of light followed almost immediately by a loud crack, both of which seemed perilously close, interrupted Silvanus's thoughts. As the rain began to pour down in buckets on the US marshal, his posse, and his prisoner, he motioned to the group to move toward the shelter of a barn that could be seen not too far off the road to the left ahead.

Approaching the barn, Silvanus came upon a farm boy who was driving two cows into the barn.

"Son, I'm a federal marshal transporting a prisoner with my posse to Indianapolis. We need to take cover in your barn until the storm settles a bit."

"Thou had better wait here 'til I speak with my father," the boy replied as he cautiously surveyed the group with their mulatto prisoner. "I'll be right back."

After tying up the cows, he then went off at a run to the farmhouse, which was about 100 yards away. He returned a few minutes later accompanied by his father who greeted Silvanus with a sober expression and said, "How may I help thee, friend?"

"As you can see, we can't proceed farther on the National Road until the storm settles down," a thoroughly drenched Silvanus wearily replied.

"Please come into the barn with thy men and prisoner. I would normally offer thee more hospitality, but I cannot support thy mission."

"I understand. The shelter of your barn is quite enough for our needs. Thank you kindly."

As the Quaker farmer and his son, who were drawn by a mixture of curiosity and compassion, approached the wagon carrying Tib, one of the members of the posse growled at them, "Keep away from the nigger!"

"Let them be!" Silvanus shouted. "They can approach the prisoner as long as they're watched closely and give him nothing besides food and drink." Turning to another deputy and speaking in a low voice, he said, "As soon as the thunder and lightning let up, ride as quickly as you can to the town of Greenfield and send a telegram to the county jail in Indianapolis informing them that our prisoner will be spending the night there and that I will need an additional ten to fifteen men for the posse.

"Thou must be quite hungry. Wouldst thou care for some cured pork and cold water?" Tib looked up from his reverie to meet the kindly gaze of their Quaker host.

"Thank you for your kindness to me. I could enjoy a little food and water right now."

In lower tones the farmer added, "We are hoping and praying that somehow thou wilt find thy way to freedom."

Tib's eyes glistened as he directly met his host's gaze and replied, "At my capture, I made a solemn vow to my wife that I would return to her and my children. I intend to keep that vow or die in the attempt."

"Marshal, it appears that our prospects of catching the train for Madison tonight are considerably diminished," Percival Thornton observed as he and Silvanus stood staring out at the downpour from inside the barn door.

"There's nothing that can be done about it," Silvanus replied. "I've been defeated by the weather and perhaps by a bit more."

"What do you mean, sir, by 'a bit more?' Do you mean that there are individuals conspiring to inhibit the progress of our mission?" Percival asked with growing alarm.

Silvanus turned to the Kentucky gentleman, gave him a piercing look and said, "Oh, I have no doubt that there are human beings trying to thwart our progress. No, that doesn't concern me. I can deal with such challenges. It's displeasing the Lord, who is no respecter of persons I'm concerned about."

"Are you questioning your duty and the law, sir?"

"Never you fear about that. I know where my duty lies. I must honor my oath of office. As for this fugitive slave law, I can't help but wonder if it isn't a pact with the devil! All I've seen come from it so far is a whole hell of a lot of suffering."

"But isn't that the very nature of justice? It must, of necessity, be blind to suffering."

"Whatever happened to the old virtue of mercy?"

"Ah, you're mistaking sentimentality for mercy. Your sentiments are commendable. However, true mercy lies in restoring the proper relationship between master and slave. There mercy can truly flourish where benevolent concern and solicitude for the inferior race can be demonstrated in the appropriate context."

"I may be mistaken but this poor devil seemed awful happy in his delusion of freedom until I captured him. Now his wife might as well be a widow with two orphaned children. A community has been ripped apart. In addition, I have a dead deputy on my conscience and God only knows what additional tragedies will follow, all because I obeyed my oath of office!"

"Please let me assure you, Marshal, that God will honor you for being faithful to your oath of office."

"Will He now? I'm not so certain about that! I expect He'd be having us mix a lot more mercy with a lot less justice, if we'd listen to Him when we write our laws."

"Marshal, that is a very interesting, if not entirely practical line of reasoning. It looks like the worst of the downpour has passed. Do you think we should start back on the road?" Percival asked, hoping to distract Silvanus from further reflections on justice and mercy.

"Pastor Jones, the marshal and his posse have finally arrived with Tib, nearly two hours after the last train for Madison left the station," Sam Johnson breathlessly reported to a gathering of free negroes and other abolitionists after running for several blocks.

"Praise God from whom all blessings flow!" was the response, which was echoed by the pastor's co-conspirators in the form of "Glory, Hallelujah!"

"With this additional time, I am still hopeful that we can negotiate a purchase price for Tib's freedom," Henry Way opined. "I will contact the agent for Tib's owner first thing tomorrow morning and send word to thee, Pastor Jones, as soon as I hear her response."

"My fervent prayer is that thou wilt not need to risk violence in attempting to secure Tib's freedom," John Burgess added.

"Amen, Brother Burgess! Nevertheless, we feel we must have a plan, in case God is calling us to act like his faithful prophets of old by smiting the Philistines," Ebenezer Jones responded.

"Eliza, you must get some rest," Mary Johnson tried to soothe her daughter after the sound of Eliza's suppressed sobbing awakened her.

"Oh Ma! I am so afraid for Tib. When I remember all the times he has cried out in his sleep, I shudder to think that his old nightmares are now becoming reality. Apparently, his old mistress will go to any length to return him to his former torment. How is it possible to hate another person so completely? I am certain that she won't allow Dr. Way to buy his freedom!" she groaned.

"My poor child! Rest assured that Pastor Jones, your father, brother, the free colored community of Indianapolis, and our Quaker friends are doing their utmost to free Tib. Hopefully, we'll hear some good news tomorrow. But ultimately, we must remember that he's in God's hands."

"I wish my faith was stronger, Ma. All I can think about is the almost impossible odds that are stacked against Tib."

"Eliza, your husband is a very intelligent and determined man. Don't forget the oath he made when he was torn from us. I, for one, will take him at his word. I'm confident that we shall see him again."

Mary Johnson climbed into bed next to her eldest daughter and held Eliza's head against her chest and stroked her hair while tears moistened both of their cheeks.

Unlike the previous morning, there was no cheerful bird to greet Tiberius as the light of the rising sun awakened him from a fitful night's sleep in the Marion County jail. What he did notice was a growing din that emanated from a very different source. The window of his cell was too high to permit a view outside of the jail, but as the morning progressed he could clearly hear the increasingly cacophonous mixture of human voices that is the audible hallmark of a mob. It was difficult for him to distinguish more than a few words due to his distance from their origin; however, "nigger" and "freedom" would frequently stand out as verbal weapons hurled back and forth in an antiphonal volley of discord. As he contemplated this development, he realized with some irony that the harmonious hymns and worship associated with the Lord's Day appeared to have been supplanted by the disharmony of the "slave's day."

"I'm sorry, Dr. Way, but the instructions I have received from Mrs. Newby regarding your kind offer to purchase the slave Tiberius's freedom are quite clear. In her telegram, she explicitly states that she will not accept any sum that would effect his liberation. I must admit, sir, that I am baffled by her response, but as her agent I must end our negotiations for now," Percival Thornton said, his usual officiousness mixed with genuine regret.

"I am also surprised, sir, that Mrs. Newby has no interest in further negotiations," Henry Way replied. "Wouldst thou object, if I accompanied thee to Louisville with the object of meeting Mrs. Newby and speaking to her in person on this subject?"

"I have no objection, Dr. Way. I must warn you, however, that once Mrs. Newby has made a decision, I have rarely seen her change her mind."

After Henry had related these developments to Pastor Jones, Ben and Sam Johnson, and John Burgess, Pastor Jones could only shake his head.

"His owner seems to be possessed by an all-consuming hatred. Unfortunately for Tib, even if we are successful in rescuing him, it looks like he'll have to take his family to Canada." Ebenezer then instinctively lowered his voice and said, "We have two plans for Tib's rescue. The first involves taking advantage of the confusion created by the mob that has been gathering outside the jail. We have bribed Tib's guard to look the other way. He has told us that at twelve-fifteen p.m. they plan to transfer him to the Madison-bound train that is scheduled to leave at one p.m. To speed his transfer from the jail to the wagon for the short ride to the train station, he will not have any shackles on his hands or feet. While we engage Marshal Beecham in conversation, several of our group of free colored persons and white abolitionists will crowd around Tib as he emerges from the jail and rush him to a nearby horse that has been saddled and bridled for his escape. If for any reason this first plan should fail, we have set up barriers made up of rails and cross ties at two points three and four miles south of Indianapolis, blocking the rail line toward Madison. If the first plan works and Tib escapes, some of our people are waiting for the telegraphic signal to take down the barriers, otherwise they will be prepared to stop and board the train."

By late morning, Tib's cellmate, a young mulatto man who had been brought into the jail about two a.m. for public drunkenness, was beginning to stir. His late arrival had added to Tib's difficulties in obtaining rest. In his drunken state he had been loud and obnoxious, swearing loudly and reeking of alcohol. Now the drunk grasped his head in his hands and moaned in a low voice, "Oh damn! What a headache!"

Tib couldn't help smiling as he looked at him, comparing their two situations. *This fellow must not be much younger than I am. In general appearance, we share many similarities and yet here he is squandering his freedom and here I am envying the freedom that he has to squander,* Tib thought.

"What're you in here for?" the drunk asked.

"I'm a runaway slave being taken back into slavery."

"Really? You don't sound like a slave."

"Appearances can be deceiving. I may have mistaken you for a drunk when you arrived here last night."

"Fair 'nough. What's your name?"

"Tiberius, but my friends call me Tib. And how are you known to the world?"

His cellmate gave Tib a puzzled look and then said, "Oh, you want to know my name. Tom's the name that friends and enemies call me."

Tib shook Tom's hand and said, "I hope you can be free some day."

"That's a strange thing for a slave to be saying to a free-born negro!"

"Friend, there are many forms of slavery."

"Marshal, I don't understand why Mrs. Newby won't even consider negotiating a price for Tiberius's freedom," Henry Way said as he, the Johnsons, Pastor Jones, and John Burgess met with Silvanus Beecham outside the jail a few minutes after noon.

"Dr. Way, her attitude puzzles me also. I was frankly startled to hear of her response from Judge Thornton. I must say that Tiberius has been a model prisoner throughout this whole business. I know this may sound ridiculous to all of you, but I truly wish him well and regret the duty that I am bound to carry out according to the law. Now, it appears that he's ready to be transferred to Union Depot for the train south to Madison."

As he spoke, Silvanus gestured toward the entrance to the jail, which had just opened while the crowd outside the jail simultaneously surged forward to see Tib. Ben and Sam could only catch a glimpse of a mulatto man emerging quickly from the jail who was then surrounded by the negro and white abolitionists, as planned.

"What's this?" Silvanus shouted as he watched the prisoner mount a horse and take off at a gallop after someone nearby gave the horse's rump a sound thump. "The prisoner is trying to escape! After him!" Turning toward his companions in conversation, he said, "Have you been trying to dupe me?" Sam, Ben, and the others had only had a limited glimpse of the back of the prisoner as he mounted the horse but were convinced that Tib was on his way to freedom. As they were about to express their joy, another mulatto who was heavily guarded emerged from the jail.

"How can this be?" It was Ebenezer Jones's turn to express surprise on behalf of himself and his companions. "That's Tib! But then, who's on the horse?"

They all looked at Silvanus, who smiled slightly, shrugged his shoulders, and said, "I must excuse myself, gentlemen. My prisoner and I have a train to catch."

With a car dedicated solely for his security, a heavily shackled Tib was surrounded by fifteen members of the posse that had now swollen in numbers to thirty-five. He had the grim satisfaction of knowing that his journey back to slavery would cost the federal government a substantial sum.

"Doctor Way, please sit with me. While we're traveling, I hope we can get better acquainted," Silvanus offered as he sat down in the car just in front of the one carrying Tib.

"Thank thee, Marshal. I would like that also."

"I can see you're disappointed about the failed rescue. I'm just doing my job and trying to honor my oath of office. You're probably wondering how it failed. You have to realize that guessing an opponent's next step is part of a US marshal's job. I just thought to myself, 'what would I do, if I were trying to rescue Tiberius?' Delaying tactics that could buy more time would help and nature helped you there. Mobs can be awfully useful for diversions, but tricky too. What you didn't know was that a mulatto drunk was jailed late last night with Tiberius. What you also didn't know was that corrupt deputies could be bought with an even higher price. So, my deputy appreciated the bribe very much which added nicely to the reward I gave him for reporting it to me."

"So, the mulatto drunk was substituted for Tiberius," Henry interjected.

"It would seem so, although you all were pretty convinced that your man had escaped."

"The human mind tends to fill in the missing information to complete a story in the desired manner," Henry admitted ruefully.

"I was counting on that."

"How didst thou obtain the cooperation of the drunk?"

"He became very helpful when he was offered release today if he cooperated. Otherwise, he was offered another five days in jail if he was unwilling to cooperate."

Suddenly, less than two miles out of Indianapolis, the train halted. Henry and Silvanus were thrown from their seats.

"Excuse me doctor, I need to check with the engineer about the cause for this sudden stop," Silvanus said as he leapt up from the floor of the car and headed to the front of the train. Returning a few minutes later, the marshal resumed his seat beside Henry and with some satisfaction said, "I am impressed by the commitment of Tiberius's friends among the abolitionists and free negroes. I expected that there might be some trouble created along the rail line and I haven't been disappointed. I sent part of my posse ahead to make sure the tracks are clear, and they discovered a pile of rails and cross ties blocking the track about a mile ahead. We'll have to proceed with caution."

For the next couple of miles, the train inched forward very slowly. The posse did a fairly thorough job of removing the two obstructions from the track, but the conductor insisted on pausing briefly to personally remove some debris at the site of the second obstruction and for his efforts was hit in the forehead by a brick thrown from some bushes near the tracks which tore a five-inch gash about an inch above his eyebrows. He was stunned and bleeding profusely but remained conscious while Henry jumped to his aid and dragged him back on the train while Silvanus ordered the engineer to pick up steam as quickly as possible. Two other bricks were thrown without hitting any targets as the train got underway.

Chapter Seventeen

Isaac and his Uncle Levi had been on the road for the past week visiting various farms in Southwestern Tennessee and Northern Mississippi, looking with varying degrees of success for potential sources of free-labor cotton and other goods and produce. Entering a small hamlet southwest of Hamburg, they heard one of the citizens mention Jamison Endicott by name. Levi asked the man if Mr. Endicott's home was nearby and received the response, "Why mister he's one o' the wealthiest planters around here. Do you know him?"

"We met and dined together on a steamboat more than a week ago. He invited my nephew and me to come visit his plantation, if our journey brought us to his neighborhood."

"Well, sir, you're in for a real treat. The Magnolias, that's the Endicott's plantation, ain't more than ten miles from here. You must take him up on his offer of hospitality. My boy, Ned, is goin' on an errand for me in that direction. He'll show you the way."

"That is very kind of thee, sir," Levi replied with some hesitation. "But as it is after three p.m. on a Friday afternoon, I would feel very awkward arriving in the evening at Mr. Endicott's home without any advance warning."

"Mr. Endicott is one of the leading planters of Hardin County and is known universally for his kindness and generosity to visitors," the man replied. "He'd be very disappointed if he knew you passed by his estate without visiting."

Levi exchanged glances with Isaac, who with his eyes gave his hearty endorsement to the plan, and said, "Thank thee kindly for thy encouragement. We appreciate very much thy offer to send a guide with us. We will take a rest from our journey and visit the Magnolias."

It turned out that 'my boy Ned' was not 'my son Ned' as Isaac first thought, but rather the slave of the affable stranger. Ned was a dark-skinned youth, above average height, who appeared to be about twenty years of age. He had a sullen, taciturn disposition, and Levi and Isaac found that it was almost impossible to engage him in conversation. Ned proceeded quickly on foot along a narrow path through some scrubby pines as they followed on horseback.

After proceeding for about four miles, Ned stopped suddenly, turned around, and mumbled, "I got's to go dis way," as he pointed to an even narrower path to the left. "Y'all keep goin' strait ahead. It's a mitey big place. Y'all can't miss it when you gits dere," and without another word he quickly disappeared along the path to the left.

"Uncle, our guide disappeared rather quickly."

"Yes, he did. I'm not certain that his master intended for him to leave us so soon. I'm guessing we could not have gone more than half the distance to the Endicotts's plantation when Ned left us."

Levi and Isaac proceeded down an uneven path through a densely wooded landscape that could barely allow two riders on horseback to ride abreast. Isaac turned to his uncle and observed, "It seems unlikely that this is the main route to the Magnolias. I'm not sure that a carriage or even a small wagon could navigate this narrow, rough path."

They went on in silence for another forty-five minutes and to their discomfort came to a fork in the path, which took the form of a perfect Y.

"Well, our friend Ned has an odd sense of what 'straight ahead' means," Levi commented. "I wonder which fork we should take."

"Perhaps, we should take the right fork since it appears to be the larger of the two."

"That seems the reasonable and logical choice, although I must say that I'm afraid logic may not be a particularly faithful guide in this part of the country. Nevertheless, the right fork it shall be."

After another half hour, the path narrowed to admit only one horseman at a time.

"Uncle, this is not too encouraging. What should we do?"

"Let's keep going for at least another quarter of an hour. Perhaps we'll find someone who can give us some directions."

A half an hour later, two tired and frustrated travelers were about ready to turn around when they overtook an elderly white woman bent under a load of kindling hobbling along the path.

"Y'all are lost," the old crone cackled as she listened to Levi's description of their journey and destination. "Ye shoulda taken the left fork back there. Ye oughta know by now not to trust directions from niggers," she said dolefully shaking her head at the obvious ignorance of Yankees. "It'll be faster fer ye to keep goin' forward at this point. About another mile or so, you'll see a narrow path goin' off to the left. Stay on that path fer about four or five miles. You'll run right into the Endicott plantation. If'n ye kin git there before dark, Endicott's niggers'll direct ye to the mansion."

Isaac and his uncle were exhausted when they finally emerged from the path at dusk and encountered a gang of Mr. Endicott's slaves who were still working in a cotton field. One of the negro slave drivers saw them emerge from the wooded path, wiped the sweat from his forehead with a dirty handkerchief, left his charges, and came over. Responding to Levi's inquiries, he said, "Massa, welcome to de Magnoleeyas. I'll take y'all to de big house."

After leaving their horses with the slave driver, Isaac and his uncle were greeted by an elderly, impeccably dressed black man who approached them from among the porticoes of a large mansion built in the Greek revival style, which was barely discernible in the gathering darkness.

"Dis way, Massa. Please come dis way. You say dat you knows Massa Endicott? Why Massa will be mitey happy to see you. He always happy to have guests. Allow me t'introduce ma self. I's Fredrick, Massa Endicott's genelman's genelman, his butler, de head of all de house niggers, at yo' service." Frederick punctuated his introduction with a deep bow. Holding a lantern up to his guests, he surveyed their features with a somewhat quizzical expression and said, "You not fum around here is you?"

Levi smiled and replied, "Thou art correct, Frederick. We are visiting Tennessee from our homes in Indiana and Ohio."

"O-hi-o. Why dats where Massa Endicott and Miss Penny was visitin'. Does all de white folk up north talk like you? Is you some kind o' preacher? You sound like yo' talkin' right outta de Bible."

Levi looked at Frederick and then at Isaac and began to laugh. "No Frederick. Isaac and I are members of the Society of Friends. This is how Friends speak. It's called plain speech."

Frederick scratched his bald head, fringed with white hair, and looked very confused. "Does you means to say dat friends in de north talk dis way wit' each other? How does you talk wit' yo' enemies?"

"Frederick, I hope and pray that we are not enemies to anyone. I am so sorry to confuse thee. We are Quakers. That's what members of the Religious Society of Friends are called outside our own community. We use plain speech in all our communication."

Isaac noticed that as soon as Frederick heard the word "Quaker" his facial muscles tightened in the lantern light and he assumed a formal air with his guests.

"Massa, I's sorry fo' wastin' yo' time. I's always talkin' too much. Please come and follow me."

Frederick directed Levi and Isaac into the parlor, which was a room to the right of the front door off the entryway. As they walked into the parlor, Isaac admired the spiral staircase that was the dominant presence on the first floor of the mansion. The parlor was decorated tastefully with a chaise lounge, sofa, and chairs arranged around a fireplace. In front of one of the chairs was a harp with a music stand located nearby. A small secretary was placed adjacent to the window and there were wooden cabinets on either side of the fireplace containing many fine books, some with expensive bindings. On the other side of the window toward the door stood a small piano. Levi sat down on the sofa while Isaac examined the titles of books in the cabinets and the secretary. Isaac was struck by the large number of religious books including compilations of sermons and Scripture commentaries that were present on the shelves. As he was about to pick up one of the commentaries, the door to the parlor opened and two women entered. One Isaac recognized immediately as Penelope Endicott, and the other was a woman not past thirty-five years of age who shared the same complexion and possessed a similar beauty to that of her daughter, but it was a beauty that had undergone a maturation that can only come with the passage of time and a fuller experience of life with its joys and sorrows.

"Welcome to the Magnolias. I am Emily Endicott, and I believe you already know my daughter Penelope."

As they exchanged greetings and introductions, Isaac stole a glance at Penelope, who, catching his glance, held it and smiled.

"I apologize that my husband Jamison is away this evening. He should be returning late tonight from a short business trip."

"Mrs. Endicott, it is we who must apologize for coming unannounced so late," Levi protested. "We did not realize that we were quite close to thy plantation until late this afternoon and then became lost on our way here."

"I am sorry that you lost your way here but now we can celebrate your safe arrival with a meal. You and Mr. Burgess must be quite famished. Please come this way to the dining room."

Colored servants silently appeared and disappeared, bringing corn bread with molasses, cold ham, and cheese. Penelope and her mother sat with their guests while they ate, which made Isaac feel awkward initially, but with their repeated urging to eat more, he complied with unfeigned enthusiasm.

"Betsy, our cook, had prepared a large berry cobbler earlier this afternoon. I hope that I can interest both of you in sharing some dessert with Penelope and me. We had deferred our enjoyment of the cobbler at supper until later in the evening and now we know why," Emily said with a smile.

"Mrs. Endicott, I am certain that my nephew and I would be very happy to become acquainted with Betsy's cobbler," Levi said with a grin, directing a wink toward Isaac.

As Isaac was finishing his second helping of the cobbler, Emily turned to him and said, "Penelope has told me of your desire to become a physician and the impressive medical skills that you have already acquired."

Isaac blushed gratefully in Penelope's direction and said, "I have a very good mentor, Dr. Henry Way, who is both a family friend and a great inspiration to me. For all the sadness and pain that I have encountered with him, Dr. Way has always offered a cheerful smile, words of comfort, and his skills at healing to ease the suffering of his patients. Even when little else could be done, he has always kept faithful vigil at the bedside of a dying person."

"This Dr. Way seems to be a rare individual, a man devoted to his profession and to the care of others. Hopefully, in the future we will have the opportunity of seeing the full impact of his mentoring when you complete your medical studies and enter practice. Always consider this part of the country in your future plans; we have a great shortage of qualified compassionate physicians here in Tennessee," Emily observed.

"Thank thee for the kind words of encouragement, Mrs. Endicott. What thou hast said will serve as an inspiration to me as I face the several years of study ahead of me." Turning toward Penelope, Isaac added, "I feel very fortunate to be thy guest this weekend. Miss Endicott has told me of her evangelistic work among the slaves, including her efforts in starting a Sunday school. I am anxious to witness thy good works, Miss Endicott."

Penelope blushed with pleasure and replied, "Mr. Burgess, I hope you will see the Lord's work and that it will not be obscured by my paltry efforts."

"My husband will be delighted to know that you are our guests. I must warn you that he will want to take you on a full tour tomorrow, so it is wise to get some rest tonight. Frederick will show you to your rooms."

"Good morning, Miss Endicott. I hope thou slept well last night," Isaac said the next morning upon encountering Penelope on the landing prior to descending the spiral staircase to attend breakfast.

"Very well, Mr. Burgess. I trust your accommodations were comfortable?"

As they entered the dining room together, Jamison Endicott, who had been deep in conversation with Levi about agricultural questions, rose to greet Penelope and Isaac as they entered. "Good morning to both of you. Penelope, you look particularly radiant this morning. And Mr. Burgess, it is a great pleasure to welcome you and your uncle to the Magnolias."

"We are overwhelmed by the warmth of thy hospitality and look forward very much to the tour of thy plantation, which thou hast so kindly offered to us," Levi responded.

"We are also looking forward to worshiping with you tomorrow," Isaac added.

"Isaac, I think you will find it very interesting. In addition to Penelope's Sunday school, there will be two preachers tomorrow. A Methodist circuit rider, Reverend Johnson Faircloth, will be joining us tonight for supper and preaching tomorrow morning, and then he will be followed by our very own homegrown preacher, Moses."

In response to the puzzled expressions on Levi and Isaac's faces, Jamison laughed and said, "I think I should explain. Moses is one of our older field hands. He has developed a real gift for preaching over the years and often draws quite a crowd to hear him on Sundays."

"Most of our servants are Baptists, including Moses," added Emily, who had joined them for breakfast after attending to some details in the kitchen. "I believe that Moses, who is a Baptist minister, will also be baptizing several people tomorrow in

Lick Creek, which runs through the plantation. Oh, I forgot that Quakers normally eschew the sacraments. Perhaps you will not be interested in seeing the baptisms," Emily said apologetically.

"We would be very interested in witnessing the baptisms. Many of our close friends are Baptists," interjected Isaac. "Quakers do not eschew the Christian sacraments. We believe that they are experienced in a uniquely personal way by each believer and that the visible forms are not a necessary part of the Christian experience," Isaac further explained as Levi gave a nod of approval to his nephew's explanation.

"I heard a Quaker minister once describe your experience of the 'Inner Light' as a central element of your faith," Penelope added. "Is that a fair statement?"

Looking at Penelope and then at his uncle, Isaac responded, "The Inner Light refers to the indwelling presence of the Holy Spirit enlightening each believing Christian. Quakers believe that communion with the Holy Spirit is directly accessible to each Christian believer and does not require the mediation of formal ceremonies. Uncle Levi, have I spoken correctly?"

"Thou hast stated clearly that which thou hast been taught by the elders and ministers of the Society of Friends," Levi confirmed with a smile.

"Is it possible then that other Christians who are not members of the Society of Friends might also experience the Inner Light?" Penelope pressed the question further.

"Absolutely! Who are we to limit God?" Isaac blurted out in his enthusiasm without looking to his uncle for approval.

Penelope smiled ever so sweetly and then asked, "Mr. Burgess. . ."

"Please call me Isaac," Isaac interrupted.

"Isaac, everything you have said about the Holy Spirit in the life of each Christian is a powerful and moving testimony to the truth. Would you begrudge some of your fellow Christians who crave demonstrable symbols of the truth of their faith through an experience of the visible sacraments?"

"Well, no, I guess not, Miss Endicott. . ."

It was Penelope's turn to interrupt Isaac in her moment of triumph. "Please call me by my Christian name, Penelope."

As Isaac sat wondering what had hit him, his face blushing a bright crimson, Emily took pity on him and said, "We have had a marvelous and highly edifying discussion to complement our breakfast. Gentlemen, if you are to have a full tour of the Magnolias, I suggest you get started very soon. Although the blossoms on the magnolia trees from which our plantation has acquired its name are perhaps somewhat past their prime, I hope you will still gain some pleasure from their fragrance as you move about the grounds."

"I inherited the Magnolias five years ago just a few months before my thirty-second birthday when my father collapsed suddenly from an apparent attack of apoplexy," Jamison explained as they walked through the extensive gardens surrounding the mansion. "My father drove himself and those around him very hard. He established this plantation through unremitting labor, both his own and that of his slaves. As a second son growing up in Virginia, he realized that his only real chance of prosperity was to migrate westward, purchase cheap land here in the Southwest, and with the support of our section's peculiar institution seize his opportunities. In fact, within ten years of his move to Hardin County in 1822, he possessed more acreage and slaves than his older brother back in the Old Dominion.

"There was a time when many of our friends and family thought that the institution of slavery would wither in the South; but that was before the incredible, almost insatiable demand for cotton developed. A bond formed out of pecuniary interest has created an unspoken partnership between the Southern planters and the owners of the cotton mills of the Northern states and England. Many fortunes have been made from the combination of African labor and King Cotton.

"Before my father died, as you may have suspected, there had already been one rupture within the family when my sister Sara married the Reverend Daniel Phillips. Sara had misgivings about the peculiar institution from her early childhood. The first time she witnessed the corporal punishment of one of the house servants, a former playmate who had been caught taking some food from the kitchen, she begged my mother to stop the whipping. When my mother explained that some corporal punishment is necessary to maintain order on a plantation, Sara offered to receive the whipping herself instead of her friend. My mother was shocked by her daughter's offer and then refused the request, insisting that Sara observe the punishment in silence without further protest. Afterward, Sara refused to eat or leave her room for several days until we all began to fear for her health. This incident happened when Sara was nearly eleven years of age, only a few months after the slave rebellion in Virginia led by the infamous Nat Turner in 1831. Some of my mother's kin were brutally killed by Turner and his fellow conspirators.

"Being five years older than Sara, I was privy to more of the discussions between my parents in the wake of the great slave rebellion. Like so many others at that time, my parents felt quite vulnerable. In fact, they were terrified of their slaves, thinking that at any time they might be savagely murdered in their beds. In 1831, we had nearly seventy-five field hands and five domestic servants compared to four members of the Endicott family, one of whom was a young child, plus one overseer. Our nearest white neighbor was five miles away. My parents felt that expediency demanded harsher measures to establish discipline on the plantation. Without fully contemplating the implications of their actions, they decided that if they were to have any kind of sense of peace and security, they must rule their human property using sufficient force to instill a respect, based on fear, for their masters on the part of the slaves. Sara could not understand or accept the practical utility of disciplinary measures, which included deprivation of certain privileges for minor offenses, more frequent whippings for moderate crimes, and threats to sell or the actual sale and separation of family members away to the Deep South for the worst forms of disobedience.

"When reflecting on our Southern dilemma, I am often reminded of a statement quoted to me by one of my cousins who had corresponded with Thomas Jefferson at the time of the Compromise of 1820, in which the former president made this observation about the peculiar institution: '. . .we have the wolf by the ear, and we can neither hold him, nor safely let him go. Justice is in one scale, and self-preservation in the other.'

"In contrast to my sister, my dear Emily has taken a more practical view of the situation. I distinctly remember a conversation we had shortly after Sara's departure north with Daniel in which Emily said, 'In accepting the responsibility for the care of these poor benighted Africans, we must be careful not to allow emotional attachments to cloud our judgment. The institution of slavery has been thrust upon us. We have inherited a great burden that we would not have chosen under any other circumstances. Now we must make the best of it, not only for our sake but ultimately for the welfare and benefit of our slaves. The radical abolitionists would liberate the slaves immediately and unconditionally. They have made no provision for their care after emancipation. Many, if not most of them, would perish through want and disease, while others would pose a real threat to public safety through their lack of discipline and lawlessness. Without considerable efforts given to preparing them for freedom, they would have an incredibly difficult time competing with the other laboring classes in this country. Unfortunately, although there are exceptional individuals, the majority struggle with the limitations imposed upon an inferior race. The only sensible and humane option is gradual emancipation and colonization on the west coast of Africa. Our Daniel and Sara seem blind to reality in their advocacy of the more radical approach to the problem. Furthermore, as with so many of the Northern abolitionists, they do a grave injustice to their own people by blaming the many for the abuses of the few. I am certain that most Southern slaveowners share my sentiments and concerns for the welfare of the Africans.'"

Jamison paused and sighed before continuing. "So, you see my friends, that I am in a delicate position. I cannot speak for other abolitionists. Perhaps you can, but I know that Sara and Daniel have never advocated immediate emancipation without due consideration for the education and welfare of those to be emancipated as well as for the public safety. Indeed, from my perspective, they are the truly brave ones in our families; but they have also paid an enormous price for acting from the strength of their convictions. If I could overcome my doubts and act with the same conviction that they possess, the outcome would be very clear. I know that such actions would destroy the happiness of my wife and only child while wounding many others whom I love. You see before you a master who is an acknowledged slave to the very institution which has given him authority over others.

"Until my dear wife and daughter accept of their own freewill the views of my sister and her husband, I try to help the negroes in small ways. I have never broken up a family in the sale of a slave. The health needs of our slaves, including the elderly, are given assiduous medical attention. I have encouraged the spiritual care of the slaves and have been gratified to see Penelope's efforts on their behalf. Ultimately, I fear for the future of our country. There are many in the South who would advocate a separation of our section from the rest of the country to preserve our institutions. If such a separation comes, I am certain it would precipitate a violent conflict. I would be the most reluctant of warriors, but should a conflict arise I know that duty and honor would compel me to offer my services to my state."

As Jamison finished relating his story that seemed more like a confession, Isaac marveled at his candor. Sensing this, Jamison smiled at Isaac and said, "I am grateful for the opportunity to share something of my family's story with both of you. You may have been startled by my willingness to speak so openly about our Southern institutions. Certainly, many of my kin and neighbors would likely censure me for speaking so frankly to guests from the North, especially with those who espouse strong abolitionist beliefs. Unfortunately, in the public debate regarding the slavery question, there has been diminishing space left for meaningful discussion and compromise. I may be more willing to speak openly with my Northern brothers and sisters about this subject than many of my fellow citizens of the South. However, I am confident that I am not alone in my horror regarding this institution and desire for its ultimate abolition. The questions, however, of how and when, remain."

Before Levi or Isaac could address the how and when of abolishing slavery, Jamison spoke again. "Emily will wonder why I have spent so much time showing you the gardens. Please allow me to show you the rest of the plantation. It will be easier to go by horseback. One of the servants is waiting with our horses."

Jamison directed his guests toward the stables. On their way to the stables they passed through a copse of large magnolia trees, which were still laden with fragrant blooms.

"It is easy to appreciate thy choice of name for thy plantation," Levi said as he pointed to the beautiful blossoms.

"Yes; I'm glad that some of our magnolias are late bloomers so that you can enjoy a whiff of their splendor while you are here."

"Here are the quarters where our slaves live." Jamison pointed out two parallel rows of white clapboard cabins. "Please take a closer look."

Levi and Isaac walked up to the first building and were impressed by the excellent state of repair of the building, which along with the others appeared to have been recently whitewashed. Looking in at the door, they both made note of the well-swept wooden floor, orderly interior, and general cleanliness. This initial impression was reinforced by an inspection of other cabins. Each hut had a loft as the only means of creating some semiprivate space out of the one large room that constituted the interior. There was a window to supplement the door for ventilation, and each cabin had a small fireplace, which served the dual purposes of heating and cooking.

"Ideally, one family shares a cabin, although on occasion two families may share living quarters," Jamison commented as they made their tour.

As they approached the far end of the slave quarters, several small children could be seen playing together. A young slave girl, probably no more than eleven or twelve years old, was supervising the younger children including two white children. Looking up, she greeted Jamison, "Mornin' Massa En'icott."

"Good morning, Mazie. How is your grandmother today?"

"She still doin' poorly, Massa."

"Perhaps, we should stop and check on Mazie's grandmother, if you don't mind, gentlemen," Jamison said, pointing the way to a larger white clapboard building at the end of the first row of cabins. "This is our infirmary and home for elderly slaves who need more care and supervision in their last years than can be provided by their families."

As they entered the building, the cleanliness and better lighting again struck them. There were windows on each side and a larger fireplace than in the slave cabins. Twelve cots were arranged in three rows of four each. Six of the cots in the first two rows were occupied by either the elderly or sick, while two additional slaves were sitting at a small table in a corner of the large room. Isaac was startled to see Penelope sitting on a stool by the side of one of the cots, bending over its occupant. She was calmly stroking the forehead of a thin, elderly black woman who lay curled up on the cot.

"Mammy Mazie, it's Miss Penny. I brought you something special that Betsy baked just for you."

Although Penelope persisted in speaking slowly to the old woman in soothing phrases, she received no response. Becoming aware of their presence, Penelope turned and smiled at her father and the guests. Isaac approached the cot and, leaning down, asked Penelope, "How long has her health been deteriorating?"

"Her memory started to fail, in small ways at first, back when I was eight years old. It's been awful to watch her decline over several years to the point about six months ago when she could no longer say much, walk, or even recognize her own child. She was my father's nurse and then the cook for many years until her mind began to give way. She is the mother of Betsy, our present cook, and grandmother to young Mazie, who received her name."

"Is she still able to eat?" Isaac asked with some incredulity.

"For the past two weeks or so she will take a few bites at a time, but only with considerable coaxing."

"Unfortunately, she frequently chokes when we do get her to eat a bit," Jamison added.

"Perhaps, if I supported her head, she might be better able to swallow," Isaac suggested.

As Isaac supported the slave woman's head, he noticed that she was clean and that her bedding was also tidy. He watched Penelope as she intently focused on the task at hand. She gently stroked the old woman's forehead again and said, "Mammy Mazie, please try this fresh cornbread that Betsy baked for you. It's always been your favorite."

She broke off a small piece and nudged it gently past Mazie's lips and was rewarded by a mechanical chewing motion on the part of the elderly slave. Penelope then cautiously offered Mazie a sip of fresh milk from a tin cup to help coax the swallowing process. Mazie took a few sips of milk, swallowed, and promptly began to cough.

"Her cough is weak," Isaac observed as he gently patted Mazie's back and attempted to adjust her position to a more upright posture.

Once more Penelope stroked Mazie's forehead and smiled at Isaac. "Well, I guess you are learning something of our plantation life. I hope you are not finding it entirely disagreeable."

"I find that what I am doing with thee right now is very agreeable. Thou hast the same gentleness that Dr. Way shows his patients. It is a great privilege for me to help thee perform this act of kindness."

Penelope paused, her eyes glistening, and gave Isaac a penetrating look. "I take it as a very high compliment that you compare me with your mentor, Dr. Way. I hope that you may always remember me in this light, my friend from the Society of Friends."

"Are these garden plots for the slaves' use?"

Levi's question roused Isaac from his musings. They had resumed their tour after helping Penelope to gently reposition Mazie on her cot.

"Families are given their own garden plot with seed and tools," Jamison explained. "In the evenings and on Sunday afternoons, if they choose, they may pursue gardening, both to supplement their diet and to provide an opportunity for the more entrepreneurial slaves to sell their excess produce to make a small income."

"How do they usually spend their income from the gardening?" Isaac asked.

"Most negroes love to wear finery for worship services and at the Christmas holidays. Much of their savings go toward fancy clothing, although we are careful to watch out for strong spirits. Some of the poor white folk in the neighborhood are a bad influence, offering to trade their moonshine for the slaves' produce. Unfortunately, there is some drunkenness among the field hands that has been difficult to completely eradicate."

Jamison noticed that Levi was looking with interest at the two young white children playing with the slave children. Motioning toward them, Jamison said, "Bobbie and Anna are the children of my overseer. That's his house over there, the two-story brick structure. His wife also helps with some of the nursing duties in our infirmary."

After remounting their horses, Jamison led them out to the cotton fields.

"Is cotton thy primary crop?" Isaac asked.

"Yes, it is our main cash crop," Jamison replied, "but we also grow other crops for our own use, such as hay, wheat, and corn, to meet the needs of our livestock and the people on the plantation. We try to be as self-sufficient as possible."

As they rode further out into the fields, the midday heat and humidity became oppressive. The loud crack of a whip interrupted Levi when he was about to make a comment to Jamison about how the intense heat must make it challenging to work on the plantation. He and Isaac both looked at Jamison for an explanation as they turned a corner at the end of a long row of well-cultivated cotton plants and saw a black slave driver again cracking a whip over the heads of field hands as they hoed.

"Don't dawdle now! You gots a lotta hoin' t'do befo' lunch," shouted the driver as he rhythmically cracked his whip in cadence with his verbal cajoling.

Jamison gave his guests an ironic look and said, "Yes, even our plantation is not a paradise. In my efforts to minimize the use of corporal punishment, I have experimented with monetary rewards and other incentives for the slaves to work, but have come to the realization that some level of intimidation is an essential part of maintaining the relationship between master and slave. When I became owner of the Magnolias, I abolished the use of rawhide whips, which lacerate the skin. We now use, only as necessary, a whip to the end of which is attached a soft, dry, buckskin cracker, about three-eighths of an inch wide and ten or twelve inches long. This is the only portion of the whip that makes contact with bare skin during a whipping. When applied by an experienced hand, it produces a loud noise and a smart sting but no break in the skin or underlying bruising."

"How often dost thou feel the need to resort to corporal punishment of thy slaves?" Levi asked.

"I first try to use any means short of physical punishment to modify disruptive behavior. Sometimes, monetary incentives are very helpful to motivate the field hands to increase productivity, especially at harvest time. If incentives are not sufficient or the slave has been surly or disobedient, I will usually threaten removal of a privilege, such as their Saturday evening social time. If the threat is ignored, then the privilege is removed for a period. If slaves are obdurate in their disobedience or if they verbally threaten or strike one of the drivers or the overseer, such offenses will lead automatically to a whipping."

"Who administers the punishment?" Isaac asked.

"Either the overseer or I will," Jamison replied with a downcast expression. "I try to make sure that any corporal punishment given to the slaves is never administered in the heat of anger. I have had to fire more than one overseer over this issue. Some of them can be cruel in the extreme. I am convinced that there is nothing more dangerous to the souls of Southern slaveowners than the power that we exert over the bodies of our slaves. We are in constant danger of becoming the worst savages, especially if we punish our slaves in a fit of passion. I thank God that I rarely must resort to real corporal punishment, usually not more than one or two whippings a year, but when I feel it is necessary, it is intentionally delayed so that its performance will not be clouded by passion. I feel utterly wretched when I must discipline one of my slaves in this way. The punishment is administered without fanfare and I have made every effort to prevent Emily and Penelope from being involved, either in witnessing or participating in the act. The cracking of the whip over the heads of the work gangs by the drivers is a bit of theatrics, hopefully a preventative, sparing me to some degree the unpleasant and noisome task of an actual whipping."

Jamison's description of slave discipline at the Magnolias was interrupted as his overseer, a young man about thirty years of age, rode up. Tipping his hat to Jamison's guests, he made his brief report.

"Mister Endicott, everythin' seems to be in order with this field. I'll be watchin' the other gang personally in the next field over. They've got a bit more work to do to catch up with this gang."

"Thanks, Charles, for your report and good efforts. I would like to introduce you to my guests, Mr. Levi Coffin of Cincinnati, Ohio, and his nephew, Mr. Isaac Burgess of Newport, Indiana. Penelope and I had the pleasure of meeting them on our return trip to Tennessee from Cincinnati. This is my overseer, Charles Simpson."

As Charles shook Levi's hand, Levi said, "I am glad to meet thee."

In response to the puzzled look on his overseer's face, Jamison laughed and said, "Charles, you may not be familiar with the plain speech of Quakers. Mr. Coffin and his nephew are members of the Society of Friends. Mr. Coffin is a friend of my sister Sara."

Charles gave Levi and Isaac a suspicious look, but caught himself and, smiling, said, "I hope that you're enjoyin' your visit to the Magnolias."

Swinging his horse around, he headed for the other cotton field.

The Reverend Johnson Faircloth smiled across the table at his niece, Melanie Faircloth, and then raised his glass to propose a toast. "I would like to toast the fine company this evening, especially the lovely representatives of the fair sex, who grace this company with their presence." He smiled condescendingly as he noticed that the two Quakers raised glasses filled with water during the toast. "How long have you served as Miss Penelope's governess, Mellie dear?" her uncle asked by way of making conversation.

"Uncle, as you know, I have been here with the Endicotts for nearly five years," his twenty-three-year-old niece answered.

Melanie Faircloth was a young woman with auburn hair and attractive features that were diminished somewhat by her overly thin figure and nervous disposition. She had the misfortune of coming from a poor family, but with deep historical roots, even pretensions to greatness. One of her great-great uncles had reportedly been a friend and neighbor of George Washington. Although she had had some ardent suitors, none of them rose to her expectations and she had been forced by necessity to leave her native Virginia and seek employment as a governess. She had remarkable gifts in modern languages and music, which she shared with Penelope. Her pupil was a quick study and had gained considerable proficiency in French and Italian, as well as in singing, dancing, and performance on the piano and harp. The young governess had also shared her own views of the world quite freely with her pupil, including her sympathies and prejudices. Penelope, at times, would frustrate the governess's best efforts to educate her regarding her proper place within the aristocracy of the South, since, after all, Penelope also shared with Melanie a strong pedigree among the first families of Virginia, with the added advantage and blessing of a fortune. It seemed to Melanie that all her efforts were wasted when Penelope, against her sincere counsel and advice, would obstinately insist on her projects with the servants. It just wasn't proper for a young mistress of a plantation to be on such familiar terms with her slaves, even personally nursing the sick and elderly.

"Reverend Faircloth, I think you will be surprised to see the improvements in our negroes that Penelope has been able to achieve through her Sunday school," Emily said with some pride.

"Melanie has written to me of your prodigious efforts on behalf of the negroes," Reverend Faircloth commented mildly. "It seems a most disagreeable business trying to teach them anything. Melanie has also described how you even personally care for the sick and aged among your servants. Are you not afraid that they might misbehave, take liberties, or not show you proper respect? Are they not better suited to care for each other without our direct assistance?"

"Reverend Faircloth, I distinctly remember being taught during my religious instruction as a Methodist that although negroes may come from an inferior race, they nevertheless possess immortal souls and will stand with us before God's judgment seat. Are we not called to treat them as brothers and sisters in the faith?" Penelope became flushed as she spoke.

"To be sure, Miss Endicott, to be sure. God's love and mercy clearly extends even to this unfortunate race. Their hope of future peace and joy in the Kingdom will also help them be better servants in this life. I am certain that your efforts to help them be sensitive to the dictates of the Gospel will bear much fruit. I just hope that you can pursue such noble actions safely with decorum in a manner befitting your station in society."

"The more I have spent time among the sick and suffering negroes on our plantation, the more I am reminded of the Lord's statement, '. . .what you have done to the least of these my brethren, you have done unto me.' Could it be possible that the Lord himself might come to us here in the person of a humble slave on the Magnolias plantation?" Penelope was now speaking faster and with passion.

"Miss Endicott, this is a most interesting and novel interpretation of the Lord's words that you have shared with us. Indeed, it is much food for thought. Melanie has also told me of your extraordinary musical gifts. Would it be possible to hear you sing and perform on the harp with Melanie accompanying you on the piano?"

Reverend Faircloth did his best to divert the conversation to safer topics while thinking to himself, *This young woman has dangerous, even incendiary notions. It is my duty to advise her father to restrain her enthusiasm.*

"Reverend Faircloth, would you prefer tea or coffee?" Emily asked as they settled into the parlor to hear the two young women perform. Still blushing from her impassioned exchange with the Methodist minister, Penelope was arranging her harp and music when Isaac caught her eye and gave her a big smile of approbation. She tried to ignore him and busy herself with the sheet music, but a subtle smile involuntarily crept across her face.

"Miss Melanie and I will first perform a happy little song by the German composer Franz Schubert called, 'Death and the Maiden.' It's about how Death comes as a friend to a very sick young maiden," Penelope explained in a cheery voice. Melanie caught her uncle's attention and rolled her eyes. As the somber but beautiful piece ended, the guests and Penelope's parents clapped.

"Miss Endicott, you sing and play very well," Johnson Faircloth said as the clapping subsided.

"I am grateful for the excellent instruction that your niece has given me. She has been a most patient teacher," Penelope responded with a smile.

Reverend Faircloth felt it his duty to add, "You seem to have chosen a rather melancholy subject for your art this evening. Is there something more cheerful you could offer us?"

"Why, Reverend Faircloth, do you find death to be too melancholy, too morbid a subject for music and song? Would you not agree that it is the one common experience we human beings share?" Penelope responded as a faint smile played on her lips.

"But, to leave no one discomfited this evening, I would like to end my performance with one last, extremely cheerful, if not silly song, a recent composition from our own popular American composer, Stephen Foster."

She then sang:

> Nelly Bly! Nelly Bly! bring de broom along,
> We'll sweep the kitchen clean, my dear, and hab a little song.
> Poke de wood, my lady lub, and make de fire burn,
> And while I take de banjo down, just gib de mush a turn.
> Heigh! Nelly Ho! Nelly listen love to me,
> I'll sing for you, play for you, a dulcet melody.

"Dear friends of Christ," Penelope began, "let us learn together another of the beautiful psalms to the Lord."

Penelope then turned to Isaac and whispered, "It is illegal to teach negroes to read and write. Thankfully, for the work of the Sunday school, those skills are not necessary, since they have amazing memories and are quite eager to learn the Scriptures by rote."

She then began to recite Psalm sixty-eight: "Let God arise, let his enemies be scattered: let them also that hate him flee before him . . . as wax melteth before the fire, so let the wicked perish at the presence of God. But let the righteous be glad; let them rejoice before God . . ."

After repeating the first few verses several times, Penelope asked her audience of fifty-six slaves, almost half of whom were in bondage on the plantation, if they would like to recite it out loud together. Isaac was struck by how quickly and enthusiastically they memorized the psalm.

". . . A father of the fatherless, and a judge of the widows . . . he bringeth out those which are bound with chains . . . thou, O God, hast prepared of thy goodness for the poor . . ."

After memorizing the first half of the psalm together, Penelope paused to ask her students its meaning. There was silence for almost a minute during which Isaac began to feel considerable discomfort, but Penelope only waited patiently with a smile on her face.

Finally, she broke the silence, "Please don't be afraid to speak up. The psalms are for all Christians. This psalm speaks directly to the hope that all Christians cherish."

"Well, Miss Penny, it be about de triumph o' de Lawd ober de ebil. Dese words be mitey pow'ful," an elderly white-haired woman responded.

"Please, Miss Penny, read us de rest o' de sawm," cried another slave.

"I do not know if we'll have enough time to finish memorizing it together this morning, because we are fortunate to have Reverend Faircloth visiting the Magnolias today. He will give a sermon and then Moses will follow with his message and the baptisms in Lick Creek. But let us, at least, hear the powerful message present in the rest of the psalm."

Penelope proceeded to finish reading the psalm, inserting commentary as she went.

"'. . . Thou hast ascended on high, thou hast led captivity captive. . .' This passage is telling us how God, through the death of Jesus, has delivered us from the slavery to sin. For those of you who will be baptized later today this passage should have special meaning," Penelope explained.

Then she continued. "'. . . *He that is* our God *is* the God of salvation . . . Ethiopia shall soon stretch out her hands unto God . . . the God of Israel *is* he that giveth strength and power unto *his* people. Blessed be God.' These final verses of the psalm speak of the great hope that we all have as children of God. He is the God of our salvation. There is no question that the salvation he is offering is for all of us here. The message is very clear: '*Ethiopia* shall stretch out her hands unto God . . .' Ethiopia refers to the African peoples. God is waiting for you to stretch out your hands to Him," Penelope said with fervor, her eyes shining, as Reverend Faircloth, Levi Coffin, and her parents joined the gathering outside the plantation house.

The heat of the Tennessee sun, combined with the droning of Reverend Faircloth's voice, made it very challenging for Isaac to stay awake. He noticed that he wasn't the only one present who was struggling with the strong allure of sleep. Many of the negroes and whites were also nodding off.

"'. . . God will reward his faithful servants in the kingdom to come, but it is essential to be faithful to one's earthly masters so that the promise can be fulfilled. St. Paul gives these instructions in the third chapter of his letter to the Colossians starting with verse twenty-two: 'Servants, obey in all things *your* masters according to the flesh; not with eyeservice, as menpleasers; but in singleness of heart, fearing God: And whatsoever ye do, do *it* heartily, as to the Lord, and not unto men; Knowing that of the Lord ye shall receive the reward of the inheritance: for ye serve the Lord Christ.'

"You see; it's really quite simple. When you serve your master, you are actually serving Christ himself. That's why it is absolutely necessary to not hold anything back. In this life, you must willingly give your wholehearted service to your earthly master, as if he were Christ himself, so that you can enjoy the indescribable joy of heaven in the next life."

Reverend Faircloth paused to wipe the sweat of his forehead with his handkerchief and surveyed his audience. Other than a few nods of approval from his white listeners, silence was the most remarkable feature of the response attending his sermon. In addition to the slaves on the Magnolias plantation who regularly attended worship services each Sunday, there were almost another fifty slaves from neighboring farms, plus close to eighty white people, made up mostly of slaveowners and poor white farmers, who would come during good weather to hear the slave preacher, Moses. In the colder months or during inclement weather they would gather for worship in a small brick church about a quarter of a mile from the Magnolias plantation house. Isaac noted with some interest that many of the slaves were better dressed on Sunday than the white worshippers. When Penelope announced during the Sunday school that Reverend Faircloth would be preaching before Moses, Isaac thought he saw a shadow of disappointment cross the faces of the slaves. This quickly passed and was replaced with an impassive expression that betrayed nothing more of their thoughts as they silently listened to the Methodist preacher's message.

After making a rough count of those present, Isaac turned to Penelope, beside whom he was seated on the large veranda, and asked in a low voice, "Do all of thy slaves attend worship services on Sundays?"

"Alas, no. There are a few miscreants who sneak off and make trades from their garden produce for spirituous liquors that are distilled by some of the poor whites in the neighborhood. They are often drunk by the end of services on Sundays. My father has decided that he should not interfere with their behavior, since Sundays are their only day off from their duties. He feels strongly that we should not compel them to attend worship services; rather their belief and worship as Christians should come by their free choice."

"Are most of the slaves on thy plantation Methodists?"

"Very few are Methodists and those are mainly from among the house servants. The vast majority are Baptists. Africans seem to find great meaning in the experience of baptism by full immersion. You will see later today how Lick Creek has been temporarily damned up for this purpose." Then with a laugh, she added, "Indeed, Moses our servant, who is a Baptist preacher, has always said that at Christmas time all the slaves become Methodists, since this is the only time of the year when they, as good Baptists, relax their prohibition on dancing."

Having given up on arousing any response from his audience, Reverend Faircloth sighed, wiped his face and brow, and then announced his closing hymn, "The Old Rugged Cross." To his surprise, persons of all complexions sang with great enthusiasm. As he sat down, his previously sleepy audience was now fully awake and attentive as a tall, thin, angular negro stood up.

Moses, a licensed Baptist preacher, was smartly dressed in a swallowtail coat with white cravat and matching black trousers. He wore a black stovepipe hat, which further augmented the impression created by his height and thin build. A significant admixture of white in both his beard and full head of hair highlighted his dark skin and handsome facial features. In a whisper, Penelope gave Isaac a brief account of the preacher's history with the Magnolias plantation. His actual age was a mystery, for Jamison's father purchased him some twenty years earlier for a bargain price at the time. The reason for the bargain price that the slave trader gave Jamison's father was due to Moses's character. He was informed that Moses was an "uppity nigger" and that his previous owner's overseers were never able to fully "break" him so that he would become a compliant and productive field hand. Allegedly, Moses seemed to have his own ideas about the best way to complete the work to be done, which annoyed the overseers and his previous master greatly. The elder Jamison had always felt that he was a good judge of a slave's potential. When he met the slave trader and his coffle of slaves on the road heading for the New Orleans market, he stopped him when he saw the tall, imposing Moses.

"What was the cause of your trouble with your old master?" the elder Jamison asked the slave.

"I thought I could do de work betta and fasta anudder way," Moses replied frankly.

"Do you know your chances of surviving very long aren't too good down the river?"

"I expec' so, but mebbe I won't git sech a dum massa down dere."

After looking at the many deep scars on Moses's back, the elder Jamison took the slave trader aside and offered him about half the usual price a young male slave of Moses's size would normally fetch. After some further negotiating, Jamison purchased the troublesome slave for two-thirds of the going price, since both the slave trader and he knew that Moses was a big gamble. Just the scars on his back alone would identify him as a "problem" negro for any potential buyer in New Orleans. The slave trader thought he had the better part of the deal, but he was quite mistaken.

On the way back to the Magnolias, Moses's new master said, "I need a new blacksmith. Old Joe is just about spent. How would you like to learn blacksmithing?"

"Hmm, I nebber done dat kind o' work. I expec' I'd like to try it."

"If you do a good job learning the trade from Old Joe and do quality work that is completed on time, I'll let you decide how and when you do the work."

Moses did well in his new vocation, more than meeting his master's expectations while managing his productivity in his own way. The senior Jamison was as good as his word and allowed Moses considerable discretion as he had promised. Due to his physical strength, which seemed out of proportion to his thin build and to his competent performance of his new trade, Moses rapidly gained the respect of the other slaves on the plantation. Their respect for him was initially tempered by some suspicion as he tended to keep to himself and would rarely attend the common worship services, which created the impression among the folks in the quarters that he must be some kind of heathen.

He eventually took a wife from among the younger slave women, and she bore him two children. When their children were three and one and a half years of age, tragedy struck. Typhoid fever swept through Hardin County and the Magnolias was not spared. About thirty of the slaves and even the younger Jamison were struck down with the illness. Moses and his young family all became ill. He watched his wife and two children die while he nursed them as best he could and then he in turn became sick. Struggling for a long period in delirium, he would cry out at times, frightening the old negro woman who kept vigil at his bedside in the infirmary. She reported later that once during a high fever he yelled out quite distinctly, "I's not ready fo' de firey flame, please don't let de Debbil take me!"

Remarkably, his fearful travail seemed to pass, for she reported twenty-four hours later that his countenance had shifted from the intense suffering that had dominated it early in the illness to a peaceful expression, which had emerged out of the distress of the previous days's struggles. His sleepy-eyed nurse was startled to awaken from a nap at his bedside to see him looking at her with a broad smile on his face.

"De Lawd took me to see de hot place an' den to see de hebbinly manshuns. I see'd my wife an' chillun. Deys wid de Lawd! Dey ain't slaves no mo'! De Lawd done tell me dat I's to preach de Gospel truth fum now on. He tole me dat it be hi' time dat I git religion. I gots to git to de creek so's I kin be baptized now! I can't keep de Lawd a waitin'!"

Moses's conversion and recovery had occurred more than a dozen years earlier. Although he continued to be a taciturn slave, making minimal use of words during his work as if speech were a necessary evil, another Moses emerged when it came time to preach. Over the years since his call he had gradually revealed during his sermons different elements of the revelations he had received during his near-fatal illness. The absolute certainty with which he shared these revelations and the compelling way he preached drew listeners, both white and negro, from the surrounding communities, even attracting listeners from outside Hardin County. After rising to his feet, Moses slowly surveyed his audience, apparently in no hurry to begin preaching. Then in a deep baritone voice he began to preach.

"Miss Penny, wif yo' permishun, I'd like to read fum de Holy Bible dat you's bin teachin' us dis mornin'. 'Let Gawd arise, let his enemies be scatter'd: let dem also dat hate him flee befo' him. . .as wax melteth befo' de fire, so let de wicked perish at de presence o' God. But let de righteous be glad; let dem rejoice befo' God. . .'"

Moses stood quite erect, solemnly extending his right arm and open hand, as if holding the very Scriptures from which by memory he quoted so fervently. Looking up toward the sky and grimacing from an inner pain, Moses almost shouted, "Brudders an' sistahs, I bin dere! I bin dat wax dats meltin' befo' de fire. I kin still feel de hot flame lickin' at my bones. What'll it be chillun, de flame or de joy o' de Lawd? What did de Revren' Fairclot' say? '. . . Dat we mite enjoy de indescribable joy o' hebbin in de nex' life.' Well how's we gonna do dat, if'n we's full o'sin an'all kind o' wickedness?"

Moses paused and with eyes that were burning coals glanced around at individuals, both slaves and whites in his audience, each of whom felt the intense heat of his gaze that seemed to penetrate to the very depths of their souls.

"Befo' de Lawd brung me back from death, he showed me how ebil I bin. He tole me, 'I's gonna give you one mo' chance, Moses. But, if'n you wants to be here wif yo' wife an' chillun enjoyin' mah bressin's, you gots to become a new man an' you mus' warn dem aroun' you to change dere wicked ways.'"

Looking out at his audience with an expression mixing intense fervor with pleading, Moses asked, "Ain't I bin tryin' my best to do dat very thing, brudders an' sistahs?"

"Yes, brudder Moses, you has," shouted one elderly woman, while several amens arose spontaneously from various directions.

"Don't you all see what King David's tryin' to tell us po' sinnahs? If'n we be righteous, de good Lawd's flame won't be lickin' our bones. No sirree! It'll be warmin' our hearts! Now lissen to dis: '. . . A fadder o' de fadderless, an' a judge o' de widows, is God in his holy habitashun . . . he bringeth out those which are bound wid chains: but de rebellious dwell in a dry land . . .' Ain't it clear, brudders and sistahs? De Lawd want us all to be free!"

Moses paused ever so briefly, lovingly embracing the word *free* as he again surveyed his audience, quickly adding, "Free from sin an' all de wickedness o' dis world."

"Amen, brudder Moses, Amen!"

"But wait brudders an' sistahs, dere's mo'. '. . . Thou O God hast prepared o' thy goodness fo' de po'. Dis promise fum de Lawd eben be fo'us po' colored folk. How's you know dis, Moses, you mite aks? I'll tells you how I knows it. It's right here in de Holy Bible dat Miss Penny be teachin' us. Jes' lissen to dis. It be right in dis here Sawm, '. . . Ethiopia shall soon stretch out her hands to God.' Dat means us. We be fum Ethiopia, where de black folk come fum. So's you kin see dat de good Lawd be callin' fo each of us, eben de colored ones, to enjoy de glory o' his mercies. Dat's why some o' you hab answered de call an'll be baptized today, so dat in de Great Day you kin come befo' de Lawd an' enjoy his warmth an' not be burn'd. But, don't any o' you forget what King David also say in dis Sawm, '. . .But God shall wound de head o' his enemies, an' de hairy scalp o' sech an one who goeth on still in his trespasses. . .' Don't any o' you linger in yo' sin. Flee fum de fire and fine de warmth o' de Lawd!"

Many more amens followed this challenge and then Moses led his congregation in singing several spirituals, which were sung enthusiastically by both white and black members of his flock.

Reverend Faircloth turned to Emily and whispered, "Do you really think it is wise for your daughter to be teaching the slaves the Scriptures? I am afraid they may misinterpret what they hear. I wouldn't want them to ever think that they will enjoy the same status that their white masters will enjoy in Paradise. It can only confuse them with false expectations. It should be sufficient for the most obedient servants to rejoice in the opportunity to resume their relationship with their loving masters in the afterlife."

Emily turned and said, "I am glad to hear your opinion, sir, for I must be confused as well. When the Lord speaks of the blessed poor, it is difficult for me to identify any members of the human family who are more qualified for that title than the poor Africans. It only seems just that the Lord might give them special blessings in the next life. Of course, I might be mistaken, but I doubt it."

As the singing ended, Isaac turned to Penelope and remarked, "Moses is an extraordinary man, who clearly has been touched by the Inner Light. He memorizes what you teach him very quickly and is able to interpret it in a divinely inspired manner."

Penelope smiled and replied, "I can't begin to tell you how much I've been blessed by the faith of so many of our servants, but especially that of Moses."

Levi Coffin, who had been listening to his nephew's conversation with Penelope, gave the two young people a penetrating glance and said, "I believe that these poor ignorant and degraded sons and daughters of Africa, who are not able to read the precious words of the Savior, are blessed with a clearer, plainer manifestation of the Holy Spirit than many of us who have had better opportunities of cultivation."

After a brief pause following his uncle's observation, Isaac asked Penelope, "What harm would it do to teach Moses to read the Scriptures for himself?"

"As I told you before, it is illegal to teach slaves to read and write. I try to follow the Lord's precept of 'Render unto Caesar what is Caesar's and unto God what is God's.'"

Before Isaac could respond, Moses rose again and announced that the baptism of five slaves from the Magnolias would occur shortly in Lick Creek, which was about a half mile away. For such occasions, the creek would be temporarily damned to facilitate full immersion of those to be baptized. Isaac and his uncle rode with the Endicotts in their carriage to the site of the baptisms. Reverend Faircloth and his niece declined the opportunity, citing fatigue. On the road, they passed five slaves adorned in immaculate white robes who were solemnly processing toward the creek. Moses, with a staff in his hand, like his namesake of old, led the large entourage of more than one hundred enslaved and free persons along the dusty road to the waters of salvation. As they walked, his booming voice erupted into song:

> Roll Jordan roll, Roll Jordan roll,
> I want to go to heaven when I die,
> to hear Jordan roll . . .

The water glistened and sparkled as it reflected the brightness of the rising sun that early morning in June 1852. A few clouds dotted an otherwise clear blue sky and birds chased each other overhead. By way of contrast, a disconsolate figure sat in chains and under heavy guard in the center of a ferry that was now crossing from the Indiana to the Kentucky shore. Tiberius was oblivious to the beauty of life surging around him as he hung his head and grimly pondered his fate while he once again crossed the Ohio River, now in the opposite direction from which he had in great danger crossed it nearly five years before.

Tiberius and his captors had arrived without further incident in Madison, Indiana via the Indianapolis-Madison Railroad early Sunday evening. To his great frustration, Marshal Beecham felt it necessary to house Tib overnight in the county jail since the arrival of the steamboat he had hoped to take that evening to Louisville had been delayed. During the night, he was awakened by one of his deputies who reported a rumored plot to rescue Tib either during the transfer to the steamboat or during the short voyage to Louisville the next day. Silvanus made a quick change in his plan and ordered a wagon to be immediately prepared for the overland transport of his prisoner the almost fifty miles to Jeffersonville, which was opposite Louisville on the Indiana side of the Ohio River. He had instructed his deputy to proceed with this plan in absolute secrecy and to leave between ten and fifteen deputies behind in Madison. They would be charged with making slow, deliberate, and very public preparations for securing the route from the jail to the wharf for transfer of the prisoner by water while he and the remainder of his posse would actually be transporting Tib overland to Jeffersonville. He also instructed the deputy in charge of those remaining behind in Madison to publicly announce after some considerable delay that the prisoner would be held another day in the county jail in Madison because of security concerns related to the suspected plot. Silvanus hoped that with a head start he would be able to transfer Tib safely overland to the jail in Jeffersonville by the next evening and commandeer a ferry across the Ohio River early the following morning before his prisoner's would-be rescuers would discover the ruse. He further instructed the deputy in charge in Madison to announce that he, the federal marshal, was ill and had transferred his authority to him temporarily while he was indisposed.

With his usual efficiency, at three o'clock in the morning Silvanus quietly transferred his sleepy and gagged prisoner from the county jail on foot to a wagon located a quarter of a mile away from the jail which was waiting outside Madison on the road to Jeffersonville. Tib was again secured with ankle chains in the wagon, the gag only being removed after two hours of steady westward travel had put some significant distance between him and any potential rescuers. After an uneventful journey, Silvanus was quite pleased to receive a telegram in Jeffersonville that evening from his deputy in Madison reporting on the activities of a large boisterous crowd of free negroes, white abolitionists, and curiosity seekers outside the jail. He made his final arrangements with a ferryman whose activities were monitored closely overnight for transfer across the Ohio River at dawn the next morning and then bade his horse Margaret a good night.

As the ferry neared the Louisville wharf, Tib's attention became acutely focused when he heard Silvanus giving instructions to his deputies regarding the final leg of the journey from the wharf to the slave pen in central Louisville.

"According to the instructions coming from Mrs. Newby, we'll be transferring our prisoner into the custody of a Mr. Matthew Garrison, who is a slave trader here in Louisville. His establishment is located at the corner of Main and Second Streets." Noticing that he had attracted Tib's attention, Silvanus walked over to him and said, "It looks like our journey together is about to come to an end. I wish we had met under happier circumstances and that my duty lay elsewhere. I still can't understand why your mistress wasn't interested in the very good offer that your friend, Dr. Way, made on your behalf."

"My mistress has her own peculiar reasons for refusing Dr. Way's offer, which extend beyond purely rational considerations."

"I guessed as much, and I must say that I'd rather not know the particulars. Becoming acquainted with you has made it nearly impossible for me to continue in my role as a federal marshal. When one of the finest human beings I ever met is standing before me in chains, all because of my fulfilling my duty to the law, I'm no longer certain there is any such thing as rational considerations in this fine land of ours."

Local citizens and other passersby stopped to gawk, many with looks of approbation on their faces, as the wagon carrying Tib with his escort made its way slowly to the corner of Main and Second Streets where the slave pen of Garrison's Negro Sales was located. Matthew Garrison, a portly man of less than average height, with graying hair and dressed in a manner befitting the wealth that had come to him from his trading in human lives, came out of the sales office next door to greet Silvanus.

"Marshal, you are right on time, just as you stated in your telegram. I am so pleased to see how well the new fugitive slave law is functioning to protect Southern property rights."

Silvanus scowled and replied in his most formal tone, "As a United States marshal, I, Silvanus Beecham, have the duty under the Federal Statute of 1850 to transfer the prisoner Tiberius, property of Mrs. Malvina Newby of Shelby County, Kentucky, into your keeping as per her instructions."

"Yes, yes, Marshal Beecham, thank you. You needn't be so formal. Please escort the prisoner this way."

After removing Tib's leg irons, Silvanus escorted his handcuffed prisoner through a gate into the small courtyard that served as an exercise area for slaves awaiting sale. There were several locked cells that opened onto the courtyard. The courtyard itself was crowded with human merchandise of both sexes, comprised of various sizes, shapes, and ages. The complexions of members of this community of misery extended from coal black to nearly white, while there was an equally impressive variation in age from small infants in arms to white-haired crones adorned with the wrinkles of advanced age. Around two sides of the courtyard there was an overhanging canopy made of canvas that provided some protection from the elements. In this area were crowded close to thirty souls.

Mr. Garrison turned to Silvanus and said, "Please replace the leg irons on the prisoner over here under the awning. There is no room in any of the cells for him."

Silvanus surveyed the courtyard with its filth, noisome smells, and the terrified looks of the slaves in response to his presence, and was sickened.

As he helped Tib to his spot under the awning and replaced the leg irons, he whispered to Tib, "Now that you are no longer my formal responsibility, I hope to God that you escape!"

Tib looked up at Silvanus and replied, "I mean to do just that. Sometimes, evil laws make criminals of the best of men. I will never forget the kindness and mercy you have shown me throughout this miserable business."

After the gate closed behind Marshal Beecham and Matthew Garrison, Tib was left to survey his new environment. As he looked around the courtyard he was struck by the apparent indifference, even listlessness of his fellow slaves. Except for the periodic cries of small children and infants, most of the courtyard's inhabitants were silent and seemed to lack even the possibility of emotive expression. As he studied their faces and inert postures, he could not help but reflect sadly, *There is an epidemic of despair here. I can now see that despair may be one of the worst forms of contagion.*

He closed his eyes, hoping to shut out the malign influence that was also beginning to creep over him.

A few minutes later he was startled out of a light sleep by a familiar voice, whispering in his ear.

"Tib, is dat you? Open yo' eyes fo' yo' ol' friend Sisro!"

Tib slowly opened his eyes to see a tall mulatto man about thirty years of age grinning at him. With a flash of recognition, Tib grabbed the man's arm and exclaimed,

"Why, it's you Cicero! I must say that five years ago I had hoped to never see you again on this side of the Ohio River but now you are definitely a sight for sore eyes!"

The two men rose and hugged each other with tears in their eyes.

"De nigger seller, Gar'son, crowed about dem capturin' a dangerous run'way. Glory be, if it ain't Tib hisself," Cicero exclaimed, as he tried to grapple with the reality of the situation. "O' course I's sorry dey captured you but still mitey glad to see you."

"Me, too!" Tib echoed both sentiments as he, with difficulty, wiped the tears from his eyes on his tattered shirtsleeve. During his journey south, he had never thought for a moment that he might meet a friend from his past. The gloom for both men lifted a bit as they shared the stories of their lives since the last time they had seen each other. Cicero had been a valued field hand on the Newby plantation. Apparently to settle some personal debts, Malvina Newby, who also owned Cicero, had decided to sell him since he would likely fetch a good price either locally or in the New Orleans market. His master had tried to reassure Cicero that she would have her agent do all he could to sell him in the local market, so that he might still be able to see his wife and three children annually during the holidays. Cicero marveled at Tib's description of Northern communities of free negroes, who could read and write, living and working with white people as equals.

"Ain't you fibbin' me, Tib? How kin it be?"

"I swear it's true. I have a beautiful free negro wife and two children back there, waiting for me. I will escape and return to them or die in the attempt."

"Tib, I gots to tell you somethin' you needs to know about yo' mammy and sistah."

"Have you heard something about them?" Tib asked anxiously. "When my mistress took ownership of me, she told me that they were both sold down the river. Are they dead?"

"Massa Newby nebber sol' dem. He jes' made it seem like he did. It be a big secret but deys libbin in a lil' cabin about ten mile fum de plantashun."

Old memories flooded Tib's consciousness as he contemplated the revelation he had just received from Cicero. He had long ago grieved the loss of his mother and sister, assuming they had been lost to him forever in the Deep South. He couldn't help but marvel that he had received such news at this time and under these circumstances. As he looked at Cicero, who was now sitting near him, he also realized to his shame how he had blotted out of his mind the plight of his old companions in bondage after settling into his new life in Indiana. Inquiring about the status of other slaves he had known on the Newby plantation, he learned of new births as well as deaths and sales, with the overall balance sheet yielding a very similar number of persons in bondage compared to when he fled for freedom. Cicero related that they had been told on the plantation that he had drowned in the Ohio River after being shot while trying to escape in a small boat. Cicero added, "'Twere hard fo' me to believe my eye when I see'd you."

"I'm very glad to see you, Cicero, but I'm so sorry that you're being sold away from your wife and children."

"I's hopin' dat I gits sold to a massa here in Kentucky. If'n I could jes' see my Sally and chillun at Christmas each year, I think I could go on libbin.'"

The creaking of the hinge on the gate to the slave pen heralded the entrance of the proprietor of Garrison's Negro Sales. Two hulking fellows, who were chewing and spitting tobacco, followed him into the slave pen. Garrison's assistants began rounding up slaves for the day's auction, which would begin in about an hour. Tib was surprised that both Cicero and he were singled out and ordered to form a line with other slaves.

They certainly aren't wasting any time in selling me down the river.

The slaves were directed one by one through the gate and then through a door immediately adjacent to the left of the gate into a room of the sales office where they were ordered to strip and wash themselves. One of the assistants cautiously approached Tib with a key to remove his leg irons and handcuffs while the other trained a pistol at him and said, "Don't try anything, nigger, or I'll send you to yer reward sooner than you'd like."

Cicero and Tib were standing together in the small, crowded room, stripped naked along with the other male and female slaves to be sold that afternoon.

"Quickly, now! Use the water from the buckets and the bars of soap to clean yourselves," one of Garrison's assistants urged. As Tib was rinsing the soap from his body, he heard the all-too-familiar shrill tones of a female voice that sent a shiver down his spine.

"Where is my slave, Tiberius?" Malvina Newby asked.

"He is in this side room washing up with the others who will be sold this afternoon," Matthew Garrison replied.

"He's a dangerous and crafty one, but not so clever as he thought he was when he ran away." Malvina looked in through the side room door scouring the room with her eyes until with great satisfaction she recognized her slave, Tiberius. "Well, well, you wretch. Did you seriously think that you could avoid drinking the entire cup of suffering that is your destiny? I hope you know by now that I *will* have justice. My agents tell me that you now have a wife and family. You have done well for yourself and for my purposes. 'The sins of the fathers. . .' Yes. The righteous Judge in his justice has heard my prayer and seen my sorrow. He is now extending the suffering you have justly deserved to subsequent generations."

Tib bit his lip as he tried to repress his growing anger. Malvina, a tall, thin, gaunt middle-aged woman, stared intently at him with a hollow-eyed expression, as if the skull of a corpse had received the gift of sight, and continued.

"You are an outrage against the white race and a freak among your own kind. The most uppity of niggers, insolent beyond human tolerance, and yet hardly worth another thought."

Tib couldn't restrain himself any further and responded by saying, "*Aquila non capit muscas.*" Smiling at his mistress, who was now glaring at him, he then added, "Oh, pardon me, ma'am. It's not likely that you have learned Latin since we last met. Please allow me to translate. '*The eagle does not hunt flies.*'"

Matthew Garrison looked first at Tib with curiosity and then at Tib's mistress with perplexity. Malvina glared back and said, "Never you mind this nigger. He is always putting on airs. He'd been a domestic servant when he was a child and picked up a few Latin phrases he'd overheard my husband utter."

"Spoutin' Latin may not endear him to my customers," Mr. Garrison cautioned. "What's this?" He pointed to the deep scars from prior whippings on Tib's back and the "N" branded on each buttock. "It looks like he also has a scar from a gunshot wound here," Garrison pointed to the prominent scar on Tib's left shoulder.

"You'd better keep a shirt and pants on him during the auction," Malvina advised.

"A discerning customer will read a lot regarding this slave's history from these scars."

"Yes, that is true. I want to reiterate my instructions to you to clear up any potential confusion. He is not for sale in the Kentucky market. His future lies in the New Orleans market. So, if you need to let bidders know that he has been a runaway, that's fine with me."

"As I said, the experienced customer will likely realize that he is damaged goods on closer inspection."

Looking grimly at Tib, Malvina responded, "If necessary, I am prepared to offer a very reasonable price to one of your colleagues who would purchase him for the New Orleans market."

Then taking Garrison aside, in a whisper she added, "Just make sure he is on his way to New Orleans tonight. You will receive the same handsome commission, regardless of the price you obtain for me."

Turning back to Tib and noticing Cicero for the first time, Malvina said, "Cicero, you see now how runaways eventually get caught. Don't ever get any such ideas in your head. I'll do my best to make sure you are sold to a buyer close to our plantation, if you promise to not try any such rascality yourself. If you are a good and faithful servant to your new master, I am certain we will be able to work out an arrangement for you to come spend the Christmas holidays with Sally and your children."

"Yes'm, Mistress Newby. I promises to be de best nigger I kin be."

"As for you, Tiberius, you wretched piece of flesh, I want you to fully appreciate your fate. There will be no damnable Quaker abolitionists to save you. That US marshal did his work very well. Those fools are probably only now beginning to realize that they have been duped. You will be on a steamboat traveling down the Mississippi before the 'good' Dr. Way arrives to offer me a 'fair' price for your freedom. I think you now realize that it is not your destiny to be free, but to suffer. There will be no escape, no way out for you this time," she said with a triumphant sneer.

Tib struggled to contain his emotions and found additional strength and inner calm as he recited another Latin quote in response, "*Aut viam inveniam aut faciam*," muttering the translation under his breath, "I will either find a way or I will make one."

"Oh, you are truly insufferable, going on with your prattle," Malvina said, exasperated. "Whatever you said or intended to say will not make one iota of difference. Your fate is sealed."

"Even the humble Greek letter *iota* does make a difference in the proper context."

"Ladies and Gentlemen, please take a close look at this fine young buck named Cicero. He has been the model of docility, an efficient and hard worker, ever faithful in his efforts to please his master, Mrs. Malvina Newby of Shelby County. Unfortunately, because of some pressing pecuniary issues, it has been necessary to offer Cicero for sale at this time. Mrs. Newby has one stipulation regarding the sale of her faithful servant. She is seeking a buyer whose home is close enough to the Newby plantation in Shelby County to make it possible for Cicero to visit his family during the annual holiday celebrations. Recognizing the fine sensibilities and concern expressed on behalf of her faithful servant by Mrs. Newby, are there interested parties?"

"Show us his back, Garrison," a voice called out from the crowd.

"As you can see, there's nary a scratch on his broad muscular back," Garrison pointed out with enthusiasm.

A middle-aged, well-dressed man came forward and asked, "May I look at his teeth?"

"Certainly, Captain Andrews. Cicero, show him your teeth."

Cicero obligingly grinned broadly, revealing a full set of healthy teeth. Captain Andrews, who had acquired his military rank and title from service in the Mexican War and who lived about fifteen miles from the Newby plantation, commented, "Garrison, he does seem like quite a strong, healthy fellow. I bid nine hundred dollars."

Captain Andrews's bid seemed to break the ice, for several other planters rose to offer counterbids. Within a few minutes, Cicero's value had climbed to fourteen hundred dollars, the highest bidder being from a plantation about twenty-five miles from the Newby estate. Tib was familiar with each of the plantations represented during the bidding. He was concerned for Cicero because a round trip journey of fifty miles on foot in December would not leave much time at all for him to see his wife and children. His hopes for Cicero rose when Captain Andrews, after some hesitation, offered a higher bid of fourteen hundred fifty dollars, but were quickly dashed when his competitor countered with fifteen hundred dollars even. Throwing one last look of farewell behind him toward Tib, an apprehensive Cicero was led off by his new master.

"Is this the runaway that the federal marshal delivered here this morning?" asked an elderly gentleman who had come up to examine Tib more closely.

Looking directly at Malvina, Garrison answered, "Yes he is the very same. As you can see he is healthy, strong, and clearly quite intelligent."

"And a lot of trouble!" an anonymous voice from the crowd added, to generalized laughter. "Show us his back, Garrison. Bet it won't be so silky smooth as the previous sale."

This remark again elicited loud guffaws. Malvina nodded to Garrison to raise Tib's shirt.

"Looks like he's been a heap o' trouble. Once they get a taste for freedom, it's hard to whip it out of 'em," volunteered another prospective buyer.

At this point, Garrison piped up and said, "He's still got many good years of labor left in him, but he might be better suited to the New Orleans market."

Looking over toward some slave traders who regularly transported slaves to the Deep South, he said, "What say you, gentlemen? Don't you agree that he would fetch a pretty penny in the New Orleans market?"

One rather oily character came up and examined Tib more closely, not unlike the manner in which one would assess the worst and best characteristics of a horse, and declared, "I bid six hundred dollars."

After some fitful bidding among the slave traders, the best offer was only seven hundred dollars. Garrison, who had requested a hundred-dollar commission for the sale, looked over anxiously at Malvina. She nodded her agreement with the purchase price and gave him a look, as if to say, "you will get your full commission."

After purchasing several other slaves, Tib's new master led the group off in chains to the wharf for transport to New Orleans via steamboat. As Tib was being driven forward onto the steamboat, he marveled at the efficiency with which Malvina Newby had executed her business. Once on board, the coffle of slaves was led to the stern near the paddle wheel. Within an hour the steamboat was pulling away from the wharf, just as another steamboat from Madison, Indiana, carrying an anxious Henry Way, was docking. Looking up from his gloomy meditation, Tib was surprised to see Malvina Newby at the dock watching his departure with deep satisfaction. Their eyes met briefly, hers with a look of triumph and his with a dull expression, suppressing his real emotions.

Tib's new master approached the coffle of fifteen slaves he was transporting to New Orleans and began to speak. "My name's Higgins, Josiah Higgins. I never thought it was good business to damage the merchandise that one plans to sell. I'd much rather not have to keep all o' you chained together. I always say, 'a happy slave, a happy sale.' But that means I must be able to trust you to stay in this part of the ship and follow my orders without question. In other words, no tricks. Do you understand?"

The chorus of the enslaved responded, "Yes'm Massa!"

"That's good, otherwise I won't hesitate to reduce my profits, by whippin' the hell out of any of you who misbehave."

Josiah unlocked the two chains holding the gang together and then removed the individual collars and leg irons from each slave.

When he got to Tib, he paused, shook his head, and said, "I'd probably be a damn fool to take your fetters off. Give me one good reason that I should remove them."

Thinking quickly, Tib assumed the slave dialect and said as obsequiously as possible, "Massa, you's a mitey kind massa. I promise to be de best slave I kin be fo' you."

Tib lowered his head after finishing his statement and then looked up at Higgins imploringly.

"I bet you found those Yankees weren't so friendly to niggers as you thought they'd be, did you now?"

"Massa, you knows dem well. Dey was real hard folk up dere. I's glad to be back in de South wif my own kind."

"Well, I'm gonna wait a bit with you. You'll have to show me you can be trusted before I'm removing your fetters," Higgins said as he moved on to the next slave, after placing Tib in handcuffs and leaving his leg irons in place.

As darkness settled over the river, the light of a full moon was reflected off the water. When Tib saw the moonlight shining on the river, his path became clear. He must strive in every way possible to convince his new master to remove his fetters, otherwise he would have no chance of escape. He realized that in the darkness of night he had found a true ally and friend. But, even if he could get free of his fetters, his only real prospect for escape would be to jump overboard during the night and swim for the Indiana or Illinois shore. Since most slaves could not swim, he hoped that when his absence would be discovered his master would assume he had, through negligence, fallen in and drowned.

The next day arrived hot and sultry, with a steamy mist that shimmered in the sunlight of early morning as it clung to the water. The itinerary of the *River Queen* included multiple stops for the loading and unloading of cargo and passengers at various points on the northern and southern shores of the river. As they came into port at a small town on the Kentucky side, Higgins appeared and told his slaves to follow his commands.

"You folks are gonna make me some additional money during this trip. A lot of these ports don't have enough stevedores to help with the cargo."

Pointing to the male slaves, he said, "You'll be working under my orders as stevedores. I expect you all to work hard without complaints. If you do, I'll make sure you get fed well for your efforts."

Turning to the females, which he had segregated to the side, he said, "If you make yourselves useful, I'll reward you as well."

After pondering for a few minutes, he came over to Tib, looked him over, and remarked, "You're one of the strongest bucks I've got. Here's your chance to prove you can be trusted." With that he began to remove Tib's fetters.

Tib replied, "Massa, thank you fo' gibben me a chance. I's gonna work real hard fo' you."

The opportunity to prove his worth and trustworthiness came on a daily basis, often several times a day, as they slowly made their way down the Ohio River. However, each night the handcuffs and leg irons were replaced, to Tib's chagrin and growing anxiety. The closer they came to Cairo, Illinois, where the Ohio joined the Mississippi River, Tib's concern increased. Once the steamboat made the transition to the Mississippi, he knew his chances of escape would be significantly compromised. He would then be confronted with a larger body of water to negotiate and the unpleasant prospect of slave states on either side of the river.

As the steamboat was approaching the wharves at Cairo in the middle of the afternoon of the fourth day of the voyage, Higgins approached an unfettered Tib and said, "You'll be real busy here in Cairo. There are some boxes I want you to transfer from the port side of the stern to the starboard side, since we'll be docking on the starboard side. If you can get started now, it'll save some time."

"Yes'm Massa."

Tib had never been on the port side of the *River Queen*, his sphere of existence and work having been limited until now to the starboard side of the stern. He was pleased to see that Higgins allowed him this much freedom to go unaccompanied out of sight to the other side of the steamboat. He almost cried out when during his search for the boxes he saw a small rowboat trailing behind the steamboat attached to the port stern.

Of course, most ships of this size would require a ready means of quickly collecting the mail or transferring passengers without the delays associated with docking.

Tib ruminated on his discovery throughout the several hours he spent transporting boxes and other material on and off the steamboat. By early evening, the *River Queen* had departed from Cairo and Tib felt a twinge of despair as he saw the mouth of the Ohio disappearing behind him. As he was reflecting on his limited options, Higgins came up to him and said, "You've done a good job. Now that we are finally on the Mississippi, I'll let you sleep at night without the fetters. If you keep working hard for me on the trip to New Orleans, I'll do my best to find you a good master."

"Oh, tank you Massa Higgins. Tank you fo' yo' kindness to me, a po' nigger," Tib responded.

While giving Higgins his most servile look, Tib was already working through his next steps. How could he get away in the rowboat without some assistance? Someone would have to cut the rope holding the boat once he was on board. Should he offer to take other slaves with him?

"Hey nigger, you hungry or not?"

Tib was startled out of his planning by the voice of a chambermaid, a young slave woman working on the steamboat, who was bringing food to each of the slaves, the reward for their hard labors of the day. He smiled at her and motioned for her to come closer, so he could whisper. "I have a pregnant wife and young son back in Indiana. Would you help me make my escape?"

Her eyes widened with a look of fear as she replied, "You ain't talkin' like a slave to me, like you done to Massa Higgins. You mus' be a mitey smart an' slippry nigger. You bin foolin' de white massa dis whole trip."

"Shh," Tib cautioned. "Have you ever wanted to be free?"

"I not sure what 'free' mean."

"It means that no one can tell you what to do or where to go without your permission. It means no one can pull you away from your family and send you where you don't want to go."

"You mean I ain't free when my massa sent me to de owner o' dis ship an' I can't see my man no mo'?"

"Yes, exactly."

"I wants to he'p you but if'n I git cotched, dey'll sell me down de ribber, like you."

"You won't get caught. I'll leave tonight in the rowboat on the port side of the stern. I only need for you to cut the rope holding the boat once I'm on board. You can quickly disappear with the knife and I will be long gone before anyone notices. Higgins checks on us before he retires for the night, usually around eleven o'clock. Would you come at midnight?"

"Yes. . .I'll come den," she said after hesitating a moment.

Tib then asked, "Would you be willing to help more than one of us to escape?"

"I don't know about dat. You mus' promise me dat you won't tell who cut de rope, if'n you gits cotched. I trus' you but I don't wanna havta trus' a lot mo' people."

"I understand. You have my promise and my word of honor that I will not betray you."

The chambermaid slipped quietly away to finish delivering food to the other slaves. Tib tried to rest in anticipation of the night's adventures but was unable to fall asleep easily. He couldn't help but enumerate the many challenges ahead. He would now be deep in slave territory without any knowledge of the region. The image of his young son, Benjamin, and pregnant wife, Eliza, rose before his imagination and he remembered his promise to them. Marshal Beecham appeared again, leaning over him in that last encounter in the Louisville slave pen, another image, which strangely complemented that of his family. *Even my former captor shares in my family's hope for me,* he thought as he dozed off.

"Well, it looks like you're mighty tired," Higgins declared with a grin as he thrust a lantern toward Tib's face.

Startled awake out of a dream about the farm in Indiana, Tib quickly recalled where he was and sleepily answered, "Yes'm Massa. I's glad to sleep now."

"You just do that. I'll have plenty for you to do tomorrow."

Tib pretended to go back to sleep, waiting for Higgins to leave. Once he was gone, Tib opened his eyes and quietly waited, watching for the chambermaid. After what seemed more like two hours than the one hour that Tib had guessed would be the difference in time between Higgins's visit and the advent of midnight, he was startled by a gentle tap on his shoulder. The chambermaid was back. He rose quickly and with her as a guide walked swiftly to the port side of the stern in the darkness, any noise they made being swallowed up by the whoosh-whoosh of the paddle wheel. When they were standing near the rowboat, Tib asked her, "What time is it?"

"It be about one in de mornin'. I's sorry I couldn't git away sooner. I brung you some bread an' water in a jug."

"Thank you for everything! I don't even know your name."

"It better dat way. Git in de boat."

Tib jumped from the stern deck into the rowboat with the tied-up headscarf containing bread and the jug of water under one arm. He signaled his goodbye to his unnamed savior and watched as she quickly cut through the rope connecting him to slavery. He didn't fully appreciate that she had been successful until he noticed the hulk of the steamboat moving swiftly away while he remained relatively stationary. With a silent thank you to heaven for a moonless night, he reached for the oars and began to pull with considerable strength against the stream.

Chapter Twenty-One

Levi Coffin looked across the table at his nephew who seemed to be gazing blankly into a vast uncharted wilderness and smiled.

"Isaac, art thou still pondering thy encounter with young Miss Endicott?"

Coming back to himself, he blushed and said, "Uncle, I am truly perplexed. Miss Endicott, in so many ways, embodies the very ideal of feminine beauty, both physical and spiritual. She comports herself with such grace and is uniformly kind and caring in her dealings with all persons, including, and perhaps most especially, with the slaves on her father's plantation. Her efforts in the slave infirmary and the Sunday school she has initiated for the slaves seem to be truly motivated by a deep Christian charity and yet . . ."

"She does not see the need for immediate and radical change to the South's peculiar institution," Levi finished Isaac's thought.

Isaac looked up and met his uncle's gaze and nodded. "Uncle, you have always said that the Southern slaveowners should be persuaded to end slavery voluntarily. What hope is there for such change to occur, if even the best people of the South do not seem to recognize the urgent nature of the problem?"

"I am quite certain that Penelope's father *does* recognize the acute nature of the problem. His dilemma, which has paralyzed any resolve he may have to act, is his realization that action on his part would elicit even more pain and conflict within his family than what has already occurred with the departure of his sister and brother-in-law to the North as committed abolitionists. His careful attempts to shield Penelope and his wife from the uglier aspects of slavery have not helped them face the true nature of the institution. Thus, they comfort themselves with the rationalization of gradual emancipation and ignore the successful precedent set by the Society of Friends."

Their conversation was interrupted by a hotel clerk who came up to their table in the dining room and asked Levi, "Sir, are you Levi Coffin of Cincinnati, Ohio?"

"Yes. I am he," Levi said as he turned to the clerk, who handed him a telegram dated from several days earlier. Levi and Isaac had arrived late the preceding evening in Memphis following several days of further travel in the rural areas of Southwestern Tennessee after their departure from the Magnolias plantation. He had been able to establish business relationships with several farmers who did not own slaves and was now waiting for the delivery of free-labor cotton and other produce to his agent in Memphis for shipment to Cincinnati.

As Levi examined the telegram before opening it he remarked, "It appears that my agent here in Memphis received this several days ago and that it was sent from Louisville." Levi's cheerful expression clouded over as he surveyed the contents of the telegram. "Dr. Way has sent us some very distressing news," Levi said as he handed the telegram to Isaac.

Isaac could hardly comprehend what he now read:

Tiberius captured by federal marshal. Efforts to free him failed. Sold down the river from Louisville. En route to New Orleans.

Isaac looked up anxiously after reading the telegram and said, "Oh Uncle, I feel terrible that I was not there to help in some way. I can't begin to imagine the distress that Eliza, Sam, and the whole Johnson family must feel right now."

"I am confident that Dr. Way, Ben Johnson, thy father, and many others will have done all they could to help Tiberius. We must pray fervently to God for his deliverance, as I am certain they are doing."

"How quickly can we leave for Cincinnati?"

"I share thy concern and desire to return to the North as quickly as possible, but we need to wait for the merchandise. Besides, it's possible that the steamboat carrying Tib to New Orleans has not yet arrived in Memphis. Perhaps, we can learn something of his fate and even intervene on his behalf."

Isaac looked at his uncle with admiration and marveled. Even now, when his own thoughts were giving way to despair, his uncle was still able to calmly reflect on the potential opportunities and hope that might be hidden within the tragedy. "It will be wise for us to listen carefully for any news of steamboats from Louisville arriving in Memphis in the next few days. From the date of this telegram, it is quite possible that Tib has not reached Memphis yet. It is very common for the steamboats on the Ohio and Mississippi to make many stops for passengers and cargo," Levi observed.

"Should we also watch for him at the slave auctions?" Isaac asked.

"That is an excellent suggestion. Many of the slave traders are looking for quick profits and Memphis, along with New Orleans, is a very busy center of the slave trade. Tib's new owner may decide to sell his stock here rather than making the full journey to New Orleans. Gaining an acquaintance with slave auctions will also be an important, albeit painful, part of thy education. My guess is that by now Dr. Way and the others have returned to Newport. I will send a short telegram informing him that we have received his telegram and will be watching the traffic on the Mississippi for the next several days before coming north."

In response to Levi Coffin's questions, a shipping clerk at the Memphis docks on the Mississippi River replied, "Sir, the only ship docked at present came from St. Louis and arrived about three hours ago. There was a ship that came from Cincinnati via Louisville and docked here briefly last night."

"Do you expect any steamboats from Louisville in the next few days?" Levi again questioned the clerk.

"Yes. There is usually at least one coming through almost every day. Some days several will dock in Memphis. They arrive at different times, but typically between late morning and mid afternoon."

"What kind of cargo was unloaded from the ship last night?" Levi further pressed the clerk for additional information.

"You sure ask a lot of questions," the clerk responded as he eyed Levi suspiciously.

"I'm a businessman with diverse interests. I would hate to miss any opportunities," Levi explained.

"Well, the main types of merchandise they unloaded last night were produce from Ohio, furniture and cotton fabric from New England, and tobacco and slaves from Kentucky."

After thanking the shipping clerk, Levi turned to Isaac as they walked back toward their hotel and said, "It looks like we'll be attending today's slave auction."

"Here is an advertisement posted by a George M. Noel in the *Memphis Daily Eagle & Enquirer* describing a slave auction that is scheduled to begin at one this afternoon just off Main Street," Levi observed after perusing the newspaper. "If we can possibly help Tib, it will be essential for us to observe the daily slave auctions and monitor the arrival of ships with slave cargo coming from Louisville for the next several days. Isaac, I want thee to promise that regardless of what thou may observe here in Memphis, especially at the slave auctions, thou will keep thy counsel. It is absolutely essential for us not to attract any negative attention to ourselves from the local populace, otherwise any opportunity we might have of helping Tib will be compromised. Dost thou understand me?"

"Yes, Uncle. I will try my very best to stay calm."

"As will I," echoed his uncle. "I do not look forward to witnessing this trade in human beings, but if we might learn something of Tib's fate and possibly come to his aid, the distress we will experience may be transformed into a blessing. I witnessed a slave auction as a young man when I was not much older than thee back in North Carolina and the experience has haunted me ever since," Levi said with a deep sigh.

"Uncle, if we do find Tib, what can we realistically hope to do to rescue him?"

"I am expecting to receive a telegram soon from Dr. Way. I suspect he tried to purchase Tib's freedom and would have raised funds for that purpose. Regardless of the factors influencing the last transaction affecting Tib's freedom, his new owner may be quite amenable to an early sale."

"Uncle, if Dr. Way was able to offer a reasonable price for Tib's freedom, I wonder why he wasn't successful."

"We will learn more when we return home, but I wouldn't be surprised that the answer lies within the mystery in which Tib has been enshrouded since thou first met him."

Isaac looked at his uncle and realized the truth of his statement. There was so much about Tib's past that was hidden, even, as far as he could tell, from Tib's own wife. Now he wondered if they would ever know.

"Ladies and Gentlemen, please come in and enjoy the cool shade of my courtyard."

George Noel, a prominent Memphis slave trader spoke his invitation in the most ingratiating tones possible to his prospective customers as they gathered outside his office. The afternoon air in the city had become quite sultry, with several angry thunderheads gathering overhead. The large awnings in the courtyard outside the sales office at Noel's Negro Sales offered considerable shade and protection from the intense afternoon heat. Slave auctions were something of a diversion for many of the citizens of Memphis. Today's auction had drawn a good-sized crowd, some buyers but also many curiosity seekers and poor whites envious of those who had the means to purchase slaves.

Isaac shuddered involuntarily as he entered the courtyard with his uncle. His friend Sam and he had attended several auctions in Indiana together, where horses, cattle, and other livestock were sold. When he saw the "livestock" to be sold by George Noel lined up for inspection on a platform in the courtyard his mind rebelled at the sheer incongruity and madness of the scene. His incomprehension was rapidly replaced by a deep feeling of revulsion. His friend Sam, or any of the Johnsons, could be standing there.

Indeed, he reflected, *Tib most assuredly was subjected to this same horrific experience only a few days ago.*

He grew pale, began to feel faint and stumbled slightly.

Levi was quick to discern his nephew's reaction and grabbed his left arm and whispered, "Isaac, for Tib's sake thou must be strong. Keep thy mind focused in prayer for the poor slaves while observing every aspect of this place of evil for any sign of our friend."

"I am sorry, Uncle, for my weakness. Hearing about such activities is not the same as witnessing them in person. I will try my best to follow thy counsel."

Levi gave Isaac's arm a squeeze and whispered again, "I share thy horror, but let us be hopeful that some good will come from our attendance of this most unholy activity."

Ten slaves were standing on the platform awaiting their fate. Tib was not among them. George Noel climbed up onto the platform and addressed the crowd, "Ladies and gentlemen, today it is my pleasure to present for your inspection and consideration some of the best negro stock I've seen in many weeks. Phil, step forward so everyone can have a good look at you."

Phil was a very dark-skinned, muscular youth of average height who stepped forward self-consciously with some hesitation.

"Now don't keep our customers waiting!" George Noel scolded, and then, assuming a broad smile, added, "Isn't he a fine specimen? Please have a closer look. Phil, open your mouth and give the folks a big grin. They just don't get healthier or stronger than young Phil here. Turn around, Phil." Lifting Phil's shirt, Noel proclaimed with great pride, "There's nary a scar on this fellow's back. He's strong as an ox and docile as a lamb. May I suggest we start the bidding at twelve hundred dollars?"

Enthusiastic bidding followed, and George Noel was pleased to sell Phil for seventeen hundred dollars.

And so the afternoon went, with periodic pauses for prospective customers to make a closer personal inspection of the merchandise. Of the ten slaves for sale that afternoon, five of them were young men who, like Phil, would be purchased to serve as field hands. Each one of them quickly brought a sale price close to that obtained for Phil. As George Noel turned to the remaining slaves, he was very pleased with the proceedings thus far. He had always thought it a good strategy to lead with his strongest merchandise, for with any luck the buyers would then be emotionally prepared to spend larger sums for the less valuable slaves that he would present later in the auction. The next slaves to be sold were a middle-aged couple, their graying hair indicative of the fact that their most productive years were behind them.

"Hattie and Tom, step forward so that our friends can have a better look at you. Some of you may be aware of the recent demise of Amelia Townsend, the widow of one of the finest attorneys that has ever served the people of Memphis, Augustus Townsend."

There were some nods of assent among the people in the crowd.

"Hattie and Tom were the Townsends' cook and butler for the past several years. They are being sold today as dictated by Mrs. Townsend's will. In addition to her excellent culinary skills, Hattie has quite a reputation as a fine seamstress, and complementing the value of his wife's talents, Tom has been the quintessential butler. For those of you who knew the Townsends, the extraordinary hospitality, fine dining, and excellent service that was so much a part of any visit to their home were in no small measure due to the diligent efforts provided by these two devoted servants. As you can see, they are both healthy and ready to provide many more years of devoted service to the person fortunate enough to purchase them. What do you think? Shall we not start off the bidding at two thousand dollars for this handsome pair?"

Several people came up and examined the husband and wife more closely.

"Why he's missing several teeth and she's got a limp," one prospective customer complained.

"It looks to me, Noel, that you've been tryin' to blacken their white hair. I'll bet they've been servin' the Townsends a bit longer than 'the past *several* years,'" a dandified youth said with a smirk to general laughter in the crowd.

After a considerable pause, George Noel smiled his ingratiating smile and said, "Well, I can see that I have some highly discerning customers who are looking for real bargains. Shall we start our bidding at the bargain price of fifteen hundred dollars for the pair?"

The dandified youth who had now retreated to the back of the crowd shouted, "They're not worth a thousand dollars between the two of them."

George Noel grimaced briefly as he felt the dollars slipping away. Trying to recoup the situation, he smiled broadly and said, "My business has always been built on the foundation of fair and honest dealings with all my customers. Would any of you like to suggest a fair price for this handsome pair of talented and experienced domestic servants?"

Again, another painful pause followed in which George Noel did his best to retain his winsome smile while Hattie's and Jim's faces could not hide their fear and anxiety. Finally, the silence was broken by the voice of an older man in the back of the crowd who cried out, "I'll bid four hundred dollars for the negress. I do remember her fine cooking."

"Are you not interested in also purchasing the butler? Besides his household skills, he is an excellent coachman," George said as he tried to bargain.

"I don't need a butler."

The dandified youth now spoke up. "I'll bid three hundred fifty dollars for him and to save you the trouble of asking, I don't need a cook."

"Before we consider further individual bidding, is anyone interested in making an offer for the pair?" George queried the crowd. After surveying the crowd and hearing no offer for the pair, George cheerily said, "We have starting bids for each of these fine servants. Surely, you can all sense a real bargain here. Don't be bashful. Who would like to make a counter offer for this highly talented cook and seamstress?"

"My offer of four hundred dollars is a generous one. She clearly has no value as breeding stock at her age," her initial bidder interrupted.

George Noel bit his lip, contemplating the many ways he would like to employ to silence the bidder. The crowd's silence in response to George's repeated request for additional bids spoke to the initial bidder's triumph. "Your shrewdness has won you quite a bargain," George congratulated Hattie's new owner.

To George's dismay, the young dandy was again able to smirk with evident pleasure, as the same process was repeated with his purchase of Tom.

Turning to leave, the dandy said in a loud voice, "Have my property delivered to my plantation just outside Natchez. My agent will help you with the details. I have some other business to attend to before I leave Memphis."

With a big yawn signifying that the auction had now lost his interest, he turned to leave the courtyard.

When Hattie realized that Natchez was to be Tom's destination, she no longer could contain her emotions and a terrible wailing began, which was accompanied by many tears and begging to "Massa George."

"Please, Massa, don' separate us. All our chillun bin sole away fum us. Tom all I got in dis whole world."

As Tom was about to add his own pleading, George responded angrily by saying, "Now hush, both of you. You've been sold to quality masters."

Turning to his assistants, he motioned for them to assist Hattie and Tom's transfers to their new owners immediately. While Hattie was in the throes of grief, she was led off by her new master, whose thoughts of a fine meal that evening deafened his ears to her cries of anguish. "Tom, I always lub you. Nebber forget dat an' nebber forget yo' Hattie!"

"Oh Hattie, dere's no mo' libbin in dis ol' body o' mine wif'out you!" And the tears began to roll down the contorted face of the old black man as he was led away in the opposite direction by the dandy's agent.

Isaac's growing agitation was diverted momentarily as he watched George turn to the remaining slaves on the platform. An attractive mulatto woman who appeared to be in her late twenties was standing holding her two children close to her and fighting back tears as Mr. Noel focused his attention on them. Both her children were quadroons: a pretty daughter, not more than thirteen or fourteen years of age, with long dark hair, fine features, and a complexion that could help her easily pass as a white person; and a younger brother, probably eleven or twelve years old, with similar features and complexion. Their mother didn't wait for the bidding to begin. She began to loudly implore George with tears streaming down her face, "Please, Massa, don't sell my chillun away fum me."

"Shush now, Libby!" George ordered.

But Libby wouldn't be shushed as she kept begging through a flood of tears that distorted her beauty. Becoming frustrated, George approached the distraught mother and said in loud enough tones that Isaac could hear, "Shut your mouth, woman, or I will give you something to really cry about! If you don't quiet down right now, I'll have you taken in the back and whipped while your children are sold."

Libby gulped hard and stopped begging, although the tears continued to stream down her face.

Turning back to the crowd, George again attempted to paint a pleasant smile on his face, which looked more like a smirk. "Don't let Libby's high spirits concern you. She is a highly competent parlor maid and is also endowed with great skill as a seamstress and cook. It distressed her previous owner greatly that pecuniary concerns necessitated her sale and that of her children. He has assured me that she was always anxious to please."

"By the look of her children, it seems that she indeed worked very hard to please her master," a sarcastic voice from the crowd shouted, followed by tittering and loud guffaws.

George smiled and said, "You can clearly see that she is a woman of many talents. Her daughter has also been trained to work effectively in the domestic sphere, and her son, as you can see, will shortly become a strapping young buck with lots of productive work in him. Are there any bids for the three of them together? Three thousand dollars as a starting bid for so much talent and potential seem a pittance to ask."

After a long pause, a voice from the crowd shouted, "I'll bid eight hundred dollars for the boy."

"But is there no interest in purchasing them together?" George asked.

Libby looked imploringly toward the crowd, and cried out, "Please buy us togedder. We'll work mitey hard fo' you."

After some hesitation, a tall figure stood out from the crowd and spoke, "I'll bid two thousand dollars for the three of them."

George responded, "Thank you for your bid. Unfortunately, it does not come close to the real value of these niggers. Are there any additional bids for the three together?" After another pause, he said, "Having heard no additional bids for the three together, let's return to the individual bidding. We have a bid of eight hundred dollars for this young man who in a very short time will be worth far more than eight hundred dollars. Are there some counter offers?"

To George's satisfaction, there were many counter offers, and soon enough he was congratulating the highest bidder, saying, "Yes sir. You'll be very happy with your purchase. At thirteen hundred dollars, he is a real bargain."

As George's assistants approached Libby's son to transfer him to his new master, she held him tightly to herself and started to scream hysterically, "Don't take him fum me!"

George's assistants grabbed her wrists, exerting intense pressure until she cried out in pain and released her son. While one assistant pinioned her arms behind her back, the other led her son away. The boy, with tears welling up in his eyes, turned back to his mother and cried, "Mama, don't worry about me. I'll be fine. I'll nebber forget you."

In sober tones befitting the businessman he was, George invited the prospective buyers to consider Libby's daughter.

"Please come forward and examine this young wench's many fine attributes. Abby, step forward so that the gentlemen can examine you."

Abby looked back at her weeping mother, who was still restrained by George's assistant, and timidly moved forward on the platform. She attracted a large number of men who came forward to examine her *attributes*. Her face, hair, figure, and light skin were the subjects of hungry, lascivious stares. A particularly obnoxious individual who had been examining her intently, looking in her mouth and approaching her from every angle, started the bidding. "I'll bid one thousand dollars for her."

George smiled as the bidding became fierce and intense.

You'd think she was a prime field hand the way they're bidding for her, he thought with satisfaction.

"Sold for nineteen hundred dollars to this gentleman here," George pointed to the man who had started the bidding. He, in turn, smiled, smacked his lips, and said, "She'll make an excellent *fancy girl*. Definitely a great investment."

Libby's daughter, who was now shaking with fear, started to cry in earnest at the prospect of being taken away from her mother by her new master. "Oh, please don't take me fum Mama! Cain't you also buy my mama?"

"My customers don't want her type. Come along now. You have some things to learn about your new work."

Isaac watched helplessly as Abby's new master separated forever a daughter from her mother, their tears and cries of grief etched deeply into his memory.

George was feeling triumphant when he completed the sale of Libby for one thousand dollars. After all, she clearly was still quite good breeding stock and had a wide variety of domestic skills. He smiled at the thought of the *wide variety* those skills encompassed, congratulating himself on having made a very sound investment.

"What is a fancy girl?" Isaac asked as they walked back toward their hotel after the auction.

"I believe it is a euphemism, used especially here in the South, for a prostitute, typically a slave prostitute. Didst thou not see how those men were looking at that poor girl?"

Isaac's face flushed as he thought of Abby and the others. "Those were human beings who were treated like cattle, even worse than cattle who don't know their fate! How can God let this happen? May God curse them!"

"God has not forgotten these poor people. Has he not brought thee here to witness this horror so that thou might be moved to act on their behalf? But, beware of thy anger. Who are the real slaves here? Abby, Libby, and the others may be chained in the flesh, but who can possess their souls? It is their masters who are slaves; slaves to their lust for power and wealth. Even more dangerous, they are also slaves to their anger. Beware of responding to the evil they commit with anger of thine own. They deserve our pity and prayers as much as the slaves. Are not the Southern slaveowners blind to the evils of a system they have inherited from their forebears? Oh, Isaac, ownership of slaves is a terrible burden that breeds evil! Would we be any different than the slaveowners, if our situations were reversed? We must work to end this evil by example, not judging others but acting through gentle persuasion, otherwise we will be in danger of acquiring the very evil we wish to reform."

"But Uncle, did not Christ drive out the moneychangers from the temple? While we stand by patiently waiting, more innocent people will suffer. Is there no place for righteous anger?"

"Thou must remember the scriptural admonition, 'Be angry and do not sin.' May Christ give thee *this anger* in abundance!"

Chapter Twenty-Two

"Isn't that Mr. Noel who is eating over there?" Isaac whispered to his uncle as they sat down to dine in the tavern next to their hotel.

Levi turned slightly to see the slave trader seated at a table nearby and, observing the large repast he was devouring, whispered back, "It seems that selling other human beings generates a hearty appetite."

While they were waiting for their food, Isaac watched the slave trader who seemed to be thoroughly enjoying his meal until a tall, darkly handsome man whom Isaac recognized as the man who bid unsuccessfully for Libby and her family came up and sat down uninvited at Noel's table.

Looking up, Noel said, "Oh, it's you, Forrest. Did you learn a bit about the business today?"

"You blackguard! I made the best offer I could to keep that family from being broken up. Most dogs are treated better than you treat your slaves at auction." The tall man named Forrest then reached across the table and grabbed Noel by the throat, glowering at him, and said, "I oughta end your miserable existence right now. Have you no feeling for these creatures?"

As Forrest tightened his grip on Noel's throat, the latter anxiously retorted in strangled tones, "It's purely a matter of sound economics. One must follow the money. You're new to this business and must learn through experience that you can't let emotions or your feelings rule business decisions."

Pondering Noel's words, Forrest gradually relaxed his stranglehold on the purveyor of human souls. Wiping his mouth nervously with his napkin, George suddenly lost interest in finishing his meal, put down some coins on the table, and beat a hasty retreat.

Isaac, who had been watching the exchange with intense interest, caught Forrest's attention and he came over to introduce himself. "I apologize for makin' such a scene. Weren't both of you at the slave auction this afternoon? We don't see many of your kind around here," Forrest said, referring to their distinctive Quaker dress.

Levi rose and, motioning for Forrest to take a seat, replied, "I am Levi Coffin, and this is my nephew, Isaac Burgess. We came from Cincinnati to conduct some business with local farmers here in Tennessee and will be departing for the North in a few days with our merchandise. In the mean time, we've been taking in the sights of Memphis."

"Noel's auction may not have been the best introduction to our fair city. Please allow me to introduce myself. I am Nathan Bedford Forrest, a local businessman here in Memphis."

"Mr. Forrest, I share thy sentiments toward Mr. Noel and the way he treated his slaves," Isaac volunteered as he considered the piercing eyes of their new acquaintance.

Waving his right hand dismissively, Forrest responded, "People like Mr. Noel give the South a bad name. T'aint no surprise that abolitionists agitate against Southern institutions when wretches like him behave the way they do. For the past few years I've been a trader in horses and cattle. Recently, I decided that I would start trading in slaves to show these damn rascals a more humane approach to the business. It jes' makes my blood boil when I see some wretch like Mr. Noel break up families like he did today. Mammy Lucinda, who's the nursemaid for my children, Will and Fanny, is a reg'lar member of our family. It's jes' plain unthinkable, un-Christian, to sell her husband, Ol' Joe, away from her, even if it's *sound economics.*"

"Wouldn't it be easier to not have to deal with slavery and the compromises it requires?" Levi asked.

Forrest smiled grimly. "It jes' ain't that simple. I wish it were. The problem is that negroes are at the low end of the human race. In fact, many of our finest medical scientists have shown that they have their own specific diseases and peculiarities that mark them as inferior. Some are concerned that they may not even be human bein's. If they were all freed, there would be mass starvation and chaos. They need white masters to take care of 'em and help 'em be productive. That's the only way they can be happy in this world."

"Doesn't the need to keep them in obedience as slaves lead to the very cruelties that thou hast condemned?" Levi probed Forrest further.

"Sometimes the devil gets in 'em and they must be chastised for their own good and for public safety. When they get dangerous notions in their heads about freedom and equality with the white man, there's no end of mischief. We in the South will never forget Nat Turner and his rebellion in Virginia over twenty years ago. Kindness and humanity must be balanced with firm resolve to maintain discipline in all our relations with the negro. There's nothin' more worrisome to us than the sight of an armed negro."

Looking over at Isaac, Forrest smiled and said, "I wasn't much older than you when my pappy died. Bein' the oldest I had to start workin' to support my family. I always regret not bein' able to have a proper education. What are you hopin' to do with yerself?"

"My hope is to become a doctor some day."

"That's a mighty fine profession. You and your uncle must come as my guests tomorrow evening for a lecture by the famous Professor Samuel Cartwright from the medical school at the University of Louisiana in New Orleans. He is currently visiting Memphis Medical College as a guest of my friend, Dr. Merrill, who is the head physician at the medical college's hospital. Dr. Cartwright has made quite a study of diseases peculiar to the negro. For someone aspirin' to be a doctor, you won't wanna miss this opportunity."

Before Isaac could respond, Levi spoke, "Mr. Forrest, we would be delighted to attend the lecture. I am certain we will both profit greatly from Professor Cartwright's erudition."

"Well, that's settled then. If you're stayin' at the hotel next door, I'll come to the lobby tomorrow evening at six-thirty p.m. sharp and we'll walk together to the lecture. The hall where Professor Cartwright will be speaking is not far from here. I'm glad to meet some Northern folks who are willin' to hear the Southern perspective about such an important issue."

Levi smiled at Isaac as they said goodbye to their new acquaintance.

"Uncle Levi, my first impression of Mr. Forrest was that he shared my anger against the slave trader. Oh, how mistaken I was!" Isaac exclaimed after Forrest had left.

"In some ways he does share thy anger at the mistreatment of the slaves by Mr. Noel. The difference between thy anger and his rests in the value placed in the poor unfortunate slaves. Mr. Forrest sees in them a reflection of his deep regard for the slave who is nursemaid to his children, I daresay not too different from the deep affection of a human being for a treasured pet. In contrast, thou seest in them thy friends, the Johnsons, and many other free negroes of thine acquaintance. On the one hand, they are viewed as highly valued livestock, even deeply loved domestic pets, and on the other, human persons created in the image of God, just as thyself. The remarkable thing about Mr. Forrest is how potentially violent a turn his anger can take, even when driven by the lesser motivation of highly valued, even loved property. Canst thou see from his example how dangerous anger can be?"

"Yes, Uncle. It was very difficult for me not to say something when he began to speak of the inferiority of the negro."

"I am very glad that thou did not for two reasons. If we are to discover more of Tib's fate and possibly help him, it will depend upon our discretion. We must not enter into controversy with our Southern brethren over the slavery issue, which will only arouse their suspicions and hinder our efforts on Tib's behalf. Also, I think thou will find Professor Cartwright's speculations to be interesting when thou can compare them to what thou know about the free negro community. Thou must judge for thyself if there seems to be any merit in the Southern physician's notions of ailments that are specific to negroes."

Chapter Twenty-Three

"Dr. Merrill, allow me to introduce some Northern acquaintances of mine to you," Nathan Bedford Forrest said with evident pleasure as he pointed to Levi and Isaac. "Dr. Merrill is the director of the Memphis Medical College hospital. I can truly say, hopefully without embarrassin' him, bein' the modest gentleman he is, that he should rightly be proud of this fine institution dedicated to the relief of sufferin' and the trainin' of doctors."

"Really, Bedford, you are too generous in your compliments," Dr. Merrill replied, his cheeks reddening slightly at the compliment. Turning to Isaac and his uncle, he said, "Ayres P. Merrill, M.D. at your service." Looking directly at Isaac, he added, "My friend, Mr. Forrest, tells me that you are an aspiring physician. Recruiting promising young talent to the medical profession is a real passion of mine. I hope you will enjoy this evening's lecture that will be given by the eminent Professor Samuel Cartwright. He will be lecturing on the particular challenges that diseases peculiar to the negro race pose for our Southern physicians. If your time permits, I would be very pleased to give you both a tour of the medical college's hospital tomorrow so that you can see firsthand our humble efforts to address the medical needs of both the white and negro populations of Memphis. Isaac, how have you acquired your interest in the healing arts?"

"For the past four to five years, I have been very fortunate, when not in school, to be able to serve as an assistant to Dr. Henry Way, a physician trained at Jefferson Medical College in Philadelphia. He is the physician in our town of Newport, Indiana."

Levi could not repress adding, "My nephew has already learned many practical skills from our friend Dr. Way, which he demonstrated on our journey to Tennessee." He then gave an account of the incident on the *Southern Belle* and Isaac's calm management of the wounded man.

Forrest gave Isaac a look of admiration and said, "A man like me could use a friend like you. As you probably noticed yesterday, I'm a man of strong feelings, which can sometimes get a man into conflict, although I usually have the upper hand. When the fightin's over, it'd be real nice to have someone like you to help put the pieces back together. After you finish your education, you oughta think seriously about comin' south. There'd be plenty of business for you here."

Before Isaac could respond, Dr. Merrill, who had just stepped away to guide the newly arrived Professor Cartwright to the lectern, interrupted the conversation with his announcement, "Ladies and Gentlemen, please take your seats so that our esteemed guest can begin his lecture."

Samuel Augustus Cartwright felt the thrill that always embraced him when standing at a lectern. The amphitheater created an additional sense of shared intimacy with his audience that enhanced the pleasure of lecturing. The warm glow that came from hearing his biography recited by Dr. Merrill had not yet dissipated as he surveyed the audience before him. After all, he indeed had much to be proud of in his pedigree. A native Virginian, he had studied in Philadelphia under Dr. Benjamin Rush, the preeminent physician of the early Republic, attended the University of Pennsylvania School of Medicine, served under General Jackson as a medical officer, and then had gone on to illustrious public service as a physician in Alabama, Mississippi, and now New Orleans. Although, as he approached his sixtieth year, he had acquired a bit of a paunch, his baldpate fringed with graying hair and prominent side-whiskers lent a certain dignity to his public persona.

"Dr. Merrill, I want to thank you for your very kind introduction. It is a signal pleasure and privilege for me to be here today in Memphis, speaking as a guest of the Memphis Medical College. You have asked me to speak about a subject of great practical concern for all of us residing here in the South, that is, the diseases and health concerns that are unique to the negro. Unfortunately, our Northern brethren acquire misguided notions about the condition of our negroes, which are often amplified and further distorted by abolitionist fanatics that have caused unfortunate and I believe unnecessary conflicts to arise between our sections."

"Before I discuss some of the diseases peculiar to the negro and yet so important for us who are concerned with his welfare to understand, it is essential for me to review some aspects of negro physiology and anatomy that will help you appreciate why the negro is vulnerable to certain kinds of conditions and behaviors.

"It is commonly taken for granted that the color of the skin constitutes the main and essential difference between the white and negro race; but there are other differences—deeper, durable, and indelible—in their anatomy and physiology than that of mere color. In the albino the skin is white, but the organization is that of the negro. Besides, it is not only in the skin that a difference in color exists between the negro and the white man, but in the membranes, the muscles, the tendons, and in all the fluids and secretions. Even the negro's brain and nerves, the chyle and all the humors, are tinctured with a shade of the pervading darkness . . ."

Levi Coffin instinctively placed his hand on his nephew's wrist, which had tensed as Isaac reacted to Professor Cartwright's litany of the alleged differences between the white and African races.

After pausing to cast a benevolent smile over his audience, the professor continued, ". . .the projecting mouth, the retreating forehead, the broad, flat nose, thick lips, and wooly hair, are peculiarities that strike every observer. According to anatomists who have dissected the negro, his brain is one-ninth or one-tenth less than in other races of men, his facial angle smaller, and all the nerves going from the brain, as also the ganglionic system of nerves, are larger in proportion than in the white man from the diffusion of the brain, as it were, into the various organs of the body, in the shape of nerves to minister to the senses, *everything, from the necessity of such a conformation, partakes of sensuality, at the expense of intellectuality.* Thus, music is a mere sensual pleasure with the negro. There is nothing in his music addressing the understanding; it has melody, but no harmony; his songs are mere sounds, without sense or meaning—pleasing the ear, without conveying a single idea to the mind; his ear is gratified by sound, as is his stomach by food.

"The great development of the nervous system, and the profuse distribution of nervous matter to the stomach, liver, and genital organs, would make the Ethiopian race entirely unmanageable if it were not that this excessive nervous development is associated with a deficiency of red blood in the pulmonary and arterial systems, from a defective atmospherization or arterialization of the blood in the lungs. It is this defective hematosis, or atmospherization of the blood, conjoined with a deficiency of cerebral matter in the cranium, and an excess of nervous matter distributed to the organs of sensation and assimilation, that is the true cause of that debasement of mind, which has rendered the people of Africa unable to take care of themselves. It is the true cause of their indolence and apathy, and why they have chosen, through countless ages, idleness, misery, and barbarism, to industry and frugality."

As the erudite professor droned on, elucidating the many alleged physiological deficiencies that predisposed the negro to enslavement, Isaac was seething.

The old fool has clearly never had a conversation with an educated free negro from the North. He makes his so-called science suit his needs and prejudices, certainly not reality!

"Like children, they are constrained by unalterable physiological laws, to love those in authority over them, who minister to their wants and immediate necessities, and are not cruel or unmerciful. The defective hematosis, in both cases, and the want of courage and energy of mind as a consequence thereof, produces in both an instinctive feeling of dependence on others, to direct them and take care of them. Hence, from a law of his nature, the negro can no more help loving a kind master, than the child can help loving her who gives it suck. Allow me then to summarize the major physiological principle that underlies the destiny of the negro as slave. Under the compulsive power of the white man, they are made to labor or exercise, which makes the lungs perform the duty of vitalizing the blood more perfectly than is done when they are left free to indulge in idleness. It is the red, vital blood, sent to the brain, that liberates their mind when under the white man's control, and it is the want of a sufficiency of red, vital blood, that chains their mind to ignorance and barbarism, when in freedom."

So, slavery frees the mind of the slave and freedom enslaves his mind. What incredible logic! Will none of these Southerners point out the obvious, that he is uttering absolute nonsense? Isaac thought as he sat, fidgeting.

The professor paused, mopped his brow with his handkerchief, smiled, and said, "Now let us turn to a discussion of some of the major diseases and ailments afflicting the negro. As I mentioned earlier, the natural state of the negro in bondage is one of tranquility and contentment. What then is to be made of those negroes who abscond and run away from their masters? This behavior is a reflection of a mental condition, unfortunately increasing in frequency due to the misguided efforts of Northern fanatics, that I have named *drapetomania,* from the Greek, *drapetes*—runaway slave—and *mania*—mad or crazy. The cause, in the majority of cases, that induces the negro to run away from service, is as much a disease of the mind as any other species of mental alienation, and much more curable, as a general rule. The key is the manner in which their master governs them. Awe and reverence must be exacted from them or they will despise their masters, become rude and ungovernable and run away.

"Before negroes run away, unless they are frightened or panic-struck, they become sulky and dissatisfied. The cause of this sulkiness and dissatisfaction should be inquired into and removed. When sulky and dissatisfied without cause, the general experience recommended, especially among those masters near the Mason and Dixon line, has been decidedly in favor of whipping them out of it as a preventative measure against absconding or other bad conduct. It has been called *whipping the devil out of them.* If any one or more of them, at any time, are inclined to raise their heads to a level with their master or overseer, humanity and their own good require that they should be punished until they fall into that submissive state which it was intended for them to occupy in all after time, when their progenitor received the name of Canaan. They have only to be kept in that state, and treated like children, with care, kindness, and humanity, to prevent and cure them from running away.

"By way of contrast, dyspepsia is not a disease of the negro; it is, *par excellence,* a disease of the Anglo-Saxon race; I have never seen a well-marked case of dyspepsia among the negroes. It is a disease that selects its victims from the most intellectual of mankind, passing by the ignorant and unreflecting."

It's probably safe to assume that Professor Cartwright suffers from a severe and protracted case of dyspepsia, Isaac thought, suppressing a smirk.

"*Dysesthesia Ethiopis* is a disease peculiar to negroes, affecting both mind and body, in a manner as well expressed by *dysesthesia,* the name I have given it, as could be by a single term. There is partial insensibility of the skin, and so great a hebetude or lethargy of the intellectual faculties as to be like a person half asleep, that is with difficulty aroused and kept awake. From the careless movements of the individuals affected with the complaint, they are apt to do much mischief, which appears as if intentional, but is mostly owing to the stupidness of mind and insensibility of the nerves induced by the disease. Thus, they break, waste, and destroy everything they handle. Overseers have called it 'rascality,' supposing that the mischief is intentional. But there is no premeditated mischief in the case—the mind is too torpid to meditate mischief, or even to be aroused by the angry passions to deeds of daring. Dysesthesia, or hebetude of sensation of both mind and body, prevails to so great an extent that when the unfortunate individual is subjected to punishment, he neither feels pain of any consequence, or shows any unusual resentment, more than by a stupid sulkiness."

"The complaint is easily curable. The object being to expand the lungs by full and deep inspirations and expirations, thereby to vitalize the impure circulating blood by introducing oxygen and expelling carbon. No sooner does the blood feel the vivifying influences derived from its full and perfect atmospherization by exercise in the open air and sun than the negro seems to be awakened to a new existence, and to look grateful and thankful to the white man whose compulsory power, by making him inhale vital air, has restored his sensation and dispelled the mist that clouded his intellect.

"In closing, I would like to make one final summary observation: that the blood, when rendered impure and carbonaceous from any cause, as from idleness, filthy habits, unwholesome food, or alcoholic drinks, affects the mind, is known not only to physicians, but was known to the Bard of Avon when he penned the lines: 'We are not ourselves when nature, being oppressed, commands the mind to suffer with the body.'"

As the clapping subsided, Dr. Merrill rose beside Professor Cartwright and said, "Thank you, Professor Cartwright, for an enlightening presentation. I suspect that you have stimulated much thought in the audience, which I daresay will produce a lively discussion. Are there questions or comments for the professor? Yes, Dr. Carleton. Speakers, please introduce yourselves before making your remarks."

A distinguished white-haired gentleman had stood up from his seat in the middle of the amphitheater and was now speaking.

"I am Dr. Horace Carleton, professor of anatomy here at the Memphis Medical College. Professor Cartwright, I commend you on a very thoughtful and interesting lecture. Your hypotheses about negro ailments are certainly worthy of consideration. I must say, however, that I was thoroughly baffled by your assertion, I hope I quote you correctly, that not only in the skin, a difference in color exists between the negro and the white man, but in all the anatomic layers and even the body fluids and secretions. I have dissected many negro and white bodies over the years and I have yet to find in any negro body *the shade of pervading darkness* of which you speak."

This comment sparked some laughter in the audience, while Professor Carleton continued.

"In fact, in my opinion, based on great personal experience, once a skin incision has been made or a body cavity has been opened, the internal structure of a negro is indistinguishable from that of a white person."

Professor Cartwright winced slightly as the professor of anatomy resumed his seat, and replied, "Thank you Professor Carleton for your observation. All I can say in response is look more diligently in the future during your dissections, for I assure you that the darkness *is* there for the discerning eye."

"Yes. Up near the back," Dr. Merrill said, pointing to another person with a question.

"Professor Cartwright, my name is Fitzhugh Moncrief. I am a physician who has been practicing medicine here in Memphis for the past ten years. I enjoyed your presentation, but also have some questions, first for you and then also for Dr. Merrill.

"As I am certain you are aware, Dr. Marion Sims of Montgomery, Alabama has been revolutionizing the treatment of vesicovaginal fistula and other conditions unique to women through the development of new surgical operations. I have had the privilege of visiting and observing Dr. Sims at work in his hospital in Montgomery. The foundation for his successful repair of vesicovaginal fistula was laid by his work with negro women burdened with the condition. From my observations and by his own description, the technique works equally well in white and negro women. Along with Professor Carleton, I must question your assertion of fundamental anatomic differences between the white and negro races. The empiric observations of as eminent a surgeon as Dr. Sims do not provide supporting evidence for your hypothesis.

"My second question is directed to Dr. Merrill, as well as yourself. In light of the concerns raised by Professor Carleton and myself questioning the hypothesis of a unique negro anatomy, and by extension, physiology, could you speak to the rationale for negro hospitals? From my naïve perspective, it seems that rather than treating unique negro diseases, negro hospitals have been developed to address the need to protect the significant financial investment of slaveholders, which certainly is a very compelling reason."

"Well, how shall I respond to your challenging questions?" Samuel Cartwright scratched his forehead and smiled. "With regard to Dr. Sims' pioneering research, I can only say that I suspect if the good doctor had access to apes from Africa, he would have also been able to devise the same efficacious operation. The anatomical and physiological differences between the negro and white races of which I speak are subtler than gross anatomical differences involving the genitourinary tract. I hope, sir, that you are not implying that the negro is the equal of the white—"

An exasperated Fitzhugh Moncrief rose again and interrupted, "Unless you have personally attended operations performed by Dr. Sims, you will not have seen the anatomy to which I refer. Dr. Sims has invented a special retractor and employs a unique positioning of his patients that makes it possible to see the anatomy as never seen before. From personal experience, I can assure you and the audience that there are no differences in the subtler aspects of this anatomic region in women of either the negro or white races. As for the larger issue of racial equality, it is obvious who is the master and who is the slave. However, I am not convinced that one can find the explanation for negro inferiority in anatomy or physiology."

Professor Cartwright scowled and then retorted, "Regarding your second question, it is clear from your own experience with Dr. Sims, who is working at a negro hospital, that such hospitals afford a positive good both for the negroes treated in them and for the advancement of medicine by the negroes' participation in research performed at such hospitals."

"I would like to make one additional comment in response to Dr. Moncrief's second question," Dr. Merrill added. "Regardless of one's opinion about the uniqueness of negro diseases, the three million negroes south of the Mason and Dixon line represent a major portion of the wealth of our country. Diligent efforts on behalf of their health are not only a matter of basic humanity but are also critical to the welfare of the entire population. A disaster affecting the health of the negroes would affect the economic well-being of the entire country."

Dr. Merrill then said, "I think we have time for one more question. Yes, here in the front. Theophilus, please go ahead."

A tall, thin, bespectacled man stood up, stretched and said, "Professor Cartwright, I am Dr. Theophilus Cromwell, a member of the medical faculty here at the Memphis Medical College. I enjoyed your lecture very much and the lively discussion following it. I would like to make an observation about the condition, which you have named, *Dysesthesia Ethiopis*. You quoted William Shakespeare's *King Lear* at the end of your presentation, to the effect that the mind cannot help but be affected by the body's distress. I would like to suggest that the opposite is just as likely. I have seen many white patients with severe melancholia exhibit the same hebetude or lethargy leading to carelessness in their behaviors. Is it not as plausible that mental distress in the negro could lead to changes in bodily function? Are you so certain that our servants are as happy in their servitude as you have described in your lecture?"

"Dr. Cromwell, thank you for your thoughtful questions, they will give me much food for thought. A more detailed exploration of the negro mind certainly seems warranted, although I must say that I seriously doubt that the negro has the mental capacity to develop true melancholia."

Dr. Merrill turned to Professor Cartwright and said, "On behalf of my colleagues here at the Memphis Medical College and the city of Memphis, I want to thank you again for coming and giving this excellent presentation. I am certain that I can speak for my colleagues when I say that we will all look forward in the future to reading of your further research and studies in negro medicine.

"Isaac, did you enjoy the lecture?" Nathan Bedford Forrest asked with a grin a short while later as he came up and gave Isaac a hearty pat on the back.

"Mr. Forrest, I found it to be very interesting and informative," Isaac answered, as diplomatically as possible.

Dr. Merrill, who heard Isaac's response, said, "Would you and your uncle like to have a tour of our hospital tomorrow; let's say at ten a.m.?"

Looking at his uncle, who nodded his assent, Isaac replied, "Yes, sir. I have never had the opportunity to see a hospital. All of my experience with Dr. Way has been in the homes of the sick."

Levi looked up from their table at breakfast the next morning as a young slave boy, no older than ten years of age, called out, "Tel-ee-gram fo' Massa Coffen!"

As he read the contents of the telegram, a broad smile came across his face and he said in a low tone to Isaac, "Dr. Way did indeed attempt to purchase Tib's freedom. His owner was apparently dead set on sending Tib South. The good news is that we might be able to effect with a new owner what Henry Way could not achieve with the previous one. I am fairly confident that Tib's steamboat, which Henry has been able to identify as the *River Queen,* has not yet arrived in Memphis. From the date of Tib's departure from Louisville that Henry has indicated in his telegram, the *River Queen* should probably arrive in the next day or so. Henry, may God bless him, also obtained the name of the slave trader who purchased Tib. It is Josiah Higgins."

"Look, Uncle! The young courier from the telegraph office is loitering over there," Isaac said, pointing to the young slave. "It appears he is expecting thee to send a reply. Perhaps we could hire him to watch for the *River Queen* while we are touring the hospital this morning."

"That is an excellent suggestion."

Levi motioned for the young slave to come back to their table and quietly explained the task to him.

As they were leaving the table, Levi said, "He knows to look for us at the hospital if we are not here in the hotel."

"Uncle, I still have great difficulty understanding how any of the people attending the lecture last evening could give any credence to Professor Cartwright's ridiculous notions."

"It's much easier to rationalize to one's conscience the necessary cruelties of the South's peculiar institution if one believes that the enslaved are not real human persons. Dost thou not think that the physicians, who rose to discuss the presentation, very effectively refuted much of Professor Cartwright's claims?"

"Yes, I must say I was very pleased to hear them acknowledge the same kinds of observations that Dr. Way has taught me, especially the identical anatomy that is shared between the negro and white races. Professor Cartwright's *pervading darkness* is to be found within his own brain! But what I find most disturbing is that none of them questioned the basic Southern assumption of negro inferiority."

"Sometimes, I fear that rational persuasion may never succeed where longstanding tradition and self-interest predominate. Be careful, Isaac, about making another assumption, that it is only the Southern population that views the negro as inferior. I daresay the majority of our Northern brethren share essentially the same views as those of our brethren below the Mason and Dixon line. But let us see and learn what kind of benevolent care is provided for the slaves in Dr. Merrill's hospital."

"Young Mr. Burgess, did you enjoy the 'rough and tumble' of ideas that were exchanged last evening?" Dr. Merrill asked, looking with curiosity at the tall Quaker youth and would-be physician.

"Yes, Dr. Merrill. I particularly enjoyed the discussion at the end of Professor Cartwright's presentation."

"You can see from the discussion, how men of science debate ideas and concepts. As you witnessed, some of Professor Cartwright's ideas are controversial, even here in the South. Before we enter the hospital, I would like to give both of you a brief overview of its purpose, nature, and organization," Dr. Merrill said as he stood at the entrance to a several-story, well-constructed, neat brick building, located within easy walking distance of the Memphis docks.

"This hospital has several purposes, which include provision of the best medical care possible to the citizens of Memphis, including the negroes, elevation of the quality of medical science, and to serve as a very effective teaching site for our medical students. In the discussion last evening the question was raised regarding the real purpose of negro hospitals. The preservation of the health of slaves is so plain a dictate of both *interest* and *mercy* that no planter is to be found in our country who does not aim to practice it as an object of primary importance.

"But some err from a want of knowledge and others from a want of care. From my own experience, I think there is much that could be done to improve the medical care of the negro. It seems to me that the development of negro hospitals in which the complaints that commonly afflict negroes can be studied systematically in comparison with the complaints of white Southerners can only lead to better care for all concerned. A major part of my own scholarly efforts has been committed to educating our slaveowners about the health concerns and necessities of their negroes. It is my strong belief that each plantation should have a properly designed and functional slave infirmary. Ideally, the sexes should be separated in different rooms, there should be access to good ventilation, allowing the sick to breathe clean air, and adequate means of heating should be provided during the cold months. Plenty of fresh fruits and vegetables should be available for those struggling to recover from illness, and every effort should be made to create a cheerful environment that will lift the spirits of the ill. Unfortunately, often through ignorance rather than overt neglect, many of our plantation owners have caused unwitting harm to their servants by not taking the appropriate measures to assure the health and well-being of their people, which does not redound to the credit of our section's institutions. While the urban setting is quite different from a rural plantation, I have strived to incorporate some of these same principles in the development of the wards in this hospital."

Dr. Merrill then proceeded to show Levi and Isaac the different wards and other functions of the hospital of the Memphis Medical College. He first led them down the corridor of one wing, pointing out different rooms organized as ten-bed wards for white persons that were segregated by sex. The rooms were large, with high ceilings, contained several windows admitting much light, and were well ventilated, with stoves for heating located at opposite ends of each room. The floors were swept clean and mopped by female slaves. Isaac and Levi were surprised to see rooms of identical size and quality, meeting the same standard of cleanliness in the opposite wing of the building in which were housed the sick slaves. The only obvious difference between the accommodations for the slave patients and the whites was the presence of strong shutters on the windows of the slave wards, which were closed and locked to secure the rooms at night but left open to admit sunshine during the daytime. There were also more ward attendants, including a few armed white men, constantly moving through the negro wards to provide security primarily during the day, since the slaves were locked in their wards at night. One additional difference did not escape Isaac's notice: whereas there were only two or three white patients in the hospital wing for whites, the Negro wards were full to overflowing.

Motioning toward the stairs, Dr. Merrill said, "I am sorry that we are not having classes right now, otherwise I would have been able to show Isaac an anatomic dissection. Our medical college classes usually run from the fall until the late spring. As you might imagine, the heat of summer is not conducive to keeping cadavers in any proper condition for teaching. However, Dr. Moncrief, whom you heard speak last night about the pioneering work of Dr. Sims in Alabama, will be performing a repair of a vesicovaginal fistula, a traumatic connection between the bladder and the birth canal, which can form as a result of a prolonged and difficult labor. The poor women, so afflicted, have no control over their urine and suffer tremendously from being isolated by the opprobrium of society. He should be starting very soon in one of our operating theaters on the second floor."

Isaac and Levi followed Dr. Merrill up the stairs and down a hall where their guide opened a door to their right and encouraged them to enter.

"Dr. Merrill, is it proper for us to observe without the patient's permission?" Isaac asked with some trepidation.

Dr. Merrill smiled and said, "I appreciate your delicacy on the matter, but don't be concerned Isaac; we have the full consent of her master for all necessary medical treatment and procedures, including any teaching that might occur. Please do come in."

As Isaac and his uncle cautiously followed Dr. Merrill into the operating theater, they were struck by its arrangement. The operating table was located within a large bay window, which admitted a much greater amount of light than the rooms below, especially in the late morning and early afternoon.

"Ah, discerning from the expressions on your faces, I see that you are impressed with the lighting in our operating theater," Dr. Merrell said with evident pride.

"Clearly, thou hast given great thought to its design in order to maximize the available light," Levi said with admiration.

"Dr. Way would be very envious," Isaac added.

There were at least a half-dozen other spectators, some of whom Isaac recognized from Professor Cartwright's lecture. Dr. Moncrief looked up briefly, acknowledging their presence and then instructed his two assistants to secure the patient, a young slave woman named Hepzibah.

"The candidate to be the first patient operated for vesicovaginal fistula in the city of Memphis, indeed in the state of Tennessee, is this twenty-three-year-old negro wench, a domestic servant here in Memphis who has suffered with urinary incontinence for the past three years after she experienced a complicated labor of several days. Unfortunately, gentlemen, you won't all be able to see everything that I will be doing in the next several minutes because of the limitations imposed by the need for the best possible lighting. Whenever feasible, I will pause to point out an important finding for your edification."

Turning to his patient, who was sweating profusely with a look of terror on her face, he said, "Hepzibah, be as still as possible. The quieter you are, the quicker I can operate."

A low whimper coming from Hepzibah was quickly replaced by screams as Dr. Moncrief widened his incision and began to dissect the deeper tissues. The two assistants tightened their grip on the slave as she began to struggle from the intense pain.

"Lawd ha' mercy! Lawd ha' mercy!" her cries filled the room and made Isaac shiver involuntarily.

Dr. Moncrief paused and with a stern voice said, "Hepzibah, you must be still for me to proceed."

"I's sorry Massa. I's sorry."

As he resumed operating, she began to squirm and whimper, until another rather loud "Hepzibah!" restrained her cries of misery. And then something happened that no one in the operating theater was quite prepared for; initially, it came as a soft tentative sound that seemed to float in the air above the slave woman, but it quickly gathered force and soon a beautiful voice permeated the room:

Swing low, sweet chariot
Coming for to carry me home.
Swing low, sweet chariot
Coming for to carry me home.

Dr. Moncrief looked up briefly from his dissection, thought better of saying anything other than to utter under his breath, "Well, I'll be damned," and continued operating. Periodically, he would motion silently to the observers to come forward, so he could point out, speaking in a whisper, key elements of the procedure, while Hepzibah continued to sing.

I looked over Jordan and what did I see
Coming for to carry me home
A band of angels coming after me
Coming for to carry me home. . .
I'm sometimes up, I'm sometimes down
Coming for to carry me home
But still my soul feels heavenly bound
Coming for to carry me home.

"Gentlemen, I have attempted to replicate in every detail the fine work of Dr. Marion Sims, including the use of silver wire to complete the closure of the fistula," Dr. Moncrief announced at the completion of the procedure, as Hepzibah continued to sing. "Time will only tell, whether I have been successful. Hepzibah! The operation is finished. Hepzibah?" Dr. Moncrief had not been able to interrupt the slave woman's song. Now he motioned to his assistants to relax their hold on her and he gently rubbed her shoulder and said, "Hepzibah, it's all over now." She gradually opened her eyes as her singing slowly faded away and smiled.

"Massa, de good Lawd has been kind to me. He took me to de hebbinly places, while you wuz cuttin' on me. I done seen de angels. Glory, Hallelujah!"

The remainder of the tour included seeing other procedure rooms for operations, autopsies, or anatomic dissections that were not currently in use, and a quick visit to the third floor where the lecture hall, medical library, and faculty offices were located. Near the end of the tour, Isaac could no longer resist asking Dr. Merrill a question about the operation.

"Sir, dost thou have ether available here to provide anesthesia during operations?"

"Yes, Isaac, we have a limited supply of ether. Are you asking because of Hepzibah?"

"Well, yes—"

Dr. Merrill interrupted and said, "It has been our experience, and Dr. Sims has confirmed this in his own work, that negroes are much less sensitive to pain than white persons. The remarkable manner in which Hepzibah distanced herself from any pain she was experiencing seems ample proof of it, don't you agree?"

"Perhaps, perhaps," Levi interjected. "It seems that God was indeed merciful to her, as she so powerfully witnessed."

"Isaac, when you complete your pre-medical studies, you should seriously consider attending a Southern medical school. You now have had an opportunity to see the outstanding facilities we are so fortunate to have here in Memphis, and have met some of our talented staff. Another thing to consider is that here in the South, as you could see on our negro wards, we have no dearth of clinical material and no difficulty whatsoever obtaining a more than adequate supply of cadavers for dissection, which make our anatomy classes and clinical training highly regarded by our students."

"Thank thee very much, Dr. Merrill, for the very kind attention thou hast shown my uncle and me today. Thou hast a remarkable institution. I doubt I will ever forget what I have learned from the visit today," Isaac said as they left Dr. Merrill at the entrance to the hospital.

"I think we had better walk directly to the docks and inquire after the *River Queen*," Levi said as they walked away.

As they headed toward the docks, Isaac's emotions began to overflow, and he could no longer restrain his comments. In a low tone, he said, "Uncle, if Dr. Merrill didn't have access to slaves, he would have no medical school or hospital for that matter."

"I suspect that many of the slaves we saw on the negro wards were the property of slave traders," Levi responded.

"What a glorious medical career to contemplate, to become a specialist in the care of negroes, so that their value as property will be preserved while I discover new treatments at their expense!" Isaac hissed sarcastically, almost beside himself with anger. "How can these Southern physicians be so blind? Hepzibah was clearly in great pain, which they chose to ignore. I can't explain the relief from her suffering that she found in singing the negro spiritual other than to acknowledge it as a miracle of God's mercy," Isaac said with a quaver in his voice.

Levi stopped, his eyes glistening, turned to his nephew, and solemnly replied, "There is no race of human beings more richly deserving of such an act of divine mercy than our African brothers and sisters who are in bondage."

"Massa Coffen, Massa Coffen! De Ribber Qween done arrived 'bout fifteen minit ago," the young slave breathlessly reported, as he intercepted Isaac and Levi on their way to the dock.

"Have they begun to unload the cargo?" Levi asked.

"No, Massa, not yet. Come wif me. I'll sho' you de way," the young slave said as he motioned eagerly to Levi, urging him toward the docks.

Isaac could not help but smile at the young slave's enthusiasm to lead them to the *River Queen* as soon as possible.

I guess he's hoping for a generous tip.

And he was not disappointed. Levi nearly doubled the amount he had offered to pay him that morning. The young slave bowed and, grinning from ear to ear, said, "Massa, I's always at yo' service. Jes' aks fo' Obeediah."

"Thank thee, Obadiah, for thy excellent service," had not quite left Levi's lips before Obadiah had scampered off looking for another entrepreneurial opportunity.

Levi and Isaac stood at the foot of the gangway of the *River Queen* watching the passengers disembark. When there was a break in the traffic leaving the ship, Levi hurried up the gangway followed closely by Isaac. Meeting a ship's steward, Levi asked him, "Is there a Josiah Higgins on board?"

"Yes, sir. I expect he's back at the stern tending to his slaves. You should find him there."

As they approached the stern, they could hear an argument in progress. "Why in damnation did you have a rowboat tied up, trailin' the boat, just temptin' fate?"

"It's standard practice with a steamboat of this size to have a rowboat available for small deliveries and collecting the mail. We can't always take the time to dock the ship at every little place along the river."

"Well, Captain, I hold you personally responsible for the loss of my property and I will take you to court here in Memphis to retrieve my financial loss."

"That's utter nonsense, sheer rubbish! Your *property* stole my rowboat and I will take you to court to recover the cost of its replacement. The security of your property is your own responsibility while traveling on the *River Queen*. If you have forgotten the very clear and explicit language of the disclaimer given to each passenger when they board my ship, I would be happy to show you another copy."

Turning on his heel, the disgruntled captain of the *River Queen* nearly ran into Levi and Isaac as he left Josiah Higgins in an equally disgruntled state.

"Art thou Josiah Higgins?" Levi asked as he cautiously approached the red-faced, angry slave trader.

"Yep, that's me, but you're catchin' me on a bad day," he growled.

"I was hoping to explore the possibility of purchasing one of thy slaves, a young man by the name of Tiberius, or Tib for short."

"Now ain't that somethin'. That's the damn nigger that done absconded and stole the captain's rowboat doin' it! I'd be mighty glad to sell 'im to you, if I had 'im. Never trust a runaway—it's got to be the first rule of this business and I go and get soft on 'im. Well, damn 'im to hell, that's what I say."

With some gentle questioning Levi was able to coax the story out of the distressed slave trader, learning that Tib likely escaped during the early hours of the morning, probably twelve or thirteen hours earlier. Higgins was especially upset because he didn't discover Tib's absence until about nine that morning, on account of his "bein' indisposed by too much celebratin' in the saloon last night." From further inquiries, Levi learned that the *River Queen* was under full steam after entering the Mississippi the preceding evening, its next stop being Memphis. Taking Isaac aside, Levi said in an excited whisper, "Tib was likely between the Missouri and Tennessee shores of the river when he escaped last night. It's hard to know which shore he would head toward but the way shipping traffic flows he would likely have been closer to the Missouri side. My guess is that he will be traveling north along the Missouri shore, having to hide the rowboat by day and row north against the current by night. I wonder how long he will be able to sustain that effort. He will probably shift to traveling on land within a few days but that will be in a hostile and unfamiliar environment. Even if he can get to a point where he can cross over into Illinois, his danger will not be over. The southern part of the state, like Indiana, is full of immigrants from the South who will not befriend a fugitive from slavery. We must hurry back to the telegraph and get a message to Henry Way, so he can tell Tib's family and alert our people in Illinois to be watching for him."

"It's amazing and more than a bit ironic to think we were so close to potentially buying his freedom. Now he is in great danger and all we can do is hope and pray," Isaac said with some frustration.

"The possibility of buying his freedom was just that, a possibility. Even though Mr. Higgins would be very pleased to sell Tib at this point, thou must remember it is because he no longer possesses him. If he had him in chains before us right now, he might demand a price we could not manage or one that another might accept. Tib has made a daring escape by any estimation. I, for one, believe that Tib's God-given intelligence will serve him quite well and that we shall see him once more united to his family in Indiana."

Chapter Twenty-Five

In the nearly two weeks since Tib's capture, the hopes of Eliza and her family had risen more than once, only to be dashed repeatedly, so that after learning from Dr. Way of his sale in Louisville and departure for the deep South, Eliza succumbed to a form of despair that enveloped every aspect of her existence. Her mother, father, and siblings tried in every way to cheer her flagging spirits, but found it very difficult when the possibility of their never seeing Tib again had clearly become a probability.

To make matters worse for Eliza, young Bennie, who looked so much like his father, would come up, tilt his head back, tug at her skirts while looking into her eyes, and ask many times a day, "Where's Papa?"

Her usual response to her son's pleas, that Tib had gone away to help the men who had taken him and would be back soon, no longer satisfied Bennie, who now would cry and say, "Why won't he come home? Is Papa mad at me?" which she would vociferously deny.

It was after one of these question-and-answer sessions with her son that her mother found her in the vegetable garden near the very spot where Tib had been arrested, silently weeping, tears streaming down her face, while Bennie played with their dog in the tall grass nearby. Mary Johnson embraced her eldest daughter and said, "Is there anything I can do, my dear one, to help you carry this burden?"

"Oh Mother, if there was only the slightest ray of hope, I think I could bear it all, but now I feel like I can no longer hide my anguish from our son. He thinks that he has angered Tib and that is why his father hasn't come home. How can I continue to lie to my own child? The thought of Bennie feeling that he is responsible for his father's absence tears at my soul. And yet, how can I tell him the truth?"

"But dear one, you can tell him the truth. Remind him, remind yourself, of Tib's words before he was taken from us, his expression of undying love for you and his children. As for his current fate, there is some real hope that Levi Coffin and Isaac may be able to intercept his steamboat in Memphis. Remember what your father said about the telegram that Dr. Way received from Levi two days ago. Isaac and Levi will be watching for the steamboat carrying Tib. Levi is about as clever a businessman as they come. He may be able to convince Tib's new master to sell Tib to him."

"Mother, I just don't understand how Tib's former owner could hate him so much as to not even give us a chance to buy his freedom. Tib did not tell me much about his life as a slave, only bits of his history would come out here and there, almost by accident. He promised me that he would share his full history with all of us, but that it had been so painful, he begged me to understand and wait until he was ready. Every time I would see his naked back and buttocks, I couldn't help but shudder at the tremendous suffering he has experienced. I'm afraid that the thought of him going through all of that again in a strange place without me there to comfort him will drive me mad."

"Your father is riding down to Richmond with Dr. Way this afternoon to check for a telegram from Levi. I have a strong feeling that we will be hearing some important news by this evening."

"I certainly shared a very strong *feeling* with you, just now, Mother," Eliza pointed to her large belly, laughing for the first time in many days as she made reference to a prominent kick from her baby.

"I think we should take the baby's kick as a good sign."

Louisa and Hattie Johnson were quilting with Rebecca at the Burgess home that afternoon. Several of the colored and white women from the Newport area were gathered, as was their frequent practice, in the parlor, working on a variety of projects from knitting socks to making quilts and blankets for the almost steady stream of refugees who flowed through the community on their way to Canada and freedom. Rebecca and her mother Priscilla had hoped that the activity and conversation would help lift Hattie and Louisa out of the gloom afflicting their family.

Hattie, who was now eighteen, had developed into an attractive young woman. Ordinarily, she would be chattering away about the three or four young men, including Pastor Ebenezer Jones's eldest son (whom she favored), who had been attempting to steal her affection. Louisa, at eleven, and Rebecca, who had recently turned twelve, were on the cusp of maidenhood, but still found the attractions of childhood to be very strong. Louisa had certainly maintained, if not further sharpened, her wit and tongue, but had also learned some discretion in regard to their application.

Without looking up from her work, Hattie said, "I hope father and Dr. Way hear from Mr. Coffin and Isaac today."

Priscilla Burgess smiled and added, "My prayer is that there will be some good news for thee. My brother will look for any opportunity to help Tib."

Rebecca raised her head and with a look of sadness said, "I miss his singing very much. Is there a part of him, I wonder, that still can sing in the midst of all his troubles?"

"No one can take that away from him!" Louisa blurted out as a tear rolled down her cheek.

Sam was walking dejectedly into town from the Johnson farm to pick up some flour for his mother from the Burgess's general store. As he walked, he could not help but ruminate on the events of the past two weeks and how impotent he and many others felt in their failed attempts to liberate Tib. The news that Isaac and his uncle were in Memphis was the only ray of hope they had had in several days. The way the US marshal had always been one step ahead of Tib's would-be rescuers was galling to him. Where was justice in all of this? Clearly, mercy had been banished long ago. He had so much to discuss with Isaac in addition to wanting to hear of his friend's travels and experiences in the South. He wondered what Isaac thought about the proper means of abolition after observing slavery in its undiluted state. Would he still espouse the pacifism so central to the Quaker religion? It was all well and good to try to persuade people to see truth, but that presumed their willingness to listen. The South's insistence on passage and implementation of the new Fugitive Slave Act was proof positive that they weren't willing to listen. Something more direct was needed to get their attention and that *something* could only be based in action. Perhaps it could only happen through violent action, a *second* American Revolution, in which the sons and daughters of Africa would finally claim the promises cherished within the Declaration of Independence.

As he was about to turn into the store, he could see some riders in the distance approaching at full gallop. Pausing, he then recognized the familiar forms of his father and Dr. Way.

"Samuel, we have the first really good news in many days!" Ben Johnson shouted as he brought his horse to a halt outside the Burgess general store.

As if moved by a powerful form of intuition, Louisa had been drawn to the window of the Burgess's parlor. When, upon looking down the street in the direction of the general store, she recognized her brother speaking with the newly arrived Dr. Way and her father, she screamed "They're here!" and ran out of the building and headed down the street, followed by Hattie, Rebecca, Priscilla, and the whole women's sewing society.

"Tib's escaped from his owner!" Ben shouted with joy. "He's either in northwestern Tennessee or southeastern Missouri, heading north along the shore of the Mississippi River. He stole a small rowboat in the middle of the night and slipped away from the steamboat. Levi thinks he had at least a ten- to twelve-hour head start."

Shouts of "Thanks be to God!" and "Glory Hallelujah!" rose from the gathering crowd.

Several minutes later, Ben entered the front door of his farmhouse and, seeing his namesake sitting on the floor, gathered Bennie up in his arms. Walking into the kitchen where Mary and Eliza were preparing the evening meal, he announced to his grandson with a big grin, "Bennie, your Papa is coming home!"

Meanwhile, the subject of all the rejoicing in Newport, Indiana was struggling at the oars of his stolen rowboat as he rowed against the powerful Mississippi current. The exultation he had initially felt had been replaced with the sober realization of the task before him. He had been relieved to find that the Missouri side of the river was sparsely inhabited as he had rowed north. His greatest fright, thus far, had been the rapid appearance of steamboats heading southward. He quickly learned to hug the shoreline, even stop rowing, and beach the rowboat, in case, someone on board a passing steamboat might perceive his movement. As dawn had approached on his first night's journey, he searched quickly for a place with sufficient underbrush to hide and secure the rowboat that would also provide him with a place to rest during the daylight hours. Bluffs that overlooked the water's edge characterized this portion of the shoreline. Fortunately, there was plenty of vegetation that extended down to the water. Tib was able to climb out of the rowboat and pull it under cover of the thick underbrush and overhanging limbs of trees that extended their welcoming embrace out over the water. Once he had secured the rowboat, he cautiously climbed up the side of the bluff and scouted the area briefly. Feeling intense relief in finding no human habitation in the vicinity, he returned to the rowboat and was sound asleep as the first rays of dawn spread their warmth over the *Father of Waters*.

Tib was awakened by the whoosh-whoosh of a steamboat's paddle wheel as it passed close to him on the Missouri side of the river, heading south. The air was quite close, humid, and very warm as he peeked over the side of the rowboat in time to see the stern of a steamboat, the *Natchez*, heading south. He guessed that it must be nearly mid-afternoon and began to ponder the best course to take. Should he leave the rowboat and head north overland or try making more headway by rowing directly up the river? Taking stock of the limited food and drink that his unnamed rescuer had brought him on the *River Queen*, he realized how hungry he was and how little there was remaining to satisfy that hunger. About two-thirds of a small loaf of bread was remaining, along with a small round of cheese that he had not yet touched. He could easily replenish the water in the jar, which he drank during the intense rowing of the prior night, as long as he stayed close to or on the river.

I can probably make this amount of food last for another two days at most, or perhaps less, if I keep rowing heavily against the river's current.

His best chance was to find plantations along the way where he hoped he would find sympathetic slaves who might be willing to help him, so that he could eventually cross over into Illinois. If he could only get as far north as the confluence of the upper Mississippi and Ohio Rivers at Cairo, it would be a great comfort to confirm his location before trying to cross the river into Illinois.

For two more nights, he rowed against the current making modest progress in exchange for the exhausting effort. After finding another hiding place before dawn, he realized that he would have to abandon the rowboat to search for food as his supply had dwindled to a few bites of bread and cheese remaining. During his scouting in the predawn light, he quietly moved up an embankment that ran down to the river and was startled to see the outline of a large brick mansion built in the Georgian style several hundred yards away, with a dozen or more crude cabins, the slave quarters, in the foreground. The closest cabin was not more than a hundred feet from him. As he hid himself for sleep in the rowboat that night, he lay awake for almost an hour silently deliberating about the next steps he should take. As he finally drifted off to sleep, he had made his decision: he would not only search out food here but would also make contact with the slaves to enlist their help to get his bearings and make more definitive plans. He suspected that he would make much quicker progress overland than rowing upstream. Now he was faced with the challenge of having to trust strangers who would not have any particular reason to want to risk brutal punishment to help him.

A group of weary slaves was huddled around a small fire in the gathering darkness, cooking their rations of rancid bacon and corn meal. They spoke very little as they focused all their remaining energy on preparing their humble repast. An hour break for lunch and midday rest was the only respite field hands could hope to enjoy on the long summer days that began just before dawn with the sound of the slave driver's horn and ended with the last rays of the setting sun. As one of the slaves began to slowly savor his food, he looked beyond the fire and his circle of companions, idly surveying the trees and bushes separating them from the Mississippi River.

Suddenly, he let out a yelp like a wounded animal and cried out, "O Lawdy, dere's de debbil out dere lookin' at me!"

"Well, Ned, it about time dat you got religion. Dat ol' debbil bin watchin' you fo' long time now," a woman, who appeared to be his wife, said with a hearty laugh.

"Look, Beulah, ober dere! Cain't yo see 'im?"

Ned pointed toward the river. Beulah looked up slowly from her meal and seeing nothing, smirked at her husband.

"Dere ain't nothin' dere but yo' fear chasin' you, you ol' fool!"

A few moments later, to the shock and fright of Beulah and the others, Ned's fear materialized in the hungry form of Tib, who cautiously approached the group from his hiding place in the bushes.

"Hey dere, nigger, you done gib us a mitey big skear," Beulah spoke up for the group. "My man here thought you be de debbil, an' mebbe fo' us po' niggers yo be de ol' trickster hisself! Dere's no good come fum helpin' run'way niggers. I s'pose you be hungry?"

Tib nodded in response to Beulah's question.

"Where you escape fum?"

"I bin sole down de ribber fum Louisville, Kaintuck. When we gots to de Mississippi, I stole a rowboat fum de *Ribber Queen* an' bin comin' north fo' tree nite."

"Gib me one good reason why we should he'p a run'way like you," Beulah said as she eyed Tib suspiciously while at the same time reaching into her pocket and pulling out some treasured cornbread, half of which she offered him. "Ol' massa Noocum be mitey happy to hab anudder strong nigger like you. He still smartin' sumthin fierce when my sistah's man done run off fo' de north mo' den two month ago." Beulah pointed to her sister, who was sitting on her other side. Beulah's sister gave Tib a brief look of intense interest and then quickly lowered her eyes.

Taking a big risk, Tib dispensed with the slave dialect and said, "Is it not true that your sister wants to follow her husband to the north and freedom? I can help her do just that."

Beulah rose, boldly approached Tib, and grasping him by the shoulders said, "Well, you be flesh and blood. Dat's good. I wuz beginnin' to believe wif my Ned dat you be de debbil. So's how come you talk like de slave one minute an' like de massa de nex'?"

"It's a long story but the important thing for your sister is," and giving Beulah's sister a piercing look, Tib continued, "I can read and write very well. If you can steal some paper, pen, and ink, I can forge a pass that will allow her to travel north without any trouble from slave patrols. That should give her an advantage of many hours, especially if I write more than one pass that misleads her pursuers. Of course, I will need to see your master's handwriting and signature so that I can study them a bit before attempting to forge some passes. I have a pregnant wife and young son in Indiana, who are free negroes. I am on my way now to return to them. There is no reason why I couldn't help your sister escape as well."

Beulah's sister gave her an imploring look and then fixed her gaze on Tib.

"Well, it looks like we got a smaht negro heah, Florrie," Beulah said with a grin. "If'n you kin write as good as you say, why don't you write free paper fo' yo'self an' Florrie?"

"I wish it were that easy. Unfortunately, manumission papers often include the owner's seal and signatures of witnesses confirming the owner's wish to free his slave. I would need a lot more information, including samples of at least two of your master's friends' signatures to copy as well as access to his seal. Even if I could forge manumission papers, I would recommend only using them once we are out of the local area. They might be more useful in a free state. I would still plan on heading for Canada, Florrie."

Flora, or Florrie as she was called, looked up at Tib, smiled gratefully and said, "Yes'm! Dat's where my man John tole me to meet 'im."

"I will also need to see a map of this part of Missouri, if you can borrow one from your master. If someone can steal a piece of paper here and there rather than all at once, I think there will be a better chance of the theft not being detected."

"Don't you worry about dat. Our Auntey Mae be de cook at de big house. She'll he'p us wif gittin' de paper. Massa Noocum won't miss it."

"Does your master give you Sundays off from work?"

"Yes'm. He be very religious. De niggers on dis plantashun git off fum when de work be done on Sattaday nite until dawn Monday mornin'. He don't seem to mind when some o' de niggers don't come to church, like my wicked Ned. Massa Noocum say dat de niggers should have one day o' dey own.

"But," she continued, turning to Ned, "dats de Lawd's day not yo' day. So's you better keep watchin' fo' de debbil or he'll git you yet!"

Beulah stood up again, a commanding figure, in spite of her average height, adjusted her headscarf and then spoke sternly to all those present.

"You must all play de dum niggers Massa Noocum tink you be, for dis plan to work. Dat mean no openin' yo' mouths aroun' nobody. Dat include you, Ned. I lub you wif all my soul, only hebbin know why, but sometimes you be one dum nigger. Jes' keep yo' mouth shut!"

Beulah made a gesture of forcibly clamping her lips together directed at her husband, grinned, and then kissed him. He meekly replied, "Yes'm, Beulah dear."

Florrie was dark-skinned like her sister and about the same height, but her build was slighter than the sturdy, muscular form of Beulah. Along with the difference in physique there was a marked contrast in personalities. Although Beulah appeared to be about thirty years of age and Florrie appeared to be about the same age as Tib, Beulah had assumed a maternal role in their relationship, especially after their parents had been sold many years earlier. Florrie's husband had urged her repeatedly to come with him when he made his escape but her natural timidity had prevented her. Tib's arrival came almost as a revelation to her. She realized that he might represent the only chance she would ever have of seeing her husband again and sharing his dream of freedom in Canada.

As the others went back to their cabins to retire for the night, Florrie and Beulah lingered behind with Tib. Beulah came up to Tib, looked him in the eyes and said in a soft but firm voice, "You promise me now dat you'll protect my Florrie and git her to Kan-uh-duh. Promise!"

"I promise that I will do everything in my power to help her arrive there safely."

As tears started to form in her eyes, Beulah gently touched his shoulder and said, "I believes you. May God bless you so dat you kin see yo' family agin. Tomorrah, befo' de sun go down you wait here for a big woman. Dat be Auntey Mae. She'll bring yo' food. She'll be standin' out here singin' de *Gospel Train*, if it be safe fo' you to come git yo' food, but she'll be singin' '*I'm a rollin thru an unfriendly world*,' if'n it ain't safe. Dere'll be mo' food fo' you den. Dis all I got to gib you now," and she handed Tib the rest of her treasured corn bread.

Late in the afternoon of the next day, Tib was waiting hidden within the bushes as instructed, hoping that no one would hear the loud growling of his stomach. After about fifteen minutes, a tall, heavy-set slave woman appeared, sauntering among the cabins in the quarters but gradually moving in Tib's direction.

As she moved closer, he could hear her singing in a deep clear voice:

> De gospel train's a'comin'
> I hear it jest at hand
> I hear de car wheel rumblin'
> And rollin' thro' de lan',
> Git on bord lil' chillun
> Git on bord lil' chillun
> Git on bord lil' chillun
> Dere's room fo' many a'mo'. . .

Once she was out of direct view from the mansion, she pulled out a parcel wrapped in a brightly colored headscarf and deposited it near some bushes about twenty feet from where Tib was hiding. As if nothing out of the ordinary had just occurred, she sauntered slowly back toward the mansion still singing to herself. Tib waited another ten minutes watching for any signs of activity in the quarters or at the mansion before creeping through the bushes as close as he could before quickly retrieving the parcel and returning to his hiding place.

Thank you, Auntey Mae! he thought with deep gratitude as he admired the fresh corn bread, two generous slices of ham, jar of fresh milk, and three apricots—a veritable feast. In the bottom of the parcel under the food was a crumpled piece of paper plus four clean pieces of paper, a small inkpot, a pen, and, amazingly, a small map of Missouri. His admiration for Auntey Mae now extended beyond the food as he marveled at how quickly and efficiently the different items had been procured. Realizing that the food would need to last for the next twenty-four hours, he ate slowly, savoring small portions of each item as he studied the crumpled piece of paper and its contents. Apparently, the master of this plantation felt secure in the sanctity of his study and the illiteracy of his slaves. For to Tib's literate gaze, the crumpled document appeared to be a short letter that had been intended to formally end a relationship between the plantation owner and another party, possibly a mistress.

June __, 1852

Dear M,
Although our friendship has been a real source of joy to me personally, and I hope also to you, I most sincerely regret to inform you that we can no longer enjoy each other's company on the same amicable basis, as has been our custom.
    Sincerely,
    Hiram Newcomb

Clearly, Mr. Newcomb was having difficulty terminating the relationship that he had proposed to end in the discarded letter. It seemed highly likely that the relationship in question was not sanctioned by the standards of his community, which may have been the impetus for Mr. Newcomb to write the letter, although he was not quite prepared to commit himself to the course of action outlined in the letter. Tib wondered if Mr. Newcomb's wife knew of his dalliance and decided to not practice copying Mr. Newcomb's handwriting on the crumpled letter.

A distracted master could be the friend of a fugitive slave, Tib thought as he concentrated on studying Hiram Newcomb's elaborate calligraphy. *I don't know what kind of a master, let alone human being he is, but he certainly has excellent penmanship,* Tib laughed to himself as he laboriously practiced copying Mr. Newcomb's script in the waning light.

Later that evening, Tib informed Beulah of the contents of Mr. Newcomb's letter. Her eyes got big for a moment and then narrowed as a sly smile formed at the corners of her mouth.

"Dere's bin sum speculayshun 'bout Massa Noocum an' some white gal ober at de nex' plantashun fo' mo' den a year now. I don't tink Missus Noocum know about it. Mebbe she suspec' sumfin, doe. If'n you kin git de paypuhs all done befo' nex' Sattaday, you an' Florrie kin git away dat night, an' Auntey Mae kin he'p Missus Noocum find dis lettah afta church on de Lawd's day. Dat'll make tings mitey discombobulatin' aroun' here fo' awhile."

Beulah chuckled to herself as she envisioned the chaos created by her mistress's discovery of the letter.

"I don't want to take advantage of private information to harm someone's marriage," Tib said as he began to have second thoughts about sharing the information with Beulah.

"Don't you worry yo'self 'bout dat retch," Beulah growled. "He sold my mammy an' pappy down de ribber when I wuz only thirteen and Florrie only five year. I bin mammy fo' Florrie after dat. Last year he sold my Dick down de ribber when he got fo'teen year, my big hansum boy," her eyes filled with bitter tears as she related the misery inflicted on her family by the philandering Mr. Newcomb. "He tole Florrie dat, on accounta her not habbin babies, he would sell her down de ribber in anudder year. She s'posed to find anudder man, now dat her John run away, an' try real hard to hab babies."

"I am sorry, Beulah, for all your troubles. You go ahead and use the letter as you think appropriate. Certainly, if your master leaves the plantation on Sunday after fighting with his wife, the overseer will be hard pressed to deny that Florrie was given a pass from her master to go visit a relative at a neighboring plantation. By the time the deception is discovered, she and I will be going in a very different direction."

Tib thanked Auntey Mae through Beulah for the food, the writing implements, and especially for the map.

"You gots to git dat map back to Auntey Mae tomorrah. De massa could miss dat."

"What is the name of this place, Beulah?"

"Why we at Noo Mah-drid."

"Ah, it's right here on the map, New Madrid," Tib pointed in the firelight.

"Well, you kin eben read a map, tink o' dat!" Beulah exclaimed with admiration.

"It looks like Charleston is about thirty miles away and close to the Mississippi River, crossing to Cairo, Illinois. Ah, here is another town to the north and west. Do you know anything about Dexter?"

"Yes'm. Dere's a plantation dere, jes' south o' town. De Sulliban place. We gots a cuzzin dere."

"Perfect. What is your cousin's name?"

"Meg."

"Margaret?"

"No, jes' Meg."

"Do you know Mr. Sullivan's full name?"

"Tom, Tom-ass, sumpin' like dat."

"Are you pretty certain it's Thomas?"

"Yes'm."

"Do you know any plantations near Charleston?"

"No, but dere's one north o' dere in Cayp Jerarrdoe, where we gots anudder old cuzzin, by name o' Lu-sin-dah."

"Oh, I see it here: Cape Girardeau. And you say her name is Lucinda?"

"Dat's it."

"Do you know the master's name there?"

"Well dat be interestin'. Tain't no master dere. Dere's a missus runnin' de place. Her man died an' she say to herself, 'I kin run dis place,' an' so she do; but she's a mean one. She whip her slave fo' de plezhur o' it."

"Do you know her name?"

"Missus Sallee, Sallee Blak."

"Sally Black?"

"Dat's it and dere ain't no white womun mo' blak in de heart den ol' Missus Sallee!"

"Beulah, this map has been extremely helpful. Please thank Auntey Mae for everything. If it's possible, I could really use one or two more pieces of paper."

"You be real quiet tomorrah. We gots a lazy oberseer but he allez cums tree day afta de Lawd's Day to inspec' de kwarters, to make sho' we ain't up to no mischief. So, we ain't up to no mischief when he come, hee hee," Beulah laughed.

She told Tib that Auntey Mae or one of the other slaves in the kitchen might be a bit later with his food the next day to avoid any unpleasant encounters with the overseer.

As he tried to sleep that night, he pondered the tasks before him. He would carefully mimic the elegant penmanship of Hiram Newcomb and produce two passes, one for the local slave patrol and one for the patrol they would likely encounter closer to Charleston. For the purpose of their travel together, he would now identify himself as Florrie's "new man," Bob. The purpose of their journey would be for him to meet Florrie's dear cousin, Meg, who was a slave on Thomas Sullivan's plantation just outside Dexter, Missouri. The favor granted to Florrie and her new man was a sign of Mr. Newcomb's benevolence as a master. For later use near Charleston, he would craft a similar pass, but this would grant permission for the couple to visit Florrie's sick elderly cousin, Lucinda, at Sally Black's plantation outside Cape Girardeau. How they would cross the Mississippi at Cairo, he had not worked out yet. His clothing was badly damaged from the last two weeks of rough conditions he had endured, and Florrie would definitely appear like a slave in her cotton dress made from "Negro cloth." Also, they had no money, or at least he had no money. He would have to explore this issue with Beulah the next night. If they carried the manumission documents that he would create and wore better clothes, they might be able to successfully make the crossing into Illinois. As he lay in the rowboat, he finally drifted off sometime after midnight, only to be awakened with a start by the slave driver's horn just before dawn.

Tib was fairly satisfied with his morning's work. He had managed to find a relatively smooth, dry surface in the rowboat on which to write and slowly, methodically he wrote the passes that he had composed mentally, using his best effort to copy the florid handwriting of Mr. Newcomb. After comparing both of his forgeries with the letter written in Newcomb's own hand, he felt reasonably satisfied that they would fool most people who were familiar with the plantation owner's handwriting and signature.

As he sat finishing the remains of the feast that Auntey Mae had brought him the afternoon before, he sighed as he realized that forging the manumission documents would be a more challenging and lengthier task. He would need to know the names of two of Mr. Newcomb's close friends, who would serve as witnesses on the documents. He realized that the chances of seeing their signatures would be extremely low, so that the manumission documents would have to be wielded by a person acting with great confidence, to minimize the degree to which they could be scrutinized by suspicious eyes. He had seen manumission papers a few times in Indiana and remembered their basic structure.

First, the owner identified himself; second, the owner identified his property that he wished to manumit, including the timing and circumstances of the manumission; third, the owner signed the document with or without affixing a personal seal, if he possessed one; and fourth, trusted individuals signed as witnesses, confirming the decision of the owner. Tib patiently forged manumission documents for Florrie and then for himself, following as closely as possible his memories of such documents but leaving blank the portions for witnesses.

Late in the afternoon, when he felt he could write no more due to the limited lighting and lack of witnesses' names, he hid the documents in the headscarf he had obtained on the *River Queen*, placing the collection inside his shirt, and then silently ascended the bank to determine if the overseer was still present in the quarters and to wait for Auntey Mae.

"Stop, you damn rascal!" a heavy, lumbering white man yelled as Tib came to the top of the embankment.

His heart pounding in his chest, Tib panicked until he realized that the overseer's back was turned to him and his wrath was actually directed at a young slave boy not more than eight years of age who had fled in the opposite direction.

"Damn niggers! You show 'em a little kindness and then all you receive in return is abuse." His bald head shining with perspiration and his face flushed from his futile efforts to catch the boy, the overseer shouted, "Bring my hat back to me right now!"

The little boy, who was clothed only in a gunnysack, turned around, giggled, dropped the overseer's hat, and quickly rejoined several other children, both negro and white, who were playing together in front of a larger cabin, presumably that of the overseer. The fat overseer sighed, ambled over to pick up his hat, dusted it off, and, muttering something about "bein' awful thirsty," entered the large cabin as his children and the young slaves scattered while Tib breathed a sigh of relief.

A half an hour later, Tib's patience was rewarded by the appearance of Auntey Mae, singing and sauntering as before until she had deposited her parcel for Tib out of sight of the mansion and the overseer's cabin. When dusk was settling over the plantation about forty-five minutes later, he was waiting for Beulah.

"I am again very grateful to your Auntey Mae for the food and the extra paper. I have the passes written and have nearly finished the free papers for Florrie, but I need the names of two witnesses. They should be good friends of Mr. Newcomb. If I could see their signatures that would be ideal."

"Well, dere be a couple good frens o' Massa Noocum dat cum to see 'im 'bout evry week or so. Dere's Massa Jas-pur Tooms and Massa Ashlee Tayt."

"Jasper Toombs and Ashley Tait?"

"Dat's right. Wait doe'. Dere's sumfin mo'. Dat Tayt, dere be tree o' dem."

"You mean he is Ashley Tait, the third?"

"Yes'm. I dunno 'bout no sig-na-chur fo' dem genelmen."

"I will wait another day or two before placing their names and signatures on the free papers, in case Auntey Mae is able to find something. How is Florrie? I will need to go over the plan with her in detail in the next night or two and then review it all again before Saturday night. Does she have any money saved? We will need to pay for the ferry across the Mississippi and may need to buy some food. Does she have access to better clothes?"

"She be here tomorrah night fo' sure. You sure do tink 'bout evryting. You a right smaht negro. You might jes' git my Florrie to Kan-uh-duh!"

"I hope to do just that."

"Well, Florrie still got de Sunday clothin' fo' her John an' fo' her self." Beulah grabbed Tib by the shoulders, sizing him with her fingers and said, "I tink you kin git inta John's Sunday bes'. Florrie got ten dolla. Will dat be enuf?" Tib smiled in the darkness and said, "That is wonderful. I can now see our way to Illinois."

By Friday evening, Tib felt they were as ready as they could be. No signatures were available for either of Mr. Newcomb's friends, so assuming that their penmanship was likely not as fine as Newcomb's, he wrote legible witness statements for each, trying to create uniquely different styles of handwriting, which he reproduced on his own false manumission document. He gave the reason for their manumission as "for their years of faithful service and in honoring a promise made long ago."

Looking directly into Florrie's eyes, Tib asked, "Now again, who am I?"

"Mah new man, Bob."

"And if we get stopped by a patrol on Sunday, where are we going?"

"We's goin' to see my cuzzin, Meg, at de Sulliban plantashun jes' ou'side Dextah."

"And, later when we turn toward Charleston, where are we going?"

"We's goin' to see my ol' cuzzin, Lu-sin-duh, at dat horribul Missus Sallee's plantashun neer Cayp Jerrardoe."

"That's excellent, but please leave out the bit about the horrible Mistress Sally."

"But, dat's God's awful truth. She be horribul!"

"Yes Florrie, but the slave patrol doesn't need to know about that."

Turning to Beulah, Tib said, "If we succeed, it will be largely due to your efforts, the help of Auntey Mae, and others unknown to me. I cannot thank you and them enough. It seems unjust to be leaving you and your husband behind."

"Don't you fret 'bout Ned an' me. I's happee if'n Florrie be free an' wif her man agin. Ol' Ned an' me'll find a way to Kan-uh-duh some day. An' when we do, I wants you to teach me to read an' write."

"It will be my joy and pleasure," Tib replied with a smile.

"Now, dere's no sense in tryin' to go befo' early mornin'. You jes' make de patrol real suspishush an' Florrie need to res' befo' all dat walkin'. Sho' me where you hidin' an' I'll make sho' you be up befo' de sun on de Lawd's day wif Florrie ready to go wif you."

Chapter Twenty-Six

The reflection from the light of a full moon was fading on the water as the gray in the eastern sky advanced. Crickets were still chirruping nearby as a low whistle penetrated the air around Tib's sleeping form, prodding him to stir briefly. The signal was repeated and this time he came to full consciousness. Faithful to her word, Beulah was waiting in the darkness for him. All he could remember before falling into a deep sleep the night before was thinking, "Will the music in the quarters ever stop?"

Within fifteen minutes he had said farewell to Beulah and the stolen rowboat and was now quickly and stealthily moving through the perimeter of the Newcomb plantation with a tearful Florrie at his side. Florrie, who had made the journey north to the Sullivan plantation on prior occasions, guided the way as they eventually joined the road between New Madrid and Dexter. Each of them carried provisions and better clothing in old sacks slung over their shoulders. Tib instinctively felt for the forged documents hidden within his clothing and smiled.

Looking over at Florrie, he said, "How do you feel this morning?"

"I's awful sor'ful, but happy at de same time."

"Florrie, think about your John and be hopeful. We need to be cheerful, happy negroes for the slave patrol."

Florrie, laughing, replied, "Yes'm. I's jes' anudder happy nigger slave."

The grayness in the eastern sky was now being transmuted into various shades of pink, which in turn were quickly swallowed up by the golden light of dawn. Tib could finally see Florrie's face clearly and she responded to his look with a big smile.

"If we can make good time, I expect we will come to the road to Charleston in about six or seven hours, hopefully not long after noon," Tib said as they walked along.

As the sun cleared the eastern horizon to their right, Tib noticed a solitary rider on horseback up ahead, who was approaching them. A sleepy-looking white youth who could not have been more than eighteen hailed them.

"Niggers, yer out awful early on a Sunday. Where's yer pass?"

As Tib pulled out his forged pass, he said, "Massa, we fum Massa Noocum's plantashun. Florrie an' me jes' jump'd ober de broom. De good massa allo' us to go see Florrie's cuzzin, Meg, at Massa Sulliban's plantashun up by Dextah way fo' a couple o' day."

"Lemme see that."

The patroller snatched the forged pass and held it up close to his eyes, rotating the document, and scrutinizing it intently for what seemed an eternity.

"Well, niggers, it looks like it's all in order. Mind yerselves, now!"

The young slave patroller handed the forged pass back to Tib and continued on his way, while Tib and Florrie went in the opposite direction. When they had passed out of sight of the slave patroller, Tib began to laugh so hard that Florrie gave him an anxious look.

"I'm sorry Florrie. I didn't mean to alarm you. It's just that the fool handed the pass back to me upside down. He could no better read it than you, Florrie! After all the risks Auntey Mae took and my careful effort to forge Newcomb's handwriting and signature, I end up being stopped by an illiterate slave patroller!"

By mid-afternoon, on what turned out to be a very hot, humid Sunday, they came to a fork in the road, the left fork going on to Dexter and the right heading to Charleston. Tib expressed great relief when he also read well-marked signs confirming the route.

"I expected us to get here sooner but I clearly misread the distance on the map."

They had been fortunate in only encountering a few other negroes on the road after meeting the slave patroller. None of the negroes they met were familiar to Florrie, which was all the better.

Once they had transferred to the Charleston road, Florrie asked, "Bob, can we stop an' rest a bit? I's real hungry."

Tib motioned for Florrie to enter some woods that were adjacent to the road. "We can cool off in the shade, get some rest, and eat without being seen from the road."

After they had been resting awhile, Florrie casually said, "I expec' Missus Noocum find de lettah fum her man to his gal 'bout now."

"So much for the peace and quiet of a Sunday afternoon."

"You don' wanna be dere when Missus Noocum git rile up," Florrie added as she rolled her eyes.

"Beulah was right. I'm sure no one will notice your absence until tomorrow morning, and even then, the overseer won't be able to act until he can check with Mr. Newcomb about the pass that you were 'given.'"

"Ebry time Massa Noocum fight wif Missus Noocum, he go off, sometime fo' two o' tree day."

"Hopefully, by the time they begin to search for you in earnest, we'll have traveled many miles in Illinois."

Tib noticed how Florrie was slowing down as the afternoon waned. "How are your feet, Florrie?"

"Dey's awful sore."

"Do you think you could go on for just a bit more? I think we're close to Charleston. We might be able to find some shelter in a barn closer to town. The sky looks threatening."

"I's sorry dat I's so slow."

As Tib was about to reassure her, he heard horses and looking up saw two white men approaching on horseback. "Niggers, show us your pass."

"Here de pass, Massa," Tib said, as he handed the forged pass to Sally Black's plantation to the slave patroller.

"Hmm. You been walkin' a fair piece t'day, if you've come from Newcomb's plantation. Well, yer almost to Charleston and it's about another twenty miles or so on to Cape Girardeau," the patroller said as he handed the pass back to Tib.

"Tank you Massa, tank you!" Tib said as the two slave patrollers rode away. He looked back at the two horsemen with satisfaction and whispered to Florrie, "It seems they believed the forgery. All of the risks and effort were worthwhile, afterall."

After trudging along for possibly another mile through densely forested country, they came to a clearing and saw a small farmhouse by the side of the road. They also noticed a barn that was further back from the road. The house, although never grand, had definitely seen better days. Paint was peeling off the siding and some of the shutters on the windows were broken and hanging askew. Both a flower garden in the front and a vegetable garden on the side were overgrown with weeds. A figure in a faded dress rose from the vegetable garden as they approached. It was a white woman, who appeared to be in her late thirties or early forties. Her hair was disheveled, patches of dirt on her face were smudged in places, as if she had been crying, and her overall expression was one of profound gloom. When she saw the two travelers, her expression brightened, and she motioned for them to leave the road and meet her.

As Tib and Florrie cautiously approached, the white woman came toward them, limping as she walked, motioning to move around to the side of the house closest to the barn. Turning around and scanning the house quickly, she then turned to greet her visitors.

Looking at the weary, footsore travelers, she smiled and said, "You mus' be right hungry. Would you like some ham an' cornbread?"

"Yes'm Missus, we awful hungry," Florrie responded.

"Don't call me Missus. I ain't missus no-body. I'm a slave jes' like you. Call me Veronica," the woman said as the gloomy expression returned to her face.

"But, how kin you be a slave?"

"My mama was a slave, dat's how. I got near a quarter nigger in me," Veronica explained matter-of-factly. I'm de last slave o' Massa Archibald Thayer, one-time justice o' de peace an' now an ol' drunk," she said and then spat in disgust.

Brightening again, she changed the subject. "Where are you goin'? Are you run'ways?"

"No. We goin' nort' to Cayp Jerrardoe to see my woman's cuzzin, Lu-sin-dah, at Missus Sally Black's plantation. We jes' jumped ober de broom," Tib smiled broadly and as convincingly as he could. "Wanna see de pass fum Massa Noocum?"

"No. It's a cryin' shame but I cain't read nor write. When I see'd both o' you, I thought, 'Here's mah chance to escape fum Massa Archibald.'"

As Veronica was speaking with Tib and Florrie, she would involuntarily wince in pain several times a minute.

Finally, Florrie couldn't restrain herself anymore and went up to Veronica and gently exposing her shoulders, exclaimed, "Veronica, you got bruzes all ober yo' body, don't you?"

Veronica nodded as big tears flowed down her cheeks. Her story came tumbling out between sobs.

"More'n twenty year ago, believe it or not, I wuz a pretty girl of sixteen. Mah ol' massa decided when he sole mah mama dat he would sell me to be a fancy girl. When Massa Thayer outbid all de others, I thought dat I would be safe, cuz he said dat I would be parlor maid in his house. But he wanted a fancy girl all for hisself an' he made that right clear after I arrived in de house. Missus Thayer jes' looked t'other way; nary a peep from her about all his night visits to mah room. Dat devil kep' me wif chile all de time. O' de twenty chillun he gib me, de las' four died at birth, anudder four died as chillun fum fever, an' de res' he sole down de river, including my las' chile, my sweet Abigail, to pay fer his drink an' gamblin'.'"

Veronica went on to explain that after her master lost all his field hands paying for gambling debts, he then began to sell his slave children to support the education of his white children. Finally, his drinking became the one constant feature of his existence after his wife died. When he was drunk, he would often come home and beat Veronica, finding her a safer outlet for his rage than his wife while she was still alive since he had acquired a healthy fear of his wife's brother who lived in a nearby town. Veronica's distress had reached its zenith just three days before when her master sold her remaining child, nine-year-old Abigail, to a slave trader, declaring that she would make a first-rate fancy girl.

"I'm runnin' low on cash. The nigger brat'll fetch a pretty penny."

Veronica's pleading to spare her remaining child only further enraged Archibald Thayer. He beat the poor woman severely, tying her up in an adjacent room so that she could hear him complete his transaction with the slave trader the next day, helpless to intervene on behalf of her daughter. All that was left to her was to mingle her wailing and weeping with that of her daughter before she was dragged from the house.

"Sorry to burden you wif my troubles, but you kin see dat livin' in de big house wif de massa kin be a speshul kind o' hell."

Florrie clasped Veronica's hands in her own and said, "We don't wanna git you in trouble wif yo' massa. Mebbe you better not gib us de food."

"Don' you worry 'bout dat. I'll help whomeber I pleaz. If he kill'd me now, it'd be a blessin'. Dere's fresh straw in de barn, if you'd like to stay de night. You wait in de barn an' I'll bring de food in 'bout half an hour."

While they waited for Veronica to return, Florrie begged Tib to help Veronica escape. Tib, who had been deeply moved by Veronica's story, asked Florrie, "Are you sure you want to take on the additional risk of telling her our secret and then including her in our plans?"

"We has to help her. De good Lawd has put her right in our path."

"Yes. I feel it is our duty to help her as well, and as I think about it, we might be able to do something very bold with her help."

"Veronica, we discussed your plight amongst ourselves and we both agreed that we should offer to help you escape," Tib said without further use of the slave dialect.

Veronica's eyes got big, and a look of awe spread over her face. "You talk like no nigger I eber heard speak."

Tib smiled and said in reply, "You should never assume anything about us 'niggers.' Some of us can be rather crafty fellows. I, for one, can read and write."

"Why you kin speak better'n ol' Massa Archibald eben when he put on his bes' mannahs," Veronica said with admiration.

Tib continued, "We are runaways hoping to cross the Mississippi River into Illinois early tomorrow. As I have been thinking about including you in our plans, an inspiration has come to me. Because you can easily pass as a white woman, I would like to propose that you take Florrie as your personal chambermaid and me, Bob, as your valet on a journey to visit relatives in Indiana on your way to eventually settling in Kentucky. If you don't mind *borrowing* that buckboard wagon over there," Tib said, pointing to a wagon stored in the barn, "you could sit up with me in front with Florrie riding in the back. It should be much easier to cross on the river ferry, if you, as a white woman, oversee your loyal, obedient slave property on a well-planned journey.

"The best parts of this plan are that we could then take a steamboat from Cairo, Illinois to Madison, Indiana, usually a trip of about three days, and then continue our journey via the Madison-Indianapolis railroad. We'll find plenty of help from the Underground Railroad in Indianapolis for the rest of the journey. Most steamboats will reduce the fare of passengers who help with the work on the steamboat. You should be able to travel second-class and hire us both out to the captain of the steamboat. I have experience as a stevedore on a steamboat and you could teach Florrie about the duties of a chambermaid before we get to Cairo. You would need to find a better-quality dress, if possible, and make yourself look and act like a slave-owning white woman who knows how to give orders.

"My only major concern with the plan is your master. Would it be possible for you to help him get very drunk tonight?"

Veronica laughed. "He's mighty good at dat all by hisself. I'll make sure he's blind drunk. Dere's some laudanum he take fer pain in his back. I'll make sure he git a big dose wif de last bit o' whiskey he drink tonite. We better leave right early in de mornin' before de sun come up so no one'll see me dat know me. I'm 'bout de same size as Missus Thayer. I'll pack sum o' her things dat are still in de house. I certainly kin find a dress o' her I kin wear."

"I have one last question: Do you have any money for the journey? There shouldn't be much expense with the steamboat because of your slaves working for the captain, but the fares on the railroad are another issue. One second-class fare for you plus negro seating for us will probably cost close to ten dollars."

"Don't worry 'bout dat, Bob. I'll git some money fo' de trip."

"Should we be worried about your master coming out to the barn?"

"Jes' stay up in de hay loft out o' sight. If I do mah job right, he won't be leabin' de house at all. I'll be out befo' dawn to git you up. Tank you, Bob an' Florrie! Tank you fo' takin' me wif you," Veronica said, tears welling up in her eyes as she was leaving.

Tib woke up with a start, initially uncertain of where he was until the steady breathing of Florrie nearby reminded him that he was with a fellow fugitive in a hayloft. As his eyes became accustomed to the gloom, he could perceive the edge of the loft and the ladder descending from it. He quietly got up and climbed down the ladder and crept softly toward the barn door. Peeking out, he noticed the gray predawn light in the east and a solitary lamp burning in one of the windows of the Thayer house. As he watched, the lamp moved from the window, which he took to mean that Veronica was on her way to awaken her guests. A few minutes later, he could see a solitary figure coming toward the barn.

"Good morning, Veronica," Tib said in a whisper, startling the woman.

"You gib me quite a fright, Bob."

"Sorry. I just wanted to greet you on your first day of freedom."

"I like de sound o' dat."

After awakening Florrie and attending to a very abbreviated toilet, they were gathered in the buckboard wagon with the two remaining horses on the farm hitched up and ready to go. Veronica was dressed nicely in a fine dress, had washed, and her hair was neatly tucked away in a bonnet. Tib turned to Veronica, complimented her on her appearance, and asked about her master and the money.

"He's snorin' away, wouldn't move, even when I pinched 'im. Mah dear Abigail is payin' fer our trip to freedom," she added somberly. "Dat ol' retch git a lot o' money fer her, nine hundred dollahs."

As they left the farm and were heading past the entrance to the farmhouse, Veronica grabbed Tib's arm tightly and whispered, "I fo'get to do one more ting; wait here for jes' a minute."

Before Tib could even ask what had been forgotten, Veronica had climbed down from the wagon and rushed back to the farmhouse. She came back out the front door two minutes later, hurried back to the wagon, climbed on board, and said, "We better git goin' as fast as we kin go. See de dawn comin' ober dere," and she pointed to the east where, indeed, the gray was giving way to pink. Tib roused the horses to a trot as they passed some other small farms over the next mile, wondering why Veronica had gone back into the house. The farmland abruptly ended after about two miles of bumpy riding in the wagon, when they entered a wooded area.

Tib turned to Veronica and said, "We should probably give the horses a rest now that we have left the farms behind. Wait! What's that?"

Tib pointed to smoke rising in the distance behind them.

"Jes' keep goin' toward Charleston. Don't you concern yo'self wif sech issues," Veronica said firmly.

"But shouldn't we go back?" Tib asked. "Perhaps your master's farmhouse is on fire."

"Dats justice for de ol' justice o' de peace," Veronica said with great conviction as she stared at the road ahead.

Florrie spoke up and said, "Bob, dis ain't yo' or mah bizness. You promise Beulah to git me to freedom. Dat's yo' bizness."

Tib hesitated and then reluctantly turned around in his seat and headed the wagon at a steady pace toward Charleston, Missouri. The forest gave way after a few minutes to open space as they entered the outskirts of the little town, named in honor of its namesake in South Carolina. Tib kept the horses at a steady pace as they passed through the still-sleeping town. As they reached the eastern outskirts, he was again relieved to see clearly marked signs, one to the left pointing toward Cape Girardeau and one straight ahead to Cairo, Illinois.

"What do dey say?" Veronica asked.

"Straight ahead is the road to Cairo and to the left is the road north to Cape Girardeau," Tib answered.

"While we are traveling, I think I better help you practice speaking like a white woman." Looking her over in the light of dawn and noticing that she was wearing a black dress with matching black bonnet and veil, he said, "I would also suggest that you present yourself as a widow, let's say, Mrs. Mabel Simpson coming from the west side of Missouri, near Kansas City, with your two faithful servants to visit relatives in Indiana on your way to relocating in Kentucky. If you are pressed for more information, just say that you are hoping to find your Simpson cousins who farm near Indianapolis and that you haven't seen them for several years. Since they came from Kentucky, you expect they will be able to advise you where you can live comfortably in that state with your slaves."

"Dat'll be good. My first massa libbed in de west o' Mizoori for 'bout tree year befo' he sole me. I know sumfin 'bout dat country," Veronica said with some relief. "What do I do when I s'posed to sign mah name?"

"What do I do when I am supposed to sign my name?" Tib corrected. Veronica laboriously mimicked Tib's diction. "You will give the agent your name and then make a mark, an 'X,'" and Tib drew an X in the air, "on the ship's register. Do you know numbers?" Tib asked with some concern.

"Yes'm. I know de money real good."

"Yes. I know money very well," Tib again corrected.

Veronica and Tib looked at each other and both began to laugh.

"Well, lessee if you kin make a silk purse outta dis sow's ear," Veronica said with a smirk.

"All you need to do is convince others that you are a slave-owning white woman. Avoid long conversations and always listen more than speak," Tib cautioned with a smile.

The trip from Charleston to the ferry across the Mississippi River took about three hours, during which Tib aggressively coached Veronica on her speech. "Talk slowly like white folk do, and if pressed to talk more, just act like you are about to cry. After all, you are in mourning."

"That won't be a pro-blem," Veronica enunciated slowly. "All I havta do is think about Abigail an' I'll be-gin to cry."

"You are doing much better with your speech," Tib gently encouraged as he looked into her sorrowful eyes.

To their relief and delight, their plan unfolded without any major challenges. Veronica performed her part well, playing the role of grieving widow and slaveowner, confident in her servants' loyalty and total obedience. In Cairo, she sold the horses and wagon together for a bargain price and then negotiated a very modest steamboat fare to include a private, second-class stateroom for her with the understanding that her servants would work for the ship's captain during the journey. When the ship's captain asked her if she would like her slaves to be in chains at night to prevent any attempt at escape, she said, "No, sir. They've been my only comfort an' consolation durin' my recent loss. I'd trust them with my life."

The captain had responded, in a consoling voice, "As it should be, ma'am, as it should be. They sound like model servants."

Veronica acknowledged his words with a slight nod of her head and a sniffle, as she attempted to hold back a tear.

By the time they arrived at Madison, Indiana early on Thursday morning, Veronica had begun to enjoy her new identity. The captain gallantly offered to send the ship's steward on ahead to arrange for her rail transportation to Indianapolis. He asked her for some money to cover the fares and then took the steward aside and explained that Mrs. Simpson would need a second-class ticket and that since her negroes were utterly trustworthy, they could ride separately in the negro car. Tib found the return trip from Madison to Indianapolis much more pleasant without the chains and guards and Florrie couldn't stop talking about how frightened she was by the speed of the train.

"Dis goin' so fast I 'fraid dat I gonna shake apart," she said. "De only udder time I feel sumfin like dis were when we colored folk get to dancin' all ober durin' de worship."

The train arrived in Indianapolis shortly after five in the afternoon. Tib surreptitiously handed a folded piece of paper to Veronica after they had reunited on the platform of the station and in a low voice asked her to hire an errand boy to deliver it to the Methodist church, which was close to the station. He had made good use of the remaining paper, pen and ink, which he had kept hidden during their escape, while on the train ride to Indianapolis to prepare a cryptic message for the Methodist minister, a prominent white abolitionist in Indianapolis, that some valuable cargo had just arrived at the railroad station that would require delivery to Richmond. A young negro boy was pleased to be given the errand and trotted off down the street toward the Methodist church, which was a few blocks away. Thirty minutes later, the minister himself came with another white man and could barely suppress his surprise and joy at seeing Tib. While Tib stood obsequiously behind her with Florrie, Veronica approached the minister and said slowly and distinctly, "Sir, I was hopin' to find a way to travel with my servants to a farm near here. I have some kin in the area I want to visit."

"I am always happy to be of service to another Christian in need," the minister said with a big smile. "Please come this way, while we discuss the details. I am certain we can arrange a way to transport you to your family's farm."

Veronica thanked him, paid the errand boy, and motioned for Tib and Florrie to follow her as she followed the two white men out of the station.

Once they had passed out of the main thoroughfare and were able to enter a shaded alleyway, the minister shook Tib's hand enthusiastically and whispered, "I can't believe it's you! We all thought we would never see you again."

Tib beamed back and replied, "I certainly wouldn't have been able to return here so quickly without the company of these two very courageous women." He introduced his two companions and said, "It was our good fortune that Mrs. Simpson looks as white as either of you gentlemen."

The minister's companion, another Methodist named John Tubbs, was a conductor on the Underground Railroad. He turned to the three fugitives and said in a low tone, "I think we can carry through with your bold plan. I will be Mrs. Simpson's cousin who has come to pick her up and take her back to Richmond to see her cousins. I am a farmer and have purchased some supplies for my farm, which are in the back of my wagon. The two of you can ride in the back of the wagon while my 'cousin' Mabel will ride up front with me. I may have to explain to any acquaintances of mine why there are slaves with us, but I will tell them that my cousin hasn't fully learned the evils of slavery yet and that I hope to persuade her to free her slaves. Pro-slavery folks will see us and only approve."

Turning to the Methodist minister, Tib said, "I can't thank you enough for your help. We all will be indebted to you and Mr. Tubbs."

The minister smiled and replied, "I will go to the telegraph office and send a message similar to what I just received from you on to our people in Richmond. Someone will relieve John as you approach Richmond. You should be prepared to lie in a hidden compartment in the relief wagon."

Turning to Tib, he said, "You are too well known in that town to pass through unnoticed. Indeed, I only hope we can get you out of Indianapolis before someone here recognizes you."

"Yes. It is the only prudent thing to do. Richmond is such a hotbed of pro-slavery sentiment, as well as abolitionism. It might be wiser to not draw any attention to Florrie, either. Mrs. Simpson can continue to ride up front in the wagon while Florrie and I will be hidden in the secret compartment."

As they rode into the night, Tib couldn't help but reflect on the differences between this journey on the National Road and the earlier one he had taken under heavy guard not so long before. After an uneventful overnight journey, at dawn the next morning, John Tubbs came up beside another buckboard wagon waiting by the side of the road on the outskirts of Richmond. He tipped his hat to the silent figure seated at the head of the wagon, while Tib and Florrie, with Tubbs's help, quietly transferred into the secret compartment in the back of the new wagon. At the same time, Mrs. Simpson introduced herself to the new conductor, who, though a man of few words, managed to say, "Good mornin', ma'am."

After Tubbs arranged some straw and kindling to hide the fugitives in the secret compartment, he quietly whispered, "May God protect you!" and the new conductor was off, moving at a steady pace into Richmond.

The town was beginning to stir, but the few people on the streets thought nothing of the middle-aged couple riding at the front of the wagon and even less about the cargo in the back. Three hours later, the wagon rolled into Newport, Indiana on a sunny Friday morning and the driver parked his wagon at the side entrance to Levi Coffins's old home and knocked.

Rebecca Burgess opened the door and, seeing Veronica, smiled at the man and said, "How art thou, Mr. Billings? Is this a new stockholder on the railroad that thou hast recruited?" she asked, as she looked with curiosity at the white woman.

Then a low, deep, musical sound began to emanate from the back of the wagon and Rebecca screamed as she recognized Tib's voice, "Wade in the water, wade in the water children . . ."

With tears streaming down her face, Rebecca tore away at the straw and kindling, opened the secret compartment, and, nearly dragging Tib out, clung to him as he stood up blinking in the sunlight.

"Oh, the loveliest white face I could ever hope to see!" Tib smiled through tears at his young Quaker friend. "Rebecca Burgess, please allow me to introduce you to Florrie and Mabel. Mr. Billings has been kind enough to deliver *three* fugitive slaves to your door this morning."

Rebecca quickly surmised the essential features of the ruse that Tib had employed in their escape, and said, "Tiberius Johnson, thou art the cleverest of men."

Tib protested that it was truly a joint effort, but Mabel pointed at Tib with a big smile and declared, "That is one smaht negro!"

Florrie couldn't restrain herself anymore. "So you ain't Bob no mo'?"

Tib gave both fellow fugitives a meaningful glance and said, "Mabel and Florrie, my real name is Tiberius Johnson, but my friends and family usually call me Tib. Rebecca, I think we had better thank Mr. Billings and go find my wife and family, don't you?"

Rebecca nodded and wiped her face with her apron, as a shocked and overjoyed Priscilla Burgess came out from the house, embraced Tib, and was introduced to his companions.

"Isaac should be back from Cincinnati later today or tomorrow. He will be so happy to see thee alive and well," Priscilla said.

While Priscilla ran off to find her husband and Dr. Way, a joyful Rebecca led the way to the Johnsons' farm. Tib quietly turned to his fellow fugitives and said in a low voice to Veronica, "I think it would be wise from now on that you remain Mabel Simpson."

"Yes. I understand. Thank you fo' ev'ryting!" Mabel said, and Florrie echoed the sentiment.

"Ladies, it should be safe for you to rest here, at least for a few days, before going on to Canada," Tib said.

Bennie had been rolling around in the grass with the Johnsons' dog before looking up the road that went past the farm to see several people coming. But it was only one person that truly caught his attention. He was up and running as fast as his little legs would permit, shouting, "Papa, Papa!"

By this time, Tib was running toward his son, and as if by some keener sense of hearing given only to mothers, Eliza, who had been behind the farmhouse heard a faint "Pa-Pa" and began to also run. Tib had already scooped up Bennie in his arms as he saw his wife come around the side of their farmhouse running toward him.

"Eliza, please let me come to you. It's not safe for you to run in your condition," Tib shouted.

As husband, wife, and son hugged each other in a tight embrace, Eliza said through her tears of joy, "Tiberius Johnson, what took you so long?"

Tib looked at his wife and with mock chagrin, said, "Well, I guess I was spending too much time seeing the sights of Missouri," and then laughter became intermingled with their tears.

"Eliza, I apologize for my unwashed state. I must smell to high heaven."

"I will take personal pleasure in restorin' you to a state of cleanliness," Eliza said with a gleam in her eye. It wasn't long before concentric rings of Johnsons and other friends had formed around Tib, Eliza, and Bennie.

Looking on with envy, Mabel whispered to Florrie, "If only I could find some part o' my family."

Later that evening, Tib recounted the details of his escape from the *River Queen* and the subsequent adventures that he had shared with Florrie and Mabel to a small group of family and friends gathered in Ben and Mary Johnson's parlor, which now included the newly arrived Isaac. Tib related Mabel's losses, but not her relationship with her former master, stating that she was a widowed domestic slave who had very recently lost her last child to the slave trade.

Pastor Ebenezer Jones spoke up for the group, directing his remarks to both Mabel and Florrie, "Ladies, on behalf of all of us here in Newport, both colored and white, you have our deepest sympathies for your losses and all the suffering you have endured. We can have you safely in Canada West within two weeks. Florrie, we will have our agents watch out for your husband. It is our fervent hope that you will be safely reunited soon under the protection of the British crown in a land where slavery does not exist. Mabel, I hope that you will be able to eventually find peace of mind in that northern land of liberty."

Mabel, who had been weeping quietly during Pastor Jones's brief speech, rose from her seat next to Priscilla, causing him to pause. She then interrupted and said, "I want to thank you, Pastor Eb-uh-neezer an' all o' you for de many good things you said, jes' now. But, I kin nebber find peace wifout tryin' to rescue mah lil' Abigail from de slave trader. Can I stay in your town awhile an' learn readin' an' writin' an' how to talk an' act like a white woman? I mus' go find mah Abbie an' buy her freedom. I'll work right hard so's I won't be no burden for you," she added with great emotion, tears streaming down her face.

"Of course, thou can stay, if thou wishest," Priscilla interjected, as she hugged the distraught fugitive.

"Her frail, elderly master is in no real condition to initiate any meaningful pursuit," Tib added.

"Well then, it is all settled. Mabel will stay with us and learn how to *become* a white woman from the South," Pastor Ebenezer chuckled.

Henry Way, who was listening to the exchange with great interest, spoke up and said, "Mabel, we are delighted to welcome thee to our community and will do all that we can to help thee learn to read and write. But I must caution thee about the dangers confronting an unaccompanied woman pursuing such a mission in the Deep South by herself. Please allow us to help thee in thy search."

Mabel raised her tear-stained face and smiling weakly, said, "Nobody bin so kind to me befo'. I thank all o' you wif mah whole heart."

Turning to Florrie, Pastor Ebenezer said with a big smile, "Young lady, we will be sending you soon to Canada."

Hearing the pastor address her in such a manner, Florrie's eyes got big and she spluttered her response, "But, but. . .Pastor Eb-uh-neezer, no-body, no how, ebber call Florrie, 'Lady.'"

Ebenezer began to laugh, a deep, hearty, infectious laugh rising from his belly, until everyone in the room, including Florrie, was laughing with him, although the look of puzzlement on her face had intensified. "Florrie, you are among free persons of color. We are not slaves and you are no longer a slave, either. Therefore, I pronounce you from this day henceforth and forevermore, to be a young lady," Pastor Ebenezer said with dignity as he winked at the bewildered fugitive.

Once the laughter had quieted down, the pastor's wife, Henrietta Jones, rose and said, "Twilight's coming on soon. Ebenezer, I'll take our two guests home so that they can settle in for the night."

"Before you go, I would like to say one more thing," Tib interjected. "None of the three refugees that came to you today would be here but for the extraordinary fact that our very different journeys collided and merged into one journey. Indvidually, our chances of success were low, but together something like a miracle has happened and so here we are. During my travail, I've seen many strange inexplicable things happen and been reminded of duties long since ignored. All I can say is that God has a strange way of getting one's attention."

After Mrs. Jones had departed with the two fugitives, Tib turned to those remaining—including John, Priscilla, Isaac and Rebecca Burgess, the Ways, Pastor Jones, and a few other trusted souls from the Baptist church, as well as the Johnson family—and said, "I had promised Eliza when we married that I would eventually lift the shroud of mystery that has hidden my past. This experience has made it abundantly clear to me that it is now time for me to share my full story with all of you who have given me a name, a home, a purpose, and most of all, love. If tomorrow evening after dinner is convenient, perhaps I can then begin to enlighten you about this strange man whom you have have taken to your hearts." Winking at Isaac and Sam, he added, "You boys won't have to keep our little secret about the Latin tutoring much longer, either."

"Although it is traditional to begin the story of one's life with the circumstances of one's birth, I must beg your indulgence and impose upon your patience, while I relate some important particulars about my parentage." Tib began, as he looked around the room at his listeners. "I would guess that most of you have surmised, correctly I might add, that I represent an example of that phenomenon known as amalgamation. Amalgamation is a social phenomenon that is both feared and loathed in the North, with most states like Indiana even outlawing marriage between white and colored individuals. While similarly decried in the South, it is also the subject of great denial on the part of slaveowners. The large numbers of enslaved indivduals who come in various shades of black, brown, yellow, and even white belie the aggressive and vociferous denials of Southern leaders to the contrary. The vast majority of instances of this phenomenon are characterized by the abuse of a female slave by either her master or another white man with the access and liberty to assert his will and desire regardless of her wishes or consent. It should be evident from what I have just said that perhaps more than any other members of the human race, the enslaved are acutely aware of their voicelessness in the matter of choosing their parents and yet they bear the full weight of the societal opprobrium connected with amalgamation in their very person."

Tib paused and with a tone of bitter irony, continued, "Please allow me then to introduce you to my father, the eminent Horton Newby of Shelby County, Kentucky, scion of an old Virginia family and owner of more than one hundred souls. As a point of clarification, the detailed narrative that I am relating to you comes out of a close intimacy that I once enjoyed with my father, which ended abruptly in my fourteenth year. Other details I learned later, as will become evident.

"Horton was born in 1806, the third son of Phelps Newby, himself a third son. However, Horton was the first of Phelps and Anna Newby's children to be born in Kentucky. Although he was born on the same soil of his current plantation, the circumstances of his birth were considerably more modest. It was through the ruthless tenacity, vigor, and shrewdness of his father that the Newby plantation achieved its wealth and preeminence.

"Being a third son, Horton was initially destined for life as a clergyman. He and his older brothers were provided with an excellent classical education by well-educated tutors, selected with care by their father in preparation for their matriculation at Princeton, a bastion of the conservative form of Presbyterianism to which their parents subscribed. The elder Newbys' Presbyterianism was more than merely an inherited family faith. True to the conservative pre-destinarian views of their forbears,

Phelps and Anna lived in the sure knowledge that it was their destiny to subdue and civilize the wilderness of Shelby County. This sense of lordship over the created order they successfully imparted to their children, while varying degrees of Presbyterian piety were also transmitted.

"While Anna Newby deeply cherished the notion of having a Presbyterian clergyman in the family, there were some disquieting features of Horton's character that did not bode well for his future as a man of the cloth. It was true that of the three brothers, he had received the greatest intellectual gifts. He was particularly adept with both ancient and modern languages and enjoyed reading history and philosophy, all of which would serve a clergyman well in his ministry. What particularly distressed his mother was his lack of piety, indeed his frank skepticism regarding religious faith.

"From an early age, Horton would all too frequently remind his parents, when caught in some misdemeanor, that his behavior was already foreordained. His glibness of speech in combination with a certain charming quality to his personality often limited the consequences for behaviors that in another child would have led to censure and a severe punishment.

"By the time he entered adolescence, he had grown to be tall, almost six feet in height, with a handsome appearance, easy smile, and winning manners. Although his interest and commitment to intellectual pursuits continued, he also began to respond to baser desires. One day he noticed his eldest brother, Phelps II, leading an attractive young slave girl by the hand away from the Quarters. Out of curiosity, he followed them, carefully avoiding detection as they entered a secluded area surrounded by a thicket. He watched with horrible fascination as his brother had his way with the young slave girl.

"Later that afternoon he confronted his brother, who initially became angry at the thought of his younger brother spying on him but then laughed and reassured Horton that such activities with one's female slaves helped dissipate the animal passions in young men, thereby protecting the virtue of Southern women. Horton realized the self-serving nature of such rationalizations and was initially disgusted with his brother's behavior, resolving that he would not succumb to such temptations. But the seed had been sown.

"About two years later, his earlier resolution wavered and finally crumbled when his admiration for a young slave girl degenerated into lust. He convinced himself, however, that their relationship was founded on love and that the young slave was a willing partner in their romance. He also flattered himself that she had succumbed purely in response to his considerable charm, choosing to forget the persistent attentions and multiple gifts he had showered upon her or the fact that he had intervened personally to stop a whipping of her father by the overseer.

"In any event, he convinced himself that he possessed a deep regard and affection for her. With that deep affection came additional privileges. Eventually, his young slave mistress was promoted, through his efforts, to the domestic staff of the plantation, which increased his access to her but also brought their relationship to the notice of his parents. Although his father shrugged off the affair as nothing more than the youthful 'sowing of wild oats,' his mother became increasingly concerned.

"When the pregnant slave girl eventually gave birth to a mulatto son, Anna Newby made a fateful decision. Horton, who was unaware of his mother's concerns about his relationship with the slave girl, was actually very pleased by the birth and did not hide the fact, insisting on further privileges for 'the mother of my son.' It was at this time that he began his tradition of naming slaves after ancient Roman worthies and so he gave his first son the name, Cicero.

"At Anna Newby's insistence, within a week of Cicero's birth, Phelps quietly made arrangements for the sale of Cicero's mother. Horton's first knowledge of the fate of his slave mistress was early one morning when her screams drew him downstairs and out the front door of the plantation house just in time to see her being dragged away. Her cries alternating between 'Mah baby, mah baby!' and 'Massa Horton, don' let dem do dis!' rent the air. Before Horton could intervene, his older brothers pinioned his arms while his mother approached him and in a calm voice said, 'Horton, it is better this way. You can never recognize this child as your son or this slave as your wife. This dalliance has gone on too long. Cicero will be cared for by one of the other nursing mothers in the Quarters. His mother will be sold to the Deep South and you will be leaving for Princeton tomorrow.'

"I don't think my father ever forgave his mother for what she did that day. The experience not only embittered him and increased his already intense cynicism, but also most certainly affected his future relationships and helped shape my fate. My father spent most of the next four years at Princeton. During the last year of his college studies, Anna Newby arranged for him to meet a young woman from a plantation in a nearby county. His mother had decided that the sixteen-year old Malvina Fairclough, the daughter of sober-minded Presbyterian parents, would be a very suitable match for the future Presbyterian minister. Anna's hope was that betrothal to a young lady of good family would help her son settle down before his return to Princeton for theological studies after completing his undergraduate degree in the spring.

"Horton, who had met Miss Fairclough on several social occasions during the past summer, good-naturedly agreed to his mother's plan for a Fairclough visit during the Christmas holidays. His past experience had taught him that his mother intended to have her way in the domestic sphere, which included planning the marriages of her children. Although the young Malvina was a bit dour for Horton's taste, her favorite topic of conversation being the latest collection of sermons she had just read, she was not unattractive and yet sufficiently plain to fulfill the requirements of being a minister's wife. Through a dutiful display of his charm, the young lady was wooed, and the betrothal arranged. Reflecting later concerning the arrangement, he ruefully admitted how unsuited for the ministry, and by extension marriage, to the pious Malvina Fairclough, he was.

"A week before his graduation from Princeton, his world was turned upside down by news from his mother informing him that cholera was sweeping through Shelby County and that his father and brothers had taken ill with the disease. With his professors' blessing and after early completion of his examinations, he bade farewell to Princeton two days later; it turned out for good. By the time he reached Shelby County, his father and both brothers were dead, his mother was dying, and he was sole heir to the plantation.

"Even in her last hours Anna Newby continued to exercise absolute authority. While keeping vigil at her bedside the first evening he had returned home, Horton had drifted off to sleep only to awaken a few minutes later to discover that his mother was staring intently at him.

"'I suppose you'll never become a minister, now that you will be inheriting the plantation with all of its responsibilities,' she said wearily as she attempted to focus her thoughts. 'Horton, you must promise me, here and now, that you will honor your betrothal to Miss Fairclough.'

"'Why wouldn't I honor the betrothal, Mother?'

"'Do you love Miss Fairclough?'

"'I hardly know her, Mother. Did you love father when you were married?'

"'Horton don't be impertinent. The Faircloughs are not so grand as the Newbys, but they are a hardworking family and Miss Fairclough will bring a handsome dowry. Your father negotiated a transfer of ten slaves and two hundred acres of prime farming land that abut our plantation on the county line that will come as her dowry. It has been the Newby family destiny to provide leadership in this community. I sincerely hope that you will carry on that tradition with this marriage.

"'One more thing, Horton,' she said with a little bit of the old fire still in her eyes, 'Stop trying to hide from God. You will never escape from the Almighty.'

"After that last conversation, Anna Newby slipped away into a delirious state from which she never awakened.

"Two days later, my father, at age twenty-one, was at the same time an orphan and the master of a large estate. Horton, true to his word and perhaps recognizing a very good dowry when he saw one, married Malvina Fairclough the next spring after a suitable period of mourning. The ten slaves that came as part of Malvina's dowry more than made up for the losses of Horton's human property that occurred during the cholera epidemic. He found it a bit ironic that, as fate or destiny would have it, the illness had disproportionately carried away most of the slaves' masters while largely sparing the slaves. The Newby plantation only lost three slaves to cholera.

"Marriage to Malvina added six prime field hands and four wenches to Horton's slave population. Only one of the wenches, who had been trained as a parlor maid on the Fairclough plantation, was assigned as a house servant. Her name was Liddie. At fifteen, Liddie had never experienced the rigors of work in the fields, primarily spending her youth assisting her aunt, who was the Fairclough cook, in the kitchen and later working in a wide variety of capacities in the Fairclough mansion. She was an energetic worker who was reasonably competent at mending clothing, cleaning, and even filling in as cook when necessary. Liddie had an ingratiating personality, bright smile, and dark beauty that with just the right admixture of servility helped her avoid most punishments. While her coloring was quite dark, her facial features were delicate, symmetrical, and even. 'Almost European,' her former master had declared. Already, at an early age, she had a very attractive, even voluptuous figure, and was aware of the stares that followed her whenever she was in the company of men. In short, other than her dark skin and wooly hair, she met, if not exceeded, the standards of beauty that the flower of Southern femininity claimed as their own.

"The Faircloughs thought it was esthetically unacceptable to have to endure the crudeness of the slave dialect in their home, so they went to considerable expense to have their domestic servants tutored in grammatical English, while at the same time taking great pains to prevent them from achieving literacy. Thus, Mr. Fairclough was particularly proud when he explained to Horton these unique qualities that had been cultivated in Liddie.

"'This is a truly remarkable achievement, Mr. Fairclough, truly remarkable indeed,' Horton enthused. 'You have created the semblance of a literate slave without the actual nuisance that would attend such a phenomenon.'

"Later, of course, my father would discover what a nuisance a literate slave could be, but I am getting ahead of my story.

"The new Mrs. Newby was generally pleased with the change in her life that attended the marriage to Horton, including her pregnancy. Like her deceased mother-in-law, Malvina also felt a deep sense of her personal destiny that was now being shared with Horton. Perhaps the first sign of disquiet in their relationship was when her husband did not seem to share her vision of the glorious future that was clearly their destiny together.

"'Horton dear, don't you believe that Providence has ordained that we should subdue the land and civilize this part of His creation?' Malvina asked over breakfast one morning, eight months after their marriage.

"'My mother would have heartily agreed with you, Malvina. Indeed, my father and brothers had no doubts about their place in the world. Ironically, they have all been struck down in their certainty, leaving the family sceptic behind to ponder the meaning of it all.'

"'But Horton, can't you see that you were spared to take up the responsibilities of leadership, not only here on the plantation but also in the wider community?'

"'I am grateful to be spared the ministry; but at what cost? I guess Providence just decided it was time for my two older brothers and parents to get out of the way, so that I could fulfill my destiny unimpeded by their presence.'

"'Horton, sometimes you distress me so, with such cynical comments. We cannot know the ways of Providence but here you are, the sole master of a great plantation, blessed with an excellent education and a devoted wife who would be at your side as you search out the path God has given you.'

"Horton looked across the table at his young bride and with a wry smile replied, 'Malvina, I certainly intend to succeed as a planter, but the question that continually perplexes me is why me? Rather than being the master of over one hundred slaves, I could just as easily have been born one of the poor devils.'

"'Horton, that is unthinkable! You have such peculiar notions. They are a cursed and inferior race. Slavery is their destiny; it is not yours. How could you ever place yourself on equal terms with such creatures? Is this some kind of abolitionist sedition you heard when you were at Princeton?'

"Horton laughed. 'No, my dear; let me assure you that I never heard such heresy at Princeton. Don't you ever wonder at the apparent randomness of the miseries that afflict mankind?'

"'I've never been plagued by such notions. Horton, your problem is you think too much. I'm sure there is a passage in the Bible that says just that. You need to stop worrying about questions you'll never answer and get on with the work at hand.'

"'Malvina, I believe you are referring to verse twenty-four of chapter twenty-six in the book of Acts where Paul is making his defense of the Christian faith before King Agrippa and the king interrupts him to say that he must be out of his mind, that too much learning was driving him insane.'

"'There, you see Horton, even the Scriptures are admonishing you.'

"'You mean King Agrippa, who was admonishing the Apostle Paul.'

"'Exactly. The old king had some very good advice for Paul, which you should also take to heart. Oh! Now the baby is upset. He's kicking something fierce.'

"'I think I had better go speak to the overseer and give you and the baby some peace,' Horton said!'

"About two months later, Malvina was delivered of a baby girl who received the name Julia. Horton was secretly pleased that he could extend his Roman naming scheme to his free daughter as well as his slaves. Although Malvina was pleased to see Horton actively engaged in managing the plantation, for which he seemed to have some real ability, she was becoming increasingly frustrated with his lack of enthusiasm for social activities, especially church attendance. Reluctantly, he attended Julia's christening but was quite resistant to Malvina's pleas for regular attendance on Sunday mornings. It was nearly an all-day outing, between the sixty-minute, one-way buggy ride to the nearest Presbyterian church, followed by the very long service, and then the ride home. Malvina would often return home between three and four in the afternoon after leaving for church at nine in the morning.

"The relationship between Horton and Malvina, which, at best, had never developed beyond a dutiful affection, underwent a progressive chill due to their growing conflict. One Sunday morning after Malvina had left for church, Horton headed toward his library, which he considered his one place of refuge. Quite often on Sunday mornings, safe within the solitude of his library, he would read the Bible, an activity that he would, of course, never admit to Malvina. Unfortunately for Malvina, she was in almost every way possible, from her attitudes and extreme piety to even some mannerisms, becoming for Horton another incarnation of his mother. He found himself beginning to resent what he perceived as Malvina's intrusions into his inner life.

"He was startled abruptly out of his reverie by an incongruous sight that met his eyes upon entering the room. The slave Liddie was intently examining an open book that she held in her right hand. When she heard him enter, an anxious look crossed her face as she quickly closed the book and returned it to its place on the bookshelf.

"'Master Newby, you startled me just now while I was tidying up,' she said by way of explanation.

"'Liddie, Sunday is your day off. You needn't be working in here or anywhere for that matter today.'

"'It's not really work for me, Master Newby. I love to touch and handle the books.' Pointing to a large tome on a different shelf, she spoke rapturously of the fine leather binding, 'The leather smells so good and the appearance of the book is so beautiful, there must be great treasures of knowledge hidden inside. It must be a great joy to be able to read them.'

"Horton couldn't help but notice how attractive she was as she spoke passionately of her love for the books in the library.

"'I may have been mistaken, but when I entered the room, it appeared to me that you were doing more than merely admiring the binding of the book you were holding,' Horton observed as a subtle smile formed at his lips.

"'No, Master Newby, I am so sorry to bother you. I should not have been here in the library.'

"'Ah, but you can't escape so easily, Liddie. You didn't tell me what you were actually doing with that book, did you? Your former master, Mr. Fairclough, assured me that you do not know how to read or write. But I suspect he might just be mistaken about the issue of your literacy.'

"Liddie became visibly agitated and tears welled up in her eyes as she began to plead with Horton, 'I am very sorry Master Newby. I didn't mean to upset you. I must go now.'

"Unfortunately, Horton was blocking the door so that Liddie's only recourse was to fall at his feet and beg as tears rolled down her cheeks.

"Replacing his mock inquisitorial expression with a real look of compassion, Horton reached down and lifted her up and said, 'Please, Liddie, don't cry. Sit with me here. I am sorry to have frightened you so much. You will not be punished for being literate. Indeed, you should have no fears regarding that on my account. But, do tell me how you learned to read.'

"After wiping her eyes with a handkerchief that Horton offered her, Liddie eyed him cautiously and then said, 'It was very difficult for the tutor to teach me how to speak English properly without also exposing me to the books he used. Without him knowing, I would borrow his books at night and with some persistence gradually taught myself to read.'

"Horton looked at Liddie and smiled. 'Did you also teach yourself to write?'

"'Yes, Master Newby.'

"'So, tell me, Liddie, what were you reading when I so rudely interrupted you?'

"Forgetting her recent tears and looking directly into Horton's eyes for the first time, Liddie smiled, jumped up, and retrieved the book from the shelf, handing it to her master. As he perused the cover, Horton was surprised and bemused to discover that Liddie had been reading a copy of Jane Austen's novel *Persuasion*. In response to his questioning look, Liddie answered, 'Sir, I must confess that some of my special favorites are the novels of Miss Austen.'

"'Really? Why do you enjoy them so much?'

"'I enjoy the heroines in her novels very much. They are able to learn from their mistakes. Lizzie Bennett in *Pride and Prejudice* is my favorite character. She overcame an enormous barrier of prejudice both in herself and in the man she loved.'

"'I didn't realize that I had a Miss Elisabeth Bennett in the house,' Horton said with a laugh. 'Please, Liddie, feel free at anytime to borrow whichever books from my library may interest you.'

"'Thank you so much Master Newby. I don't know where to begin.'

"'I would be happy to give your reading some direction,' Horton offered.

"And so began, over a mutual interest in books, the clandestine meetings between the slave Liddie and my father.

"Horton Newby was struck by Liddie's intelligence and her ability to quickly assimilate new information. He took considerable pleasure in introducing her to other great writers and poets as well as a broad reading of history, philosophy, and even some law. Unlike his wife, over time, Liddie became the confidant and friend to whom Horton could share his deepest thoughts, hopes, and doubts. He was unable to avoid making unfavorable comparisons between the intelligence, curiosity, and thirst for knowledge of his slave and Malvina. His wife seemed bereft of interests beyond expanding the family's fortune and political influence.

"The irony that slaves might be more civilized than their masters struck him with full force one day when Malvina stopped at the door to his library, looked in with disdain, and complained, 'Really, Horton, you have too many books. I just don't see the value in collecting all these dusty volumes. Beyond some practical books on farming, why should we need anything else besides the Bible and some good collections of sermons?'

"'If you ever thought to look inside some of those *dusty volumes*, you might discover why,' Horton answered with disgust.

"After that exchange, it was only a matter of time before Horton's platonic interest in Liddie would expand to include a romantic interest as well. At first, Liddie did not even notice any change in Horton's behavior toward her. In the presence of so many books and with his help as a very effective guide, her insatiable thirst for knowledge dominated her perceptions of her master. The Fairclough library, as might be expected from Malvina's dim view of the worthiness of learning as a pursuit for its own sake, was truly impoverished compared to the veritable palace of learning represented by the Newby library.

"So, when Horton's tenderness finally broke through the magical glow of all the stories and interesting facts in which Liddie basked, she at first misinterpreted them as his ardent sharing in her admiration for the treasures of the library. But, when he placed his arm around her and began to stroke her shoulder, she woke from the bewitchment of the books and realized how dangerous her situation was. She protested vociferously, 'Master Newby, this isn't right!' and pulled away from him.

"Horton, apologizing, said, 'Liddie, I am so sorry. I didn't mean to alarm you. Don't you feel anything toward me? I have been drawn to you ever since that first encounter over Miss Austen so many months ago.'

"Liddie, who now was softly crying, replied, 'Master Newby, you have been so kind to me. How can I repay your kindness by wounding Mrs. Newby? She is the one who should be receiving your caresses.'

"'But, Liddie it is you I love. I would be a liar to say anything else. You and I are bound together with a chain whose many and varied links transcend the normal relationship between master and slave or between the African and European. We are two kindred spirits. Our shared love of books is only part of this reality.'

"Liddie could only respond through her tears, 'Oh Master. . .' as she ran from the room.

Chapter Twenty-Eight

"For the next four weeks, Liddie did everything she possibly could to avoid contact with my father. When she was in his presence, she would maintain silence and keep her eyes focused on the floor. She felt acutely the loss of those magical times on Sundays, which had been spent in the library with Horton and his books. Her self-enforced isolation allowed her to reflect on her situation and to more closely observe the relationship between her master and his wife. It was obvious to her that Mrs. Newby did not at all understand her husband and from the way they interacted, even in front of their servants, that there was considerable tension between them.

"As she reflected on her own situation, she realized as time passed that Horton was correct in his surmise about her feelings for him. She did love him, and yet she could also fully appreciate in what a cursed state she now found herself. There she was, a poor African slave, much too educated for her own good, trapped within an attractive black body while yearning to be a demure Austen heroine, and in love with a married man who could have his way with her as easily as sell her to another. What was she to do?

"One evening when Mrs. Newby was away for several days visiting her family and after Horton had apparently retired for the night, Liddie crept into the library in search of a book. Her self-inflicted isolation had included an interdiction on visits to the library. Now that four weeks had passed since her last visit, her desire for something to read had overwhelmed her fear of an encounter with Horton.

"As she entered the room, holding a candle as her sole source of light, she was surprised to see that the fire was still blazing in the grate and was alarmed when she could recognize a very familiar figure sitting quietly in a large wingback chair whose silhouette was outlined in the firelight. Before she could beat a hasty retreat, Horton spoke.

"'Liddie please forgive me. I knew if I couldn't draw you to me, that eventually the books would. It seems like the past four weeks have been utterly devoid of life. The books in this library are nothing more than dead objects without your presence.

I cannot begin to tell you how much I miss our reading and conversations together. Please, tell me honestly, from your heart, that you have at least some small regard for me.'

"As a solitary tear glistened, running down her cheek in the candlelight, Liddie replied through quavering lips, 'Oh Master Newby, you know that I love you. But I must not love you, a married man.' Liddie continued with a note of bitterness in her voice, 'As my master, of course, you can force your attentions on me. Even if you were to divorce your wife, the law would never sanction our marriage.'

"Horton interrupted with passion in his voice, 'Liddie, I would never force my attentions on you. I am more your slave than you mine. My love for you transcends all the external distinctions of our physical existence.'

"'To my own condemnation, I believe you. But the painful truth remains that I am your property and any children we may have together will also be your property. Promise me, give me your solemn promise, Master Newby . . . I guess that I may now call you Horton, that you will free our children and me no later than the first child's eighteenth birthday.'

"Horton rose from his chair and, kneeling before Liddie, clasped her feet and declared, 'Dear Liddie, I promise with all my soul that our children will be raised and educated with all the privileges of my rank as a planter and I will emancipate you and your children, as you have requested, on the eighteenth birthday of the first child.'

"And so, my mother freely gave that hidden portion of herself, which her master did not possess by right of ownership, her love, to that same master, my father.

"It did not take long for Malvina Newby to discover that some major changes had occurred in the relationship between Liddie and her husband. Whereas Horton had been for the most part indifferent to the domestic servants on the Newby plantation, delegating their management to Malvina, he began to be overly solicitous to the young parlormaid.

"One day, several weeks later, when Liddie had completed her duties much more slowly than usual, Malvina took a switch and began to beat her for laziness. Hearing her cries, Horton came quickly, grabbed the switch out of Malvina's hand, and said, 'Woman, if you ever so much as lay a hand on her again, I will apply this same switch to your back! Can't you see that she has the morning sickness? Liddie, you are relieved of your duties for the rest of the day.'

"Malvina was none too pleased at this interference by her husband in the domestic sphere and let him know it. 'Horton, it has always been customary on a plantation for the mistress to assume authority over the household. How dare you threaten me or infringe on my authority, especially in front of the servants!'

"'I apologize for my intervention in your management of the servants, but you must accept this as a special exception from now on.'

"From that time, Malvina watched Liddie and her husband very closely. She quickly had her suspicions confirmed when she overheard the other servants tittering about Liddie and the master. She was disgusted but accepted the fact of her husband's slave mistress, having been all too familiar with the practice from witnessing her mother's acquiescence in the face of her own father's and brothers' behavior. Having a personal distaste for marital relations, she hoped that Liddie could satisfy her husband's needs and spare her the bother.

"What began to distress her was Horton's treatment of Liddie in front of the other servants. As Liddie's belly began to swell, he would go out of his way to compliment her on her beauty and even pat her abdomen affectionately. After witnessing such a display, Malvina remonstrated Horton in private.

"'Your behavior with Liddie in front of the other servants and especially in front of me, is uncouth and frankly despicable. What you do with the slave in private to satisfy your needs is your affair, but I object most strenuously to these open displays of affection in public.'

"Horton replied, 'How can I do otherwise in the presence of the woman I love?'

"'The woman you love? Humbug! Pure animal lust, unalloyed with anything higher, is what you feel for that nigger! Love is about responsibility and that responsibility lies elsewhere, with your lawful wife and daughter.'

"'Malvina, you are trying my patience. I would not quibble with your partial definition of love, for indeed it is grounded in responsibility, but there is so much more that you cannot begin to understand. The responsibility I feel in my love for you and Julia will not impede the equal sense of responsibility that I bear in my love for Liddie and our child.'

"Thus, the battle lines were drawn before my birth as my father pressed the boundaries of Southern propriety. I was born in 1830, almost two years after my half-sister Julia. My mulatto complexion was the final nettlesome confirmation for Malvina of my father's role, not that he made any pretense of hiding it. Indeed, I was doted on from the beginning. Horton insisted that Liddie be freed of any further domestic duties and purchased a slave to serve as her personal body servant.

"My earliest memories of my father were only positive. He was affectionate and kind, but would also discipline me when I was naughty. The living arrangements in the plantation house were a bit of a mystery to me for several years. My mother and I (and later my sister) occupied one portion of the mansion, while Malvina and Julia occupied the other. Only my father seemed to be able to migrate safely and freely between both regions. Notwithstanding all of Malvina's objections, Julia and I, from an early age, were playmates in the neutral territory known as the nursery. I was blessed with a bright mind and quick intelligence, which were sources of delight to my parents but additional irritants to Malvina. I began to read at the early age of three and was already reading with greater success than my five-year-old half-sister. Although my parents spoiled me, I remain grateful to both of them for the disciplined approach to learning that they introduced in my routine from an early age. Horton spared no expense in obtaining first-rate tutors for his children. Of his three children and as his only son, my scholarly abilities were a real source of pride to him. He strove to give me the best classical education possible through the efforts of the tutors in combination with his own careful supervision.

"As I approached my fourteenth year, my father told me that he was quite satisfied with my academic preparation to date and that if it were possible, I was well prepared to matriculate at his alma mater, the next year. Ah yes, *if it were possible*. I had been sufficiently sheltered during my childhood that I didn't quite realize that no manner of education, however great, could ever wipe away the ancestral curse of my African heritage. There were a few instances, of course, when I was younger that I perceived there might be a problem.

"Just before Julia, at the age of twelve, refused to play with me any more, Julia, Livia, my six-year old sister, and I would frequently play together out in the yard behind the mansion. Inevitably, we made contact with the other children from the slave quarters and learned the slave dialect sufficiently to facilitate our games together. After being knocked down and receiving a bloody nose in a fight, in the proud innocence of a spoiled child, I declared to the miscreants who had wounded me, 'you shouldn't treat me that way. I'm the son of Master Horton.' The quick response was hearty laughter as they pointed out in crude but accurate terms that 'you jes' anudder nigger like us. Ain't you eber look at yo'self in a mirror?' Quickly seeking justification and confirmation of my exalted state, I turned to Julia and said, 'Julia, tell them I'm not a nigger.'

"'But that is exactly what Livia and you are. Niggers, plain and simple.'

"And with that revelation from my half-sister, my cherished assumptions about my place in the universe were destroyed. So, although I felt understandable pride at my father's declaration that I was nearly ready for Princeton, I realized that Princeton wasn't ready for me.

"As Julia approached the age at which young ladies of the planter class are displayed socially, the tensions in the household rose to new heights. Malvina was increasingly frustrated and angry that Horton's *unusual living arrangement*, as the openly adulterous relationship with his slave mistress in the same house with his white wife came to be known in the surrounding community, prevented them from hosting any social events to highlight Julia's coming out. Horton tried to reassure her that he would make sure Julia attended all the other social events hosted at the neighboring plantations once she turned fourteen.

"'Whether we host social occasions here or not, seems to me to be entirely irrelevant. After all,' he was fond of pointing out, 'I do possess one of the largest plantations in this part of Kentucky, which will certainly pique the interest of many a suitor when he considers that Julia is the sole heir.'

"Julia, for her part, was mortified by the attention lavished by her father on his nigger children. Malvina had taught her well. The abrupt change in our relationship still surprises me when I think of it. I cherish many fond memories of playing with her in the nursery up until that fateful day when my real status was confirmed from her own mouth.

"Julia, though not considered a beauty, had delicate, even features, auburn hair, a slight figure, and on a good day a winsome smile. Unfortunately, she had a weak constitution and was sickly from an early age. As she acquired increasing doses of her mother's sense of injustice and wounded pride, her good days diminished proportionately so that it became a rare day, indeed, that her lovely smile would once again grace her lips. At first, I grieved the loss of my playmate, but by way of compensation shifted my focus toward more scholarly activities while my younger sister Livia began to command a part of my attention.

"Livia was as robust and vivacious as Julia was weak and retiring. I'm afraid she was even more spoiled than me. She had many of the charming qualities of my mother, which endeared her to my father but also made it very difficult for him to say no to her caprices. Although she also had a quick mind, it was more often applied toward avoiding the acquisition of knowledge than its pursuit. In spite of this proclivity toward play at the expense of learning, Livia progressed in her education so that before we were separated from each other at age ten, she could read and write tolerably well.

"Now I must turn to the part of my story that started the whole chain of events, which ultimately culminated in my escape from slavery to find a small paradise in Indiana only to be forcibly returned to bondage and yet escape again to be sharing the tale with you here tonight. As I mentioned earlier, Julia was sickly. Before she could attend many cotillions and other less august social gatherings, her health took a turn for the worse. It seemed as if every minor ailment that wafted through the plantation threatened her very existence. Invariably, what might manifest itself as a sore throat and runny nose in the rest of the household would put Julia in bed for a week. My father called in various physicians, each with a different opinion. Some recommended bleeding or at least the generous use of purgatives to cleanse her system. Others recommended strange dietary interventions while still others spoke vaguely about the need for more rest. My father became increasingly frantic and irritated with such vague expostulations.

"'The poor girl has been in bed for the past week, getting weaker by the day and you advise more bedrest?' he half-shouted at one physician with venomous sarcasm.

"Then, inexplicably, Julia got better despite the ministrations of the medical profession. She began to get out of bed, take small walks, regained an appetite, and even smiled briefly in my direction. At least that is what Livia insisted on reporting to me, even though my attempts to visit Julia and express my concern for her were uniformly rebuffed by Malvina, who now guarded her daughter more like a jailer than a mother.

"Over the next two years Julia's health waxed and waned. She was even able to attend a cotillion, although her energy was largely spent after two dances. My father, who had proportionately focused more of his time and attentions on me than on his two daughters, realizing his error, began to be more attentive to Julia, who warmed to his presence even as she declined further in health. During her periods of convalescence, he spent many hours reading at her bedside, trying in every way to cheer her into better health. He even chided her gently about her rejection of Livia and me. Her response was telling. She complained bitterly of the pain that he had caused her mother and her by openly flouting his relationship with his slave mistress in which he showered so much of his affection on her progeny.

"'Papa, you have wounded Mama and me deeply by treating those niggers like normal people.'

"Initially, he protested that the members of his slave family were normal people. But, when he saw that his arguments in defense of Liddie and her children only heightened Julia's agitation, he desisted and tried to avoid the topic in the future.

"As Horton grieved over the decline of his eldest child, he became more pensive, seeking relief from his conflicting thoughts by putting more energy into the management of the plantation. Liddie, who noted the change in his behavior with apprehension, expressed her sincere desire to help. Horton could only peer into her eyes with a sense of helplessness and say, 'Liddie, dear, I must work through this pain on my own.' Liddie protested that she could not help but share in his pain out of her love for him. His response was only to say, 'I created this pain, I must bear it alone.'

"Shortly after Julia's sixteenth birthday, her condition worsened such that she was now spending most of her time in bed. Horton alternated taking turns with Malvina and Jenny, Malvina's personal maid, in keeping vigil at Julia's bedside. Jenny, who was quite religious, told Julia of the exciting changes occurring among the slaves on the plantation as a result of a revival that had been going on nearby.

"'Why Miss Julia, eben dat ol' sinnah, Harry got religion. He done gib up likker fo' good, or at least fo' de past week. De Speerit jes' grab de sinnahs dere an' throw dem to de ground. God's power's dere fo' all to see!'

"Despite all the comforting denials to the contrary from both Malvina and my father, Julia recognized that she would not get better. Jenny was the only one of her attendants that did not interrupt her or change the subject when Julia would begin to speak of her mortality. Jenny would listen sympathetically, nod her head and say, 'Miss Julia, dats de way o' dis misrabul an' sor'ful world. But, if'n a po' sinnah git saved, den de Lawd Hisself will come to dat sinnah when he die an' grab 'im away fum de debbil an' say, "dis one mine, he saved by mah blood. You cain't hab 'im. I's takin 'im home wif me to de pearly manshuns!"'

"'Oh Jenny, I wish I had your simple faith and could die in such hope,' Julia cried as she grasped the old slave's hand tightly.

"'But Miss Julia, you kin hab de bressed hope!' exclaimed Jenny. 'Dere's nuthin keepin' you fum goin' to de rebibal.'

"'But Jenny, mother doesn't approve of revivals. Presbyterians just don't go to revivals.'

"Jenny gave Julia a sorrowful, questioning look that was mixed with pity and replied, 'Den how dey eber gonna git saved?' But before Julia could attempt to answer her question, she added, 'But Miss Julia, Massa Newby would take you. I knows he would do anyting fo' you.'

"Later that evening during Horton's time to keep vigil with his daughter, Julia gave her father a look filled with the intensity of chronic suffering. With a worried smile he responded, 'What is it my dear? Are you in pain?'

"Pointing to her heart, Julia replied, 'No father, I am physically comfortable. My pain is of a deeper sort. It is here in my soul. I want to find peace with God before I die.'

"'Oh, dear one, don't speak of death. You will recover, I am certain of it.'

"'Stop father! You know as well as I do that I will not recover, that indeed I am dying. I have been speaking with Jenny and she has urged me to attend the local revival to find peace before I die. I know that mother would not approve, but I ask you to lay aside all your cynicism and take me to the revival. For I fear not only for my own soul, but I also fear greatly for yours, father. What if the Methodists are right that we are more responsible for our choices and ultimately our salvation than we would like to admit?'

"'Ah, you speak of the doctrines of Arminius. Yes, they are a very interesting contrast to orthodox Calvinism.'

"'Father, please listen to me. I am not interested in debating the fine points of doctrine with you. I want to prepare for my death.'

"As Horton's eyes met his daughter's intense gaze, he encountered a gravity there that frightened him. 'Of course, Julia, I will take you tomorrow, if you feel well enough.'

"'Thank you, father. Now I must speak plainly with you of the fears and hopes of a dying daughter. Before I die, I hope to see you and Mama reconciled. Can you not see how much you have wounded her with this shameful relationship that you persist in having with Liddie?'

"'I see, dear one, that you advocate very effectively on behalf of your mother and that I have caused you deep pain for which I am very sorry. Regarding Liddie, Tiberius, and Livia, if I have sinned, it is in that I have not been able to set a total boundary around my love for you and your mother. Perhaps I have loved indiscriminately, and too much.'

"'Father, can you with certainty identify as love actions which have not only wounded those to whom you are bound through holy matrimony but also those tangled within your net of desire? You have elevated the slave Liddie and her children to a condition that can only lead to their suffering. Her children think of themselves as the children of a Southern planter, and indeed they are: the *slave* children of a Southern planter with no rights that will ever be respected by the laws of Kentucky. You create false expectations in their minds and that of their mother while trampling on the dignity of your actual wife and daughter.

"And now I must speak of my fears. If Jenny is right, I want more than anything to die in the knowledge that not just I but my whole family has been saved. That is why you must take me to the revival with an open heart, father. It is not too late for a convinced skeptic to find salvation,' Julia said as tears were streaming down her face.

"As tears also welled up in his eyes, Horton declared with fervor, 'Oh Julia, if my being saved could bring you peace and joy, I pray that such a miracle will happen!'

"Clasping her hand with both his hands, he moistened it with his tears."

"The revival was being co-sponsored by both the local Methodist and Baptist communities. Rather than competing directly with each other for the souls of local sinners, a truce of sorts had been declared among the local Methodist and Baptist clergy 'to achieve harmony in the Lord's vineyard,' as one of the Methodist ministers described it. This, of course, did not mean that the truce extended to other denominations. After all, many Episcopalians and Presbyterians in the county, besides Horton and Julia, were in desperate need of being saved and they were all fair game. In terms of bragging rights, the Baptists knew they would likely save more souls, because there was a decided preference among slaves for baptism by immersion over the less robust sprinkling of the other denominations.

"My father urged Malvina to join Julia and him in attending the revival, but she refused, reminding both of them that serious Presbyterians did not attend such festivals of profligate emotionalism. He then invited my mother, Livia, and me to attend but insisted that we follow in another carriage, which I now assume was to avoid upsetting Julia, but at the time seemed strange to Livia and me, since we had traveled in public around the county and in Northern Kentucky in the same carriage with our father on many prior occasions. My mother, who seemed uncharacteristically anxious, ushered us toward the seating in the negro section of the large tent. I had usually been able to avoid this situation because of my father's unconventional insistence on having his mulatto children and slave mistress sit with him in public, which typically entailed sitting apart from everybody else. So, on this occasion, I felt abandoned and to some degree humiliated having to sit with my dirty and uncouth African cousins. From our seats, we had a good view of the proceedings as well as of my father and half-sister. Julia appeared quite flushed; whether from the excitement of the moment or the onset of another fever, we could not tell.

"'Brothers and sisters,' a tall, wiry white man, a real frontier preacher, began to address the crowd of three thousand distressed souls, as he roamed back and forth on the podium at the front of the tent. 'Why have you come this evening? Are ye here fleein' from the wrath to come? Yes, I expect so. Felt the flames lickin' at your feet did ye? It kin git purty hot out there in the world. Well how else do ye think the Savior kin git our attention? He just lets that ol' Devil tempt us to do some tomfoolery and before we know it, we're in a heap o' trouble.'

"'Now I bet ye wanna say, "well that ain't fair o' God to let ol' Scratch git us into trouble." But ask yerselves this, brothers and sisters: How many of us would give God a second thought, if everythin' were goin' right? Now don't ever think that your station in this life is gonna protect you from that fire. No sirree, the Good Book is right clear on that point. The Apostle Paul himself says, "There is neither Jew nor Greek, there is neither bond nor free, there is neither male nor female: for ye are all one in Christ Jesus." Yes, masters, he's talkin' to you. Yes, slaves, he's talkin' to you: *neither bond nor free.* For our colored friends out there, "bond" means "slave." So, before the throne of God Almighty what station ye happen to occupy in this life don't amount to nothin'.'

"A resounding 'Amen!' coming from the negro section briefly interrupted the preacher, who smiled and continued.

"'The Good Lord ain't worried if you were a slave or a rich planter in this life. No, but He's a heap worried about the kind o' life that slave or planter lived, what kind o' choices he made. Ye see brothers and sisters, it ain't so important what we're fleein' from, it's who we're fleeing to that matters. Yes, our feet feel the heat so that we will run for our lives, run to the Source of life. I hope and pray with all my soul that some of you—no, all of you—will give your hearts to Jesus. I don't mean tomorrah or mebbe someday, depending on the weather. No! I mean tonight, right now. Let his mercy touch you and melt your hearts of stone! Now let us sing together:

> On Jordan's stormy banks I stand,
> And cast a wishful eye
> To Canaan's fair and happy land,
> Where my possessions lie.
> I am bound for the promised land,
> I am bound for the promised land;
> Oh, who will come and go with me?
> I am bound for the promised land . . .

"The crowd became very animated as they sang the hymn following the preacher's message. But no one was more animated than my half-sister. Julia sang with more than great enthusiasm. With tears rolling down her cheeks, she sang with conviction, the conviction of one who was already there, standing on Jordan's stormy bank. It was clear to me at that moment that my father was overwhelmed by the sheer power and force of his dying daughter's conviction. Julia clutched Horton's arm as they began to sing the third stanza, which, as she fixed her eyes on his, he felt compelled to also sing:

> No chilling winds or poisonous breath
> Can reach that healthful shore;

> Sickness and sorrow, pain and death,
> Are felt and feared no more.
> I am bound for the promised land,
> I am bound for the promised land;
> Oh, who will come and go with me?
> I am bound for the promised land.

"Julia poured out her soul into that song and with it her energy. She collapsed in her father's arms, her fevered brow resting on his chest. He carried her from the tent, motioning for us to follow, and thus our revival abruptly ended as we returned home with my dying half-sister.

"Reluctantly, in his desperation, Horton called again for the physicians, as Julia was consumed by a high fever, her rare lucid moments swallowed up in a sea of delirium. A consensus of sorts was achieved among the medical savants that Julia was in the advanced stages of pneumonia and that her remaining time in this life was limited to no more than a few days at most. Horton, Malvina, and the slave Jenny resumed their bedside vigil, mopping the sweat from Julia's forehead, moistening her lips with small amounts of water, and holding her hand. Horton even began to exercise a long-neglected gift of song and softly sang hymns to Julia, his voice breaking at times in his grief.

"Near midnight on the third night after attending the revival, Julia slowly awakened as Horton finished singing the final stanza of "What Wondrous Love Is This":

> And when from death I'm free, I'll sing on, I'll sing on;
> And when from death I'm free, I'll sing on.
> And when from death I'm free
> I'll sing His love for me,
> And through eternity I'll sing on, I'll sing on,
> And through eternity I'll sing on.

"Smiling weakly, she said, 'Thank you Papa. Amid all my strange and frightening dreams, I could still hear your voice singing hymns and I knew that God was near.' Suddenly, struggling to raise herself up in bed, she spoke in sober tones, 'Papa, please call Mama, Jenny, Tiberius, Livia, and Liddie here. I must say goodbye to each of them and ask their forgiveness before I depart.'

"Shadows dancing on the walls cast by the flickering light of Jenny's candle were the wraiths that guided us to Julia. In our sleepiness, Livia and I were struggling to leave the world of dreams only to wake to a living nightmare. As we turned a corner, my mother's face was illuminated for one brief moment, revealing an expression of profound sorrow that made me gasp involuntarily and anxiously ask, 'Mother, are you so sad because Julia is suffering? Is she dying?'

"'Oh, my dear Tiberius and Livia! Yes, I am truly sad that Julia is suffering, and her death is approaching very soon. But I fear that her suffering and death are yet the beginning of greater suffering that will afflict all those whom I love.'

"Jenny ushered us into a room lit by several candelabra, which I learned later had been brought at Julia's request. She had asked Jenny to 'lighten the darkness, so that I may see each person clearly.' The dominant feature of the room was the large four-poster bed that was enshrouded with a canopy and curtains of red velvet. The curtain nearest the door was pulled back, revealing the slight form of my half-sister and my father, sitting at her side, his face wet with tears. Standing stiffly beside her husband, Malvina's face was even paler than usual and was utterly devoid of emotion. No tear moistened her cheek. Her eyes seemed fixed on infinity. The only acknowledgment of our entrance was a slight disdainful curling of the lips, which passed fleetingly, a small wave in an otherwise silent ocean.

"'Papa, is everyone here?'

"'Yes, my dear one.'

"'Please come closer. I want to see each of you.'

"Only death's embrace could gather my father's two families in one room with such intimacy. Two families which had for so many years coexisted uneasily under the same roof but within their own defined domains.

"Turning to Jenny, Julia directed her first remarks to the faithful old servant, 'Oh Jenny, I have felt God's mercy and love ever since you spoke of the revival. It was as if He was speaking directly to me through your love and concern. I am so thankful that Papa was with me and that Tiberius, Livia, and Liddie were also present to hear the preacher's message. For the last several days I have been standing on Jordan's stormy banks waiting to make my crossing. But, one unfinished task has prevented my departure for that distant shore.'

"'Livia, would you come and give your half-sister a last kiss? Please forgive me for the wounds and sorrow that I have caused you.' Without any hesitation, Livia rushed forward and, embracing Julia, kissed her on the cheek and through tears said, 'Of course I forgive you, dear sister.'

"My turn was next as Julia looked at me expectantly. I approached more hesitantly, but Julia reached out and pulled me into her embrace. 'Oh Tiberius, the dear playmate of my childhood, please forgive me for the sorrow I have caused you.'

"Overcome with emotion, all I could say was, 'Dear Julia, I love you and will miss you greatly.'

"Julia quickly responded, 'But Tiberius, don't grieve, because we will see each other again in a far happier place where there is neither slave nor free, for we will all be one in Christ.'

"Looking next to my mother, she said, 'Please, Liddie, come hold my hand. I forgive you for all the sorrow you have caused Mama and me. Please forgive me for the hateful feelings I have harbored toward you.'

"My mother clasped Julia's hand in hers, nodded her head in assent, and wept gentle tears not only for the dying girl but in anticipation of the misery to come, which she, but not her children or their father, could yet appreciate.

"'The suffering in this household has come about because of an impatience with God's ways,' Julia said as her face became flushed with emotion. 'I implore you all to accept your different roles in this life as they have been ordained by God. Yes, there still are slaves and free in this imperfect world, while our hope has always resided in the next where all the barriers that separate us will be no more. Is it not possible to restore a normal home life, father and mother? Can you not once more be a husband and wife who love each other fully without compromise?'

"'Liddie, Tiberius and Livia, can you not see that the life you have lived in this house has been nothing more than a sham? Your hope lies not in this life but the next.'

"'Papa, can you not see that your youthful passion has committed these three souls to a life of suffering? Although the changes you must make will be extremely painful, I am convinced that in that very suffering you will find healing and redemption.'

"Silently, my mother gathered Livia and me, drawing us away from Julia's bedside toward the door to her room. Before we left the room, Julia could be heard saying to my father, 'Promise me, Papa, that you will restore the proper relationships in this house, that you will honor Mama and no longer humiliate her by your adultery.'

"As if struck by a hard blow to the back, my mother staggered when the response came, a soft but clearly audible, 'I promise.'

"Recovering quickly, she dragged Livia and me out of the room, down the stairs, and across the main hall back to her room on the opposite side of the mansion, shutting and locking the door behind her. Trying her best to suppress sobs she spoke haltingly in a whisper as she held us close to her.

"'Oh, my dear children, please forgive me. I believe your half-sister's prediction is correct that great suffering will come to us. In my love for your father, I have hoped for too much. The dying can place great demands upon the living. It is their prerogative and your dying sister has seized this opportunity to restore what she sees as the proper order of nature.' Kissing both of us on the forehead, she added, 'Neither of my beautiful children are prepared for what I fear they will soon experience.'

"'What do you mean, Mother, by *proper order of nature*?' Livia asked, a puzzled look on her face.

"'In Julia's mind, or at least her mind under the influence of her mother, the proper order of nature is a delicate way of saying that negroes will never be the equal of white people, that it is in their nature to be slaves and nothing more in this life.'

"'But Julia spoke of there being neither slave nor free, that we are all one in Christ.'

"'Yes. I believe she is truly sincere in her belief and the love she has expressed for both of you and even in her desire to forgive me. But she was also clear in stating her belief that the fulfillment of the vision of oneness in Christ occurs in the next life.'

"I interrupted at this point and said, 'But, Mother, the original Greek speaks in the present tense, not the future.'

"Stroking my hair with her right hand and looking sadly into my eyes, she replied, 'Tiberius, I think that just about sums up the relationship between master and slave. The master extorts service from the slave in the present while promising peace and joy in the future, a future to be found only beyond the grave.'

"Oh, how poorly I understood the inextricable link that exists between death and life! In death, my half-sister gave sharp definition to my life and to the lives of all who were, through the gravitational pull of affection and blood, within her orbit.

"According to Jenny, after extracting the fateful promise from my father, Julia lapsed into a feverish sleep. About five in the morning, Jenny, who was keeping vigil, was awakened to hear a wide-eyed Julia, who was staring intently at a point on the opposite wall, cry out, 'Is that you Auntie Bea? But I don't know how to swim. Yes, yes, of course I trust you. I am coming!'

"Those were her last words.

"Auntie Bea was the slave cook who had doted on Julia, Livia, and me when we were younger. She had died two years earlier. Jenny told me that when she reported Julia's last words to Malvina, her only response was, 'Oh, she died in delirium.'

"When my father heard Jenny's report, he responded by looking upward and saying, 'Auntie Bea please take care of my Julia.'"

"Later that morning I was called to my father's library, where all the tangled relationships of the Newby plantation began, for a private discussion. My father looked haggard from sleepless nights and intense grief. 'Oh Tiberius, how I miss Julia!' he said through fresh tears.

"We embraced as I replied, my voice breaking, 'I also miss her very much. Perhaps Auntie Bea really did escort her across that last river and she is now in a place of joy and peace.'

"Looking directly into my eyes with an intense, almost hungry expression, he said, 'Tiberius, I hope so with all my heart. I hope so. If only I could overcome my doubts. I crave the peace that your sister clearly had . . . I mean has.'

"My father then proceeded in a meandering fashion to make a confession of sorts. He told me of his early life, his skepticism, his mother's disappointed wishes for him, his relationship with the young slave woman before his departure for Princeton, including the revelation that Julia, Livia, and I had a half-brother named Cicero who was one of the field hands.

"I stopped him at this point in his narrative and asked, 'Why did you treat Livia and me differently from Cicero?'

"Horton gave me another sad look and replied, 'Tiberius, your mother is the love of my life. I was now the master and not the master's errant son as in the case of poor Cicero. I could impose my will in my kingdom, otherwise known as the Newby plantation, and I did just that. I didn't give a fig about social conventions. The deeper moral questions I had rationalized by reassuring my conscience that I would always treat my legal wife and daughter well, respecting their needs and interests, while it was only right that I should also be able to truly love your mother and her children, including treating them with the same care as I gave Julia.

"But Julia's illness, suffering, and death have forced me to take a long penetrating look into the mirror of my conscience. All that I can see is that I have caused untold suffering in Julia's and Malvina's lives while setting a foundation for inevitable suffering in my slave family. I have placed your mother, Livia, and you in a state of limbo, never to fully realize the privileges of the planter class, always to be frustrated in your hopes, but also never to be accepted by your African brothers and sisters. For this sin, I shall spend eternity in the second circle of hell, forever buffeted by the wailing winds of lust, yearning for the illusive vision of what I thought I had. What my pilgrimage with Julia in her suffering has taught me is that I should do all I can to make things right.'

"'I think that *making things right* is what Mother described as restoring the *proper order of nature*, which translated means negroes will never be the equals of white people. Is this what you mean, Father?' I asked bitterly.

"'When did she speak of this to you?'

"'Last night, after we said goodbye to Julia, she became quite anxious and expressed her concern for our future.'

"My father cradled his forehead in his hands and groaned deeply. 'How can I convince you that this is the reality you must accept in this life?'

"'Why then did you ever show me another reality? Why did you introduce me to the world of learning and ideas?'

"'It was my folly and hubris. Please forgive me.'

"'Forgive you for giving me a good education? Never! Father, are you mad? Is it not clear to you that I have considerable intellectual gifts, which you have helped develop? How can that be folly and hubris?'

"'But all that learning will ill prepare you for the reality of slavery.'

"'And why must slavery be my destiny?'

"'I have pondered and struggled with this question for a long time. How can a mere accident of birth condemn a man to a particular fate? I resisted it, passionately resisted all the orthodox Calvinisim that was infused into me by my mother. Livia, you, and the other children borne by my dear Liddie who did not survive infancy, are products of that resistance. Peering into the face of death with Julia has forced me to finally submit to that terrible logic. My children by Liddie are by nature slaves, and I have fought a futile battle against reality making claims to the contrary.'

"'Father, I just don't understand. What are you planning to do with us?'

"'Averting his gaze from mine and focusing on a spot on the carpet in front of the fireplace, he replied in a soft monotone, 'I promised Julia on her deathbed that I would make things right between her mother and me. Malvina agreed to reconciliation on two conditions: the first being that I immediately transfer ownership of you to her and the second that I sell your mother and Livia, thus effectively separating myself from those I love the most in the world.'

"'Father, please don't act in haste. Surely, your grief is speaking in this decision. You will only regret such drastic actions.'

"'But, son, can't you understand that this is for your salvation, for the salvation of your dear mother and sister, as well?'

"'Are you saying that forcing us to suffer will save us? Don't we have any choice in the matter?'

"With tears in his voice, my father replied, 'This is the terrible reality we must face together. Neither of us, nor your mother or sister, have a choice in the matter. The only choice we may have is how we respond to this terrible calamity. Can we accept it patiently and endure, or will we resist the inevitable?'

"This was the last conversation I had with my father.

"Another similar conversation between my father and mother occurred in the library shortly after I left. Livia and I quietly eavesdropped outside. Most of the conversation was distorted by the overflowing of emotion and tears, but one part I will never forget. My mother had become quite agitated and cried out, 'Horton, you solemnly promised me before we came together that you would free my children and me on the eighteenth birthday of my firstborn child. Have you forgotten this promise? Malvina will work out her revenge on our son. Do you really want that?'

"'No Liddie, you are mistaken. I don't believe she bears him any ill will. She feels she can help him make the transition to agricultural work more easily than I can, and I think she is correct. Don't you remember that I told you long ago how when Malvina and I were married, she learned of my first slave son, Cicero, a product of my youthful passion, and how she requested that I transfer his ownership to her shortly thereafter? She has treated Cicero very well since.'

"'Yes. I should have taken that as a warning of what was to come. You say that I am the love of your life and yet you plan to sell Livia and me down the river. You might as well kill us now!'

"At this point I put my arms around Livia and directed her back to her room so that her sobbing would not be heard. I closed the door to her room and held her in my arms, rocking back and forth, both of us crying bitter tears. After what might have been an eternity of sorrow shared by two siblings, we felt the additional embrace of our mother, which only intensified our wailing and tears. Finally, she pulled us apart and spoke in earnest, sober tones, searching out our souls with her eyes.

"'My dear children, I again must beg your forgiveness for bringing you into this world of suffering. I am a weak and sinful woman, who still loves your father despite his betrayal. I believe he loves us very much but is so deranged by grief for Julia that he is making cruel decisions he is convinced are kind, even righteous, and which he believes will save our souls. I hope that he is right, but all I can see at this moment is the great suffering that will fall upon us because of his actions. We have little time left together, I fear.

"Tiberius, I cannot begin to say how proud I am to be your mother. My prayer for you is to endure and find the freedom you should have received at birth. Your intellectual gifts and learning will ultimately be a blessing to you and others.

"Livia, my sweet child, my comfort and joy, I will do everything I can to prevent us being separated. My love for both of you is undying and I hope that we might meet again in this life in a place where there is neither bond nor free but where all are one in the freedom of God's mercy.'

"My mother was right. That was to be our last meeting. The tread of boots on the wood floor outside our door announced the beginning of my *higher education* in the form of the newly hired overseer, whom some of you have met in the courtroom in Richmond. I might have been well prepared to attend Princeton as my father had so recently opined, but I was not at all prepared for my first meeting with Thomas Blavey that afternoon.

"'Where's the uppity young nigger buck?'

"'In there, Mr. Blavey,' the voice of Malvina Newby, my new mistress, could be heard saying.

"In response to loud banging on the door, I reflexively got up and opened the door. The overseer rushed in, grabbed my arms, and pinioned them behind my back before I realized what was happening. Handcuffs were applied, and then, unlike Moses, who willingly left the house of Pharoah's daughter, I was dragged kicking and screaming from the room with my sister and mother clinging to me. Once he had separated me from my family, Blavey pushed a revolver into my ribs and ordered 'git movin' now, nigger!'

"I passed my new mistress, who in her state of fresh grief still managed to have a very satisfied expression on her face. At the foot of the stairs in the entryway stood my father with a helpless look of sorrow on his face. Unable to restrain myself, I cried out, 'Father, Father!' But there was no response.

"Before being forced out the front door, I shouted back, '*Absens haeres non erit!* You think 'out of sight out of mind,' but I assure you, Father, that I will haunt your thoughts. You will find no rest or peace by what you have done.'

"Blavey paused, looking back for direction from Malvina. Looking up at him, she replied to his implied question, 'Yes, you may discipline him.'

"'Yes, Ma'am, it'll be my pleasure,' was the reply from the enthusiastic overseer while my father groaned audibly, turned around, and fled upstairs.

"Wasting no time, Blavey directed me toward the Quarters to a whipping post, which I had largely ignored in my earlier life of privilege but with which I was soon to become intimately acquainted. In what would become a familiar pattern, I was ordered to strip to the waist after the handcuffs had been removed.

"As Blavey was about to tie my hands together around the whipping post, I heard a familiar voice shout, 'Wait! I don't want you damaging those valuable clothes. Have him strip completely and then administer the punishment for his insolence to Mr. Newby. Here is some clothing that is appropriate for his station.'

"And having said this, Malvina handed Blavey some coarse garments made from the *negro cloth*, typically worn by slaves. I had very little idea of pain before that day but was rapidly educated in a topic that had been largely of theoretical interest to me before. My practical experience of living had begun. As I knelt, naked, with my arms tied around the whipping post, I was not sure what to expect but resolved in youthful pride that I would show no emotion that might gratify my new mistress, who stood close by, watching with interest as Blavey prepared for the whipping.

"At Malvina's bidding, Blavey rounded up the slaves working in fields close by the mansion so that they might witness the spectacle. In some of the faces I recognized former playmates that Julia and I had played with a few years before. Everyone stared impassively ahead, almost as if I didn't exist, while Blavey readied himself and then applied the first lash. I involuntarily yelped at the sudden pain, a sharp searing pain that in its reality beggared any descriptions I had read in books. I tried to steady myself and anticipate the pain as it came with further lashes.

"For a while, I thought I had the upper hand in my battle with Malvina as Blavey counted off the lashes. But, as he approached twenty lashes, I found myself thinking, 'Surely he will stop soon,' and that was my undoing. The hope for the lashing to cease became an all-consuming desire and before I knew it, I was begging and pleading for mercy. The rate of lashing decreased a little, which increased my hope, but I then perceived in my pain that Malvina had motioned to Blavey to reduce the rate so that I might be able to fully savor the vision of my mother's and sister's anguish as they were being dragged away from the mansion by a slave trader to be sold south.

"My mother and sister caught sight of me in my naked and bleeding state and cried all the more loudly for me by name, 'Tiberius, Tiberius! Please, Mrs. Newby have mercy!'

"Malvina was deaf to their cries as she motioned first to the slave trader to load up his cargo and then to Blavey to continue at the previous faster rate of lashing. Finally, sometime after fifty lashes, I mercifully passed out. My next memory from that first whipping was awakening to the intense sting of the briny water that Blavey poured on my raw back.

"One of the young slave observers, who was near me, spat and said, 'Dam uppity nigger fum de big house. We tole you befo': you jes' a nigger like de rest o' us.'"

Chapter Thirty-One

Seeing the distress on the faces of his listeners and hearing some stifled sobs, Tib paused in his narrative and said, "I am so sorry to cause any of you distress with the more lurid details of my story. I promise that I will not describe any more of my punishments but will only say that the first was unfortunately only one of many similar punishments that my mistress saw fit to use in her efforts to break my 'uppity' spirit.

"After lying for some time in the dust near the whipping post, a large field hand came with another smaller fellow and they carried me to a slave cabin in the Quarters. To my shame, I had never even looked inside a slave cabin until that day when my world was turned upside down. They gently placed me prone on a worn mat that lay on the dirt floor. The tall mulatto who had organized my care leaned down and with a grin said, 'Welcum to de kwarters. Dey call me Sisro here.'

"Looking more intently at his face, I replied, 'Are you the only Cicero here on the plantation?'

"'Expec' so. Sisro ain't dat common a name. What's yo' name?'

"'Tiberius.'

"'Dat's a mou'ful. I tink we'll call you Tib. How's dat wif you?'

"'That's fine with me.' And so, my half-brother gave me my nickname.

"In a few minutes, some other slaves entered the cabin. An older woman looked down at me and, speaking to Cicero, said, 'We alreddy tight in heah. What you thinkin' 'bout bringin' dis trouble heah?'

"'Oh Auntie, he no trouble. He ain't bin a real nigger befo'. I'll show 'im all about bein' a nigger.'

"'Well, you kin care for 'im den. Jes' keep 'im ober dere wif you an' outta mah way.'

"'Yes'm Auntie.' Turning to me, Cicero whispered, 'I nebber knowed my mammy. She sole down de ribber when I wuz born. Dey say dat my pappy's a big massa somewhere aroun' here but I dunno nuttin' about 'im.'

"And so, my half-brother, who was unaware of his kinship with me, became my guardian angel, protector, and mentor. You might even say he rounded out my formal education. Where book learning and scholarship ended, he taught me to survive in a hostile world. With Cicero's patient guidance, I learned the rudimentary skills necessary to the agricultural work that was my new calling in life.

"Somehow, beyond all reason, I frantically clung to the notion that my father would come to his senses and rescue me from the nightmare in which he had placed me. Cicero would see me fretting as we worked in the fields together and try to cheer me up. 'Musta bin grand to lib in de big house. I sorry dat you can't be dere no more.'

"I would start off complaining about the injustice of my treatment but a voice within me would accuse me, 'Here you are complaining of what you've lost, but what of that which your brother never had?'

"I would feel a mixture of shame and gratitude in the midst of my misery, shame for my selfishness and self-pity and gratitude for the new brother I had found. I was hesitant to tell Cicero of our true relationship, being unsure how he would react to the knowledge. Would he resent and hate me for the privileges I had enjoyed, which he had been denied? My selfish need for friendship kept me from revealing the truth to him.

"Although the work was often back breaking, the food terrible, and there was the constant threat of punishment by the sadistic overseer, life among the slaves on my father's plantation had its own consolations. I gradually lost my identity as the 'uppity' nigger and began to form friendships with the other slaves. Like the Moses of old, I finally had begun to recognize who my people were and to embrace them rather than deny them. Ironically, I must admit that Julia's death and its aftermath were the transforming elements of my life.

"One aspect of my life on the Newby plantation never improved however. Malvina Newby was confident that I was the very incarnation of all the evil in my father and gradually her all-consuming passion was to literally 'Whip the Devil out of me.' I was to be the expiation for the sins of her husband. The blows that she could never give Horton directly, I would receive. Again, I must confess the deep gratitude I owe to Cicero, who would gently wash and dress my wounds and never cease in his efforts to bring me out of my despair. He taught me more of real humanity in his own humble way than all the wisdom I accrued from the ancient philosophers.

"As I approached my seventeenth birthday in the winter of 1847, something happened that, although meant to be a new form of punishment, was the best gift Malvina Newby could have ever given me. One of the older slave women in the Quarters, whose name was Clarissa, had developed a cancerous growth that had gradually transformed the lower half of her abdomen into a large cauliflower-like mass which produced a horrible stench. Many of the more superstitious slaves on the plantation thought that a practitioner of dark magic must have cursed Clarissa and that she would inevitably die a terrible death. But regardless of the many theories that were debated regarding the cause of her suffering, all her fellow slaves were in agreement that they could not abide being in her presence. Thomas Blavey approached Malvina for advice on how to address the nursing needs of the dying woman. After pondering the situation for a few minutes, Malvina had the inspiration to assign me to Clarissa's cabin as her caregiver. Blavey took great delight in informing me of my new living and work arrangements. It came about in the following way.

"During the colder winter months, much of the work for the field hands shifted to other tasks, such as repairing farm equipment and buildings. In some ways, it was a welcome respite from the intense work in the fields during the heat of summer. The opportunity to learn other skills also provided a relief from the monotony of the summer routine. I had even learned some basic blacksmithing skills from the plantation's blacksmith, a burly young man in his early twenties, who had been given the name Caesar by my father when he was purchased with his mother as a child.

"While I was helping Caesar one morning, Blavey the overseer sauntered over to the forge, paused to spit some tobacco juice on the ground at my feet, and then, leering at me with a toothy grin, said, 'Mistress Newby has a special task for you, nigger. Follow me.'

"Shrugging my shoulders, I gave Caesar a puzzled look of farewell and followed the overseer. As Blavey led me back toward the Quarters, he chuckled and said, 'I gotta hand it to Mistress Newby. By tomorrow, you may be beggin' me for a whippin' instead of this nice little job.'

"As we approached a small cabin on the edge of the Quarters, an increasingly pungent odor overwhelmed me. I could not help thinking that a dead rotting animal must be nearby. As the overseer led me to the door of the cabin, it became quite apparent that the smell was emanating from inside.

"'Nigger, do ye know who Clarissa is?'

"'Yes.'

"'What's your nose tellin' ye?'

"'Is this Clarissa's cabin?'

"'You are a smart nigger, ain't ye? But it ain't jes' Clarissa's cabin anymore. She'll be sharin' it with you. Yer job is to take care of her until that cancer's eaten her up.'

"My desire not to give Blavey or my mistress any satisfaction overcame my horror and revulsion at the task assigned to me. With great effort, I checked my emotions, gulped hard, smiled at Blavey, and said, 'I'll be happy to care for her, sir.'

"The overseer gave me a queer look, scratched his head in disbelief, and disappointed at my lack of protest, replied, 'Well, suit yerself, nigger.'

"As Blavey walked away, I hesitated outside Clarissa's door. How would I be able to endure that awful smell, not to mention all the other tasks that would be required of me? As I pondered this question, an answer came to me in the form of another question that was as clear as if someone had spoken the words directly in my ear. 'How do you suppose Clarissa endures the smell, pain, and misery from which she cannot escape for even a moment?' With shame at my own weakness, I approached the door to her cabin and lightly knocked. A frail, feminine voice from within responded, 'Who's dere?'

"'Clarissa, it's Tib. May I come in?'

"'Cum in! Pleaz cum in, Tib. I bin hopin' fo' some company.'

"As I entered the cabin, the smell became almost overpowering. Again, I hesitated for a moment. Clarissa, who was extremely observant, noticed my hesitation and said, 'Tib, cum right in. De good Lawd send you to me. He'll help you obercum de bad smell.'

"'Clarissa, Mistress Newby sent me to care for you.'

"'No, Tib, de good Lawd choose you outta all de slaves on dis plantashun. Missus Newby jes' open her mouth an' out cum de Lawd's word. Ain't dere a place in de Bible war Gawd gib speech to an ass?'

"'Oh yes, Clarissa, you are referring to the passage in the book of Numbers when God gives speech to Balaam's ass, who asks the wicked man why he has beaten him three times.'

"'See Tib, it be right dere in de Bible. Missus Newby be de Lawd's ass jes' like de poor ass in de Bible.'

"I would have laughed heartily at her comparison of my mistress with Balaam's ass but for the intense sincerity, even absolute certainty, with which she spoke those words. As I came to know her during the next several weeks, there was something about Clarissa that only confirmed for me the profound nature of the insight manifested in that initial statement. Eventually, I came to regard Clarissa's pronouncements with awe, sensing in them an authority akin to an ancient oracle or one of the prophets of old, but I am getting ahead of my story.

"Like the other slave cabins in the Quarters, Clarissa's home left much to be desired for someone who had grown up in the master's big house. The floor was dirt and the walls were made up of wooden planks that had frequent gaps allowing the cold winds of winter to enter. There was a poorly constructed chimney that did not draw well, allowing smoke to accumulate in the small room. But for the gaps between the boards in the walls, there would have been very little ventilation, since there were no windows. Needless to say, it was quite chilly inside the cabin during the winter.

"Someone had taken pity on Clarissa, who was too weak to walk, and brought kindling and logs for a fire the night before. The last embers of that fire were still struggling for life when I entered that morning. With the fire dying and the door closed, the interior was dim, even at noontime, being dependent on any stray rays of light that might penetrate the darkness through the gaps in the walls. My attempts to keep a candle lit were frustrated by gusts of cold air that would invariably blow it out. As I assessed the challenges that I faced in caring for the old woman, I noted ironically that the draftiness of the cabin helped make the horrible stench a bit more bearable for me while causing her great discomfort. She lay under a thin filthy blanket, more a rag than a blanket, shivering constantly.

Informing Clarissa that I needed to get some more kindling and logs for the fire, I also went in search of a proper blanket and whale oil lamp that would not be so easily extinguished. Leaving that horrible smell behind when I walked out of her cabin was an indescribable sensation. I told myself that I would never take fresh air for granted again. Pondering the fact that I would have to return to that same experience soon, I tried to think of potential solutions to the problem the odor posed. *Surely,* I reasoned *the odor is emanating from the large abdominal tumor. Since it smells like rotting flesh, there may indeed be decaying flesh present that might be washed away with gentle bathing. Once the portion of the tumor that is decaying is removed by washing, perhaps the odor would also be diminished.*

"The means of obtaining a tub in which to bathe her perplexed me. It seemed that the only source for such a rare item would be the big house, access to which was strictly forbidden to me. As I was carrying a load of kindling and wood back to the cabin, passing Caesar at work in the smithy, I happened to see him plunge a red-hot iron in a wooden tub of water.

"After reviving Clarissa's fire and depositing the remaining kindling and logs nearby in the cabin, I told her, 'Clarissa, I have an idea of how to make the smell better and hopefully help you feel better as well. I will return soon.'

"'Why bless you Tib fo' eben tryin.'

"'Caesar, do you have another wooden tub like that one?' I asked a short while later, pointing at the tub of water he used for cooling hot metal.

"He looked at me quizzically and asked, 'Tib, what do you want dat fo'? You ain't in de big house no mo.'

'Caesar, it isn't for me, although a proper bath would be very nice. No, it's for Clarissa. I think if I bathe her tumor frequently, I might be able to reduce that terrible smell.'

"'Ain't you 'fraid dat de curse on her will cum on you, if'n you tech dat ting?'

"'No, Caesar, no one cursed Clarissa. She unfortunately has a cancerous tumor that is slowly killing her.'

"'Well, dis be de only tub outside o' de big house.'

"'Could I use it to wash Clarissa? I could do the bathing very early or late in the day, whichever is easier for you. I promise to wash it out with soap each time I use it and refill it with water for you.'

"'You sure you ain't afraid o' de curse on her?'

"'No, I'm prepared to take that risk.'

"'Well, den, I'll he'p you carry it in de mornin' jes' afta de sun come up.'

"With some more begging, I was able to obtain a whale oil lamp, lye soap, a real blanket that was even clean, and a large kettle to heat the water for her bath. After making all the arrangements, I sat down beside Clarissa's cot and explained my plan.

Listening intently, in the light of the whale oil lamp she then scrutinized me carefully, and said, 'Tib, you makin' a mighty big fuss ober dis ol' woman.'

"'If the good Lord really did send me to you, don't you think He would want me to do a good job taking care of you?'

"As a solitary tear emerged from the corner of her eye and wandered slowly down her cheek, Clarissa replied, 'Tank you, Tib. You go right ahed an' do de bes' you kin fo' de Lawd.'

"And thus, I became the last son, the last child, of the slave Clarissa in this life. She had lost all twelve of her own children, three from sickness, two as still births, and seven were sold down the river, as was her husband.

"I discovered that if I bathed her every day, being careful to flush the decaying material from the many crevices in the cancerous growth, that the odor was diminished substantially. Of course, over time I also became used to the smell. Each morning, after filling the borrowed tub with warm water, I would cautiously lift her slight, emaciated body and slowly place her in the tub of water. Gently, ever so gently, I would then flush the debris that had accumulated in the past twenty-four hours away from the cancerous growth while listening to Clarissa speak of her emigration from Virginia to Kentucky as a young slave of the Newbys and her subsequent life on the plantation in Shelby County. She described many sad as well as happy times, but never railed against her enslavement or her master's cruelties. These intimate times between adopted son and mother became very precious to both of us. I was afraid that I might exacerbate her suffering by the bathing, but she insisted on my continuing the baths almost to the very end of her life, speaking of the relief she experienced by being placed in the warm water and touched 'Wif lub by mah adopted son.'

"It grieved me terribly to see her decline each day. Although she would very politely make an effort to eat the food I brought her from the big house (the cook had been quietly colluding with me to help Clarissa) she continued to literally shrink as the tumor grew larger. None of this disturbed her in the least, except to the extent that she was aware of it upsetting her adopted son. She seemed to experience very little pain, only grimacing slightly when being moved during the bathing process.

"Frequently, she would sing slave spirituals to me. Eventually, as I learned the words, I found myself singing with her, forming an odd but poignant duet. Clarissa had a remarkable memory. She was entirely illiterate but could quote the substance of long passages of Scripture from memory with a deep understanding of the text. Indeed, I would enter our cabin, returning from some errand, only to find her in the depths of prayer centered on some Scripture passage. She would interrupt her prayer, turn to me and smile. If I was fortunate, she would begin to discuss her understanding of the passage, usually pointing out something that I who had been thoroughly educated in the Scriptures as great literature, had missed in my reading.

"As I witnessed her steady decline, I began to mourn in anticipation of the loss of yet one more parent. One morning when I had picked up her naked, almost skeletal form from the bath and was drying her, I could repress my emotions no longer, and began to complain and rail, whether against Fate or God, I wasn't quite sure, having thoroughly imbibed my father's skepticism.

"'Oh Clarissa, how can you bear such suffering? Why has God allowed African slaves to suffer so much? Is there no justice in the world?'

"Without a moment's hesitation, this answer came from her lips as she looked with deep compassion into my eyes, '*Be still and know dat I'm God.* Tib, don't you remember what de Scripture say about' takin' up yo' cross an' followin' de Lawd? Look to yo' heart son, stop tinking so much wif yo' head. De only way we gonna see de Lawd be when we follows 'im.'

"'Do you mean that we should just accept being slaves?'

"'Oh no, Tib! If'n you ebber git de chance to be free, promise yo' ol' adopted mammy dat you takes it.'

"'I promise, dear mammy Clarissa.'

"'Tib, de suffrin' don' go away when you free. It jes' diffrent. De suffrin' be where you find God. De Bible say dat God be lub. An' how do God lub us? He lub us on de cross. When you becum a real man, Tib, den you know dis truth. Ain't dis lub dat we found togedder, you an' me, in de suffrin dat God gib me to share wif you?'

"With no formal education, this illiterate, dying slave woman could speak of the distinction between man in the masculine and man as the human person. She knew not a word of Greek but understood this distinction that is so clearly drawn in that ancient language. She had somehow attained real manhood, had become fully human, in her suffering. What could I say in response to her? What can I say now in response to her? For that brief moment, which still haunts me, I could only weep as I held her in my arms.

"Looking up at me, she smiled, and said, 'Now, Tib, you truly my son,' and she reached up and touched my forehead with her thin frail fingers.

"All I could wish to say now to my dear adoptive mother would be, 'Oh Clarissa, I hope that I have made a beginning, a small beginning, at becoming a real man.'

"Clarissa died a few days later and I thought my heart would break. I dug her grave, moistening the soil with my tears. At one point, Cicero came and pleaded to let him help me prepare the grave, but I shooed him away, saying, 'No Cicero, I must do this alone.'

"As I placed her small, fragile body that was wrapped only in her blanket in the grave, I said the first real prayer of my life, 'Lord, you show your love in strange ways to your children, beyond the understanding of the educated and so-called wise. Take this poor slave woman, who was rich in wisdom born of suffering, to yourself, for her love for you is pure and more precious than fine gold. It cannot rot in this grave.'"

Chapter Thirty-Two

Pausing to clear his throat that was choked with renewed emotion, and looking around the room, Tib continued.

"There isn't much more to say of my time on my father's plantation. I took Clarissa's death and her benediction on my seeking freedom as signs for me to escape from bondage at the first opportunity. I think it was perplexing for my mistress and for the overseer to see me attend to what they saw as the most horrible and onerous of tasks with such commitment, even joy. Naturally, after Clarissa's death, the usual routine of punishments was reinitiated.

"Through clandestine contacts with the cook, I obtained pen and paper. It was my purpose to write passes for Cicero and myself that would help make our escape through Shelby County much easier to accomplish. When I broached my plan to Cicero, I was surprised by his refusal to come with me. He told me of his ardent love for one of the young slave girls on the plantation and his fear that she would be too frightened to come along. Unfortunately, he was correct in his concerns. Thankfully, after we confided in her, she did not reveal the plan in her terror of potential punishment.

"So, alas, I made my escape alone as you know. It was with great joy and some surprise that I saw Cicero again in the slave market in Louisville. I suspect Cicero's wife may feel differently about running away now that she likely will only be able to see him briefly once a year.

"And now, dear friends and family, you have heard the strange story of the bastard son of a Southern planter."

"Tiberius Johnson, you are a child of God and with the good Lord there are no bastard sons or daughters!" Pastor Ebenezer Jones blurted out with conviction.

There wasn't a dry eye in the Johnson parlor at that moment, as Eliza jumped up from her seat and rushed to her husband's side. With her eyes glistening, she said, "Tib Johnson, there was no reason for you to be ashamed of your life story and parentage. I am certain that there is much good in your father. You must write to him and remind him of his duty to your mother, sister, and half-brother."

John Burgess, who had been very moved by Tib's account of his life, rose and added, "I agree with Eliza, Tib. Thou must write to thy father and I will deliver the letter directly into his hand. Thy old mistress would be too suspicious of Dr. Way, if she encountered him, but I could engage thy father on some business in the nearest town and give him more information as thou would permit."

About noon the next day, Dr. Way knocked on the Johnsons' front door. When Sam opened the door, he could see from the somber expression on Henry Way's face that he had some portentous news to share.

"Dr. Way, please come in. I'll go fetch Tib," he said in response to Henry's request to speak with Tib.

"Sam, I think your whole family will want to hear this news," he said upon further consideration.

As the Johnson family gathered in the same parlor that had been the witness of Tib's story the night before, Henry handed a telegram to Tib. An initial look of concern changed slowly into a smile as he perused the telegram.

"Dear ones, Dr. Way has received a telegram with a message for me from my old friend, Marshal Silvanus Beecham. It reads as follows, 'Greetings from Madison, Dr. Way. Have just received a telegram from Malvina Newby. Upon learning of the slave Tiberius's escape, she is requesting aid in recovery of said runaway. Informed Mrs. Newby that I am no longer a US marshal. Greetings to entire Johnson family, Silvanus Beecham.'"

"Tib, you must leave for Canada right away!" Eliza exclaimed.

"Yes, Tib, you must depart as soon as possible," Ben Johnson added.

"Even though she no longer owns you, Malvina Newby can't let go of her hatred for you," Eliza marveled.

"For her, my freedom and happiness are contradictions to everything she believes about how the universe is ordered. My escape must have caused something of a sensation for her to hear of it so soon."

"Tib, you and Florrie will go on ahead and I will follow in a few days with Bennie and meet you in Windsor," Eliza said as tears were welling up in her eyes.

"I will make sure Eliza and Bennie are reunited with you safely in the Queen's dominion," Ben added.

Tib became agitated and, speaking with passion, said, "Eliza, how can I justify tearing you away from all that you have known and loved in this world?"

"All that I have loved? Aren't you forgetting someone, Tiberius Johnson? *Thy people will be my people. Whither thou goest, I will go.* You might as well call me Ruth from now on. It so happens that I would rather live in a country where my husband, where my whole family, can enjoy the full privileges of humanity. Besides, Tib, if Malvina Newby hates you as much as she has so far demonstrated, I wouldn't feel safe staying here, since as it has happened with others, she could easily send someone north to kidnap me and Bennie out of spite."

Turning to his father-in-law, Tib said, "Father, be sure and carry firearms with you when you bring Eliza through Detroit. A pregnant woman with a small child would be a very tempting target for slavecatchers who may not bother to examine your free papers."

Sam interjected, "Pa, I want to come along and help. I know how to use a pistol."

"Son, who is going to take care of the farm while we are gone?"

It was Dr. Way's turn to interrupt as he said, "Ben, I am sure that the Burgesses and many others will come forward to help while you and Sam are gone. Don't worry about the farm. Just make sure Eliza and Bennie arrive safely in Canada."

"Well, Sam, it looks like you'll be coming to Canada with us," Ben said, giving his son a wink.

"Isaac, I will have my own adventure before starting at Oberlin, after all," Sam said with some satisfaction. He had been very envious of his friend Isaac's travels in the South, feeling great frustration from the constraints placed on him by his race.

"Sam, I hope that thou and thy family will be safe as you accompany Eliza and Bennie to Windsor," Isaac replied. "My Uncle Levi told me of some incidents that have happened in Detroit in which slavecatchers waiting in that city to capture runaways have attempted to kidnap free persons of color and take them back to the South to be sold into slavery."

"I'd like to see them try to take any of us!" Sam said fiercely with a look of grim determination on his face. "We Baptists aren't pacifists. Don't you ever question the pacifist teachings of the Quakers?"

Isaac, who was walking with his best friend by the same stream that had witnessed their first acquaintance with Tib five years before, reddened in the face in response to the pointed question. "Sam, you know that I struggle greatly with this teaching of the Society of Friends. So many times, during my journey to Tennessee, I was driven to intense anger by the cruelty I witnessed. My first inclination was to attack those who were inflicting such cruelties on innocent people. Thankfully, my Uncle Levi was able to prevent me from acts of violence, which would not have changed the immediate situation but could have made it worse for the slaves."

"Isaac, you are the best of friends. I could never ask for better. But I am not sure you can fully understand my perspective. For you, the horrors of the peculiar institution are repulsive, a great evil plaguing American culture that must be eliminated, hopefully in true Quaker fashion by gentle persuasion, through reason and example. For my part, I also share the same goals, but there is something more fundamental, which relates to the nature of my very existence. I may not be feeling the overseer's lash but there is no guarantee that I would not experience such horrors; certainly not by virtue of my appearance. I am free to the extent that enfranchised white citizens of this state or any state recognize the validity of my free papers. But do I, will I, ever enjoy the same privileges that you as a white man have in this country? The happiness, health, and safety of my sister, a free woman of color, are put at risk merely because she has the temerity to love someone's *property* as her husband. I share the horror of violence that Friends feel so strongly, but I will not stand by and let my sister, her husband, and child be threatened with such horrors, even if violent means may be necessary to prevent such an outrage. You have that medallion in your house with the slave; his chained hands raised in protest, who cries out with the question that every person of color asks, 'Am I not a man and a brother?' Sometimes, it may be necessary for a brother to strike his brother to awaken in his brother's conscience the answer hidden there, 'Yes, this is my brother and *not* my property.'"

"I cannot and will not attempt to refute thy argument. Only go with my prayers for thy safety and that of thy family. Remember that thy future Oberlin roommate will be waiting for thee."

As they embraced, Sam laughed and said, "As you can see, I am working on my own rhetorical skills as a future lawyer. I don't expect you to capitulate so easily in our future debates."

"I promise thee that I will do my best to be a better rhetorical adversary."

Sam's sister Hattie joined them as Sam was finishing his impassioned speech and remarked, "Isaac, has my brother convinced you to take up arms? I'm afraid he's going to get himself killed sometime with his hotheaded notions. Samuel Johnson, I will never forgive you if you get yourself killed in some battle with slavecatchers. Please be careful and keep calm, no matter the circumstances."

"Oh Hattie, I'll be careful, but I must say that the only kind of future I can see for this country is one of conflict, a conflict centered on the fate of the negro. When that comes, I don't plan to stand by and watch."

"Anyway, Pa sent me to fetch you. He is ready to leave now."

It had been three days since Tib had left with Florrie for Canada and four days since Dr. Way had delivered the telegram from Silvanus Beecham. Taking no chances, Florrie and Tib traveled from station to station of the Underground Railroad with the assistance of different conductors, first moving east into Ohio and then northeast to Sandusky with the plan to gain passage on a steamboat friendly to freedom seekers heading to Canada. He would then travel the short distance overland to Windsor to await Eliza's arrival. Because Eliza was in the eighth month of her pregnancy, Ben had wanted to make the journey as simple and comfortable for her as possible. Although Dr. Way and Pastor Jones expressed some concern, he had elected to travel during the daytime on the larger roads to reduce the trauma to Eliza and her baby, with the plan being to catch the train from Toledo to Detroit once they arrived in Toledo.

Mary Johnson hugged her daughter close and then pulling back from the embrace, looked directly into Eliza's face, as if to absorb and retain as much of her daughter's essence as possible, and said, "How can I bear to let you go and yet go you must. It has been my joy to be your mother and friend. Will I see you again in this life?"

"Of course, you will, Mother. I have every confidence that we shall meet again and soon," Eliza replied. "You must come and visit us in Canada once we are settled."

"Yes, yes, dear one, I will come. It's so much change for me to absorb all at once; two of my children departing so far from home, my eldest to Canada and Samuel to Oberlin's preparatory college with Isaac. And with all of Hattie's suitors coming around, I'm afraid I'll lose her soon as well."

"Oh Ma, you'll still have Pa and me," Louisa declared with mock indignation.

"Yes, my dear, perhaps that is what disturbs me the most, a full and undiluted Louisa Johnson!" Mary said with a big smile, as tears dissolved into laughter.

Chapter Thirty-Three

Captain Atwood was having a vexing day. His steamer, the *T. Whitney*, had been docked at Sandusky on Lake Erie since just before eight that morning. The ship was bound for Detroit and normally should leave port at two in the afternoon, which time was rapidly approaching, it being half past one. Whenever possible, the captain's custom was to accommodate additional passengers, who were seeking freedom. He had been informed on his arrival in Sandusky that some *cargo* would be arriving today for urgent shipment. Having acquired through experience a heightened sense of the presence of slavecatchers, he noticed two suspicious-appearing characters skulking about the dock, as he waited for signs of the cargo's delivery. He had already completed the loading of the ship an hour before and only a small trickle of passengers continued to board the vessel. He did not like the situation at all. One of the two loitering characters caught his eye and even gave what to him seemed a knowing smirk in response to his look. Just as the ship was beginning to put up steam to depart on time at two, a carriage arrived in some haste and two heavily veiled women wearing black dresses and large bonnets descended from the carriage with the help of an older gentleman wearing the broad-brimmed hat and plain dress distinctive of a Quaker. Captain Atwood noticed that their arrival was being observed with considerable interest by the two loiterers on the dock.

As the women ascended the gangway leading to the lower deck of the ship, one of the two men on the dock appeared to whisper instructions into the ear of the other and they made promptly for the gangway. The ship's steward who had just waved the two ladies forward on to the ship blocked the path of the two men as they approached the top of the gangway.

"Do you gentlemen have tickets for Detroit?"

The taller of the two answered, "We'd like to speak with those ladies that jes' got on to the ship fer a minute, before you kin depart," pointing to the revolver strapped to his right hip. Before Captain Atwood could intervene, he saw the two men brush his steward aside and rapidly approach from behind the unsuspecting women who were walking slowly away from them. Once they had overtaken the women, they unceremoniously ripped the bonnets with the attached veils off their heads to reveal Tib and Florrie who at the last minute had assumed this disguise with the assistance of their Quaker conductor.

"I thought you were awful tall fer a woman," one of the slavecatchers said with a laugh as he pointed a revolver at Tib's head.

Florrie, who was shaking with fear, began to cry. Tib tried to comfort her with the words, "Don't be afraid. They won't succeed."

The slavecatcher who was pointing his revolver at Tib laughed again. "What makes you think yer gonna escape this time, nigger? Yer luck jes' ran out. Both o' you fit the descriptions of two niggers who absconded from Missouri."

Pointing to Tib, "you escaped from a steamboat on the Mississippi and then helped this nigger here," pointing to Florrie, "to escape from her master near New Madrid."

Turning to Captain Atwood, who had rushed forward, he added, "thanks to the kind offices of this here nigger's former mistress, Mrs. Malvina Newby of Shelby County, Kentucky, my partners and I've been watchin' the port of Sandusky and Detroit fer these two. Captain, we'll be obliged, if you could give us passage to Detroit along with these runaways. Then we can join our partners there an' transport 'em back to their owners."

Silently, gritting his teeth, Captain Atwood, nodded and said, "You may pay the steward your fares. Be aware that without the support of a US marshal and the proper paperwork supporting your claim under the Fugitive Slave Act of 1850, you will likely be charged with kidnapping when you arrive in Detroit."

"Really Cap'n, you cain't be serious. They's obvious runaways. What self-respectin' free man would ever dress up like a woman?"

"One who is trying to avoid harassment by villains like your self," Tib retorted. Turning to the captain, Tib added, "Captain, here are our free papers for your inspection."

As Captain Atwood carefully perused the forged documents, Tib quickly exchanged glances with Florrie and was now very thankful for the great efforts he had made so many days before to forge her owner's handwriting and signature.

"These manumission documents appear to be in order," the captain said. Flushing, the tall slavecatcher angrily demanded to see the documents. As he slowly and ponderously studied them, it became clear to Tib that the slavecatcher could not read. It was now his turn to laugh. "Captain, would you be so kind as to read the documents for this gentleman, as he obviously cannot read."

"What're ye tryin' to insinuate, nigger?" growled the slavecatcher.

"Nothing more than the fact that you are illiterate. Most literate people would not require a quarter of the time you have taken to read documents of that length. If you can read, please go ahead and read for all to hear."

At this, the captain started to laugh heartily and, retrieving the documents from the scowling man, read them out loud to the growing crowd on the ship as it left port.

After he had finished, the tall slavecatcher protested, "They're just goddam forgeries!"

"If I hear more oaths from you, sir, you will be confined to your quarters. As for your debating the authenticity of these free papers, you may take that up with the authorities in Detroit. Now kindly hand me your firearms; both of you will be able to retrieve them once you depart from the ship in Detroit. In the meantime, I do not want you creating any mischief while on board my vessel."

After Tib and Florrie were shown their small stateroom on the lower deck of the *T. Whitney* and closed the door behind them, Florrie danced around joyfully and hugging Tib said, "I neber could 'preciate how valubul learnin' could be 'til today. When we gets to Kanudah, dats de firs's thing ah wants to do, learn to read an' write."

"Florrie, I think we are very fortunate to have Mr. Atwood as captain of this ship. I suspect he doubts the authenticity of our free papers but is willing to take the risk to help us escape. I wonder what he is planning."

Captain Atwood sat observing the two slavecatchers as they drank liberally from the ship's supply of strong spirits. Usually the journey to Detroit would take approximately eighteen to twenty hours depending on the conditions on Lake Erie and the presence or absence of a head wind. Occasionally, it would be necessary to make an unplanned stop on the Canadian side of the lake to take on additional wood, if they had been battling particularly difficult conditions, to enable completion of the voyage to Detroit. As darkness settled over Lake Erie and inebriation clouded the minds of the slavecatchers, Captain Atwood executed his plan. Walking back to the boiler room, he poked his head inside and asked about the supply of wood.

"Cap'n, we should have plenty for the trip to Detroit. The lake is calm with nary a headwind," was the reply.

"Unfortunately, a headwind and rough conditions will develop overnight, slowing our progress and causing more of our fuel to be expended than planned, which will necessitate a stop for fuel at Amherstburg in the morning." the captain explained.

"Oh, I see, Cap'n. Yes, yer right the lake's getting' a bit rough, ain't it?" the sailor, one of several free men of color serving on board, said with a wink.

As dawn was breaking over a very calm Lake Erie, a knock at their stateroom door awakened Tib, who jumped up from his place on the floor where he had been sleeping and cautiously opened the door. Captain Atwood tipped his hat and said, "I hope that your voyage has been pleasant thus far. A deficiency of fuel has been detected overnight, which will require an unplanned stop at Amherstburg, Canada. I thought it my duty to inform you of this deviation from our normal route."

"Captain Atwood, I cannot begin to express our gratitude for all your efforts on our behalf."

"My great hope is that you will take advantage of this opportunity to enjoy the Queen's hospitality."

"With great pleasure, sir."

"We should be docking in about two hours."

"Hey! Are we already in Detroit?" one of the slavecatchers shouted while rubbing his throbbing temples, as he emerged from the saloon where he and his partner had been sleeping off their revels from the previous night.

The colored sailor who had discretely disposed of some of the ship's fuel the night before gave him a puzzled look and said, "Don't you remember de terribul storm las' nite wif de hi' winds? We gotta load mo' fuel to git to Detroit. Dis here's Amherstburg, Canada."

"Damn nigger! I don't believe you."

"Well cum and see fo' yo' self," and the black sailor led the way to the boiler room where the slavecatcher noted with great dismay that very little wood remained. After showing the dwindling fuel supply to the slavecatcher, the sailor chuckled, "Hee, hee. I guess you musta had a mitey good time in de saloon to jes' sleep rite thru all de trubbels las' nite."

While the garrulous sailor was entertaining the disgruntled slavecatcher, the docking maneuvers were completed, and Tib and Florrie, who had resumed their usual dress, quietly slipped onto the gangway and ran to make contact with the free soil of Canada. The slavecatcher shouted, "Damnation!" as he noticed their heads disappearing down the gangway, and, yelling for his sleepy partner, ran in pursuit.

Pausing to stoop and kiss the soil of his new country, Tib heard the shouts and oaths of the slavecatchers and turned to witness their pursuit. He urged Florrie to run on ahead while he stood his ground. Converging from all directions, citizens of Amherstburg came running in response to the shouting, including some stevedores, several of whom were of African descent, and also the local sheriff. The breathless slavecatchers caught up to Tib, still shouting, swearing, and demanding his surrender.

Tib smiled and replied, "You gentlemen must feel quite ill, having to breathe the free air of the Queen's dominion. However, I have never felt better. I am now a free man on free soil. Come and take me at your own risk. My slave-owning father, in addition to teaching me the niceties of a Southern planter's life, also taught me the basic skills of pugilism so necessary for the preservation of a Southern gentleman's honor. You now have had fair warning."

The tall slavecatcher lunged at Tib, who dodged his crude blow and, in response, landed a direct blow to his face. The other slavecatcher now tried his luck and moved in to grab Tib, who deftly avoided his grasp but in turn grabbed his adversary and threw him to the ground. His first adversary, with blood streaming from his nose and lips, again lunged at Tib landing a solid blow to Tib's chest causing him to stagger backwards briefly. Recovering quickly, Tib planted another firm blow to the man's face followed by additional blows to his stomach, bringing the slavecatcher to his knees.

"This, indeed, is a welcome sight. A white man kneeling before a negro," Tib said with satisfaction. At that moment, a gunshot rang out, followed almost instantly by a scream of pain, which interrupted Tib's speech. Turning around, Tib saw his other adversary clutching his bleeding right hand with his left and a knife in the dust at his feet. Looking at the sheriff who had come forward, revolver in hand and ready to shoot again, if necessary, Tib bowed low to him and said, "Sir, that was very fine marksmanship. Thank you for saving my life. I am clearly no longer in the American republic, but in a land where the value of every human being is assumed and defended."

The sheriff stepped forward, offered his hand to Tib and said, "Welcome to Canada West. It was my duty and pleasure." Addressing the bloodied slavecatchers, he said, "You have two choices, assuming the good captain agrees. Either you can stay here in Canada and face charges of assault and attempted kidnapping or you can return to the United States with the understanding that if you ever set foot on Canadian soil again you will experience the full weight of the Queen's justice."

The slavecatchers cautiously withdrew from the scene of combat and then beat a hasty retreat to the ship where Captain Atwood announced they would be confined to quarters for the remainder of the journey to Detroit.

Chapter Thirty-Four

Although there were several alternative points of entry for freedom seekers into Canada from Michigan such as Port Huron to the north and Trenton to the south, they were only that: alternatives to the main point of entry, which led directly through Detroit. Although a concerted effort at organizing the Underground Railroad in southern Michigan had been made by the Reverend John Cross and others in the 1840s, with the intent to speed the safe transfer of fugitives coming from western states like Missouri and Illinois, as well as those converging on Michigan through Indiana and Ohio, it was rare for conductors to know the identities of other conductors beyond the confines of their own county. This ignorance helped protect the identities and personal safety of those aiding the fugitive, while keeping the organization minimal as well as local in character.

Abolitionists with a variety of religious affiliations, including Quakers, Presbyterians, Congregationalists, Baptists, and Wesleyan Methodists, collaborated with settlements of free persons of color and the self-emancipated in the loose organization of the Underground Railroad in Michigan. This collaboration also extended to the terminus in Detroit and was further enhanced by the presence of a negro vigilance committee organized for the protection of freedom seekers, which met in the basement of the Second Baptist Church on Fort Street, a short distance from the Detroit River. For freedom seekers, Detroit was *Midnight,* while across the Detroit River the Queen's dominion had become *Dawn,* the one place in North America that recognizing their full humanity and represented the dawn of a new life.

George DeBaptiste and his friend and colleague William Lambert had lingered behind in the basement of the Second Baptist Church to chat after the formal meeting of the negro vigilance committee had ended. Both men had established successful businesses in Detroit. Lambert owned a dry-cleaning and tailoring business, and DeBaptiste, who had started in the city as a barber, having been at one time the personal valet of President William Henry Harrison, had diversified his business interests to even include ownership of the steamship the *T. Whitney.*

"Your Captain Atwood is certainly a resourceful fellow. To have the presence of mind to 'run out of fuel,' necessitating the stop at Amherstburg, was brilliant," William Lambert said with admiration.

"Yes, he is quite a fellow. I couldn't wish for a better captain for the *T. Whitney*," George DeBaptiste replied with a hearty laugh. "But I also must add that the account he gave of the manly bravery of the fugitive who turned on his pursuers once he was on the free soil of Canada West moves me greatly when I think of it."

"Seymour Finney told me this morning that the two slavecatchers from the *T. Whitney* who have been staying at his hotel are still licking their wounds three days later. However, he is concerned that they have been joined by two more partners who are clearly up to some kind of mischief."

"According to Captain Atwood, they boasted that they had partners in Detroit who were also waiting for the fugitive couple. I doubt they will want to leave Detroit empty-handed. Perhaps they will attempt to kidnap some free persons of color."

Their speculations were cut short by the distinct sound of a woman screaming in the distance.

"George," William said, giving his friend a knowing look as they both rushed for the stairs, "our question may be in the process of being answered."

As they emerged from the Second Baptist Church, George DeBaptiste and William Lambert were drawn to the sound of shouting mingled with a woman's screams about a block away on Fort Street. Drawing revolvers, they approached the source of the disturbance at a run. A crowd of people, both colored and white, including other members of the vigilance committee, could be seen rapidly gathering from several directions in response to the commotion.

"Look George! One of the slavecatchers has a revolver pointed at the head of a young woman. She appears to be due to deliver a baby any day now. There's also a small boy clinging to her, must be her son, and another young man nearby who has also been apprehended by the other slavecatcher."

An angry Eliza Johnson, with a terrified Bennie clinging to her skirt, was insisting that the slavecatcher release her and Bennie, while Sam was yelling at both of them, "We are free Negroes. Release my sister, her son, and me now!"

"Shut up, nigger!" The slavecatcher holding Eliza yelled at Sam while his associate gave Sam a blow across the face with his fist. "Y'all precisely fit the descriptions we have of some runaways from the honorable Edward Townsend of Boone County, Kentucky."

Ben Johnson, who had stepped away briefly from his family to look for accomodations for the night had been drawn back to the scene by his daughter's screams. Addressing the slavecatchers while fingering his revolver, he shouted, "I have the free papers to prove that they are not runaways. Release my daughter, son, and grandson immediately!"

"Don't you come any closer, nigger," the slavecatcher holding Eliza said as he cocked the revolver pointed at her head."

By this time, a crowd of nearly a hundred people, mostly colored, had surrounded the victims and perpetrators. George DeBaptiste turned to his friend, and said, "William, see if you can find the sheriff quickly while I negotiate with these devils."

William Lambert alerted some other associates from the vigilance committee, all of whom headed off at a run in different directions in search of the sheriff.

Stepping forward, George DeBaptiste addressed the slavecatchers. "Where is the US marshal who should be supporting you in your claim to these individuals?"

"What's that to you nigger? This ain't your goddam business. Y'all need to leave quiet-like right now, if you wanna see no harm come to these here niggers."

"Apparently, you haven't realized yet that you are completely surrounded. If you cause any more harm to them, you will answer with your lives. As it is, you will be indicted for assault and kidnapping. You may be tempted to shoot your way out of this confrontation, but I assure you that your dismembered corpses will be witnesses of our triumph over you. Now lay down your weapons."

At this point, William Lambert returned with the sheriff. Sheriff Fitch walked up to the slavecatchers and said, "What are you waiting for? Lay down your weapons at once."

"But, Sheriff, we are jes' here in Detroit recoverin' stolen property."

Motioning to Ben Johnson to come forward, the sheriff reviewed the free papers that Ben was carrying for his family and said, "These free papers are perfectly in order. You have assaulted and attempted to kidnap free people. These are serious crimes in the state of Michigan. You will receive a fair trial, which is much more than can be said for what you offer to those you try to drag back into slavery. As I already have said, lay down your weapons now or I can't answer for what this mob will do to you."

After some hesitation and exchanges of panicked looks, reluctantly the two slave-catchers laid down their weapons and were escorted to jail by two of the sheriff's deputies.

Sheriff Fitch approached the shaken but reunited family and said, "Please accept my sincere apologies for all the trouble you have experienced this afternoon in Detroit." Looking at Sam, he added, "Son, you are going to be quite sore for some time. That's an awful bruise forming on your cheek. Would you like to see a physician?"

"No, sir. But I would like to testify at the trial of these kidnappers."

"I wish you could. Unfortunately, the state of Michigan has given very few legal rights to colored people." Motioning to a white man standing nearby, Sheriff Fitch asked him, "Did you witness this altercation?"

"I did, sir."

"How did this young man acquire his injury?"

"The slavecatcher hit him with his fist."

"From what sort of provocation?"

"He only demanded that they be released as free negroes."

Turning to Sam, the sheriff asked, "Are the particulars correct as he has told them?"

"Yes, sir."

Giving the witness his most formal and imperious look, Sheriff Fitch said to Sam, "You have my word that the account of your assault will be entered accurately in the court record."

"Father, if it is still possible, I would like to cross over to Windsor today," Eliza said with some strain in her voice. George DeBaptiste, who had introduced William Lambert and himself to the Johnsons interjected, "I fully appreciate your frustrations, Mrs. Johnson. There is another ferry crossing the Detroit River that will leave at seven p.m. this evening. Do you feel that you are able to endure more travel in your condition?"

"Sir, I appreciate very much your concern for my welfare and that of my baby, and I can't begin to thank both of you enough for your intervention which brought about our rescue from those slavecatchers. But my baby is kicking something fierce right now and I can only interpret it as a message that he wants to be reunited with his father as soon as possible."

Turning to George DeBaptiste, William Lambert added with a smile, "It seems that this week has brought some remarkable freedom seekers, who are made of the sternest material, not unlike yourself, ma'am. If you only could have met the couple that Captain Atwood, who commands George's steamship the *T. Whitney*, dropped off in Amherstburg, you would have met some kindred spirits. The man, a tall handsome mulatto, who spoke English better than the captain, soundly thrashed the slavecatchers who had tried to capture him and his female companion when they tried to follow them on to Canadian soil."

Eliza's eyes flashed as she exclaimed, "I do know that remarkable man. He is my husband. He went on ahead of us through Sandusky, Ohio accompanying a young woman who hoped to be reunited with her husband who had already escaped from slavery in Missouri some months ago."

"Well, George," William Lambert said, "I think we had better help this determined young woman find her husband in Windsor, this evening. Don't you agree?"

With a wink, George DeBaptiste, replied, "Are you sure you wouldn't want to enjoy some more of Detroit's fine hospitality?" This elicited laughter all around, although Sam winced in pain as he laughed.

Before the advent of the telegraph and rail service a few years later, Amherstburg's larger population and more active trade to some extent dwarfed the village of Windsor in Canada West. Members of the Detroit vigilance committee and other operatives of the Underground Railroad made frequent crossings back and forth between the American republic and the Queen's dominion. Being quite familiar with both communities, they had built up a network of contacts on both sides of the border. It was to these contacts that George DeBaptiste and William Lambert went off separately in search of Tib, leaving the Johnsons to dine at a small inn near the wharf.

While they were finishing their meal, Sam began to recount his frustrations with the day's proceedings. "When I become a lawyer, I will fight for the rights of negroes to testify in court. Basic rights relating to citizenship must be universally applied and not something for the states to decide at their discretion and whim. Just think of it, Pa. Our own state of Indiana, a year ago, enacted a law to exclude any more colored persons from immigrating to the state. The United States constitution is fundamentally flawed and must be amended."

"Well, I can see you're not likely to be focusing much of your attention on farming with all of your plans to change the world."

"As a lawyer, I can fight for the rights of farmers, including colored farmers."

Ben smiled and said, "I will appreciate your advocacy and also a little help when harvest time comes."

"Oh Pa, becoming a lawyer won't make me forget how to farm."

"No. But it will consume most of your time and energy. I'm very proud of your scholarship and I am very pleased that you are going to Oberlin with Isaac this year. Just don't forget your connection to the soil when you're conjugating all those Greek and Latin verbs."

"I promise, I won't forget." Then, resting his uninjured cheek in his hand, Sam gazed dreamily into the space before him and changed the subject. "Oh, how I would have liked to have been there when Tib thrashed those slavecatchers."

"And what kind of tall tales are folks spinning about Tib, the Scourge of Slavecatchers?" a familiar voice asked.

"Oh, Tiberius Johnson!" Eliza screamed as she rose awkwardly from her chair to hug her husband with tears streaming down her face. Bennie, Sam, and Ben all gathered around Tib, beaming with joy and relief, while George DeBaptiste and William Lambert smiled and nodded to one another to make their exit.

Chapter Thirty-Five

If one bothered to look, a weary traveler could be seen gently prodding his horse forward on the Louisville-Shelbyville turnpike in the heat and humidity of waning daylight in late August 1852. Crickets in the tall grass by the roadside endeavored to provide some musical entertainment while frogs croaking in a nearby swamp did their best to harmonize. Both horse and rider struggled with flying adversaries; the horse's tail swishing rhythmically in vain attempts to prevent large flies from landing and biting its hindquarters and its rider often striking ineffectually and too late at mosquitoes which were overly anxious to welcome him to Shelby County, Kentucky. As the shadows lengthened, it became more difficult to dodge the many puddles that had been created by a thunderstorm, which had passed through earlier in the afternoon. Between being soaked earlier in that same downpour and now being frequently splashed with muddy water from its residue, both horse and rider were a bit disgruntled.

Although not in the habit of speaking to his horse, the loneliness of their circumstances seemed to demand conversation and so the rider spoke.

"Dinah, here we are in Kentucky. I hope we will overtake or meet some traveler soon who can give us some sense of the distance we must still travel to reach Shelbyville this evening."

In response to hearing her name spoken, Dinah perked up her head but otherwise did not comment. After another half hour of plodding along the turnpike in the gathering darkness, the rider abruptly pulled up on Dinah's reins when he was suddenly startled by the presence of other travelers on the turnpike. Because of the imperceptible nature of their dark skin in the waning light and his own distracted thoughts, he had overtaken a gang of eight to ten negroes walking along the turnpike, whom he had not noticed until he was nearly upon them.

"Good evening. Can any of you tell me how much farther I must travel to reach Shelbyville this evening?"

"You ain't fum aroun' here, is you, Massa?"

"I have come from Indiana. Why dost thou say that?"

"Well fo' one ting, no white man fum Kaintuk eber talk like dat to us po' niggers. Fo' anudder ting, you talk like some kind a preacher."

John Burgess laughed and said, "I'm a Quaker and that is how we speak. We call it plain speech."

"Well it be sum kind o' plain speakin' rite outta de Bible. We gots to turn up dis yer path to Massa Newby's plantashun. If'n you go anudder mile or so, you be in de town."

"Do all of you work for Mr. Horton Newby?"

"Yessum, Massa. Massa Horton Newby hisself be our massa." And with some pride, the slave added, "De Newby plantashun be de grandist o' all de plantashuns in dese yer parts. We's quality niggers, not like dem udder niggers fum de po' white trash farms. Why, we jes' bin gittin de pasture reddy fo' Massa Newby's hosses."

"Does Mr. Newby raise horses on his plantation?"

"Ober a hunnerd, but he also grow tobacky, corn, wheat, and sorgum fo' de markets." Then, waving farewell, the spokesman for the gang said, "Like ah say, jes' go on fo' anudder mile or so an' you'll git dere."

After groping along the turnpike in the growing darkness for more than an hour, it became evident to John Burgess that a mile or so was clearly a very rough estimate. He was thankful to finally see some lights ahead and hear noises associated with human habitation after another fifteen minutes of travel. With the overcast sky, it was difficult to discern more than the outline of buildings as he rode up the main street past the county courthouse. Farther up the street, a cacophony of raucous music, yelling, and swearing wafted toward his ears. Unfortunately for the earnest, temperance-minded Quaker, the main hotel of Shelbyville was located across the street from the largest and noisiest saloon in town.

Early the next morning, John inquired at the hotel desk about sending a message to Mr. Newby. A young slave was dispatched with a brief note for Mr. Newby proposing a meeting in town at his earliest convenience regarding a matter of great personal interest to him that also would require the utmost discretion. The note was signed Mr. John Burgess, trader in general merchandise. A postscript was added beneath his signature, which read, "Fortune favors the bold." The slave was instructed to make sure the note was delivered directly to Mr. Newby and to await his reply. Later, shortly after noon, the messenger returned with a note from Horton for John Burgess. "Please wait for me in the lobby of the hotel at 6 p.m. this evening, H. N."

Promptly, at six p.m., a tall, well-dressed gentleman presented himself to the hotel's main desk. His face was handsome but something about his eyes bore an air of melancholy. Graying at the temples highlighted his dark hair and even features. The hotel clerk directed him toward John Burgess, who was seated in a large chair reading a newspaper.

"Mr. Burgess?"

Looking up from the paper, John had his first glimpse of Horton Newby and was struck by the many similarities in appearance and bearing between father and mulatto son. Rising quickly, he extended his right hand and said, "Mr. Newby, thy son clearly bears thy image. It is my great pleasure to meet thee and deliver a letter from thy son."

"Is it possible that he lives? I was told that he was shot and drowned in the Ohio River during his escape five years ago. And yet, it is hard to believe that a Quaker businessman such as yourself would add the Roman aphorism, 'Fortune favors the bold,' to his signature."

John laughed and said, "Tib assured me that adding this aphorism would pique thy interest."

His eyes glistening, Horton replied, "Tiberius remembered my fondness for such sayings, especially that one. It was a powerful hook to draw me here. I had lost all hope that the reports of his death were false and yet here you are, an emissary for the living."

Seeing his genuine joy at the news, and feeling compassion for Horton, John suggested, "Perhaps we can find a quiet place to dine where I can give thee a full account of thy son's life in the time since he left thy plantation. I think it will be very helpful in preparing thee for his letter."

"There are private rooms available for dining at this hotel. I'll make the arrangements."

Fifteen minutes later they were seated together in a small chamber just off the main dining hall. John proceeded to review the details of Tib's first escape after crossing the Ohio River, the long convalescence and recovery from his wound in Newport on the Johnsons' farm, his romance with Eliza Johnson, their subsequent marriage, the birth of young Bennie and the second pregnancy, Tib's arrest and sale down the river earlier in the summer, the daring escape from the steamboat on the Mississippi, and his final narrow escape from recapture, followed by his subsequent safe arrival and reunion with his family in Canada West. John mentioned the role of Malvina Newby in the history of Tib's adventures without comment but noticed the pained expression that suffused Horton's face as he absorbed the news of her vengeful activities. Horton listened intently to John's account without interruption, sighing deeply when John completed the narrative and handed him Tib's letter.

"In my grief over my daughter Julia's death and in my promise to her on her deathbed, I convinced myself that Malvina would not be a cruel mistress to Tiberius," he said sadly. "My mistake became all too evident very shortly after signing ownership of Tiberius over to her. He may have told you something of his life on my plantation before and after Malvina became his mistress. The last words he shouted at me as he was being dragged off by our overseer to the slave quarters have stayed with me ever since. How true and insightful they were, although I refused to comprehend them then. 'You think *out of sight out of mind*, but I assure you, Father, that I will haunt your thoughts. You will find no rest or peace by what you have done.' He has never been out of my thoughts all these years and I have truly been haunted by those words.

Since that fateful day, I have tried to immerse myself in new activities as a means of forgetting. Indeed, I have gained some measure of success as a horse breeder in the county in the intervening time, but it brings me no joy. No amount of worldly success has inoculated me from the deep, deep regret and sorrow I feel for the suffering I have caused him and others who are very dear to me."

"But, Mr. Newby, thou canst make amends. The merciful God has intervened in extraordinary ways and on more than one occasion to preserve the life of this most remarkable man who is thy son," John interjected.

Ignoring the food on his plate, Horton stared pensively ahead of him and said, "At the time of my daughter's death, for the first time in my life as a religious skeptic of the Presbyterian stripe, I was convinced by Julia that I had disrupted the natural order of creation by elevating my slave mistress and children, and the only course of action that might bring salvation to all of us would be to accept the roles already foreordained for each of us in this life as God's will."

"Dost thou actually believe that the institution of slavery is God's will?" John could not help interrupting.

"No, not now," Horton replied. "But, in listening to the earnest entreaties of my dying child, I was convinced for at least a time. Our peculiar institution started as an economic phenomenon driven by human greed, including my own. With its perpetuation, of necessity, a series of rationalizations justifying its existence have developed. On more than one occasion, I have thoroughly discomfited my wife Malvina by speculating in true Presbyterian fashion about predestination and how I could have just as easily been born a slave as a master. Now, through painful reflection, I have come to realize that I was truly born a slave, but my master has been my unrestrained desires."

"Perhaps God has worked his merciful will through thy mistakes," John said. "After all, if Tib had not experienced the suffering of his people, the full formation of his character would not have occurred, he would not have fled the South, and would never have met thy daughter-in-law. No matter how painful his suffering has been, I believe Tib has been able to recognize the genuine love shown him by his sister Julia and her overall good intentions. He expressed a sense of complete abandonment by thee, but it was his wife Eliza who, after hearing the account of his early life, insisted that she knew there must be much good in his father and that Tib must write and allow thee to demonstrate that goodness for the sake of all."

"It sounds like Tiberius has been very fortunate in his choice of wife. Few women would be so charitable to one who has been the source of such suffering in one they love. To have such faith in one whom she has never met! That is truly remarkable."

"But, has she not met thee, at least to some degree, in thy son? Perhaps it is time for thee to read Tib's letter and discover the good within thee that thy daughter-in-law perceives from a distance."

John could not help but notice that Horton's hands shook ever so slightly as he grasped the letter that was handed to him. "Wouldst thou like to be alone while thou readest Tib's letter?" John asked.

"No, please stay and witness the fear and trembling of an old reprobate as he stands before his judge."

As Horton began to read, his caution and anxiety were quickly overwhelmed by such profound absorption in the letter's contents, that John Burgess, the hotel room, the entire cosmos seemed to melt away, as he was once again face-to-face with his son and conscience:

Father,

By now, I hope that you have become acquainted with the particulars of my life since you last saw me. The bearer of my letter is a very dear and trusted friend, a true Friend in both the religious and secular sense. You have received this letter partly as a herald and partly as an appeal.

First, it has been delivered to notify you that I am now a free man, a citizen of the Queen's dominion in Canada West. With the help of many good people and a merciful Providence, I now possess that most precious gift, freedom, which you had denied me. My wife Eliza, an extraordinary creature whose love I am not worthy to receive, has urged me to write to you and make an appeal to the good in the father whom I once knew and loved, in her firm belief that his goodness still lives and that perhaps he has acquired a clearer perspective on the fateful decisions that were made at the deathbed of my dear sister Julia.

In writing this letter, I am confronted with a profound irony. Should I be thankful for the decisions that so radically changed my life because of Julia's suffering and death? Young Moses willingly chose to leave the house of Pharoah's daughter, thereby coming to know his people and his mission in life. The reality of my situation was that I probably required a more forceful means of making the same discoveries. I would not have willingly left my "house of Pharoah's daughter." My suffering brought me into contact with some of the best people I have ever known, including my dear wife. All I can do is marvel at the chain of events and encounters that have brought me to this place in my existence.

Now, here is my appeal. During my travail earlier this summer when my mistress brought me back into slavery, I had the remarkable good fortune of meeting your other son, Cicero, in the slave pen in Louisville. He had become a real brother to me during my service as a field hand on your plantation, but for selfish reasons I did not reveal our true relationship to him. He told me some extraordinary news, which also gives me hope that you may seriously consider my appeal. I learned from Cicero that you did not sell my mother and Livia down the river but have kept them secretly in a small house not too distant from the plantation. How you have managed to keep this knowledge from my mistress is an amazing thing. At this time, I appeal to all that is good in you to finally fulfill the promise you made to my mother so long ago and free her and Livia.

Since I am already a self-emancipated man, I am also requesting in fulfillment of your responsibility to me that you purchase Cicero and emancipate him and his family. To my reckoning, that would just about cover my emancipation, which was to occur on my eighteenth birthday with the interest accruing since that time for your three slaves whom you had solemnly promised to free.

One final theological comment for your reflection, since I know you always enjoyed such speculation. My mistress has tried with all her considerable abilities to return me to slavery so that I might continue to serve as the surrogate for your penance only to experience great frustration with her repeated failures. Is it just possible, Father, that one could strike a balance between the strict predestinarian view of the orthodox Calvinist and that of Arminius, espousing free choice? It may be that we are born into a set of circumstances not of our choosing, yet we do have the freedom to choose how we live under those circumstances. Let me assure you from personal experience that, given the opportunity, I know of no person in bondage who would not rather choose and seek out freedom. May the kind Providence help you to see and fulfill your duty.

Your son,
Tiberius

A tall, middle-aged white man with graying, shoulder-length hair which struggled valiantly to compensate for a receding hairline, was striding down the main street of Buxton, Canada West in late October 1852. The seeming incongruity of his presence among so many refugees from American slavery was neither apparent in his facial expression or in that of the many persons of African descent with whom he exchanged greetings in passing on the street. Indeed, not only did he receive salutations of respect from passersby but also many expressions of genuine affection. Although a habitual earnestness, almost bordering on severity, was written in his face, when he focused his gaze on other members of his own species, the earnest intensity was overwhelmed and replaced by a gentle smile that radiated something tender, almost maternal in his character. When he opened his mouth and spoke, his accent betrayed his Scots-Irish origins.

The Reverend William King was nearly the only white person affiliated with the Elgin Settlement, the name originally given to the community founded in honor of the Governor General, Lord Elgin, whose influence was so crucial in recruiting the subscriptions for its establishment. Over time the community had acquired the name of Buxton to also honor Sir Thomas Buxton, who had played a central role in the passage of the legislation abolishing slavery throughout the British Empire.

As his mind was absorbed in contemplating the many changes that had occurred so rapidly in the community over the past few years, his eyes met those of William Parker, one of the newest and most celebrated members of the community who had arrived the previous April. Smiling, he approached Parker and, extending his hand, said, "How are you this fine morning, William?"

Parker grinned and replied, "Sir, I hope you can tell that I'm makin' progress in my learnin'. I fear my speech is improvin' faster than my readin' and writin' skills, though."

King smiled and said, "I hear very encouraging reports regarding your progress. Do not be discouraged. I assure you that the hero of Christiana, through perseverance, will prevail over any challenges posed by learning his letters at the age of thirty. My only requirement of you will be to see you write a full history of the events as you recall them for posterity."

Rather than surrender in accordance with the Fugitve Slave Act when his former master cornered them in Christiana, Pennsylvania the preceding year, Parker, with his wife, other fugitives, and local citizens resisted and fought back, killing Parker's master and later escaping to Canada West. His brave resistance had made him a hero among abolitionists. Lord Elgin had refused requests from the US government to extradite Parker, who had told him he would not be taken back alive.

"Reverend King, I want to thank you for introducin' me to Tib Johnson. He's been real kind to my wife and me, spendin' extra time in the evenin's teachin' us. He won't take any payment for all the extra time he spends with us. He just insists that it's his privilege."

"William, that is gratifying to hear. Tiberius has been a real godsend to the community and for me especially. He has had a first-rate education and is doing great service as my assistant teacher at the school. The arrival of Tiberius and his family in Buxton has given me the much-needed time to assist in other business concerns of the community while he does much of the primary teaching at the school. He has a natural gift for teaching, as well as the infinite patience and good humor that are such essential companions to the successful teacher. Actually, I am on my way now to meet with him at the school."

"Martha, that is excellent work. You are developing beautiful penmanship. I would like for you to now concentrate more of your efforts on mastering the spelling."

William King had slipped into the back of the large schoolroom and was quietly observing the gentle encouragement that Tib was giving one of the young refugee women who had been a student at the school for the past six months since her arrival in the settlement. What appeared to be a rather ordinary schoolroom by most standards was notable for two unusual features that in juxtaposition would likely disconcert most American observers who might happen to visit. The presence of so many studious negroes pursuing knowledge under the benevolent gaze of Queen Victoria emanating from the large portrait at the front of the room were two powerful reminders that the Stars and Stripes did not wave outside this school. As was his habit when Tib was about to move on to the next pupil, he surveyed the room looking for any students who required immediate support. Seeing William King silently observing in the back, he smiled and walked back to greet him.

"Good morning, Tiberius. How are your students faring this fine morning?"

"*Your* students, sir, continue to be a credit to the excellent program of instruction you have established for them. I merely bask in the glow of your success and daily discover how much I enjoy this vocation. Indeed, I am thankful beyond words for the trust you have placed in me."

"And I cannot begin to express my gratitude that a kind Providence through the auspices of a sagacious sheriff in Amherstburg has sent you and your family to me."

"Then I am doubly in debt to that wise sheriff, for not only did he direct me to you, my dear benefactor and mentor, but he also made it possible that a living Tiberius Johnson stands before you today in this schoolroom."

Grinning broadly, the Presbyterian minister clasped his young friend's right shoulder with his left hand while gripping Tib's right hand firmly in his own. "Oh Tiberius, if there were only more like you. The school is bursting at the seams. We must start another school to accommodate all the need. As you know, our community receives new refugees almost on a daily basis. The key to their successful transition to being free citizens of Canada is literacy. But the key to their full integration into Canadian society at all levels is a first-rate education that will prepare some of them and their children for the university.

"Look at the students here today. Nearly a quarter of them are white children from the neighboring community. One could question the wisdom or justice of allowing white children to consume so much of the school's resources. But I submit to you that an excellent classical education should be blind to color. By voluntarily seeking out what they perceive to be a superior education, the parents of the white children attending this school are doing more to break down the prejudices of white Canadians regarding the African race than any number of lectures I could give."

"Reverend King, the radical departure of your educational program from that in the other colored settlements has been a great inspiration for me. Clearly, basic literacy and vocational skills will be important for many, perhaps even a majority of the refugees, but your belief that colored children, if given the same exposure to a classical education, would be fully capable of becoming scholars of the highest order is nothing short of revolutionary. Your students are living proof that given the same opportunites for self-improvement, those of African ancestry are every bit the equal of those who would claim to be their masters."

"Tiberius, if there has been a proof of that principle, it is you who have established the precedent long before any of my modest efforts."

"How ironic that my father and owner, through an act of whimsy, would provide for his enslaved offspring, what you have offered through Christian charity!"

"Oh, my friend, never doubt the mysterious ways in which Providence intervenes in our humble existence. Don't forget that I was also once a slaveowner tolerating, if not fully embracing, ownership of other human souls whom I acquired through marriage. I always comforted myself with the conscious intention of freeing them at the earliest opportunity but needed the chastisement of exposure as a hypocrite by the great abolitionist, Frederick Douglass, during my theological training in Scotland, to drive me toward real action.

"No, Tiberius, I am confident that whatever the motives were that impelled your father to give you an excellent classical education, his investment will yet yield him much more than the mere gratification of an egoistic whim. As for myself, I remain especially grateful for the immeasurably valuable, albeit painful, lessons I have learned at the expense of my own dignity. Thank God for Frederick Douglass!"

"Well, I can only marvel at the faith you and my dear wife Eliza have both placed in my father. As for me, I must reserve judgment and wait patiently upon the future. What brings me tremendous pleasure and a smile every time I contemplate it, is the absolute astonishment on the faces of the white abolitionist visitors last week who heard your ten-year old scholar recite from the poet Virgil in the original Latin, provide a fluid English translation, and follow up with a lucid commentary!"

"It was a rare moment, indeed it was, to see the looks on their faces. Gone were the patronizing smugness and pity, replaced with respect and awe for the glorious image of the divine manifested in a young former slave. God has been good to us here in Buxton."

"Well, it is because of your inspiring example, sir, that I am prepared to work additional hours to support the increased need. For me the work is its own reward, although the salary provided is certainly appreciated by my wife and family."

"Tiberius, I only wish that the council could offer you more for your services. After all, here you are with a growing family. How are Eliza and young Naomi?"

"Mother and daughter are doing well. It has been nearly six weeks since Naomi's birth. She is a great source of joy for all of us, although I fear that our son Benjamin is a bit jealous of his sister."

"One of the most difficult realizations in a young child's life is the discovery that one no longer is the sole ruler over parental affection."

"Yes. Truly difficult and yet so essential!"

"Ah Tiberius, do you hear our liberty bell? It rings again from the tower of St. Andrew's church heralding the arrival of some new members of our community."

Tib smiled and said, "Sir, I don't want to detain you if you wish to go and welcome the newcomers."

"By the look on Eliza's face, I suspect I should be relieving you so that you may attend to her immediately. If you had been looking out the window as I have, you would have noticed that your wife is running rapidly in this direction."

Tib turned so that he could follow the direction of King's gaze and was amazed to see his wife almost at the steps of the schoolhouse.

"Please go, Tiberius, and attend to your wife. By the look on her face, my guess is that she has important news for you. I will take care of the students."

Tib threw a quick "Thank you" over his shoulder as he bounded out of the room to meet his wife on the steps of the school. Anxious thoughts bombarded him from all sides as he rushed into the arms of his breathless wife, whose face was stained with fresh tears.

Has something happened to one of the children? What new sorrow must I bear?

"What is it my darling? Are you and the children all right?"

"Oh, darling Tib. We are more than all right! Come and see the miracle for which we have prayed so long and hard."

Grasping his arm firmly in hers, Eliza slowly directed Tib's steps away from the school and down the street toward St. Andrew's Church, the source of the sound of liberation, which had pealed forth only a few minutes before.

"Steady, my dear husband, steady yourself," Eliza cautioned as they headed down the street.

"Eliza, why are you treating me like an invalid?"

"Tib, look carefully down the street. Do you recognize anyone walking toward us?"

Tib paused and gazed intently ahead, unable at first to comprehend the vision that presented itself to his eyes. He began to feel lightheaded and weak in the knees while Eliza's grip on his arm tightened.

"What you see, Tib, is real. This is no dream, my brave husband."

"Oh my God! It truly is a miracle," Tib exclaimed with joy as he began to run toward the reality that had been so hard at first to comprehend. Reaching first his mother, who was carrying Naomi, he lifted Liddie, still holding his daughter, from the ground, her tears streaming down onto his cheeks and mingling fully with his own. "Oh, my dear mother! To see you once again, one whom I had thought lost forever, to hold and kiss you who gave me life!"

"My handsome, noble son. How I have yearned for this moment! And now you have a beautiful wife and children, my grandchildren!" As Tib clung fiercely to his mother, alternating between kissing both her and his baby daughter on the forehead, she gently reminded him that there were others waiting to greet him. "Tiberius, I am not the only one who craves your attention, although I would be in bliss to remain so."

Reluctantly, releasing her from his grasp while coming to himself, Livia approached him holding her nephew's hand.

"Why Livia, you have become a woman and quite a beauty at that!"

"Brother, your powers of observation astound me. I might add that you seem to also meet the qualifications for being a man."

Brother and sister hugged tightly as they mixed their laughter with tears, including a thoroughly bewildered Bennie in their embrace.

Next, to Tib's great joy, his half-brother Cicero stepped forward to introduce his wife and two children.

"Oh Tib, you wuz always a brudder to me. I nebber knew dat you wuz mah real brudder, doe," Cicero said with great emotion as he hugged Tib.

"Please forgive me, brother, for I did know that you were my real brother, but selfishly kept the knowledge to myself because I was afraid you would resent the special treatment that I had received as a child and which you had been denied," Tib said with contrition.

"Oh, Tib, I dunno what I would do wif all dat fine'ry dat you had in de big house. If'n you kin he'p me an' mah fam'ly learn to read an' write, dat's all I want."

"It will be my great pleasure, Brother."

Taking up the rear of the column of pilgrims was a person whom Tib had both desired and been loath to meet. Bowing low before his father, Tib said, "Tiberius Claudius Nero at your service, Father. Is your motto still *audentes fortuna juvat*? Does fortune still favor the bold?"

"No, my son. I now subscribe to another more ancient *motto*, one recommended most heartily by a penitent murderer and adulterer: *Have mercy upon me O God. . .*"

As he said these words, Horton Newby, who had accompanied his slave family on their journey to freedom knelt before his son, lowered his head, and added, "Can you ever forgive me for the suffering I have caused you, Tiberius?"

Reaching out and touching his father's shoulder, Tib replied, "Please stand up, Father, and look at your daughter-in-law, Eliza. She is the source of your forgiveness and the consummation of my healing. When she pressed me to write that letter to you, I realized that I had to forgive you. The reality of that forgiveness, its price, only came in full force to me when I signed my name to that providential document."

Without hesitation, Eliza walked up to Horton, gave him a hearty embrace, and said, "Welcome to real freedom, Father."

Part Three

Render to Caesar the things that are Caesar's, and to God the things that are God's.

—Mark 12:17

"You should have seen how Isaac, our pacifist Quaker, calmly proceeded to dispatch each of his competitors. He has such a steady hand and sharp eye; he never missed the center of the target through all ten rounds."

Sam Johnson waxed eloquent upon the virtues of his friend Isaac's performance in a recent contest of marksmanship that was held at the county fair in Richmond, Indiana during a brief break before the beginning of the present term.

"They need men with your skills out in Kansas these days," another young man volunteered who was seated at table with Isaac.

Blushing with increasing embarrassment mixed with secret pride, Isaac could only remember his father's words of congratulation when he won the contest: "Isaac thou hast a gift. How wilt thou use it?"

Protesting his friends' bragging about his prowess with a rifled musket, Isaac said, "Sam, I am grateful to God for clear vision and a steady hand. They have helped me provide meat for my family's table, but I hope that these skills will be used to heal, not wound, others."

It was suppertime on Wednesday evening, the third of September 1856, and the dining room of the Ladies' Hall at Oberlin College was filled with the noise of many competing conversations, which were seasoned by an odd and sometimes awkward mixture of solemnity and laughter. Periodically, heated debate would rise above the usual vocal hum but would rapidly be quelled by a look or word from the Principal of the Female Department, Mrs. Dascomb, during the course of her duties in which she closely monitored the interactions between the male and female students. Meals on campus were held in common in the Ladies' Hall, affording both sexes an opportunity for social interaction outside of the classroom and worship services, which other than the Oberlin Choir were the only other sanctioned times at which the young male and female scholars could meet. Three rows of tables were arranged in the dining hall, usually with male students seated opposite female students. Matriculating students were made aware very early in their tenure at Oberlin of the many prohibited behaviors, but especially that "Students are prohibited, *on pain of expulsion*, from visiting those of the other sex, at their rooms, or receiving visits from them at their own, except by special permission from the President, or the Principal of the Female Department, in a case of serious illness." Oberlin's founders and faculty were confident that educating young men and women together would extend the civilizing influences of the latter upon the former while also affording young ladies the best possible educational opportunities by their direct participation with young men in an educational program marked by intellectual rigor. The founders' confidence in the ability of any serious and moral person to be an effective student, regardless of sex or color, made them doubly concerned to demonstrate that no scandalous behaviors should arise in their educational experiment that would compromise its success.

Along with its firm stand against slavery, Oberlin was also known for its progressive views about various other reforms, including a strong prohibition against the use of intoxicating substances such as tobacco and spirituous liquor. There was even an early enthusiasm for the dietary reforms of Sylvester Graham. Many of the students (and faculty) were grateful that the institution's foray into vegetarianism had waned by the 1850s, including Isaac and Sam. While not formally espousing women's suffrage and other more controversial aspects of the Woman's Question, Oberlin faculty insisted that women were as capable of attaining to the same levels of scholarship as any of their best male students. Indeed, they took particular satisfaction in having conferred the first bachelor's degrees offered by an American instititution of higher learning on three female graduates in 1841. With the exception of rhetoric, female candidates for the Bachelor of Arts degree took all the same courses as their male counterparts, including courses in Greek and Latin. It was felt that since the ladies would not be giving sermons or speaking publically other than in the capacity of teachers, that rhetoric would be a superfluous course of study for them. This policy was held in derision by several popular women orators, including the Grimke sisters, one of whom, Angelina, was married to a famous Oberlin graduate, the leading abolitionist Theodore Weld. Both sisters, as well as Lucy Stone, an 1847 recipient of a bachelor's degree from Oberlin, were all ardent advocates of abolition and women's suffrage, and frequently spoke to promiscuous gatherings comprised of both men and women.

Another student seated near Isaac began to expound upon recent events in Kansas.

"Have you heard about the attack last Saturday on the free-soil settlement of Osawatomie? John Brown, who is the son of one of Oberlin's former trustees and brother to an alumna, and his forces were greatly outnumbered by Missouri ruffians but fought valiantly in defense of the community before being driven off. The Missourians looted and burned Osawatomie to the ground."

Isaac looked up from his plate to hear his sister, Rebecca, who was serving at the table, answer with a grave voice, "I would like to honor Mr. Brown for his bravery and commitment to ending slavery, but I cannot countenance his use of violence. It seems as if there is only violence heaped upon violence in Kansas. The attack on Osawatomie may well be retribution for the acts of violence perpetrated by Mr. Brown and his associates at Pottawatomie Creek last May, which were in turn retribution for the attack on Lawrence. When will it ever end, this 'eye for an eye and tooth for a tooth?' Can we not try peaceful moral suasion? Violence only begets more violence."

"Those are fine sentiments, Miss Burgess, but moral suasion has failed. I think the only real means of convincing those Missouri slaveholders of their error will come at the end of a gun barrel," a grim-faced young man replied.

Rebecca, a pained expression on her face, exchanged glances with Isaac and said in reply, "I still cherish the hope that an appeal to the conscience of the slaveholder is a viable alternative. My fear is that as the conflict escalates, the clamor of the passions that have been inflamed will drown the voices of conscience and reason."

With that, Rebecca Burgess delivered more bread to the table and was about to move on when Sam spoke up, and said, "Rebecca, if only the rest of the human race were as gentle and reasonable as you. If they were, there would be no 'Bleeding Kansas.' Indeed, there would be no slavery."

Rebecca blushed slightly and smiled gratefully at Sam, but resisted the temptation to be further drawn into the discussion.

Isaac and Sam had now been at Oberlin for the past four years, two of which had been spent in the Preparatory Department and the last two in the collegiate program. They had not yet begun to fully savor their new status as upperclassmen after their recent ascension to the junior class in the college. Rebecca had been at Oberlin in the Preparatory Department the past two years and was now a freshman in the collegiate program with every hope of obtaining the same bachelor's degree that her brother and friend were seeking. Sam's younger sister, Louisa, had returned to complete her training in the Preparatory Department, having matriculated the previous year. She remained less than enthusiastic regarding pursuit of a bachelor's degree, telling Rebecca with characteristic sarcasm, "A diploma in the Ladies' Course will prepare me quite adequately to be a teacher without my having to grub around in Greek and Latin roots."

To which Rebecca had replied, "But dear Louisa, thou art denying thyself the very great privilege of intimate converse with the dead. A serious study of the so-called dead languages can open for the living the minds and thoughts of those long since departed from this world."

"Are you certain, Rebecca, that the dead appreciate such prying into their affairs?"

"If done with the utmost discretion and respect, I cannot perceive any objection on their part."

"Well, I'm glad to hear of it, although I suspect they might tolerate your discrete advances more than mine." Louisa, unable to sustain the pretence any longer had burst out laughing. Although Rebecca valiantly attempted to maintain her stiff composure for a few more moments, she also dissolved into laughter, as her gaze met the wordless sarcasm in Louisa's eyes.

The four students from Newport, Indiana were representative of the younger end of the range of ages reflected in the Oberlin student body. Typically, even students in the Preparatory Department were frequently over twenty years of age while Sam and Isaac, at eighteen, were some of the youngest juniors in the collegiate program. Rebecca, at age sixteen, and Louisa, at fifteen, also were younger than many of their counterparts in the Ladies' Department. It was not unusual for students seeking formal training to come to Oberlin after several years of service as rural teachers or unlettered ministers.

While some of the motivations for attending Oberlin were the same as for other students, the Quaker contingent from Newport, Indiana had some unique reasons for seeking an education at Oberlin. One of the strongest reasons for Isaac and Rebecca was that their Uncle Levi Coffin had given his blessing upon Oberlin as an institution that had a strong anti-slavery testimony, including its very active support of the Underground Railroad. That it also admitted women and persons of color for study were further evidence of an institution that shared many values with the Anti-Slavery Friends. Its strong stance on temperance also gave Uncle Levi further confidence that this would be a wholesome environment in which his niece and nephew could pursue their education. Although he, with their parents, felt confident of their solid grounding in the faith of their forbears, he still felt impelled to give Isaac, and then later Rebecca, some counsel regarding the prevailing religious atmosphere at Oberlin.

"Professor Finney, who is now the president of Oberlin and the principal speaker at First Day worship, is a most remarkable and persuasive homilist," Levi said. "His sermons, although intended to appeal to the reason, often have a powerful emotional aspect that can lead to excessive displays. I have seen him encourage highly emotional manifestations of repentance in the form of calls to the altar. It has been a longstanding testimony of the Society of Friends that the work of the Holy Spirit is primarily an interior work hidden within each soul and that acquisition of the Inner Light of God's presence is the work and struggle of a lifetime. Evangelists like Professor Finney will often cite dramatic conversions like that of the Apostle Paul. However, I must observe that Paul's experience on the road to Damascus was a beginning, albeit dramatic, to his new life in Christ, which was followed by great sufferings as well as illuminations that continued to the end of his life. Sometimes, the evangelistic enthusiasm of our fellow Christians who are not Friends may blind them to the quiet, ongoing work of the Holy Spirit. Nonetheless, Oberlin is a very fine Christian institution that has fully embraced the dignity and equality of every man and woman before God, regardless of their condition. Search out, then, the great treasure that lies hidden and buried there."

Another feature of Oberlin that was attractive for so many of its students, including the young scholars from Newport, was the opportunity to defray many student expenses through labor at the college or within the Oberlin community. The majority of its students came from farms with minimal financial means to pay tuition and living expenses at the college. Indeed, the motto for the school had always been "Learning and Labor." Rebecca's serving at table in the dining room of the Ladies' Hall was a reflection of that tradition. Young men and women at the college would often seek or be assigned various domestic or farming chores for which they would receive some small recompense toward their living expenses and tuition. A major feature of the Oberlin curriculum was a twelve-week winter break during which students would scatter in all directions, mostly in Ohio but even below the Mason-Dixon line, in search of teaching posts in rural schools, an important source of additional income to pay their college expenses. It was not uncommon for the many young abolitionists to establish stops on the Underground Railroad during their winter teaching activities. Sometimes, depending on the prevalent attitudes within individual communities, such efforts might be met with resistance and even overt hostility, especially in some of the communities of southern Ohio.

Wednesday evenings provided an interesting diversion for the students, whose formal instruction was largely confined to recitation sessions in the morning and manual labor and study in the afternoons. Literary societies, which were an important aspect of student life, met on Wednesday evenings. Although the title implied activities related to the study or composition of literature, the primary activity of the societies, which were established separately as male and female societies, was the exchange of ideas most often in the form of debates on various topics of general interest.

On one such Wednesday evening, Rebecca and Louisa, who shared a room in the hall with two other young women, rushed upstairs to collect their things prior to heading off to the meeting of the Young Ladies' Literary Society.

"What is the Men's Society debating tonight?" Louisa asked with a yawn.

"Oh Louisa, I think that thou witnessed a portion of the debate at the supper table. I believe the men will be debating whether the use of force is ever justified in a good cause such as emancipation of the slaves."

"It's unfortunate that you cannot enter the fray with the men. It would do them good to hear a sane feminine voice."

"I am not at all certain that my views on the subject are perceived by much of anyone these days as sane. As the suffering of over three million persons in bondage continues unabated with only greater intransigence on the part of our Southern brethren, I must admit the clear failure of all attempts at moral suasion. Must it inevitably come to violence?"

"A large portion of the crisis, I believe, is from the feeble response that Northern politicians have made to every selfish demand coming from the Southern slavocracy. Let me see, I kept some notes from Professor Finney's sermon about three weeks ago. Ah, here they are. In his usual direct manner, he describes very clearly in his sermon the abrogation of their duty by Northern politicians: 'Just as our dough-faced politicians might, but do not and will not, resist the demands of the slave power. Just such is the bondage of sinners under temptation. The Bible represents Satan as ruling the hearts of men at his will, just as the men who wield the slave power of the South rule the dough faces of the North at their will, dictating the choice of our Presidents and the entire legislation of the Federal Government.' As I see it, the North has allowed the South, like an undisciplined and thoroughly spoiled child to become a tyrant. In families where I have witnessed such childish tyranny arise; violence is almost sure to follow. But who am I to have an opinion? After all, I am only a young woman, and a colored one at that!"

"As always, thou art able to find a path of simplicity through all the complexity. Thy metaphor of the South as spoiled child and the North as indulgent parent has great merit. I also fear that thou art correct in thy prediction of more violence. We must compare notes with the men after they have their debate. Unfortunately, right now we must hurry for I am to debate in favor of the proposition: Resolved—The reading of fictitious works can be a positive influence on the mind."

Mrs. Dascomb rose and introduced the debaters and the topic for debate. Rebecca, as the proponent for the resolution, went first.

"Dear Ladies, at the outset of this friendly exchange I am anxious to clarify specifically for all of you that for which I debate. I am not here proposing that the reading of fictitious works *is* a positive influence on the mind, but rather that it *can* be a positive mental influence. Why is this distinction arising from use of the subjunctive mood so critical to my argument on behalf of fictitious literary works? When my esteemed opponent stands here before you to condemn fictitious works, I want you all to be fully certain that I share many of the same concerns that she will appropriately raise as objections to the reading of such materials. For ninety, nay perhaps even ninety-five, percent of the so-called popular fiction of our current era, I also share her deep misgivings regarding the baleful influence that may be exerted on the minds of innocent persons. In my opinion, literature of any kind that wishes to be considered literature in the truest sense must do more than entertain. It should, like the Scriptures, witness to the truth. It must challenge the sleeping conscience to awaken, the hardened heart to melt, and the ignorant mind to be illuminated.

"What is the central feature of fiction from which it draws its power? Is it not the narrative? Christ never spoke his greatest truths as dry lectures but as parables. And what are parables if not stories? I think that our greatest theologians would not disagree that at least some of these stories may have had fictitious elements in them, and yet they speak of sublime truths in ways only stories can. Why is this so? It is precisely because stories capture one's imagination, engaging both the intellect and emotions.

"Of course this is why fictitious works can also be very dangerous. All forms of mental activity should be subject to the light of reason and subject to the dictates of a conscience guided by the Spirit of God. With this rule to guide us, let us assume for a moment that even one piece of fictitious literature exists that meets these criteria. If there is such a one, I have won my argument.

"Let me now present my evidence. Here in my hand I hold a copy of Mrs. Stowe's book: *Uncle Tom's Cabin*. This volume has likely done more to advance the cause of the oppressed slave in this country than any number of other polemical works that have been written to foster the cause of abolition, and yet, strictly speaking, it is fictitious in nature. Has it not spoken to the minds and hearts of many who had previously been indifferent to the suffering of those in chains? I submit to you that through Mrs. Stowe's artistry, the truth has shone more brightly and is yet awakening many to the suffering and humanity of the slave."

Her unfortunate opponent, a Miss Evangeline Watts, who happened to be a great enthusiast of Mrs. Stowe's writing, nearly capitulated before she began and made only a feeble effort at demonstrating the irreparable harm that fictitious works cause to the human mind. She was the first to congratulate Rebecca on a brilliant argument at the end of the meeting.

Before adjourning, Mrs. Dascomb announced, "I think you will all be pleased to hear that next week Miss Sarah Jones and Miss Judith Abercrombie will debate the topic of fashion, a subject of perennial interest to our society. It will be the fourth debate in our series on the Bloomer Costume. Resolved—The Reform Dress, popularly known as the Bloomer Dress, is not indecent."

Tib involuntarily shivered in the crisp, cold autumn air. The light of a full moon illuminated the outline of the two-story, whitewashed frame house that he and his family called home. Other than the two to three acres close to the house, he and Eliza had not had time to cultivate more of the fifty acres they owned within the Elgin Settlement. The remaining acreage was timber, some of which was gradually being harvested for the growing lumber industry in Buxton. This had provided much needed additional income for the family.

He smiled as he gazed at the land and the house, both tangible signs of his Canadian citizenship, for he had risen early this October day in 1856, along with many other former American slaves residing in the community, to cast his first ballot as an enfranchised citizen of the Queen's dominion. Indeed, he had gone to considerable trouble to arrive in time from Toronto for the voting. For the past two years, with Reverend King's support and urging, he had temporarily relocated his growing family, Eliza, Bennie, Naomi, and another daughter, Phoebe, to Toronto so that he might obtain the university education that had been previously denied him. He was surprised and pleased when after several rigorous oral examinations in the spring of 1854, the University of Toronto offered him advanced placement. With another two years of intensive study and assuming timely completion of his thesis, he hoped to have received both his bachelor's and master's degrees with a specialization in history in the summer or autumn of 1858.

As he dreamily contemplated the shadows cast by the moonlight, he reflected on a conversation that he had had with William King two years earlier.

"Tiberius, your people will need first-rate scholars and academics. Now that your father is teaching here in Buxton, I think that we can spare you for this more important task. I have been in correspondence with Dr. Martin Delany, a negro physician and prominent abolitionist. He has some very interesting ideas about how to elevate the African race, including promoting their emigration not only to Canada, but also to Central America and the Western coast of Africa."

Tib remembered how he had protested, "But Reverend King, his notions do not seem to differ fundamentally from those of the older colonization societies."

"Tib, regarding his African plans, I think they differ in at least two important points. First, the emigration, as opposed to colonization, would be planned and organized by the emigrants, not through some benevolent scheme of repentant slaveowner. And second, the goal for the African endeavor, if I understand him correctly, would be to attack slavery at its origin through education and the modeling of alternative means of prosperity for the native Africans, such as more advanced farming techniques, rather than dependence on the sale of one's brothers and sisters into slavery."

"Sir, I subscribe to the simple-minded notion that as I am a native of the United States, born in the sovereign state of Kentucky, I should have the same rights as any other person who calls that his native land. I am eternally grateful for the citizenship bestowed on me by her Majesty's government, but if there ever is a general emancipation of slaves in the United States, I know where my duty lies. They will need colleges and universities to elevate them in the land, *their land*, which they have cultivated and developed at such a dear price. In the meantime, with the many thousands of emigrants from the slave states arriving in Canada West, I hope that my additional formal education will be put to good use."

He had spent a very pleasant evening before retiring early the previous night, visiting with his mother, his sister Livia, and her husband, all of whom were living at the home while he and his family were staying in Toronto. Livia had fallen in love with one of the young refugees whom she had been tutoring in reading and writing skills. Despite the distractions associated with their growing affection, he progressed rapidly in his studies with her help and after several months was quite proficient in his use of the English language. His passion for reading astounded Livia, who had often taken her own literacy for granted. It seemed to Tib that Frank and Livia, who had been married six months earlier, still retained the joyful glow of a newly married couple. Now that he had found steady employment working with many of the other men of Buxton on the Great Western Railway, Frank could express a sense of calm contentment with their present circumstances while outlining ambitious plans for the future.

When Tib arrived in the late afternoon on the previous day, his mother Liddie had been very glad to see him but was clearly disappointed that he had not brought Eliza and the grandchildren. Apologizing for the brevity of his visit, he said, "Mother, I'm sorry but my professors gave me a very brief leave of absence for this trip, which really precluded bringing the whole family. I promise to bring all of them for the Christmas holiday, when we will have much more time to spend together."

"It's very difficult for me, Tiberius, to endure any separation from my dear ones after being finally reunited again four years ago. Your mother will try to be more patient. I am so thankful and proud that you are able to pursue a university education. I know your father is also very proud of all your accomplishments."

"Mother, please tell me then of your relationship with Father. How are you bearing up with his continued presence here in Buxton?"

"We have cordial conversations after church almost every Sunday in Reverend King's parlor and recently we have begun to share and discuss books as we once did. It is remarkable to see him working with such energy and purpose in the school. He is quite appreciated by the students for his excellent instruction and the great patience he shows in his teaching. He has even persuaded me to assist as a volunteer tutor for some of the students, which I quite enjoy.

"I think at first when he lingered here so long in Buxton after delivering the remainder of his slave family to freedom, he was quite at sea. The revelation that he had been secretly harboring his former slave mistress and daughter nearby, almost under her nose, was more than Malvina Newby could tolerate. She certainly did not believe his protestations that our intimacies had ended when Livia and I were sent away on that fateful day. Thus, when he confessed to her that we were living nearby under his protection and that he planned to finally honor his promise to free us, she exploded in a rage and insisted that his infidelities had continued and that she could not bear the thought of being in the same house with him.

"Although Malvina would never believe me, it is absolutely true that our intimacies ended abruptly with my departure from the plantation. Indeed, as you know, I was so angry with him that I rarely responded to his expressions of concern for our well-being on the quarterly visits he made to our secluded cottage. Somehow, I guess, he had hoped that he could be reconciled with Malvina, his lawful wife, while still cherishing his love for me. As my coldness toward him persisted, especially after his report of your supposed death in the Ohio River, he would still come, bringing books as well as other gifts, having, I believe, finally lost all hope of regaining my affection. He would sit with us in silence for several minutes, a look of profound sadness suffusing his face and then, rising to go, would bow gravely to each of us and depart."

"Over several conversations, I have gradually learned that when your father made his decision to free us, he anticipated Malvina's reaction and decided in an effort to mollify her to give her power of attorney over the plantation in his absence and to name her favorite nephew, Gordon Fairclough, as heir to the estate in the event of their deaths. He dreaded returning to the hostile environment that he knew awaited him at home but also felt very awkward about staying here. As in so many other things, Reverend King, in his sagaciousness, recognized the brokenness in your father's soul and has gone about mending it through employing him in meaningful labor. I have had the privilege of seeing him laugh with and cry over persons for whom at an earlier time in his life he might not have given a second thought, and indeed would have viewed as mere chattel. The old spark of cynicism that you and I know so well has been extinguished and replaced by a sense of childlike wonder and awe. It is as if he is seeing the world, and especially all its complex and varied human relationships, in a new, transformed light."

"Oh Mother, you still love him, don't you?"

"Tiberius, I never stopped loving him, but this is a new and greater love, a love purified through suffering. We are both struggling in our own ways to find a new and deeper intimacy, no longer dependent on physical relations. I am finally beginning to know the man that Horton Newby was always meant to be. Neither of us has spoken of it and indeed may never speak of it, but we both know that our former intimacy must now be supplanted by that of equals, both in the sight of men and of God.

"Horton has recently spoken to me of the different Greek words for love. He mentioned the word *philia*, which is often translated as 'friendship.' He waxed eloquent about the limitations of English to convey the full depth of meaning conveyed by *philia*. The intimate bonds of true friendship extend well beyond mere ties of affection but reflect deep connections between two souls. This was the diffident manner in which the new Horton could declare his deep love for me. I was quite moved by such shyness and humility, coming from a man who once held full sway over my entire being."

"Has he spoken to you yet of *agapē*, Mother?"

"No. Is that another Greek word for love?"

"Yes. It was appropriated by the early Christians and came to mean a love without limits, a love expressed by a God who would die for the sake of his creatures, a self-sacrificial love."

"Is it possible that when one reaches the greatest depth of *philia*, one has arrived at *agapē*?

"I cannot say. But, when you and Father have fully plumbed the depths of *philia* together, I think you will have the answer."

Tib's musings upon the prior evening's conversation were interrupted by the familiar voice of his half-brother Cicero.

"Brother, are you ready to cast the first vote of your life?"

Grinning as he shook Cicero's hand, Tib replied, "I am as ready as you and a lot of other new citizens of Canada West are. And I'd dare say it's about time!"

"Tib, would you mind much if our father came along? He'd really like to see you."

Somewhat startled and bemused by Cicero's request, Tib replied, "I never knew our father to be fond of early rising."

"Tib, I know you still struggle with. . .Oh what's the word? Am-bi-va-lent, that's it. . .with ambivalent feelin's for Father. But you know he's really done a heap of good here in Buxton. I can now truly say that not only do I have a father, but also, I've got one I can be really proud of. Did you know he'll be comin' to live in my home later this month?"

"No, I didn't. So, he is finally leaving Reverend King's place. He's been enjoying his hospitality for over four years now, ever since he arrived in Buxton."

"He didn't really have another place to stay at that time, since your mother and Livia were staying with you, and Milly and I didn't have a place of our own yet. It's taken me nearly four years to no longer think of him as 'de massa,' but as my father instead. I'm just beginning to appreciate the Newby part of me."

"Well, I am very glad that you are getting to know him and that he is really becoming part of your family."

"Part of *our* family, you should say," Cicero chided Tib.

"Yes. You're absolutely correct. Please forgive me, Brother. I would very much like to see him."

"Good. We'll collect him at Reverend King's home where he should be waitin' for us."

The moonshine that had illuminated Tib's early-morning reverie was rapidly being swallowed up by the gray predawn light in the eastern sky as they approached Reverend King's home.

"Good morning, Father. I am impressed by your rising at such an early hour to join us on our pilgrimage," Tib said as he gave Horton a hearty handshake.

"Tiberius and Cicero, it would give me the greatest pleasure to personally witness my sons' initiation into the liturgy of the body politic."

"Father, what do you mean by *liturgy of the body politic*? You're stretchin' your partially lettered son's knowledge to the limit," Cicero complained.

"Cicero, I apologize for my fondness for the use of obscure turns of phrase. With the utmost sincerity, I meant to say that it would be a great source of joy for me to see both of you recognized as full citizens of your adopted country by the simple but fundamental act of voting."

"Father don't apologize. How else will I learn? So, liturgy means voting?"

"Well, not exactly. It actually refers to a common act of the people, which could, of course, be a religious service, but in the context of the body politic refers to a common political action, like voting."

"Oh, I see. Thank you, Father, for teachin' me. Tib, every time I'm around Father I learn somethin' new. It's such a glorious thing, this business of learnin'!"

"Father, it seems quite clear to me that Cicero is a very quick study. Indeed, quicker than I ever have been."

"Tiberius, he is indeed very quick, but I think the real difference lies not so much in quickness of intellect as in the intensity of appetite and thirst for knowledge he possesses. These have been held in check for so long by the systematic suppression of learning that is such a foundational principle underlying the subjugation of the negro in the South that when the dam holding them in check has been removed, the flood is almost overwhelming, a truly extraordinary force of nature.

"I have seen many others like Cicero for whom the hunger and thirst for knowledge, for mental development, is equally as strong. Whether thirty years of age or three years of age like Cicero's young Sally, I have never seen such enthusiasm, commitment, and gratitude for the basic experience of learning. I am in awe every day I spend with my students."

Tib was startled but pleased to hear direct confirmation from his father's own lips of the change that Liddie had seen developing in Horton's character. He thought he would test the depth of the change by a little probing of his own.

"Father, have you ever reflected on the possibility that the metaphor you so aptly employed just now might work in two directions? Is it possible that the suppression or dam of which you speak has also affected the slaveowners as much as their slaves? It seems that it not only has blinded the slaveowners of the South to the potential and desire for learning inherent within their human property, but also has distorted their own ability to learn to the point of being imprisoned within a false world of knowledge of their own making, the boundaries of which are formed by that same dam holding back the colored person?"

"Oh Tiberius, there is nothing like perspective to help open one's eyes. The longer I have experienced the honest freedom of Buxton, the more horrific my life as I knew it in Kentucky has become. You are absolutely right that the peculiar institution has not only been the dam holding back the inherent humanity of the negro, but it has also done the same to the white citizens who have blindly, unquestioningly defended it, stopping their ears to any arguments to the contrary. They have become moral and intellectual slaves to a system that denies the fundamental necessity of human beings to seek the truth. Lies must be added to lies to maintain some level of composure in the face of the reality that stares the white Southerner in the face.

"Sadly enough, even here in the Queen's dominion, there are elements of that same prejudice toward the African race that are so common throughout the United States. For example, the Member of Parliament from Chatham, Edward Larwill, who has been such a thorn in the flesh to Reverend King and the whole Elgin Settlement, continues his irrational vituperations against the refugees."

"But Father," Cicero interjected, "Reverend King has emphasized that there is strength in numbers, and we mean to prove that today. Three hundred newly enfranchised citizens from the Elgin Settlement are marching to Chatham early this morning to help elect a new member from Chatham. Archibald McKellar, who had been a past supporter of Larwill, has come to appreciate the great success of our settlement and has now become one of our greatest defenders, much to Larwill's chagrin. He is now standing for Parliament from Chatham. It is our fervent hope that our votes will unseat Larwill in favor of McKellar and demonstrate that there is indeed strength in numbers. As colored Canadians, united together, we will have a voice in our government."

"Cicero, you have very eloquently stated why I, as your father, am so anxious to witness this historic event. How extraordinary to see three hundred men of African descent—indeed, former slaves!—exercise their rights as newly enfranchised citizens of Canada! With such commitment and mutual support, I believe it may not be many years before you will be able to elect one of your own to public office here in Canada. That will be a grand day, indeed!"

As they continued their march along the forest road to Chatham, the light of dawn was now revealing the different shades of red and yellow that had been hidden quietly in the darkness of night among the remaining green of the autumn leaves. The three men looked with awe on the transformation of the scene about them and felt instinctively that its beauty augured well for the success of their endeavor. By late morning, the people of Chatham were surprised, and some were alarmed by the arrival of over three hundred colored men who promptly reported to the polling place of the town and presented their evidence of citizenship. Horton Newby watched his sons and marveled at the complete order and solemnity that attended the whole contingent from Buxton as they proceeded to perform their civic duty like any other citizen of Canada West. As he watched, he could only reflect that what they were accomplishing was indeed a liturgy, not just the liturgy of the body politic, but also a liturgy of freedom in which the God of freedom watched the proceedings and smiled. As the member of Parliament from Chatham was soon to learn, there was strength in numbers, including colored numbers. Edward Larwill was defeated in his bid for reelection that day through the common action of the men from Buxton.

September 14, 1858

Dear Isaac,

I am quite anxious to hear thy news of Ann Arbor and about thy first days as a medical student there. Thou must be quite happy to be matriculating in two weeks, to finally be engaged in direct pursuit of thy dream of becoming a physician. Art thou satisfied with thy lodgings? I am curious about thy impressions of the Friends' Meeting there. As Uncle Levi would ask, hast thou had an opportunity to purchase stock in the local Underground Railroad yet? Sam, Louisa, and I as well as thy other friends here at Oberlin already miss thee greatly.

Until yesterday, I had nothing remarkable to report to thee. Classes began as usual without any major difficulties. Professor Dascomb's science lectures are proving to be every bit as interesting as thou hadst promised. I'm not certain at this point which I find more interesting, natural philosophy or chemistry. Of course, the subjects complement one another. Just the possibility to begin to understand in some small way the laws that govern the material world has been thrilling to me. The courses in advanced anatomy and physiology are proving to be not only as fascinating as their predecessors were last year, but also quite practical.

As thou knowest, Dr. Dascomb is always giving useful applications from his practice of medicine to illustrate the importance of the information he shares with us. His recent discussion of the use of tourniquets to control bleeding from injuries to the blood vessels was most edifying. Hopefully, I will never need to use this knowledge in practice; however, I am very glad to learn of it. It seems to me that thy professors might give thee advanced standing in thy medical studies, since Dr. Dascomb is so thorough and comprehensive in his teaching. I will be very curious to hear about the new knowledge that thou hast gained during thy formal medical studies. Although I sometimes feel that my days may be too full, I am glad to be continuing, on thy advice, my study of French. The new instructor is much more effective at drawing *les mots Français de ma bouche.*

Sam has thoroughly embraced his work with Mr. John Mercer Langston and finds reading the Law to be as fascinating and challenging as he had hoped. Mr. Langston, being one of the very few colored persons admitted to the Bar, is a great inspiration, especially for Sam. His stories of his father's exploits as an officer during the Revolution are always fascinating to hear. It seems that his efforts to obtain voting rights for the negroes here in Ohio have not yet borne fruit, but he cheerfully keeps his hand to the plow, providing an excellent model of patience for us all. With all his duties and responsibilities reading the Law with Mr. Langston, Sam has made a point of continuing his participation in the Oberlin Choir. Professor Allen was clearly pleased to have Sam remain in the choir since his deep bass voice would have been sorely missed.

Since thou hast left Oberlin, it seems that Sam has been even more solicitous toward me. He makes a great effort to still take meals with Louisa and me in the Ladies Hall, has not missed a Friday choir practice yet, and stands close to us during services on First Day in the church. He truly is another brother to me, especially in thy absence. However, he seems infinitely more tolerant of my prattle than thou hast ever been, Brother, which remains a mystery to me. Sam has been following all the recent political developments with great interest. Thou rememberest how his mood was so downcast, even despairing, after Chief Justice Taney's ruling in the case of the unfortunate slave Dred Scott last year. For some time, he could only speak of his fears that the Supreme Court's decision was the first step toward enslaving all negroes regardless of their status and location within the United States. Certainly, in my own experience here in Oberlin of late, the slavecatchers seem to have been thoroughly emboldened, perhaps as a consequence of this judicial decision.

On a positive note, Sam seems to have gained new vigor and energy from following the current debates in Illinois between Mr. Lincoln and Senator Douglas. Undoubtedly, he is frustrated by what he sees as the half measures proposed by a politician, but nonetheless is inspired with new hope because despite this, Mr. Lincoln has brought the issue of slavery, its potential extension through the Dred Scott decision, and even its future existence, squarely before the American public. His mentor, Mr. Langston, has counseled patience, but has concluded in his private discussions with Sam that Mr. Lincoln's "house divided" speech, which was so much a part of Senator Douglas's attack on him in the first debate, is prophetic. To use a medical metaphor, of which I hope thou wilt approve, the abscess of slavery is coming to a head. The question remains: How much pain and suffering will attend its drainage?

Louisa, as ever, remains my rock of good cheer. Without naming the unfortunate victim, I must share with you an amusing anecdote of an incident of which Louisa and I were witnesses that caught one of the other young ladies here completely by surprise, and yet again illustrates Louisa's unique gifts. For our unnamed friend, it was truly mortifying but for me it was confirmation of all my concerns regarding hoop skirts. Here is what happened. Being delayed by many dishes to clean after breakfast last Thursday, Louisa, our friend, and I were hurrying to our first recitation. Rather than continue on the longer route along the plank sidewalk around Tappan Square, our friend suggested in a very determined voice that we should take a shortcut across the square. Without further reflection, she plunged ahead on to the grass of Tappan Square only to find herself unable to make any forward progress. Quick-eyed Louisa discovered that the heroine of our adventure was most firmly attached to the plank sidewalk by a protruding nail that had transfixed one of the lower hoops of her skirt. After a variety of attempts to liberate the incarcerated hoop, all of which proved to be dismal failures, our heroine, looking around and blushing crimson in embarrassment, asked, "What will become of me, if Mrs. Dascomb discovers me trapped here by my hoop skirt?" In an ill-conceived attempt at comforting our distraught friend, Louisa said, "Really dear, it could be much worse. After all, Mrs. Dascomb has always been a kind and understanding principal of the Ladies' program. The real question we need to consider is this: What if some young man or men from Tappan Hall discover you here in such a predicament? As thou might expect, a flood of tears began to emanate from the eyes of our friend as she begged us to extricate her from her dilemma. At this point, Louisa volunteered, "This will likely require a drastic operation from which your hoop skirt might not survive." In her misery, she wailed, "Do whatever you must to this accursed skirt!" With such a mandate, Louisa ran back to the Ladies Hall and obtaining a rather large knife returned with a look of grim determination on her face that barely concealed her mirth. Brother, I think thou wouldst truly admire Louisa's skillful and rapid amputation of the offending hoop. Unfortunately, the operation created a permanent disfigurement of the hoop skirt. Indeed, a significant portion of the lower half of the skirt was left affixed to the plank sidewalk, leaving our classmate no choice but to run as if the Furies were chasing her back to her room in the Ladies Hall. Needless to say, Louisa found the whole affair to be uproariously funny. Louisa has even paraphrased Professor Finney's ferocious sermon on "the wages of sin," homilizing somewhat irreverently to our friend ever since regarding the 'wages' of wearing hoop skirts! When we made a second effort to attend our first recitation, we noted with some surprise that the remnants of the dismembered hoop skirt were no longer in evidence. Since the incident there has been much gossiping among the students as to the purported identity of the victim. Neither Louisa nor I have given any evidence of our knowledge regarding the incident, however.

One final note on the affair, I would like to add. With a perfectly sober expression on her face, Mrs. Dascomb announced at breakfast on Friday morning that she would like to have some volunteers from the Ladies' Literary

Society debate the following: Resolved—Hoop skirts are hazardous to the health and safety of women.

Finally, dear Brother, I alluded earlier in this letter to something of great moment that occurred yesterday. I will now present thee with the details of a most singular incident that I was fortunate to witness, the ultimate outcome of which remains uncertain. The community has continued to be on tenterhooks since that incident on the twentieth of August when slavecatchers tried unsuccessfully to apprehend a colored woman and her two children. Thankfully, as thou knowest, her screams alerted the community and she was rescued. Since that event, suspicious characters speaking with strong Southern accents have been observed to be staying at Mr. Wack's establishment. Also, the town clerk, Anson Dayton, who has never been a friend of the negro, has been seen at Wack's hotel speaking with the strangers from the South. Well, all these suspicious activities came to a head when yesterday, in broad daylight an escaped slave, John Price, who had been living and working in our community for two years, was captured by the slavecatchers from Kentucky. He would have been taken back into slavery if it had not been that our fellow student, Ansel Lyman, providentially witnessed his being carried off in a buggy at the crossroads where the north-south road between Oberlin and Wellington intersects with the diagonal road between Elyria and Columbus. Three men in the buggy turning onto the road to Wellington held poor John Price. When he saw Ansel Lyman walking with another man, he had the presence of mind to start crying out for assistance. Being outnumbered, especially since his walking companion was also no friend of negroes, Ansel wisely did not react to his cries immediately but after they had passed out of sight, he quickly returned to Oberlin and raised the alarm.

It was truly amazing how quickly the word of Price's capture spread in Oberlin. Brother, it is a pleasant irony that Price's kidnappers could not have chosen a more dangerous witness of their nefarious deed. Since the time he spent fighting with Osawatomie John Brown in Kansas back in 1856, I think thou wouldst agree that Ansel Lyman has been the most militant of abolitionists. Certainly his blood was up when Louisa and I heard him haranguing the growing crowd on South Main Street. He was calling for the formation of a posse of citizens to give chase and rescue Price. It seemed clear to everyone that the slavecatchers's goal was to transport Price to Columbus for an expedited hearing before a federal commissioner under the Fugitive Slave Act to return him as quickly as possible to his master in Kentucky. To this end the next southbound train to Columbus would be leaving by about five p.m. from Wellington. It being the early afternoon, we all realized that there was limited time in which to act. A general exodus, almost a stampede, from Oberlin followed thereafter. I must admit in my weakness and curiosity, I succumbed, along with Louisa, to the temptation to follow the mass of people heading to Wellington in search of poor Mr. Price. A Miss Adelia Field, an Oberlin graduate and principal of a seminary in Tennessee, who was visiting the community with her mother, allowed us to crowd into her buggy along with some other students. I must say that she had the grimmest look of determination on her face. Turning around to all of us, before whipping her horses into action, she said, "Today, you will witness the sterner stuff of which Oberlinites are made. When the Higher Law of the Gospel is in direct opposition to the laws of man, there is no question where our duty lies. I am glad, indeed thankful, that each of you will be able to come and witness this historic moment. No refugee from slavery, who has sought protection in Oberlin, has ever been returned to bondage! And by the mercy of God, Mr. Price will not be the first."

For the entire nine-mile ride to Wellington we were enveloped in a cloud of dust from all the traffic on the road. The dust in no way seemed to daunt Miss Field's enthusiasm for the chase. Indeed, her elderly mother was even more vehement in the directions she constantly gave her daughter to "press forward with all possible speed! Do not spare the horses when a man's life and freedom are at stake!" By the time we arrived at the outskirts of Wellington about forty-five minutes later, the horses were in a lather, foaming at the mouth, in their exhaustion. Oddly enough there was already a crowd of people in Wellington, but partly for a different reason. There had been a fire earlier in the morning that had destroyed a harness shop and several adjacent buildings on the west side of Main Street near the main public square which had drawn farmers and curiosity seekers from neighboring farms. As we approached the public square, it was crowded with men both colored and white with many women in attendance as well. Each new buggy arriving from the north was met with cheers. When we slowly moved forward among the many horsedrawn conveyances, we were startled to hear a woman from the town shout, "What are we coming to? A fire in the morning and war at night." By three p.m. there may have been as many as five hundred men crowded into the public square surrounding the Wadsworth Hotel where the slavecatchers had secured their prisoner in an attic room. What followed after our arrival in Wellington is still a confused jumble of events in my mind. Perhaps Louisa can give thee a better sense of what happened. Unfortunately, there was much shouting and oaths coming from the crowd in the square as the afternoon progressed. At the same time rumors flowed through the crowd like the turbulence seen in river rapids, sometimes producing shouts of exaltation when it appeared that the rescuers from Oberlin were making headway in their negotiations with the slavecatchers or at other moments a collective groan would arise as when someone claimed that members of the state militia were on a train from Cleveland that would arrive at approximately five p.m. to enforce the federal statute. Crowds that can rapidly become unruly mobs are frightening entities. The mood of the crowd in the square would change at a dizzying rate.

To his great disappointment, Sam was with Mr. Langston attending to legal business in another county, which precluded their involvement in the event. However, Mr. Langston's brother, Charles, a respected teacher who happened to also be visiting Oberlin, was present during the events in Wellington and made every effort to calm the situation as he negotiated with the slavecatchers on behalf of Mr. Price. I believe one attempted strategy was to seek a warrant for the arrest of the slavecatchers as kidnappers under Ohio law. Later, we learned from Charles Langston that the slavecatchers had, in general, laid their plans well, having obtained the necessary power of attorney and federal warrant for Price's capture. My guess is that the vast majority of the people that crowded the square were unaware of the federal warrant and I daresay would not have cared if they had known. Between frustration with the delays associated with the legal wrangling and the impending arrival of the five o'clock train from Cleveland, allegedly bringing the state militia, the crowd in the square became increasingly restive. Men began to shout, "Bring him out!" and wave firearms and other weapons, demanding that either Price be released or that the hotel be stormed immediately to achieve his release by force. At one point, the slavecatchers thought they could convince the crowd that John Price was willing to return to slavery by having him appear on the balcony outside the attic window of the room in which he was being confined. It was clear that he spoke out of fear of his captors and this ploy only angered the crowd more. Indeed, one colored man from Oberlin urged Price to jump to freedom while he trained his rifle on one of Price's captors. Price's hesitation gave his captor enough time to grab him and pull him back into the attic. This incident produced an even louder outcry from the crowd to intervene with force. When the train from Cleveland finally arrived without troups aboard there was a general sigh of relief. However, it was becoming clear that with only about an hour of daylight left, any attempt at rescue would have to be accomplished soon or the opportunity would likely be lost with an overnight delay that could change the situation dramatically on the morrow.

The situation changed rapidly from this point onward with calls for volunteers to storm the hotel. For all the bluster coming from the crowd, only five men joined William Lincoln, one of whom was Ansel Lyman, in response to his call for volunteers. Soon, they disappeared into the hotel and we could then hear noise from an apparent scuffle followed soon thereafter by shouts of "Forward, forward!" Later, after an anxious pause we heard a shot and more shouting from within, it being unclear whether this was from Lincoln's group or another that had attacked from the rear of the hotel. Feeling utterly impotent to help and unwilling to countenance violence as we waited anxiously for the outcome of the incident unfolding across the square in the Wadsworth Hotel, I joined Louisa, Miss Field, and her mother in prayers for the safe rescue of John Price and that no harm might come to either rescuers or captors in the process. Amazingly, by God's kind providence, our prayers were answered when some minutes later we heard a triumphant shout coming from the hotel and then witnessed John Price being escorted to a waiting buggy by another Oberlin student. After being deposited in the buggy, he was whisked away toward Oberlin to the general relief and exultation of the crowd who witnessed this happy culmination to the day's adventure. As the crowd dispersed, many of whom were returning to Oberlin, including Miss Field and her passengers, Louisa gave me a look devoid of her usual good humor and whispered, "I thank God for Price's rescue, but this is not the end of the affair. I hope that the rescuers are circumspect about describing the events of the rescue and their involvement, for I am quite certain that the full fury of President Buchanan's administration will be directed at Oberlin in response to this challenge to its authority." Rarely, does Louisa speak with such bluntness unalloyed with humor. I fear, dear Brother, that she is correct in her apprehensions for our college. Many in our struggling and divided country will see in this action nothing less than an act of revolution. Pray for thy alma mater.

Your affectionate sister,
Rebecca

It had been more than ten days since he had received Rebecca's letter and Isaac, who was not as prompt a correspondent as his sister, was beginning to feel guilty each time he saw the letter accusing him on the small side table he used as a desk in his room. He had just returned from the first clinical demonstration of his medical course and was still reveling in the experience. An exhilarating walk in the crisp autumn air had further heightened his euphoria late that Saturday morning. The profusion of beautiful colors that were bursting forth among the trees of his new town added to his enthusiasm. As he sat down to write, he comforted himself by reflecting that, after all, Rebecca had asked about his medical school experience in her letter. He could now in all honesty tell her about his first few days of instruction.

October 9, 1858

Dear Rebecca,

I apologize for the tardiness of my correspondence, but I wanted to give thee at least a small report of my experience as a medical student thus far. Perhaps I should first give thee a brief description of my journey here from Adrian and address some of thy other questions about the town and locale before attempting to describe the university and its medical and surgical department.

Mrs. Laura Haviland sends thee her greetings and wellwishes. She is hoping that thou wilt be able to assist in the teaching program at the Raisin Institute again this winter term. I assured her of thy continued commitment and interest assuming a stipend can be found to support thy efforts. Though she is fifty years of age, I marvel at the vigor she demonstrates in all her activities. There is a steady stream of refugees that flows through Adrian in a northeasterly direction ultimately through Detroit toward freedom in Canada West. Ann Arbor is a well-situated intermediate stop for many of them and should provide me many opportunities to purchase additional stock in the Underground Railroad.

Before I departed from Adrian, Mrs. Haviland gave me explicit directions for my journey north to Ann Arbor so that I might witness a most singular sight. The stagecoach to Ann Arbor that follows the road between the town of Saline and Ann Arbor passes directly by the home of a Captain Lowry who is an ardent abolitionist and stockholder of the Underground Railroad. His home is about six miles south of Ann Arbor. This gentleman has a reputation for being absolutely fearless in his antislavery convictions and has demonstrated this by erecting a sign by the side of the road to welcome all fugitves from slavery. The stagecoach driver made a point of stopping so that all of us on the stage could read the sign. It appeared to portray the images of a male and female slave with the caption: *liberty to the fugitive captive and the oppressed over all the earth, both male and female of all colors.* I was subsequently informed that all his closest neighbors are also abolitionists, so the sign and its owner remain unmolested. In any event, I now know the location of one of the local conductors and may come to know the man and not just his art.

The Huron River bisects the town of Ann Arbor. The main portion of the town, including the university, is located south of the river while a growing business district is located just north of the river. After six years in Oberlin, having to endure the monotony of the extremely flat terrain, it is a positive joy to experience the undulating and varied landscape of this town, with its lovely river, which adds considerably to its character and charm. There must be no more than a few thousand inhabitants. Considering that several hundred students are present in the community during the educational sessions, according to the housekeeper here where I rent a room, there have been concerns in the community about public rowdiness and disorder at various times. Unfortunately, there are saloons in the western portion of the town that supply beer and wine, primarily to the German portion of the population but also to some students. Thankfully, stronger forms of spirituous liquors have been banned in the town.

There is a greater variety of Christian communities represented here than in Oberlin. The major protestant denominations, including the German evangelical church and Catholics, have churches in the community and there are two Friends meetings, one in Ann Arbor and the other in the nearby community of Ypsilanti. Both Friends meetings are of the Hicksite persuasion, unfortunately. After attending First Day meeting last week, I found their views to be too far divergent from the orthodox tradition among the Indiana Yearly Meeting of Friends. Some of them view Elias Hicks as another Christ. They seem to be gradually wandering away from Christianity. Although I cannot in good conscience worship with them, there are clearly many good-hearted souls in their community who share our desire to assist the freedom seeker. I feel confident that in this commitment to those fleeing bondage, I will find a common ground for collaboration with the Friends meetings here. As thou knowest, Mrs. Haviland has been worshiping with the Wesleyan Methodists for some time. They own considerable stock in the Underground Railroad in this area. She has assured me that apart from externals, their faith and practice is closer to the orthodox Friends understanding. The Wesleyan Methodist church here in Ann Arbor will be the next religious community I visit.

The students are encouraged to seek lodging in the community as the buildings previously used for dormitories have been converted to other uses at the direction of President Tappan. By the way, in anticipation of thy question, I don't know of any familial connection between Reverend Henry Tappan, the president of the University of Michigan, and the Tappan brothers who have provided so much generous support to Oberlin College. I have not learned anything yet regarding President Tappan's views on slavery. His major concern seems to be the reproduction of an excellent Prussian form of higher education here on the frontier. One of the central elements of his program is public or state support for university education, so that it might be accessible to average citizens with limited means, for which I am heartily thankful. The fee for matriculation in the Science, Literature, and Arts or Medical and Surgical Departments has been ten dollars. Most other medical schools charge between sixty-five and one hundred twenty-five dollars per term. The ten-dollar fee at the University of Michigan is for both years of study and that is true for residents and non-residents of the state! Since last year, the administration has felt the need to add an additional annual charge of five dollars plus the deposit of one dollar per term for potential costs related to damage of equipment. As thou canst see, even with the recent increase in cost, a medical education here is a bargain. This may in part help account for the large number of students enrolled in the Medical and Surgical Department. I am told there are over two hundred students currently hoping to qualify as physicians, while only a small percentage of them will complete all the requirements and graduate.

Like so many communities here in the Western states, there are many who share our abhorrence for slavery and others who, if not overt defenders of the South's peculiar institution, clearly regard those among us who would advocate for a rapid end to the institution as dangerous agitators. Like Anson Dayton and some of the other Democrats in Oberlin, they perceive abolitionists as serious threats to the union of the states, rather than recognizing that it is slavery, with all its attendant evils, which is the actual threat. So, I am learning that discretion is an essential virtue for the Underground Railroad stockholder here in Ann Arbor. To illustrate this, I must share another anecdote with you that I heard from a fellow student only this morning after our clinical demonstration. One of the former regents of the university who served earlier in this decade, a Michigan Supreme Court justice named Abner Pratt, was quite hostile to abolitionists. Indeed, two faculty members with strong antislavery views left the institution because of his harassment. In contrast to this, apart from the usual gibes about our plain dress and speech, I have so far been treated kindly by most of the students and faculty. In fact, when I first arrived in Ann Arbor and applied to the university administration for assistance with finding lodging, the clerk, a kindly, bespectacled older gentleman, looked up at me and, after a thoughtful pause, said with the slightest of smiles, "Hmm, A.B. from Oberlin and a Quaker—might you be of the abolitionist persuasion?" When I answered in the affirmative, his smile widened as he said, "I thought so. One of our medical school professors, Dr. Alonzo Palmer, shares your dislike for the South's peculiar institution. He is also a member of the vestry at St. Andrew's Episcopal Church and teaches Bible classes there as a lay reader. He will be returning next month from visiting some of the great medical institutions and physicians of Britain and France. Before he left for Europe last April, he instructed me to keep watch for a likely student who might be a suitable lodger in his home. You appear to fit the bill, young man. You can share your convictions regarding slavery and attempt to convert each to the other's religious persuasion—truly a match made in heaven." The elderly clerk chuckled, apparently at his own cleverness, and then sent me off to find a red brick house on Division Street with the Episcopal Church located across the street as my landmark. Later that afternoon I met his housekeeper, a stout and cheery woman of middle age. Confirming my association with the Society of Friends, she said, "You'll do nicely, young man. Dr. Palmer has a warm spot in his heart for Quakers. In his younger days, a kindly Quaker lady nursed him through the typhoid fever." Dr. Palmer is a widower, having lost his young wife to consumption back in 1846.

So, dear Sister, by the good graces of a clerk of the University of Michigan and a very pleasant motherly sort of housekeeper, I am now ensconced in a comfortable room. As thou might guess I feel some trepidation that it happens to be the home of one of my professors, whom I have not yet met. The monthly rate for my lodging is quite reasonable. After meeting Dr. Corydon Ford, the Professor of Anatomy, I have hopes of finding employment as one of his assistants in the Anatomy Department. He informally questioned me about my knowledge of the subject, my training under Professor Dascomb at Oberlin, and my practical medical experience to date, and seemed very pleased with the excellent preparation that I received at Oberlin as well as the practical understanding imparted to me by Dr. Way. He thought that my experience coupled with the A.B. from Oberlin should afford me the opportunity for advanced standing in my medical studies.

Thank thee for the news of Sam and his work in the Law. He has found his natural element and I am certain Mr. Langston will be an excellent mentor. I am glad that he has continued attending choir practice and is still singing with Louisa and thee in First Day services.

Isaac paused at this point in his writing and thought to himself, *Oh, Rebecca, canst thou not see that his devotion to thee may be more than that of a friend?* As he pondered whether to make any comment regarding the subject, he felt anger rise within him as he remembered the newspaper accounts of Mr. Lincoln's third debate with Senator Douglas. *Why do these politicians speak lies and half truths? Mr. Lincoln's hostility toward slavery is well known and yet he feels the need to explicitly state that negroes represent an inferior race and to assure his audience of his hostility toward amalgamation. He may make humor at the seemingly absurd notion that there might even be desire for unions between the colored and white races in Illinois and yet, the products of such illicit unions in the South bear witness in their great numbers to that very desire. Clearly, Southern amalgamation may primarily reflect the base desire of those who are in authority over those with whom they force their union and yet is it not possible that were there true equality between the races a mutual desire of a higher order could form? I know what Uncle Levi would say, 'The mass of Americans, both north and south, do not have the personal knowledge and acquaintance of educated, free-born negroes that we enjoy,' and yet I can only feel intensely the anger mixed with shame that Sam must have experienced reading these accounts of the debates. Perhaps I would not be so distressed, other than the fact that Mr. Lincoln and the Republican Party represent the best hope for the rights of negroes that exists within the government,* he thought sadly. Isaac then resumed his letter.

Sam is indeed a wonderful brother to us both, as Louisa is a sister. Thank thee for sharing the very amusing incident of the hoop skirt. I will not hazard a guess regarding the victim's identity since I would not want thee to feel any pressure to prevaricate on her behalf, although I am fairly certain who she is. Thou may tell her in consolation that some of the young gentlemen in Oberlin have more than once remarked on how pretty she looked in her calico dress, even though it lacked the added attractions of a hoop skirt.

One amusing anecdote deserves another. This morning I had my first introduction to the professor of surgery, Dr. Moses Gunn, who lectures and gives clinical demonstrations on Wednesdays and Saturdays. He travels here by railroad from Detroit where he has a large and thriving general practice. Before the clinical demonstration began, one of the second-year students, who had the opportunity to hear Dr. Gunn's lectures last year (all students are expected to attend the lectures of the medical faculty twice during their medical education), whispered to me, sharing some of this remarkable physician's history. The tradition handed down among the students is that Dr. Gunn, who was a fellow student and friend of Dr. Corydon Ford at Geneva Medical College in New York, became aware of the plan to open a medical and surgical department at the University of Michigan while he was still a student in New York. He formed a plan of his own to be the first professor of anatomy and surgery at the new medical school. Promptly, upon graduation, he made the arduous journey from New York to Michigan dragging a large trunk along with his other earthly possessions. Once he was settled in the town, he began to offer private anatomical demonstrations in his medical office to interested students, for the trunk contained the corpse of a condemned criminal that he had obtained from the local penitentiary in New York prior to his departure for Michigan. Needless to say, such foresight and enterprise did not go unnoticed by the university's regents who offered him the professorship of anatomy and surgery. Later, as he developed his medical practice in Detroit, he was able to convince the regents to split his appointment into two positions. He would retain the professorship of surgery while a separate professor of anatomy would be recruited. And thus, his friend Dr. Corydon Ford was recruited from Geneva Medical College to the latter position. Dr. Ford's lectures yesterday were excellent. He does much of his teaching directly from dissected specimens and is able to breathe life and vitality into dessicated muscle and sinew with his clear and lucid style of presentation.

Dr. Gunn and other faculty have offered free medical care to local citizens who are willing to have that care provided in the presence of medical students from the university. This morning, a very brave woman of middle age presented herself for examination in the large teaching amphitheater on the upper floor of the Medical Building. The lighting is remarkably good due to sunlight coming through the glass dome above the room. There must have been at least one hundred students staring down intently from the galleries at the poor woman while she was questioned and then examined by Dr. Gunn. The professor introduced himself and explained that all of those in attendance were his students who were grateful for the opportunity to meet her and learn from her experience. He then proceeded to ask her to tell us about her problem. In English marked with a heavy German accent, she introduced herself as Maria Schwartzkopf, the wife of a local German dairy farmer. The couple had emigrated from Bavaria to the United States twenty-five years earlier and spent nearly twenty years here in Michigan on their farm outside of Ann Arbor. Her health had been remarkably good for most of her life and she had borne thirteen children, of whom ten were alive and well. However, over the past six months she had not been well. Dr. Gunn interrupted her story at this point and asked her to be more specific regarding her symptoms. In what manner was she feeling unwell? She then described a gradual process of becoming increasingly fatigued, which in the last six months was accompanied by poor appetite and weight loss. She stopped and looked at Dr. Gunn as if searching for something and then spoke in German, not being able to recall the words in English in the anxiety of the moment. Dr. Gunn, who speaks German translated for her indicating that she always had enjoyed eating. Indeed, she had been rather stout most of her married life and was quite distressed at this change in her constitution. In recent weeks, these symptoms were joined by the emergence of pain and nausea. The pain was in the central portion of her upper abdomen and was exacerbated when she attempted to eat. After some gentle expressions of reassurance spoken in German by Dr. Gunn, Mrs. Schwartzkopf cautiously allowed him to discretely expose her abdomen and successively other portions of her anatomy for examination. He directed those of us who wished, to approach one at a time, and follow his lead as he identified findings of potential interest. When my turn came, as I approached her, our eyes met for an instant. Although I know very little of the German language, no translation was necessary as I witnessed the deepest anguish and fear of a soul in great distress. That momentary look, a visual plea for help that, although unspoken, shrieked with all the terrors of human mortality, will haunt me for the rest of my days. Her brief self-revelation abruptly ceased, and her face again resumed a stoic expression while yet another student approached to examine her as an interesting "specimen" of the human condition.

As I came closer, I was struck by the intensity of her weight loss. The subcutaneous fat overlying her facial bones was markedly diminshed, imparting to her an almost skeletal appearance. The wasting extended to all aspects of her anatomy. Her arms, legs, chest, and abdomen were almost devoid of any mass of muscle or adipose. It was almost as if I was encountering a living wraith. Dr. Gunn gently directed my examining hands to two seemingly unrelated findings: a tender but firm mass occupying much of the central portion of the upper abdomen and a firm, nontender, immovable nodular mass at the base of the neck on the patient's left side.

After the examination was completed, Dr. Gunn explained to the patient that he wanted to confer with his "colleagues" briefly before rendering an opinion and then showed her to a waiting room outside the amphitheater. After returning to the amphitheater, he surveyed the room and asked, "Well, gentlemen, what do you think? What is your diagnosis?" One student from the second year suggested that it might be an advanced stage of consumption. Another volunteered "asthenia due to melancholia." The professor then shook his head with a pained expression on his face. "What did you feel, when I directed your physical examination?" One student answered, "a very firm and apparently tender upper abdominal mass, from the patient's reaction."

"What is the significance of the firm mass found at the base of the left side of the patient's neck? Are any of you familiar with the work of the German scientist and physician, Rudolph Virchow?" After noting the blank expressions on many of our faces, Professor Gunn again gently shook his head with a renewed look of pain on his face. "Well, gentlemen, I hope that after today, Dr. Virchow's name will be etched deeply within each of your memories. It is his pioneering work in morbid anatomy that will transform medicine. Regarding the possibility of advanced consumption involving the abdominal cavity, in her history our patient has given us no reason to believe that she has suffered from a prolonged course of consumption with its antecedent pulmonary manifestations. Indeed, she has declared most emphatically that she was in excellent health until about six months ago. What about the suggestion that her marked asthenia and weight loss might be the result of melancholia? She has every right to be melancholic but for a very different reason. Did any of you perceive her poorly concealed attempts at hiding her intense fear? She conveys a sense of impending doom, does she not? This unfortunate woman will die soon from advanced cancer of the stomach. The firm tender upper abdominal mass that each of you felt is tumor encasing the body of the stomach, the so-called *linitis plastica* or leather bottle stomach. Professor Virchow first described the significance of a mass presenting at the base of the neck in this context about ten years ago. It is usually a manifestation of far-advanced gastric cancer, although it sometimes can signify advanced cancers from other abdominal organs that have spread via the thoracic duct to its confluence with the left subclavian vein in the base of the neck. There is nothing we can offer this poor woman but the truth and laudanum."

The professor was about to leave the amphitheater to bring the unfortunate woman back to hear her prognosis, when several anxious students raised questions, most of which related to his last statement indicating that only the truth and laudanum could be offered to her. Several of the second-year students indicated that their preceptors would sometimes conceal the truth of a painful diagnosis rather than add to the distress of an already anguished patient. Professor Gunn paused thoughtfully after hearing these objections and replied, "Are you saying gentlemen that it is better to die ignorant of one's fate, if this is even possible, with no opportunity to prepare to meet one's Maker?" With that, he left the amphitheater and brought the patient back into the room. She now bore a continued look of apprehension on her face mingled with flashes of hope, probably created by what to her must have seemed a very prolonged discussion of her treatment options. After taking her seat, she looked up hopefully at Dr. Gunn. He in turn slowly drew up a chair, sat down facing her and gently taking her hand in his, silently gazed into her face with a profound look of sadness. Rebecca, it was as if for some ill-defined moment in time the world had stopped its movement around the sun and the other inhabitants of that large room had vanished utterly. Only those two souls remained, in some ineffable form of spiritual communion, not a word passing between them, only a lifetime's joys and sorrows intimately shared through a gaze more pregnant with meaning than any speech given by man. We knew the prognosis had been fully communicated when a soft sobbing could be heard, and Professor Gunn had leaned forward to touch Mrs. Schwartzkopf's shoulder and express his sorrow and regret. As he helped her leave the room, there was complete silence in the amphitheater, as if no one even dared to breathe. The closest analogy I might convey to thee of the experience was its similarity to the deepest and most profound movement of the Spirit in a silent meeting on First Day. When Professor Gunn returned to the amphitheater, there was a large communal sigh of relief so that as one organism we could again breathe. Looking up at us, he smiled with a tinge of sadness and said, "Gentlemen, you were absolutely correct in being concerned about my statement that there is nothing left but the truth and laudanum. Sometimes, professors must determine if their students are awake and attending to their lectures. The most important medicine you will ever administer is compassion and unlike the homeopath, you must administer it liberally and in large doses. But I hope you can understand that deceit in the name of compassion is an unnecessary evil and can never be alloyed with the truth."

Dear Sister, perhaps thou canst see that there are other forms of the human drama, more intimate in their nature, but no less powerful than the heroic rescue of John Price, that are played out in the lives of those around us. Indeed, tragedies and triumphs are unfolding in our midst, if we have but eyes to see and ears to hear.

With great affection, thy brother,

Isaac

P. S. I must protest when thou sayest that I am less tolerant of thy so-called prattle than Sam. Dear Sister, thy *prattle* served up in heaping portions is most nourishing for the philosophically minded among us. If there is any difference in our tolerance, it may relate to Sam's being much more a true philosopher than thy humble brother.

Sunday afternoons were one of the few times in the week when the Reverend William King could sit down in his favorite chair by the fire and relax. The relaxation would normally take the form of reading a book, quite often the Bible but sometimes other edifying works of literature. Or, at least that was always the plan, for invariably, after a few minutes, the warmth of the fireside, the comfort of the chair, and the world of ideas would combine to produce a potent narcotic and he would drift off into the realm of dreams. This afternoon he gradually became aware of an annoying sound that was harsh and rhythmic in nature. Finally, he realized that there was someone nearby loudly snoring.

How rude!" he thought. *I must awaken the fellow and ask him to snore elsewhere.*

Unfortunately, the more he tried to rouse the disturber of the peace, the more frustrated he became.

Won't anyone help me stop this man's incessant snoring? he implored.

"Reverend King, I am so sorry to disturb your rest. Please wake up! Abigail Simpson has come with an urgent request for you to speak with her mother."

Oh, what a relief! The old rascal has stopped snoring, he thought as he slowly returned to consciousness in response to the pleas of his housekeeper, Jenny. Cautiously opening an eye, the identity of the old rascal became apparent to him and he quickly shook off sleep, feeling rather sheepish.

"Jenny, how long have you been trying to awaken me?"

"Not too long, sir, really no more than a few minutes. You seemed so tired with your snoring and all; I hated to disturb you. It's just that Abigail's mother has been doing poorly with the pneumonia and she's been asking for you."

"Ah, poor soul, there is something very sad about that woman. I have yet to see her smile," he said, as he rose from the chair. He found Abigail waiting patiently for him in the hall.

"How is one of my finest students this cold Sunday afternoon?" he asked as he gave Abigail a big smile.

"Oh, thank you Reverend King, I'm very well, but I'm quite concerned that my mother is worse. She only speaks of her imminent death and makes me fear for her survival."

The young octoroon bit her lower lip and began to cry as she related her anxiety for her mother's welfare. As William King hugged her gently and tried to comfort her, he reflected on the fact that there had always been something mysterious about the quiet and reserved quadroon, Mabel Simpson, and her lovely daughter. Both could have easily passed as members of the white community, but had gradually found their way to Buxton from New York, arriving in town in the spring of 1855. Mrs. Simpson had sought out Tiberius in Toronto before moving on to Buxton with his encouragement. When the subject of Mabel and her daughter would come up in conversation, Tib would speak highly of both mother and daughter but never offered any more details of their past history than to say that he came to know Mabel during their escape with Florrie from Missouri and that she was a very brave woman who had suffered much. Being a curious individual, as humans often are, such a vague history only further piqued his interest.

As he looked down into the dark eyes of the slender young beauty with raven black wavy hair who would turn sixteen in two months, he wondered if some portion of the mystery was about to be revealed to him. When they had first arrived four years earlier, Abigail was illiterate and spoke the slave dialect while her mother could read tolerably well and spoke grammatical English. He remembered how Mabel had brought her daughter to the school and begged for her admission so that she might learn to be a "civilized young woman." He smiled to himself recalling his response to the earnest woman's plea.

"Madame, I will endeavor to teach her whatever she is capable of learning and to the degree to which she pursues such knowledge, but as to her being 'civilized' at the end of the process, that is something I cannot guarantee. I am, at best, barely civilized myself. True civilization, in my humble opinion, comes as a grace from God for which we must continually strive, realizing that ultimately it is a gift. If, after all her learning, your daughter discovers greater humility rather than pride, she will be civilized."

Smiling at the tearful young woman who had rapidly mastered a great portion of his curriculum in her efforts to be *civilized*, he said, "Abigail, my child, let us go to your mother and bring her some comfort in her travail."

It was not unusual to have a heavy snowfall in early spring in Canada West and late March of 1859 was no different from preceding years. Abigail and Reverend King trudged in silence through several inches of fresh snow that had fallen the night before until they reached the small cottage where Mabel and her daughter lived on the edge of the town. Before entering the cottage, Abigail turned to the minister and said, "Earlier this afternoon the doctor told me that he was certain the crisis will come in the next day or so. I don't know what I will do if she dies. She is all the family I have in this world."

"Courage, Abigail. Pray that God's mercy will enfold your mother and that his will be done. Remember that we are all children of God. We can never truly be orphans. Your mother is a strong woman. If she will continue the struggle, I feel that she will prevail in the crisis with the Lord's help."

"But, Reverend King, that's just it," Abigail replied. "I have never seen my mother so utterly despondent and bereft of hope. The last two nights she has cried out in her sleep, 'I am damned!' I am so frightened for her when she is in this state of mind."

At this, Abigail began to cry again. After composing herself, she showed Reverend King into her mother's room and quietly left him alone with her mother, who was lying awake in bed. Not sure of what he might encounter, William approached Mabel wondering if her nocturnal exclamations were products of a delirious state brought about by the pneumonia or if they were more representative of a deeper spiritual struggle.

"Ah, Reverend King you have come! Thank you for struggling through the snow on a very cold Sunday afternoon to visit me. I was afraid I would die before having this opportunity," she said with a look of great intensity on her flushed face. "Please come closer and sit with me. The doctor came earlier and said there should be no risk of contagion. He says I have pneumonia and that I am approaching the crisis. Within two days I will either be getting better or will be in the grave." She firmly grasped at his hand with her clammy fingers, turning aside briefly to cough and then with an imploring look, asked in a hoarse whisper, "Would you hear the confession of a great sinner? In my early years, I was the slave of a Catholic family. They had me baptized, catechized, and confirmed. The sacrament of confession was a great comfort to me as a young girl. I felt it was the one place that I could tell the truth, because only God heard and the priest, as witness, was sworn to secrecy. Well, when the judge, who was a Protestant, bought me, he wouldn't let me be a Catholic anymore. He said they're all damned to hell. I know you are a Protestant minister, but there is something about you; you've been so patient and kind to Abigail and me, I thought I would ask."

"Protestants believe that an intermediary between man and God is unnecessary. You could always confess directly to God. He is always ready to hear your sorrow and anguish."

"But, isn't there a place in the Good Book, where it says, 'Confess your sins to one another,' or something to that effect?"

"Yes, Mrs. Simpson, you put me to shame. It is written, just as you say, in the general epistle of James." William paused, swallowed hard, and then added, "Although I am not a priest of the Catholic Church, I will endeavor to listen in the same manner as the priest who brought such comfort to you in your youth, neither judging nor censuring you, but being a friend and witness to your woes as you open your heart to God."

"Reverend King, maybe I shouldn't burden you with my sins. They'll only drag you down to the Pit with me."

And then with beads of sweat forming on her forehead, Mabel said, "It was really quite presumptuous of me to ask you here. You are too pure a soul to be polluted by me and besides; I know that I am damned for all eternity. There is no hope for me. I must submit to my fate. But I will say this, even as the flames lick at my wretched frame, I will remain forever grateful to God that he helped me rescue my Abigail and that she is in the care of such good people as Tib and yourself."

"Mrs. Simpson . . . Mabel, there is no sin so great that God cannot forgive it. Do you remember the sinful thief who was crucified with the Lord? Although he had committed horrendous sins, he was forgiven everything and given that great assurance, 'Today, shalt thou be with me in Paradise.' Now, I find myself in the odd position of insisting that you make your confession. Please dear woman, for the sake of the peace of your soul and for your eternal salvation, tell me your story."

And so, Mabel told William of being auctioned in her youth as a fancy girl and her initial relief at being purchased for the purpose of being parlor maid to a judge only to find that she was destined to be his personal fancy girl. She described her bitterness at being almost continually pregnant by a man whom she loathed, how he would not even allow her to love her offspring from his forced union with her but would sell her children when it became expedient for his personal finances. She enumerated the many different methods she had contemplated for his murder after each beating she received at his hands or when her children were sold away from her. In her account of his drugging and murder by fire, she made it clear that it had been premeditated and that she made every attempt to conceal it from Tib and Florrie until it was too late for him to be rescued and that she bore full responsibility for the deed. She told of her long stay in Newport, Indiana during which the kindly Quaker girl Rebecca taught her to read, write, and speak like a genteel lady, all with the intention of preparing for an attempt to rescue her daughter from slavery and from a similar fate to what she had experienced.

"Did not the Quakers offer you assistance in finding Abigail?" William interrupted her narrative.

"Of course they did. Through their contacts they helped me track her to New Orleans, but I made a fateful decision that I would use whatever means necessary to rescue Abigail. I did not want to involve those good and kind people in any plot that might corrupt them or put them in danger of criminal prosecution. So, one day I quietly slipped away from Newport, Indiana and headed south by railroad and then by steamboat to New Orleans. I had very carefully husbanded the money that was obtained from Abigail's purchase and had even added to it. That money was now invested in a desperate plan in which I played the role of a woman who owned her own house of ill repute. In this guise, I made the tour of the houses of prostitution of New Orleans looking for likely candidates for my establishment. By this time, Abigail was eleven years of age. I was greatly concerned that in another year she would be put to a very different work from the household chores that were assigned to young slave girls in such establishments prior to the initiation into the real work of the place. It took me several months of persistent and patient searching before I was rewarded with my first glimpse in over two years of my daughter. After careful observation of her work routine I was able to meet her very briefly under clandestine circumstances in the alley behind the house of ill fame. She almost screamed with joy at our first meeting but quickly adopted a silent and seemingly unconcerned demeanor at my request. I explained to her that I needed to negotiate with her owner to buy her freedom and that she must say nothing about it to anyone. She gave me a description of the interior of the house and the location where she usually slept in an attic chamber with two other young girls, who were to also share her destiny.

"Fancy girls could fetch prices above one thousand five hundred dollars in the New Orleans slave market at that time. I was confronted with the painful realization that the one thousand dollars that I carried with me would not be sufficient to purchase her freedom. Purchase of a less attractive, older fancy girl with less earning potential than my daughter would have to be the pretext for my acquaintance with Abigail's owner. Meanwhile, I purchased tickets for the next day's steamship voyage to New York, acquired a substantial amount of arsenic to rid my premises of rodents, and laudanum for my chronic abdominal distress. Abigail's owner's debauched sensibilities were only exceeded by his greed. When I made my brazen approach at the entrance to the house of ill fame late that afternoon, one of the fancy girls eyeing me with disgust, referred me to a room upstairs on the second level where he greeted me with interest and invited me to sup with him as we discussed the potential purchase. He had already imbibed generous amounts of wine prior to my arrival, the continued consumption of which I encouraged while pouring more glasses for him as I feigned drinking similar quantities myself. When he departed briefly to call for the object of my possible purchase, so that I might examine her in detail, I added an admixture of laudanum and arsenic to his wine. After carefully examining the fancy girl with an eye to her future potential in my establishment, I inquired about other candidates that might also be suitable, to create the impression that I might want to purchase more than one slave. Being informed after his inquiries that the other potential candidate was with a customer at present, I turned to my host and proposed a toast to a successful conclusion to our business. He quaffed the entire glass without a pause. Thankfully, the laudanum began to take effect before the full force of the arsenic was felt. I watched as he sunk into a distressed slumber marked by a combination, in equal portions, of moaning and snoring. Meanwhile, the raucousness in the house had increased, providing an excellent opportunity for me to slip quietly upstairs in search of Abigail, who had just returned from emptying a chamber pot.

"As we were about to slip out the front door one of the more mature ladies of the establishment came running up to me and said, 'Our massa is moaning a powful lot up dere,' pointing to the room in which I had met with him. She gave me a suspicious look and added, 'He don't look like he gonna wake up fum dat sleep.'

"I smiled at her and replied, 'If you have ever dreamed of being free, this might just be the day to claim your freedom.'

"Her look of suspicion turned to joy and she gave me a big hug, saying, 'Honey, I bin waitin' fo' dis moment a long time. Tank you fo' yo' good deed. I's gonna tell de genelmen dat de massa is poorly an' dat he might hab de cholera. I don't tink dey'll be so interested in de ladies when dey hears dat and den we's gonna scatta to de four winds.'

"Several of the light-skinned ladies obtained berths on the same steamship with Abigail and me. We arrived without incident in New York and after making some inquiries I learned of Tib's move to Toronto and Abigail and I went to visit him there to seek his counsel. As you know, he referred us to you and this wonderful town. Neither Tib nor Abigail know about my murderous deed in New Orleans. . ."

"Or, your rescue of several slaves in that same city," interjected William.

"Well, Reverend, that is very kind of you to describe it that way, but the fact is I planned the murder of that wretched man and did not forsee the opportunity to help those other poor souls. I must also confess that I am glad that his death brought about their freedom. If my soul can be sacrificed to help save not only my daughter but also these others, my damnation will be worth the agony."

"Why are you so certain that you are damned, Mabel?"

"Well I lived in sin with that terrible man for so many years that it made me mad with hate to the point that I drugged him and burned him alive. Then I planned the murder by poison of my daughter's master. I am an adulterous murderer."

"What of it, my dear? So was King David and he is one of God's great saints. It seems to me that you hate the sins you have committed. Is that not so?"

"Yes, but I'm afraid I'd do them all over again, if I was in the same situation."

"I understand, but want to tell you something. I am not certain I would have acted differently than you if I had been caught in the same set of circumstances. Remember what the good Lord said to the sinful woman when all her accusers realized they had no business judging her, 'neither do I judge thee but go and sin no more.' Mabel Simpson, you have made your confession to God. You have sinned mightily but have also loved greatly. I believe he has heard you, that he loves you, and that his message to you is 'to go and sin no more.' My friend, we both need to tarry longer in this world to repent of our sins and rejoice in God's mercy. You have no business condemning yourself. That's God's business. I have one small request of you, if it would not be too much of an imposition."

"What is that, Reverend?"

"Please indulge me and show me a beautiful smile. I have seen it in your daughter and I know that you have it hidden within you."

With shining eyes, Mabel, for the first time in many years smiled broadly, drew William's hand to her lips, and kissed it. He, in turn, bent down and kissed her on the forehead. Her crisis had passed.

When William returned home, he found Horton Newby waiting. They would not infrequently dine together on Sunday evenings since Horton's move to Cicero's home as a means of continuing their friendship, but this was an unplanned visit. Horton rose and said, "William, I apologize for the intrusion on your solitude. Jenny told me that you were engaged in your pastoral duties and I thought I would wait until you returned, but I see that the hour is getting late."

"Nonsense, my friend. Please stay and dine with me." Calling for his housekeeper, he said, "Jenny, please set another place for Mr. Newby."

"It is already done, sir. You may dine at any time."

"Oh, Jenny, what an amazing creature you are! You are so thoughtful and kind to me."

Jenny, an elderly mulatto woman, smiled and replied, "Reverend King, it is a joy for me whenever I can make your life a little easier. You have done so much for us."

"Horton, you look troubled. How can I help you?" William asked as he reached for another piece of bread.

"William, I have lived here in Buxton for over six years and only rarely have I received a communication from my wife Malvina. Wisely or not, I gave her power of attorney in my absence, and so she has managed the plantation for these several years. As a gesture of goodwill before I left Kentucky in 1852, I acceded to her demand that her favorite nephew, Gordon Fairclough, be made heir of the estate in the event of our deaths. I have just received a letter from her in which she informs me that the plantation has experienced a series of reverses without providing any specifics and more importantly she states that her own health is failing, indeed her physician thinks she may die from advanced consumption within the next few months. It is only with great trepidation that I consider the situation that awaits me in Kentucky, but I feel it is my duty to return to my native state and face my past."

"Now that Tiberius is back from Toronto and with Cicero's help, the teaching will continue in your absence," William said. "Providence is giving you an opportunity in this crisis."

"Yes, William, I agree and appreciate your subtle allusion to that important element of opportunity that was always connected to the original meaning of the word's Greek antecedent, *krisis*. Not only will I be facing my *krisis*, my judgment, but also, I hope and pray that it will indeed be the *opportunity* for my redemption. Over the years that I have lived and taught here in Buxton there has always been that still small voice nagging with its importunate whisper, 'Kentucky, O Kentucky, how many have you left behind?' It may take me several months to complete my business there. Malvina's nephew was always a feckless youth, interested neither in learning or industry. I can only begin to imagine what he may have convinced his aunt to do on his behalf. Without informing me and to my shame, she even sold my first son, Cicero, to pay for some of her nephew's gambling debts. Certainly, he will not take kindly to seeing the human property that he is expecting as an inheritance taken north to be emancipated.

"Also, I was quite distressed to learn in her letter that about a year ago Malvina had rehired Thomas Blavey as the plantation's overseer. He is a truly vicious and unscrupulous man, whom I had discharged from service before I left Kentucky. Now I shudder in contemplation of the present state of affairs on the plantation. From my intimate knowledge of the slaveowner's mind, I realize the need for a careful plan involving deception that unfortunately must also anticipate the possibility of violence on the part of my fellow Kentuckians who will not take kindly to any serious tampering with Southern institutions. From their perspective, it's one thing for the tender conscience of a master to impel him to free a slave mistress and his children by her. It might even be considered as a generous act worthy of some muted praise. But to indiscriminately emancipate all the slaves on one of the largest plantations in the state? At the least, it would be considered the act of a fool or madman, and at the worst, a nihilistic act of revolution, a denial of all the South's heritage and traditions. No, William, I will be entering voluntarily into Daniel's den of lions and I assure you they will be quite famished."

"Horton, I will pray for your safety and the success of your efforts on behalf of your slaves."

"Thank you, William. That means a great deal to me. Please pray for sound judgment on my part. What do you know of John Fairfield?"

"Only bits and pieces of information that I have heard from some of the Detroit conductors of the Underground Railroad. His history seems to be shrouded in mystery. He is said to have been the heir of a plantation in Virginia but out of an early and deep antipathy for slavery, he rejected his appointed place in Southern society and became an outlaw to his own kind. He has dedicated all his energies to freeing as many slaves as possible. Some say that he has brought hundreds, if not thousands of slaves to freedom from the South. His methods are considered controversial, especially among our Quaker friends, who respect his bravery and commitment to the oppressed slave but eschew his methods, which reportedly include arming slaves and encouraging their use of violence rather than surrender to their pursuers when threatened with capture. He is also known for the many bold and clever ruses he has used, including impersonation of plantation overseers and slave traders, which have helped him gain direct access to the slaves and has made his rescue of larger numbers of slaves possible."

"I have heard much the same reports about his exploits. It is my plan to meet with him in southern Ohio before I enter Kentucky and seek his assistance in developing and executing a plan to deliver my slaves to freedom. His boldness and understanding of the Southern slaveowner's mind will be invaluable. I will do everything possible to avoid violence and bloodshed, but I am prepared to risk my own life in an action that my conscience has long demanded and that I can no longer delay."

"For what it's worth, my friend, you go with my blessing. I will also pray that no violence will be necessary, but that God's will be done."

"William, if I do not return to Buxton, there is something that rests heavily on my soul that I must share with you. Thanks to my daughter-in-law, Eliza, much healing has come to the relations I enjoy with my African children. At the heart of it all, is my connection with Tiberius. Without his letter and the kind offices of his dear wife, I would never have known my older son, Cicero and his family. The strange irony is that Cicero has never remonstrated with me for the great evil and suffering he experienced as one of my slaves. He has only expressed joy in becoming acquainted with his father, while receiving his freedom and education have been additional unanticipated gifts in which he has reveled with childlike joy. He is the humblest of men and yet no less intelligent than his younger brother. I marvel at his mathematical gifts and his fascination with natural philosophy. Unfortunately, the limits of what we can teach him in these areas have been reached some time ago."

"Yes, Horton, he is a remarkable man," William interjected. "With your blessing, I will urge him to seek formal training in Toronto like his brother but in the areas of mathematics and natural philosophy, in which he takes so much pleasure. With his passion for learning and wonder at the mysteries of the universe, like his brother he should be a tremendous educator and asset to his people."

"My daughter, Livia, has gradually warmed to me as my friendship has been slowly renewed with her mother, but she, like Tiberius, has maintained a wall of separation that I feel acutely. Both of them have been very polite, even cordial at times, but I crave the warmth of love that I share with Cicero. If my life should be cut short, preventing my return to Buxton, one of my greatest regrets will be this gaping wound that remains festering between Liddie's children and me."

"Horton, I think you have misjudged the situation. Surely you must be aware that Liddie and her children have a very different history with you than Cicero and his family."

"Yes. Painfully aware."

"They remember a time in which they shared the complete trust and intimacy of a family with you as the head. Since that was shattered, it has been less than seven years in which healing of the old wounds has been initiated. The problem is that neither they nor you can return to the previous intimacy, for which you *all* yearn. A new intimacy must be born that can engender a greater trust, one that will transcend the old wounds. Do not despair, but be patient. I am certain that the path of healing for you and your family goes through Kentucky. Go in hope."

As William King finally retired for the night after his rather eventful Sunday, he lay back on his bed and pondered the two very different encounters he had experienced.

How complex is the individual cosmos in which each person resides! he marveled as he began to drift off to sleep. *It's all very fascinating and very tiring. I hope that old rascal will have the decency to not return and disturb my slumbers tonight,* he thought as he remembered the unwelcome guest with his loud snoring, who had disrupted his afternoon nap.

Chapter Forty-Two

May 13, 1859

Dear Isaac,

Thou must be quite relieved and pleased to have completed the first half of thy medical curriculum. I know that our parents are very proud of thee. I am delighted to hear from thy letter that thou wilt be able to work with Professor Gunn as thy preceptor until the beginning of the next term at the University of Michigan in October. Between thy work in thy spare hours with Professor Palmer in his medical practice in Ann Arbor and Professor Gunn's private practice in Detroit, thou wilt gain a wide and varied experience of medicine. Wilt thou continue to work in the Anatomy Department as an assistant to Professor Ford next year? Dost thou find the experience of spending so much time among the decaying bodies of the dead to be distressing? Although I can fully appreciate the necessity of anatomic dissection to the acquisition of a real, practical knowledge of human anatomy, I cannot help but be concerned about the toll such intimate contact with death, particularly on a daily basis, would take on a person with thy sensitivity and compassionate nature. Dost thou fear becoming hardened or calloused to suffering and death as a result?

Although Professor Dascomb has relied on drawings and illustrations from various texts for most of the anatomic instruction he has given us, he was able to acquire a cadaver recently and has been making some very effective demonstrations using a careful technique of dissection. While the educational experience has been unparalleled, I cannot escape from a sense of desecration. Who was this person, whose body has been forced to yield its secrets to us? What right do we have to intrude in such an intimate manner in the physical being of this individual, who once lived, breathed and walked the earth with us? It is difficult for me to believe that this person voluntarily offered up his mortal remains for such a purpose. I hope that the sense of awe (and horror) that enfolded me when first I met this remnant of a man will never leave me, while deep gratitude will always accompany my ambivalent sentiments.

Before relating the details of what Sam, Louisa, and I witnessed in Cleveland, I would like to introduce thee to another student from the Ladies' Course, whose friendship Louisa and I enjoy: Miss Arabella Phillips. Although she started her studies at Oberlin after thy departure, she has been seasoned by more than ten years of practical experience teaching in various schools. She has come to Oberlin to receive additional training in support of her work as a teacher. She is a strong-minded, conscientious person of great integrity who is not afraid to speak her mind. To give thee a sense of Miss Phillips's personality, I would like to describe an incident that occurred in the autumn term before Professor Finney and his wife left for an evangelistic tour of England in January.

As I mentioned, Miss Phillips is in the habit of speaking her mind on almost any subject of interest to her. Having lived independently for several years in her role as a teacher in country schools, she has been accustomed to defining her own system of prayers and devotions. Indeed, she has been a model of piety and Christian charity. After having the opportunity to experience the many public prayers offered daily both in individual classes and in the regular worship services, she observed during breakfast one morning that she reckoned she had to pray at least twenty-one times in a day and that seemed a bit excessive. Some of us explained to her that the large number of public prayers was a cherished tradition at the college, which she would likely become accustomed to over time. Her rather pointed response was, "I prefer to do my praying in private, as the Lord enjoins us to do."

Louisa and I had witnessed her bold assessment, as did others, but then forgot all about it until an incident one week later that occurred while we were walking with Arabella. Professor Finney, who must have seen Arabella from some distance, made a point of changing direction and walking across Tappan Square, intercepting us as we were traversing the boardwalk to one of our recitation sessions. Completely ignoring Louisa's and my presence and focusing all his attention on Arabella, he stiffly bowed and gave her a most distressing greeting, saying, "Good morning, Daughter of the Devil!" Louisa and I gasped at the harshness of his greeting while Arabella did not in the slightest degree lose her composure. With a gentle but ironic smile suffusing her face, she extended her hand to the professor and said, "I'm glad to see you, Father." This witty response caught Professor Finney completely by surprise. At first, he blushed profoundly and then, beginning to weep, he apologized profusely to Arabella, imploring her to give her heart to God. She gently replied that she was hopeful of God's mercy and that she thanked him for his concern. Such is the character, wit, and intelligence of Arabella Phillips.

Our scholarly activities have been somewhat overshadowed by events related to the fate of our brave Oberlin rescuers. Louisa's prediction and concerns regarding the federal government's interest in the case could not be overstated. As I am sure thou hast seen in the newspapers, it seems that

President Buchanan's administration is making war in earnest on Oberlin. The grand jury that made the indictments last winter was stacked with Democrats. They made an especial effort to indict leading citizens of Oberlin. None of these eminent members of our community were even present in Wellington for the rescue of John Price. Nevertheless, they were charged with aiding and abetting the rescuers. The grand jury even had a special recess so that witnesses could be found to implicate them.

As thou might guess, Sam has been following every detail with intense interest. His mentor's brother, Charles Langston, has been a central figure in much of the drama being played out in the courtroom in Cleveland the past few days. Several of us were given leave from our regularly assigned instruction to attend the proceedings. Professor Dascomb told us, "Sir Isaac Newton and his laws can wait. The history of our poor benighted country is unfolding in Cleveland. It is your duty to be witnesses for future generations."

Sam thinks it was a brilliant counterstroke by the Rescuers' defense team of calling a grand jury in Lorain County in February to indict the agents, who captured John Price, for kidnapping under Ohio law. I don't know if the newspapers in Ann Arbor at the time reported the inspiring words of Judge Carpenter: "Every man, woman, and child in Ohio, of whatever birth, descent, parentage, complexion, or conformation, is presumed in law to be free." He went on to say that when ". . .the slave. . .crosses our boundary, he is baptized in the air of freedom; and that baptism is irrevocable."

Alas, the legal machinations involving the case have become increasingly convoluted. One thing has been quite clear from the beginning, however; just as the grand jury was stacked with Democrats, the same outcome has occurred at the actual trial in Cleveland. The jury is made up entirely of Democrats, as is the judge. There has been little hope of a fair trial from the beginning of this whole business.

Isaac, I rejoice in John Price's safe arrival in Canada, though the means and manner of his escape after the rescue in Wellington, rightly remain a mystery from most of his friends and enemies alike. As thou knowest, Charles Langston's fate was sealed with the conviction of Mr. Bushnell. He was convicted on the tenth of this month, but before the jury met, the prosecuting attorney, George Bliss, dropped any pretense and gave clear evidence, in his closing arguments, of the real target of the federal government's fury: "The students who attend that Oberlin College are taught sedition and treason in connection with science and literature, and they graduate from that institution to go forth and preach opposition and treason . . ."

Now I would like to turn to the sentencing of Charles Langston that occurred two days ago and give thee my firsthand account of the dramatic scene that unfolded in the courtroom before our eyes. Although Mr. Langston's younger brother, John Mercer, as an attorney, offered to speak on his brother's behalf, Charles indicated his strong desire to address the court himself, and what an address it was! He described the condition of colored persons in the United States, the state of prejudice toward them among white persons, his efforts on behalf of John Price, and how, as a noncitizen, he and other persons of color could not expect legal redress. Here is an excerpt for thee to contemplate.

"I have not had a trial before a jury of my peers. The Constitution guarantees—not merely to its citizens—but to *all persons* a trial before an *impartial* jury. I have had no such trial. The colored man is oppressed by certain universal and deeply fixed *prejudices*. And the prejudices which white people have against colored men grow out of this fact: that we have, as a people, *consented* for two hundred years to be *slaves* of the whites. We have been scourged, crushed, and cruelly oppressed, and have submitted to it all tamely, meekly, and peaceably; I mean as a people, and with rare individual exceptions; and today you see us thus, meekly submitting to the penalties of an infamous law. Now the Americans have this feeling, and it is an honorable one, that they will respect those who rebel at oppression, but despise those who tamely submit to outrage and wrong; and while our people submit as a people, they will as a people be despised . . . Let me . . . tell a United States Marshal that my father was a Revolutionary soldier; that he served under Lafayette, and fought through the whole war; and that he always told me that he fought for *my* freedom as much as for his own; and the Marshal would sneer at me, and clutch me with his bloody fingers, and say he had a *right* to make me a slave! And when I appeal to Congress, they say he has a right to make me a slave; when I appeal to the people, they say he has a right to make me a slave, and when I appeal to your Honor, your Honor says he has a right to make me a slave; and if any man, white or black, seeks an investigation of that claim, they make themselves amenable to the pains and penalties of the Fugitive Slave Act." And then he raised his voice and with a vehemence driven by anguish for his people, shouted, "Black men have no rights which white men are bound to respect!"

The atmosphere in the courtroom was electric as he shouted out those words. It was extraordinary to witness the response of Judge Willson. He was clearly moved by Mr. Langston's speech, so moved in fact that it was difficult for him to regain sufficient composure and power of speech to pronounce sentence. When he did pronounce the sentence, he spoke of "mitigating circumstances" that resulted in a sentence of twenty days in prison and a fine of one hundred dollars plus the costs of prosecution. The full penalty could have been six months' imprisonment and a fine of one thousand dollars!

Perhaps I might close with this observation made in a recent homily given by one of our best students in the Theological Department here at Oberlin. Surely, thou must remember Anthony Burns? He is the former fugitive slave for whom President Pierce sent federal troops to Boston to forcibly return him to slavery in Virginia in 1854 under the Fugitive Slave Act. His freedom was eventually purchased and since that time he has been studying here at Oberlin for the ministry. He is scheduled to finish his training for the ministry here at the same time I graduate. In his sermon in First Church, he reflected on some of the terrible experiences he had endured both in slavery and during his time as a fugitive. Even when he was taken in chains back to Virginia on that fateful day in 1854, he said that he never felt abandoned by God. "I felt the encouragement and strength of many thousands of prayers on that voyage back to my master and was confident that God's mercy would prevail, whether I died in chains or not. The bonds of love are stronger than any chains wrought by man."

Dear brother, I have resolved to join more fervently in a rebellion against the slave power, a rebellion of prayer.

Ever thy affectionate sister,
Rebecca

The intoxicating scent of lilacs roused the drowsy traveler as his horse plodded along the Louisville and Shelbyville Road in early May 1859. Inhaling deeply their perfume, he entered a long-forgotten memory from a more innocent time of slaves planting these same bushes at the direction of his father when he was a boy. How pleasant it all seemed, shrouded in the haze of memory; the happy and contented slaves reveling in their work under the benevolent direction of their master, his father. Or, at least that is how the childish memory had been preserved with due care taken to filter out any unpleasantness.

Shaking off his somnolence and nostalgia for an ephemeral past, Horton Newby resumed an erect posture in the saddle and began to attend to everything that his sensory faculties presented for review. The lilacs were the first tangible evidence of the eastern boundary of his plantation, which ran up to the Shelbyville Branch, a modification of the original turnpike made after the advent of rail service between Louisville and Frankfort in the early 1850s. When the lilacs were first planted, this was but a small track through the wilderness.

The warmth of the midafternoon sun that enveloped him, for all its pleasantness, brought with it an indefinable sadness, a yearning for a state of being that was now utterly foreign to him. That sensuous Kentucky sun lacked the ascetic chill of the northern sun he had come to know in Canada West. He shuddered involuntarily as he sensed its passionate character. He realized that the memories associated with the very elements making up this corner of the cosmos were almost too intoxicating, too powerful for him to resist. He must never again grow accustomed to them. He would strive with all his being to keep them foreign. While making this mental resolution, he heard voices ahead on the road, speaking in the slave dialect. One voice stood out among the others as being quite familiar.

As he overtook the gang of ten slaves, he greeted them, "Well, my friends, what is the news of your plantation?"

A particularly tall, well-built slave who was nearly six feet in height turned and scrutinizing Horton for a moment, asked tentatively, "Can dat really be you, Massa Newby? We all thought you be dead long ago."

"As you can see, Caesar, I am still alive, and since I've grown accustomed to living, I hope to remain above ground a bit longer."

Another slave laughing, said, "Why dats Massa Newby fo' sure. He got de same qweer humor dat our ol' Massa had."

They were quite startled when he got off his horse and approaching each one of them offered to shake their hand. Horton then asked, "Are you glad to see me return?"

After some hesitation, Caesar, the blacksmith, replied for the group and said, "Dey was bettah times when you was still de Massa here. When you left, a lotta bad tings happen."

Looking directly at Caesar and sensing his continued reticence to speak further, Horton pressed him, saying, "Please tell me more. I come back as your friend, not your master. I have been in the land of freedom, in Canada, these past several years."

"Well, Massa, befo' you left dere was about a hunnerd niggers on de plantashun. Ober de past tree year, Missus Newby sold forty niggers down de ribber cuz she need to pay fo' her nephew gamblin'. Anudder ting, Massa, she sold about hab de hosses."

Horton had been prepared for some bad news regarding the state of the plantation, but the extent of the disaster staggered him. With some anxiety, he asked, "Have any of you lost family members when Mistress Newby sold slaves from the plantation?"

"Ned, here, didn't lose nobody. O' course he ain't got no fambly to lose," Caesar said in a voice tinged with bitterness.

"But, the rest of you have lost family members, is that not so?"

Caesar, again speaking for the group, said, "Yessum, Massa. Mah Sally was sold a year ago. Fred ober dere," Caesar pointed at a scrawny-looking fellow who bore a particularly disconsolate expression on his face, "he lose his wife an' tree chillun four year ago."

Horton, whose well of emotion was overflowing simultaneously with grief and anger, interrupted him, and raising his voice, almost shouted with a fierceness that surprised the slaves, "There will be no more families separated, no more loved ones sold down the river while I have breath in me! I am very sorry for what has been done to you in my absence. Can you all keep a secret?"

A deep laugh rose in unison from the slaves, as if emerging from a composite being. Caesar looked directly into Horton's eyes and said, "Niggers hab a speshul gift for keepin' secrets. Dats how we manage to lib in dis hebbin dat white folk call de peculyer insteetooshun."

"Forgive me, of course, any peace you experience in this life depends on deception and secrets. Here is the secret to be kept. I have come back to Kentucky to bring all of you out of slavery. With such a large number of slaves, we will have to use deception to get you out of the state safely. My nephew currently expects to inherit all of you and the plantation, when Mistress Newby and I die. From your report, he has clearly been abusing his inheritance before his time. As you may know, your mistress is dying. Several things must be done before I can take you north to freedom after her death. My will must be changed, the remaining horses must be sold, the plantation with the land will be put up for sale, and my plans to depart to Texas with my slave property in search of a new plantation will be shared with the community. Mr. Fairclough will not take kindly to the thought of losing his inheritance and will likely seek any means of obtaining whatever property I take with me, including violence. In a few days, I will meet with you again, first with this smaller group, and once you feel the others can be trusted to also keep the secret, all of the slaves on the plantation. For the present, I must beg each of you to keep what I have told you now a well-guarded secret. Your freedom and my life may depend on it."

After walking with Horton a bit further, the gang of slaves left the road to take a shortcut back to the slave quarters, while he continued on the road until he reached the main entrance to his plantation. He trotted up the long, tree-lined drive and, jumping off his horse, handed the reins to an elderly negro, who with a speechless look of amazement on his face, received them, bowed ceremoniously to the master he had not seen in several years, and led the horse away. Rather than immediately enter the mansion, Horton first walked toward a large tulip tree that was in full bloom about one hundred yards away. Within a gated enclosure shaded by the tree was the family burial plot. He removed several low hanging blossoms from the tree and placed them at the base of his daughter Julia's grave marker and remained standing there deep in thought for several minutes before he realized that another person had joined him and was also standing silently beside him before the grave. Sunlight filtering through the leaves of the tree overhead danced among the shadows on the marker and almost seemed to create a halo around Julia's name inscribed in the stone.

"I loved her very much as I know you did, Jenny. The words she spoke to me on her deathbed came to me almost as a divine oracle. My decision and the actions I took in response to that oracle caused so much suffering and yet they may have in some way set in motion the chain of events that confirm the truth of her words. Oh Julia, how I miss you and wish you could see the good that has been wrought out of the evil that initially attended those fateful words!"

"But, Massa Newby, I'm certain dat she does see de good dat has come outta all yer fambly's trubbels. Don't you know dat she's restin' in de bosom ob Abraham, jes' like de good Lawd say? An' fum Abraham's bosom she be watchin' ober us."

"Yes, Jenny. Of course, you are right. Your faith puts me to shame. Please pray for your wicked old master."

"Massa Newby, I nebber stopped prayin' fo' you, an' I's gonna keep on prayin' fo' you until all de wickedness is clear outta you. Why do you tink yer here now? De prayin' brought you all de way fum Canada; it sho' did! It took a whole lotta prayin' befo' Missus Newby wrote dat lettuh to you, but she sho' did, an' dat's de good Lawd's doin'!"

"And what of Mistress Newby's consumption, Jenny?"

"Yes, Massa, dat's anudder miracle fum de Lawd. How else do you tink de Lawd could git her to pay attention? I knows dat de Lawd spoke to Elijah in de still, small voice. Fo' de big saints, all de Lawd has to do is wispah, cuz dey's always lissenin' fo' him. But fo' de rest ob us sinnahs he gotta shout sometime to wake us up. I tink he got Missus Newby's attention now doe."

Turning slowly away from his daughter's grave, Horton walked back to the mansion with Jenny. "How is Mistress Newby today?" Horton asked, pausing on the porticoed piazza before going inside.

"She bin poorly dese las' sevrul days, Massa. Took to her bed an' ain't left it since den. She bin spittin' de blood fo' weeks an' she so thin dat you won't reco'nize her."

"Jenny, I'll go with you directly to her room," Horton said while looking around in the entryway. Noticing some sudden motion out of the corner of his eye, he recognized with some disgust the familiar form of Thomas Blavey, who had clearly been startled, rising suddenly from the desk in his office that was to the left of the vestibule.

"Mr. Newby, this is an unexpected pleasure. I apologize for not greeting you upon your arrival. We were under the impression that you would be arriving in two days," Blavey said obsequiously while giving Horton a furtive look.

"The opportunity arose for me to return to Kentucky earlier than I had stated in my correspondence with Mistress Newby," Horton responded brusquely. "Mr. Blavey, I would be grateful if you could have the plantation's accounts, since my departure seven years ago until the present, ready for my review tomorrow morning."

"Sir, it may be difficult for me to locate all of the records that quickly."

"Really, Mr. Blavey, someone of your abilities should be able to manage it. I would also appreciate your tidying my office, as I plan to resume its use in the morning."

"Yes, sir," came the anxious reply.

As Horton headed instinctively toward the large central spiral staircase, Jenny motioned for him to follow her down a hallway to the right on the main floor. Turning her head, she whispered, "Missus Newby ain't bin up de stairs in a long time. She's awful weak. She bin sleepin' in dis room heah." And Jenny pointed to a door about halfway down the hall, which in the past had been the door to a guest room. When he entered the room, Horton was struck by the stark contrast between his wife's arrangement of the room in which she was awaiting her death and that which their daughter had chosen years before. Whereas Julia in her last days and hours craved illumination, Malvina seemed to find comfort in the shadows. The dark purple curtains were drawn tight across the large window and wherever a few stray rays of light slipped past the barrier; they could do so only as foreigners, apologizing in haste for intruding on the customary gloom of the place. A solitary candle was the reluctant concession to practical considerations and Jenny's insistent pleas.

"Malvina, it's Horton. I've just arrived."

"You really did come. Please come closer so that I can see you."

"Malvina, it is a bright sunny day outside; actually, quite beautiful. Please allow me to open these curtains so that you can enjoy the light of spring," Horton said as he moved toward the window to open the curtains.

"No! Please don't open the blinds. The darkness suits me," Malvina protested in a shrill whisper, which was swallowed up in a fit of coughing. Horton dutifully complied and coming closer was shocked by what he saw in the candlelight. The woman lying on the bed before him was hardly recognizable as the wife he had known. Malvina had always been rather thin but now appeared to Horton in the form of a skeleton, which for the sake of modesty had retained a veneer of skin. Her hair was completely white with clumps of thin strands scattered in no apparent order about her head and face. Flecks of blood stained the corners of her mouth. Her breath came fitfully, at times in gasps that were often triggered by frequent paroxysms of coughing. Malvina had always had a pale complexion but now her face, even her lips, provided such a profound contrast to the scarlet stains produced by the drops of life-bearing liquid that she had the appearance of a marble statue to which an artist had affixed a garish paint to achieve some macabre effect.

"Horton, other than a few more gray hairs around your temples, you appear the same as when you left seven years ago. The Canadian climate must agree with you, or is it that nigger wench? She must be keeping you nice and warm during those long winters!"

Horton, who had been expecting a greeting of this nature, swallowed hard, and replied, "Malvina, I see that although you are quite ill, your sharp wit continues as strong as ever. I suspect it would be useless for me to protest, but I will make this rebuttal to the aspersions you cast on Liddie's character. She has not shared any physical intimacies with me since that fateful day when I handed Tiberius over to your care. My greatest hope remains that she will someday forgive me for all the suffering I have caused her and her children. Likewise, I have sought and continue to hope for your forgiveness for my role in your unhappiness."

"Jenny keeps after me about being saved. Her persistence wears on my patience at times. There's just no point in trying to explain orthodox Presbyterianism to niggers. Sometimes, when she is talking of how she feels God's love, I marvel. How could she experience such things, bearing the curse of Canaan as she does? She also has this annoying habit of speaking openly with me about my impending death. Such impertinence!"

"Only the impertinence of love. Malvina, do you remember from the gospel readings in church how Christ was always helping the poor and even said, 'Blessed are the poor in spirit for theirs is the kingdom of heaven?' Perhaps those very souls that we have thought were cursed bear the greatest of blessings from God. Can't you see that Jenny loves you?"

"Horton, that's preposterous. I never sought the love or even the slightest affection from my servants. It is their fear and obedience that I expect, I demand. It is my right as their owner. In return, they can expect benevolence on my part, nothing more. It is most disagreeable when she displays such concern for my welfare. I swear to you that I have never requested it of her."

"Malvina, it is something that she has chosen to give you, it is her grace which, like the merciful God in whose love she takes so much joy, she bestows on you freely. This is the act of a free woman. When through some inexplicable miracle she chooses to love you despite yourself, she is no longer your slave. In fact, she is not even your equal. She has risen far above folk like us. That is what makes you uncomfortable when she treats you so. Rather than fight it, why don't you bathe in the experience awhile. You might find you like it after all."

"Horton, this thinking of yours would undo the Divine order of nature. Everything and everyone in their place, that's what I have been taught and—"

"It's small comfort at this point in your life, I daresay," Horton interrupted.

A tear started to roll down Malvina's hollow cheek as she gave her husband an intense look and grasped at his hand.

"Like the rest of my family, I grew up with the assurance, no, the certainty, that it was our destiny to be leaders in this commonwealth of Kentucky and that destiny clearly extended to a heavenly Kentucky, where we would continue to preside eternally in the higher ranks of the elect following a rich and productive life here. But in reality, every project I have touched in my life has gone to ruin. First, the sorry state of our marriage is not entirely a result of your sins. I could have been a better, a more loving wife. I know that I drove you into the arms of your slave mistress by my coldness. You are a man with a passionate nature. I could have asked you to teach me in the arts of love. Julia also spoke to me privately before she died. Although she extracted that fateful promise from you, she also requested a promise of me, which I did not fulfill. She implored me to freely forgive your slave family and to take no revenge against them. But, as you know all too well, that I would never do. My hate for them, for you, was so great that I lied to my own child on her deathbed! Every attempt I made to make them and you suffer has ultimately been foiled. Gradually, as the grip of this illness has tightened over me, I came to realize the horrible truth. God has set himself against me. I am not one of the elect. Rather, I am damned for all eternity!"

Horton gripped his wife's hand tightly and, with a searching look, tried to penetrate the heavy curtain of despair written in her eyes. He was about to attempt to speak some words of comfort but another fit of coughing interrupted the effort. Jenny entered the room in response to the sound of Malvina's coughing and said, "Massa Newby, de doctor gib us some med'cine fo' de cough."

She handed a small vial of laudanum to Horton, who then mixed several drops in water and slowly encouraged Malvina to swallow it. She gradually drifted off into a restless sleep, as Horton and Jenny watched at her bedside. Jenny then whispered to

Horton, "De doctor said dat one o' dese times she gonna die wif de coughin', dat she'll be drownded by all de blood!"

"Mr. Blavey, there are gaping holes in your accounts," Horton said with some astonishment. "Perhaps through negligence and sloth, some of the earlier records have been misplaced as you claim. However, some of the most dramatic disparities are recent. In fact, they seem to coincide with the decline in Mistress Newby's health. You have another day to discover the missing records. I will send for my attorney, who will be here tomorrow to review the records as an impartial observer. Later, this afternoon you will take me on a tour of the plantation. I must say, I am afraid of what I may find, as you should be, sir."

"Oh Blavey, there you are! I've been looking all over for you about that cash I need. Oh! Is that you Uncle Horton? Back so soon from Canada?"

"Yes, Gordon, although I'm not so sure most people would say that returning from a seven-year hiatus qualifies as *so soon*. It seems that both you and Mr. Blavey have been discomfited by my early arrival. I wonder why," Horton said as he looked at his nephew, Gordon Fairclough, who had precipitously discovered his uncle's presence under awkward circumstances. "Have I interrupted some important financial transaction between you?"

Gordon Fairclough, the only male issue of Malvina's younger and favorite brother was a twenty-five-year-old gentleman in search of a fortune. Somewhat puny in build, his physiognomy shared many features in common with his deceased cousin Julia, but unfortunately lacked her better features, particularly her winsome smile. Gordon Fairclough's mouth was chronically contorted by a nasty habit of whining, which left its imprint in the form of a peculiar grimace, never quite a smile or a pout. Not being particularly inclined to work and finding himself well-suited to a life of leisure, he had discovered that money was a necessary requisite for such a vocation, and thus, when not spending or gambling it away, he was in search of it. Today, he was in search of it. Gordon found that a small lie now and then could be quite expedient, and having considerable practice in this arena, he thought that one might be very helpful right at this moment.

"Oh, Uncle Horton, I am so glad you are back a few days early, I rode over to check on Aunt Malvina. I was about to ask Blavey here for some cash so that I could go and purchase some more medical supplies for her."

"Mr. Blavey was just about to leave. Why don't you go right now and visit your aunt? I am certain she would appreciate it very much. As for her medical supplies, thank you for your offer but your assistance will be unnecessary. I will take care of such purchases in the future."

As Blavey and Gordon both hesitated, Horton gave Blavey a stern look and said, "Mr. Blavey, you have considerable preparations to make for my tour this afternoon. Please attend to them immediately. Gordon, your aunt is waiting."

Reluctantly, both men went off in different directions, as instructed. Horton thought to himself, *If Malvina's illness and my absence could have been drawn out another year, these two rascals would have used up almost all of the resources of this plantation!*

After less than three minutes had elapsed, Gordon Fairclough tried to quietly bypass Horton's office on his way out the front door.

"Gordon Fairclough! That was a very short, an indecently short, visit to your aunt. Come in here!" Horton commanded. With an involuntary curl of his upper lip, Gordon reentered his uncle's office and sat down in the chair to which he was directed.

"Uncle Horton, she was sleeping. I didn't want to disturb her."

"Have you ever heard of keeping vigil at the bedside?"

"Uncle Horton that would be most unpleasant. It is very dark and gloomy in there. Auntie Malvina always wanted me to be happy."

"Is that how you badgered her out of a large portion of your inheritance? It seems the price of Gordon Fairclough's happiness has risen steeply of late. How many slave families have been broken up to pay for your profligate spending and gambling, you wretch? It seems Mr. Blavey and you have had an interesting collaboration, you in manipulating a dying woman and he in embezzlement. How much have you promised him in future favors for the money he has advanced you from the plantation's accounts? Of course, for such kind services on your behalf should he not be entitled to receive, or shall I say take, some personal compensation?"

"Uncle Horton, you seem out of sorts. Perhaps it is due to the long journey and Auntie's poor condition. She has always been generous to me. Unfortunately, I have been unlucky in some of my endeavors—"

"You mean in your gambling!"

"Well, it is what all the young gentlemen of good family do in this region."

"Shame on me for interfering with such a fine vocation! Be aware, young man, that you have already received your inheritance. From this moment, you should seek further support for your gentlemanly pursuits elsewhere! If you find it too troubling to sit with the dying aunt who has indulged your fancies so generously, you may leave."

"Mr. Blavey, how do you account for the dreadful state of the negro quarters? At least half of the cabins have roofs that will leak horribly this winter. Did you not give the slaves their allotment of clothes this year? Many of them by the state of their gums and teeth appear to have the scurvy. Have they not had access to any fresh fruits and vegetables? Both the fields and the horses that remain have been neglected. What explanation can you give for such poor management?"

Horton was now quite angry with the overseer as he surveyed the wreckage of what had been one of the great plantations of Kentucky.

"Mr. Newby, I had to make many economies because of the frequent requests for money from your nephew. Missus Newby just wasn't able to refuse him anything."

Horton knew this was true, but he could also divine an active complicity with his nephew on the part of the overseer.

"Although a significant portion of the waste and destruction on this plantation is a result of my nephew's activities, my careful review of the accounts has satisfied me that he has had a willing collaborator in his mischief, especially during recent months as your mistress's health has precipitously declined," Horton declared as they rode back from the horse pasture. "Although I am confident I could have you charged with embezzlement based on the gross irregularities I have seen in the accounts, I will not press charges at this time. Your services are no longer required here. You may pack your things and leave tomorrow morning."

Thomas Blavey did not argue with Horton, although he almost asked for a week's pay, since the first week of May had almost passed, but thought better of it, knowing the likely answer to such a request. However, such sound reasoning did not keep him from nursing a growing sense of injustice as he packed his belongings that night. After all, hadn't he held the place together while the master was having his fun with his nigger wife up in Canada? It wasn't his fault that the old woman doted on her nephew. And so, what if he took a little extra cash now and then. He deserved that extra pay for his years of devoted service to Mistress Newby. It was a real shame she wasn't well enough to speak up for his rights.

The next several days Horton spent in working with the slaves on the plantation, accounting for the value of the disposable property, and consulting with his attorney over a revised will. The nights were spent in alternating shifts, keeping vigil at Malvina's bedside with Jenny. Because of concerns about the bleeding that might be stirred up by her coughing fits, her physician had recommended heavier and regular doses of laudanum. As a consequence, she was less coherent but occasional moments of lucidity would be interspersed with wild dreams and delirium. She would not infrequently cry out in terror.

One night she startled a sleepy Horton by screaming, "Get away from me. I'm still alive! You can't have me yet!"

With a look of sheer terror on her ashen face, she continued to flail her arms at the unseen adversary even after Horton grabbed her arms and spoke reassuring words so as to calm her.

Jenny took these occurrences as signs of a bitter spiritual struggle over the fate of Malvina's soul. Jenny's theology was sufficiently unsophisticated to entertain the possibility of a struggle to the very last breath so she wasn't about to give up on her mistress, predestination or no predestination. Horton was moved to see Jenny praying fervently at his wife's bedside. Her prayers were not marked by any particular eloquence of language or diction, but they carried a vitality that came from the depths of a soul that knew suffering. There was no diffidence in her address to the Deity. She was bold, direct, and personal.

"Lawd Jesus, I knows dat you sez to acks an' you'll receeb, seek an' you'll find, an' knock an' de door will be open fo' you. Well, Lawd, dis here woman done some pow'ful wicked tings in her life. An' now she got some kind o' crazy noshun dat she cain't ebber be saved. But I knows dat if'n you kin take away eben de hate fum my heart, dat you kin save dis po' sinful woman. I acks you now, Lawd, to accept dis woman's soul. Tank you, Lawd. I promise to help her be fit fo' de hebbinly manshuns. You jes' keep her 'til I git dere. Now, Lawd, if'n you don't mind, could you gib dis ol' sinner a sign dat Missus be yourn an' not de debbil's?"

Two evenings later, as Horton came to relieve Jenny at three in the morning, she was absorbed in gently rubbing Malvina's forehead with a moist cloth while softly singing, "Deep ribber, my home is ober Jordan . . ."

As her song came to a close, Malvina's eyes opened and looking directly into Jenny's eyes, an extraordinary change began to transform her face. Starting with her eyes and spreading slowly to the corners of her mouth, something was struggling to form against the habitual gloom embedded within her countenance. After some ill-defined fluttering motions, the change solidfied into the sweet innocent smile of a child that persisted against all odds for a whole minute. Malvina then, in a hoarse whisper, tried to speak. It came slowly, not unlike the smile, but out came the softly spoken but distinct words, "I love you, Jenny."

Three hours later, Malvina began to cough large amounts of blood. She expired a few minutes later.

Chapter Forty-Four

"Well, my young Quaker colleague, how would you treat this injury?"

"Unfortunately, Professor Gunn, I see no alternative but amputation," Isaac replied as he looked back at the crushed limb with exposed bone in the wound.

He had been working for his preceptor, Dr. Moses Gunn, in his general practice in Detroit since early May. As the month of September was rapidly approaching, he could reflect with great satisfaction upon the wide variety of illnesses and injuries he had seen and been allowed to treat under the professor's supervision.

"Why have you come to this determination? What are your findings that indicate such a course of action?"

Looking again at the negro youth lying on the hospital cot, he made mental note of the history of the accident as it had been reported, what he had seen when he first examined the patient twenty minutes before, and what he saw now. The injured youth could not be more than thirteen or fourteen years of age, his clothes were in tatters, and he appeared emaciated. He had been brought in from the street about an hour earlier, screaming in pain and bleeding profusely from a gaping wound in his left leg about four inches above his ankle. A tourniquet had been placed by the time Dr. Gunn and he had arrived after they had been summoned by one of St. Mary's Hospital staff.

The driver of a large dray loaded with produce was quite distraught when he brought him to the hospital, complaining that "I shouted at him to get out of the middle of the street, but he didn't seem to hear me above all the other noise at the waterfront. My horses had been affrighted a few seconds earlier by a loud noise and were running like the wind. I tried hard to rein them in but to no avail. I'll never forget the look of terror on that boy's face when he turned and saw what was coming toward him and could only make a desperate leap for safety."

When Dr. Gunn and Isaac had first tried to examine the youth, his already evident pain was matched by the fear in his eyes.

"Mah leg, mah leg! Kin you save it?"

His condition had changed rapidly since his first medical evaluation twenty minutes earlier. He now appeared listless and his pulse had increased markedly.

"Dr. Gunn, I believe his condition is changing rapidly for the worse. His pulse has increased to one hundred and ten beats per minute, he has become listless, both of which are signs of the shock induced by this magnitude of trauma, and the crush injury has produced multiple fragments of bone, as can be seen in the open wound. I don't believe that an injury of this severity can heal with meaningful recovery of function. I recommend immediate administration of a stimulant to arrest the shock, followed by amputation as the safest and best course of action to preserve his life. If he lives, he should be able to regain considerable function with an artificial limb. With chloroform anesthesia, we should be able to reduce his chances of being propelled into another bout of shock."

"That is sound reasoning Mr. Burgess. I agree with your plan. What technique of amputation would you propose?"

"Flaps, sir. My preference would be to create anterior and posterior flaps of skin and muscle so that the stumps of the tibia and fibula will be adequately covered."

"Very well, Mr. Burgess you may proceed with the amputation. I will administer the chloroform and one of the aides here in the hospital will assist with retraction of the tissues at your direction."

"But, Dr. Gunn, shouldn't I be assisting thee in performing the operation? Dost thou feel that I am ready to perform such a procedure?" Isaac asked with some anxiety.

"Mr. Burgess, you have assisted in four other amputations already during your work with me this spring and summer. I daresay that you have more practical experience in this area of surgery than most physicians will acquire in their entire careers. When I determine that you are ready, you are ready. Now let us proceed."

Isaac had indeed been quite fortunate in his experience with Dr. Gunn. He had assisted in leg amputations for gangrene in two elderly patients, another amputation just below the hip joint for trauma, and amputation of an arm for a cancerous tumor. Dr. Gunn's practice had grown considerably over the past several years and consequently so had his reputation for being willing to treat difficult cases. Although he had been trusted to perform smaller procedures, this was the first time that Isaac was given the opportunity to perform a major operation. He was grateful for Dr. Gunn's confidence in him but also felt great trepidation when he realized he was now responsible for the young man's fate. Raising the flaps went fairly smoothly, although he was spattered with blood before gaining full control of the bleeding arteries. As he began to saw through the bone, he felt a singular thrill that could only be described as a strange mixture of horror and delight. He moved quickly and confidently through the procedure, much to his own surprise, when later he could reflect upon what he had done.

At the completion of the amputation, his eyes met those of his mentor who then verbalized the unspoken communication, saying, "Well done, Mr. Burgess. You have a calm and steady hand. If ever this damnable conflict over Southern property rights comes to war, you will have an opportunity to further refine the skills you have acquired. By the way, you do plan to write and submit your thesis this next term, do you not?"

"I hope to, sir."

"Well, I propose you write about amputations. You will be able to approach the subject with the authority of experience and not just from reading medical texts and journals."

Isaac, who had been struggling with which subject to address in the written thesis that was required of all candidates for the medical degree was very grateful for the suggestion. "Thank thee, Dr. Gunn; I will write about amputations for my thesis."

While checking on their young patient after the procedure, a well-dressed middle-aged colored man, who was well known to Isaac, approached them and, addressing Isaac, said, "I think you should know that your young patient is a fugitive slave. His parents and sister are in great anxiety regarding his condition."

Isaac, turning toward Dr. Gunn, replied, "Mr. Lambert, please allow me to introduce thee to my professor, Dr. Moses Gunn."

Dr. Gunn gruffly acknowledged William Lambert's offer of a handshake with only a silent nod and then speaking to Isaac, said, "I need to finish my rounds. I trust you will be able to help this gentleman find a suitable arrangement for the care of your patient. You can meet me later for lunch at my residence."

Isaac, whose face had reddened with embarrassment, apologized to William Lambert for his professor's brusque manner.

"You needn't apologize for his behavior. My guess is that like so many of the white community here in Detroit, he doesn't want to be seen consorting with negroes and abolitionists. The important thing is that he did not refuse to provide care to this boy."

Isaac explained the nature of the injury, which necessitated amputation, but also his hopes for the ultimate survival and recovery of his patient.

"Unfortunately, Mr. Lambert, he is not in any condition to travel the remaining distance to Canada at the present time. I would prefer to keep him here in Detroit for another week so that he can regain sufficient strength while I observe him closely for any complications that might develop with his wound."

"His injury has thoroughly complicated our plans for his family's escape to Canada," William said as he scratched his forehead in perplexity. "We have reliable reports that slavecatchers, who have been pursuing this family, will arrive in Detroit in the next day or two."

"Dost thou think that the rest of his family would be willing to go on ahead to Windsor?"

"I have been trying my best to convince them of that course of action with limited success. They refuse to leave him behind. Perhaps if they heard from his doctor, they could be persuaded. They are being lodged for the moment in the basement of the Second Baptist Church."

"Mr. Lambert, my hope is to keep him safely here in the hospital as my patient for another week and then with thy help I would accompany him on the journey across the Detroit River to Windsor. But it will be much more difficult to accomplish this if we also need to hide other members of his family at the same time. Before we go to speak with the family, allow me to discuss the situation with the Superior, Sister Mary de Sales, and enlist her aid. I have always found her to be supportive of any person in need."

William Lambert paused before introducing Isaac to his patient's family while searching for the right words to convince them to trust the tall Quaker with the life of their son and brother. Isaac, who had recently turned twenty-one, had grown a full beard and mustache after starting his medical studies, which made him look older than his actual age.

William cleared his throat and spoke, "This is Mr. Burgess. He is a medical student and assistant to Dr. Moses Gunn, one of the best doctors here in Detroit. He is a friend to the negro and has helped many others like you on their journey to freedom. Please listen to what he has to say about your son's injury and his recommendations for his care." Then, pausing as he remembered his close collaboration with Isaac over the past several months, he turned to each of the family members with an earnest expression on his face, and pointing to Isaac, declared, "I would trust my own life to this man."

"Mistah Burjis, how's mah boy, Dick; will he lib?" his mother asked with intense anxiety in her voice.

"I hope and pray that he will live, ma'am. The injury to his leg was very severe. Unfortunately, we had to amputate, I mean cut off the lower part below his knee," Isaac explained as he pointed to his own leg.

His patient's mother began to wail, with his sister joining in shortly after, while the father could only bow his head with an utterly disconsolate expression on his face.

Isaac was deeply moved by their sorrow and replied, "I am so sorry. I truly wish we could have saved his leg. But, with your prayers and help, let us work hard to save his life. He cannot be safely moved for at least a week. With the help of the Sisters at St. Mary's Hospital, I believe he can be hidden from the slavecatchers, but you must go on to Canada now. Hiding all four of you will be much more difficult and if they catch you, the risk of Dick being captured will be much higher. Unfortunately, I cannot allow you to visit him at the hospital because not all the members of the staff are sympathetic to the negro. Please trust me in this. God willing, you will be reunited with your son and brother in about a week. Go ahead and prepare a place for him to recover as a free man in Canada."

Isaac earnestly searched each of their faces as he said these last words. Dick's mother wiped her eyes and said, "Bless you, Mistah Burjis. I trust you. Bring mah boy to me in de land o' freedom."

Near the end of lunch later that day, Isaac hesitated as he mustered the courage to speak. Anticipating his question, Moses Gunn, smiled and said, "I sense, my young colleague, that you were distressed by my less-than-cordial response when you introduced me to your friend, Mr. Lambert."

"Yes, sir. I never perceived thee to be hostile to the cause of freedom for the negro."

"You are correct, Isaac. Slavery is a damnable humbug. It is a blight on the history and honor of our country. Unfortunately, the right to hold property in human beings is protected by the Constitution. It is my sincere hope that someday our brethren in the South will adopt a process of gradual emancipation so that the hypocrisy, which threatens our identity as a freedom-loving people, will be finally erased. I have never chastised you for your enthusiasm for abolitionism. Indeed, I admire and respect your commitment to principle and the philanthropy that motivates your actions. But I also see a real danger in these activities. If there is no more room for compromise, if another Henry Clay does not soon arise, I fear that disunion and civil war will be the inevitable result of the agitations of the abolitionists.

"There is a practical consideration that I would also like to lay before you for your reflection. You may dismiss it as the venality of a man commited to personal success and material well-being over higher values, but I must express this concern, nonetheless. It has been my good fortune to develop a thriving clinical practice here in Detroit of which you have been an indirect beneficiary in the educational experience you have enjoyed these past few months. That *good fortune* of which I speak has a foundation built on good relationships within the community I serve. How can I serve the whole community, if I alienate a majority of that same community by openly espousing radical views? In the time we have worked together, have you ever seen me turn away any patient in need, even when they were unable to pay for my services? The ability of some to pay generous fees for my services has allowed me to offer my services to all in need, including negroes. If I were imprisoned for publicly helping a runaway slave, how would that benefit the other people who need medical services here in Detroit? My advice to you is to be very cautious and circumspect in your work assisting fugitives. I would hate to see a brilliant career of service to the many cut short by zealous service to a few."

As Isaac listened to Dr. Gunn speak, he could not help but reflect on the enthusiastic account of the final acquittal of the Oberlin Rescuers that Rebecca had given him earlier that summer. He still recalled with great satisfaction how the legal counterstroke by abolitionist lawyers under Ohio law, in which the Kentucky slaveholders who had captured John Price were prosecuted as kidnappers, had ultimately resulted in a legal standoff and release of the Oberlin Rescuers.

"Dost thou not see some value in the attention given in the public eye to the evils of slavery by the recent events at Oberlin?" he asked.

Moses Gunn smiled faintly as he replied, "The Oberlin incident is just the kind of action that will only further inflame the passions and intransigence of Southerners regarding this issue. It will be used as additional evidence of the North's intention to deprive them of their rights in property. I am afraid that the efforts of moderate Republicans like Lincoln to limit the extension of slavery will be lost in the furor created at both extremes of the political spectrum. All I can say as your friend and mentor is this: please be discrete in your activities."

As Isaac checked on Dick's condition later that evening before retiring for the night, he wondered if the "opportunity" granted him to operate on the young runaway was another way that Dr. Gunn had chosen to distance himself from the potential risk of prosecution under the Fugitive Slave Act. He resolved to take full responsibility for the medical care provided to Dick, should any legal action be taken.

"Mr. Burgess, thank God that you have come!" Sister Mary de Sales, the Superior responsible for St. Mary's Hospital, blurted as Isaac arrived in the hospital in response to her summons five days later. "Slavecatchers have been in the neighborhood looking for witnesses of the accident. It appears someone has told them something about an injured negro youth being brought to St. Mary's five days ago and they are suspicious that he may be one of the fugitives they are pursuing. They tried to gain access to the wards an hour ago, but I told them that under no circumstances would I allow them entrance at that time, since they would completely disrupt our care of the sick. Their leader was quite uncivil. He threatened to obtain a writ to search the hospital and said he would return soon with a US marshal to make his search anyway, if I didn't cooperate. In the calmest voice I could summon under such threats, I told him that he could come back for a quiet tour of the hospital but no earlier than eight p.m. after we have finished our rounds and fed the patients this evening. This seemed to satisfy him, and he said, 'We'll return at 8 p.m. sharp.' As they were leaving, I heard one of his associates say that capturing the injured slave would guarantee the surrender and return of the others, even if they were in Canada. What shall we do? We have less than six hours before they will return."

The Sisters of Charity nun, with her white cornette and black habit, made a curious contrast with the earnest young Quaker medical student as they spoke together in low tones in a hallway near the main entrance to the Catholic hospital. The hospital had been in operation for about nine years, providing care to all comers regardless of their faith or color, but was especially a refuge for the poor who had no means to pay for their care. Isaac looked into the kindly nun's face that was tightly framed by her cornette and tried to be as reassuring as possible.

"Sister Mary, we share common cause in our efforts to do God's work for the poor and downtrodden. Surely, He will support us in this time of trial. Clearly, it will be dangerous for Dick to stay here tonight, but even though his recovery since the operation has so far been uneventful, I am not certain that transporting him to Canada this soon is a safe option. Let us go and visit Dick. Perhaps an inspiration will come as we attend to our patient."

"Dick, how art thou feeling this afternoon?"

"Mistah Burjis, mah leg don't hurt so bad as yestiday but de stranjist ting happin. I kin feel mah foot itchin' eben doe it ain't dere!"

"Yes, Dick. Sometimes patients will feel their feet even after they are gone. It's almost as if there is a memory of a limb's presence that is retained. Is it painful?

"No, jes' itchin rite now. I jes' don't know war to scratch. Will I eber walk agin?"

"At first you'll need crutches, but I hope that eventually you will be able to wear an artificial leg and walk tolerably well."

While they were chatting, in the bed across from Dick, a young negro began to have a coughing fit and cried out in delirium, "Mammy, Mammy!"

Isaac and Sister Mary excused themselves and went over to attend to the other patient.

"Ned, you are in the hospital. You have an inflammation of the lungs. Don't be afraid, please try and swallow this medicine to help reduce the coughing," Sister Mary said as soothingly as she could. Turning to Isaac she whispered in his ear, "He has definitely taken a turn for the worse."

"Yes. His fever has increased substantially, which is also confirmed by his rapid pulse. It's at least one hundred and twenty beats per minute. I am not sure he will last another hour, let alone through the night," Isaac whispered with some anxiety.

As he pondered the fate awaiting Ned, he couldn't help but notice that although he was about two years older than Dick, he was essentially the same size and skin color. Other than having two intact legs, he could meet the superficial criteria that most slavecatchers were typically given to guide them in identifying escaped slaves. A plan began to form in his mind of how he might deceive the slavecatchers. He tried not to think about how the sad fate of one human being might save another as he considered all the factors involved. Remembering how Tib's brands and old scar were used in confirming his identity, he realized he would have to examine Dick and Ned for any unusual marks or scars.

"Sister Mary, couldst thou help me examine both of these patients?"

Both Ned and Dick's backs had the crisscrossing pattern of scars from whippings and fortunately, neither of them had any brands or other unique external marks that Isaac could identify. As he was finishing the examination of his two patients, another nun came up to Sister Mary and whispered in her ear. A renewed look of anxiety appeared on Sister Mary's face, which aroused Isaac's curiosity. After leaving the ward together, she told Isaac that a friendly informant had brought news that the slavecatchers had begun to patrol the street outside the hospital.

"Sister Mary, we must find a means of transporting Dick out of the hospital this evening. Their leader has planned well. They will be watching for any movements to and from the hospital tonight. Couldst thou send a messenger to Seymour Finney with my compliments, requesting that he send a wagon to the morgue of St. Mary's Hospital as soon as possible?"

"Are you sure you want to receive assistance from Mr. Finney? He entertains slavecatchers all the time in his hotel—"

"And fugitive slaves in his barn," Isaac finished Sister Mary's sentence as her eyes grew large.

"Yes. It is true. What better place to house slavecatchers than in a hotel managed by a member of the Underground Railroad? Please keep that bit of knowledge to thyself. Mr. Finney does not want to lose his public reputation of being a friend of the peculiar institution. It has served our cause very well."

While they continued to make their rounds, Isaac caught up with Dr. Gunn and assisted him with a dressing change. Sister Mary returned in a few minutes and whispered to Isaac, "It appears that Ned is close to death."

Looking meaningfully at Dr. Gunn, Isaac said, "Sir, my duties here are likely to detain me through the night. Please give my regrets to Mrs. Gunn as I will very much miss her company and the fine meal that awaits us."

Moses Gunn smirked at Isaac and said, "I expect to see you alive and present for rounds tomorrow. Don't go and do some fool thing and get yourself killed for an ideal." And then pausing for a moment, he added, "You're a brave one for all your foolish notions."

"Sister Mary, he is gone," Isaac said sadly as he looked at Ned's face and the peaceful immobility that had enveloped it. "I need to work quickly. Couldst thou help me transfer him to the operating theater?" he asked in a whisper.

"Mr. Burgess, I will help you with the whole business," Sister Mary insisted.

"But, Sister, thou dost not know what I am about to do. I would like to spare thee any involvement in my sin."

"Mr. Burgess, do you take me for some sort of naive fool because I wear the habit of a nun? I know what you are about, sir, and I must insist that I help you with this task. Besides, since you are not of the Catholic faith, I can confess both of our combined sins together as my own and perhaps gain absolution for both of us."

Isaac was at a loss for words and not understanding her theology, but nevertheless appreciated the sentiments and help of his monastic friend.

"Well, Sister Mary, this will be one operation that I will not add to my list of accomplishments this summer. Indeed, I think this must remain a secret that we will keep to the grave," Isaac said as he began to recreate Dick's amputation on Ned's lifeless corpse. Speaking to the subject of his postmortem ministrations, he said, "Ned, in death, thou art truly blessed. How many can boast that after death they have saved a life?"

Sister Mary de Sales thought to herself, *Oh these Protestant heretics, such good-hearted souls and yet they know nothing of the communion of the saints!*

"Ah, now I think we are finished," Isaac said with some satisfaction. "We will let him rest in the morgue until he is introduced to our Southern friends later this evening. Now we must go and explain to Dick in a very quiet and circumspect manner the necessity of his 'death' for the benefit of his fellow patients."

A surprised but quiet Dick listened to the whispered instructions Isaac gave him and awaited his feigned death with calm and composure. But he insisted that he was ready to make the full journey to Windsor that night and would accept any additional risks. After some silent meditation over the risks at Dick's bedside, Isaac whispered in his ear, "So be it, my friend. I think thou wilt tolerate the experience."

On cue, about half an hour later, when he heard Isaac speaking with Sister Mary in the hallway outside the ten-bed ward, he cried out, tried to raise himself up in bed, and fell back apparently lifeless. Isaac and Sister Mary rushed in, made loud exclamations of surprise at this sudden inexplicable turn in events, finally attributing the phenomenon to a late recurrence of shock. Sadly, Isaac told Sister Mary that he needed help to transport the body to the morgue. Thus, two tragic deaths were vividly etched upon the memories of the remaining patients, several of whom, in their fear, began to vocally speculate as to the identity of the next victim, which only added to the general anxiety on the ward.

Seymour Finney's wagon was waiting in the stable adjacent to the morgue. One of Finney's assistants was sitting patiently whittling a piece of wood while awaiting further instructions. After finding the false bottom in the wagon, Isaac instructed Dick to lie still while Sister Mary and he helped position him in the compartment. They then placed two coffins containing patients who had died earlier that day for early delivery to the pauper's cemetery. After one last whispered exchange with Sister Mary, Isaac also climbed into the hidden compartment within the false bottom, lying next to his frightened patient. Isaac bid Sister Mary a good night and, whispering instructions to Dick to be absolutely silent until he gave the signal, told Finney's assistant to take them to the docks on the Detroit River, which were on the way to the cemetery.

As the wagon rolled out of the stable, Isaac reflected on the fact that of all the times he had helped to ferry passengers using false-bottomed wagons, this was the first time that he had shared their accommodations. It was a painful ride between the irregular surface of the street and the cramped, rigid confinement of the hidden compartment. There was also something unnerving about having the two coffins lying side-by-side immediately above them. In the gathering gloom of dusk, he could make out very few details of their route through the narrow slats of the wagon. After only a few minutes, two horsemen clattered up to the wagon and ordered Finney's assistant to halt.

"You were comin' from the hospital, weren't you, you damn rascal! Open up those coffins right now!" barked one of the riders with a thick Southern drawl.

Taking his time, Finney's assistant scratched his head, looking doubtfully at the slavecatchers, and replied, "Are you sure you want me to do that? Have you ever seen a corpse before? I don't want you to be alarmed by what you see."

"Open 'em up an' stop yer talkin'!"

"As you wish, sir." Slowly, the assistant pried open the lid of each coffin and revealed, to the disgust of the slavecatchers, the corpses of two elderly white women. "Now gentlemen would you mind helping me secure the lids on these coffins. I think you have seen all you wanted to see."

"We don't have time fer the likes of you, secure 'em yerself!"

And with that rather thoughtless remark the slavecatchers rode off in another direction. After securing the lids, Finney's assistant continued the journey to the pauper's cemetery interrupted by a brief detour to the nearby docks. With a rapid succession of three raps on the wood of the wagon on Isaac's side, the assistant announced their arrival at the docks. Shortly after this signal the wagon stopped and he carefully assisted Isaac out first, so he could in turn help carry Dick to a nearby rowboat. One of William Lambert's friends from the Second Baptist Church was already waiting in the boat to row them across the Detroit River. Isaac thanked Finney's assistant, climbed into the rowboat with his patient, and in a whisper, said, "Let's row for freedom!"

Meanwhile, St. Mary's Hospital, or more specifically, Sister Mary de Sales, was playing host to the three advocates for Southern rights who, as promised, had arrived back at the hospital at eight p.m. sharp for the promised tour.

"I am Sister Mary de Sales of the Catholic Sisters of Charity. My duties as Superior of this hospital include administration of the philanthropic activities that God has appointed for us to perform here as well as to serve as leader of the sisterhood, who provide service to Our Lord in the persons of the sick and poor. The hospital has been serving the people of Detroit for approximately nine years. All of us who work here feel it is our great privilege to be given this sacred trust—"

The leader of the slavecatchers interrupted her at this point and said, "Ma'am, jes take us on the tour. We want to see all of yer nigger patients."

"But, sir, this is an essential part of the tour of St. Mary's Hospital. Our work—I should say, the Lord's work—depends upon the generous support of people like yourselves, who have come to see the great need and to witness the miracles of healing that God brings about for his suffering children who come here for succor."

Again, the leader of the slavecatchers interrupted her in his frustration, and said, "Looky 'ere, ma'am, we jes' don't have time fer all this here folderol."

But to his surprise, one of his associates spoke up and said to him, "Now wait a minute, Joe. I'd like to hear what this nice lady has to say. All you were gonna do was head to the nearest saloon as soon as we git done here anyway."

Sister Mary looked at her guests, a faint smile forming at the corners of her mouth, and continued, "It was through the great and benevolent support of our bishop, his Grace. . ."

A patient recitation of the nearly unabridged history of St. Mary's resulted in the actual tour beginning at nearly eight-forty p.m., after Joe's associate, Ernest, had all his questions answered to his satisfaction.

"Gentlemen, here is the first ward I would like to show you. As you can see, the sisters keep it very clean and tidy. Oh, please let me introduce you to the patients. May I have your attention, please? These gentlemen have come all the way from . . ."

"Kentucky, ma'am," Ernest volunteered.

"Kentucky, to visit our hospital. They are anxious to learn all they can about our work. Isn't that wonderful?"

Several patients' voices were raised in unison, "Yes, Sister."

"Isn't it wonderful, gentlemen, how much hope your visit has brought our patients?"

"I jes' wanted to see the nigger ward, not all these other folks," Joe growled.

"Oh, shut up!" Ernest retorted.

"I am sorry to cause any discord among you gentlemen," Sister Mary added blandly. "I just wanted to show you that we provide the same loving care for all our patients. Please follow me to the negro ward, where you will see the same cleanliness, order, and attention given to the colored patients as to the white patients."

"Well that's a good thing, since the niggers are a damn sight more valuable than most of the white trash in this place," Joe muttered under his breath.

As Sister Mary blushed in response to Joe's assessment of the value of St. Mary's patients, Ernest intervened, "Now, Joe that jes' ain't the way you should be talkin' around ladies. Where's your manners, Joe?"

"Sorry, ma'am," was Joe's grudging response.

Ignoring his rudeness, Sister Mary allowed the slavecatchers to search the negro ward closely. To their disappointment, none of the patients were young enough to meet the description of Dick's appearance they possessed.

In frustration, Joe exclaimed, "Ain't there any other niggers in this hospital?"

While Sister Mary hesitated, a patient who was lying in the bed next to the one that Dick had lately occupied, nervously cleared his throat, which caught Joe's attention.

"You there, boy. Can you tell me about any other niggers that have been here?"

With a look of panic on his face, he replied, "Dere was two mo' colored folk dis mornin' but dey up an' died dis aftanoon."

"Was one of 'em injured?"

"Yes'm. Dat would be Dick. Dey cut off his leg afta he got run ober in de street."

Giving Sister Mary a sharp look, Joe demanded, "Why didn't you tell us about this earlier?"

"Sir, most people who ask for a tour of St. Mary's Hospital don't request a visit to our morgue. Would you care to see poor Dick?" Sister Mary offered.

"Take us there right now. . .uh, please," Joe added when he saw the scowl on Ernest's face.

Later, as he examined the corpse of the young negro with his amputated leg, Joe's only comment was, "Damn niggers!"

Ernest took Sister Mary aside and apologized for his associate's outburst, "I'm awful sorry that he talks that way, ma'am. He can get real angry sometimes and then he forgets himself. Thank you kindly for the wonderful tour of your hospital. You are doin' a powerful good work here, even if you're Catholics."

Then as the slavecatchers departed, Ernest slipped a fifty-cent piece into the hand of an astonished and speechless Sister Mary, and said, "I wish I had more to give. Unfortunately, since we didn't catch the niggers, I can't afford to give more right now, ma'am."

Across the Detroit River in the early hours of the next morning, a sleepy but very happy reunion occurred when Isaac was finally able to reunite Dick with his family and congratulate them all on their newfound freedom. After considerable urging, Isaac accepted their offer of some strong coffee before returning to Detroit. His energy was fading fast and he knew this was one circumstance that necessitated a break from his usual practice of eschewing all stimulants that he had so faithfully followed as a student at Oberlin. He was grateful for the opportunity to wash his face and brush the straw off his clothes before starting early morning rounds with Dr. Gunn.

A nun came up to him and, handing him a note, said, "Mr. Burgess, Sister Mary de Sales left a message for you."

Her terse message, which elicited a smile from Isaac, read: "Had a very pleasant and satisfying visit with our guests."

"Mr. Burgess, I am pleased to see that you are alive and apparently well, although a bit bedraggled, I'd daresay," Moses Gunn said with a smile while directing a look of curiosity at the note in Isaac's hand.

Isaac grinned and in reply said, "It has been an eventful and productive night, sir."

"Indeed. My sources tell me that you have been traveling with the dead lately," Dr. Gunn commented cryptically.

It was Isaac's turn to be curious. "Dost thou have dealings with Mr. Finney?"

"Not particularly. But I do have dealings with his laconic assistant, whom you also seem to know. What you don't realize, is that our quiet friend and assistant to the enterprising Mr. Finney has other forms of employment as well. It is safe to say, that he is quite a versatile fellow with eclectic professional interests. I assume you finished your expedition with him last evening under the impression that he was delivering two recently deceased patients to the pauper's cemetery. Am I not correct?"

"Yes, of course, sir."

"Have you ever wondered with all your work there, how our anatomy department has maintained a steady supply of cadavers for our medical students? Perhaps Dr. Ford hasn't shared this part of our school's illustrious history with you."

"As assistants to the senior demonstrator, we were told that there are longstanding arrangements with hospitals and the city morgue here in Detroit that provide us with unclaimed corpses, or corpses whose relatives cannot afford the burial costs."

"I see. Well, I suppose that half-truths are sometimes more palatable than the whole truth. Isaac, herein resides the fundamental moral dilemma of modern medical education. I assume that you accept the utter necessity of anatomic dissection as a cornerstone of the training of competent medical practitioners?"

"Why yes, of course."

"It only follows that an ongoing supply of fresh material in the form of relatively well-preserved cadavers is essential to the educational process. Do you agree?"

"Yes."

"Ah, but here is the rub. The public, more specifically, members of polite society, are not so enchanted with the notion of having their eternal repose disturbed at its outset by the grubbing around in their earthly remains by curious would-be sawbones. Our medical school's very existence hung in the balance after an incident—which is now only spoken of in hushed tones as apocryphal lore, mind you, nothing more than mere legend—of a body being unceremoniously exhumed by resurrectionists for use in our anatomic teaching back in '51. The fact is, whatever the truth of the accusation that resurrectionists were operating in Ann Arbor on behalf of medical education, a local mob gathered quickly with the intent to burn down the main medical school building. Our only recourse was to arm the medical students and have patrols of students, rifled muskets in hand, guarding the building at all times.

"Finally, the excitement dissipated, and we were left with the ongoing problem of supplying teaching material for practical instruction in anatomy. One of our early demonstrators in the department came up with the obvious solution based on the fundamental human principle of 'out of sight, out of mind.' Mr. Finney's assistant is a part of the medical school's network of discreet individuals who provide us with high quality anatomic material for teaching. Rather than cause unnecessary distress to the kind sisters of St. Mary's Hospital, we prefer to allow them to remain under the impression that a decent burial has been given to the white and colored Protestant patients who die under their care. The fate of deceased Catholic patients is followed too closely for us to avail ourselves of a broader, more ecumenical sampling of corpses. Similar arrangements exist with the city morgue and other medical establishments for the poor of Detroit. Now, I think you may have a better understanding of the origin of the cadavers that arrive, packed in ice, at the railroad depot in Ann Arbor."

Isaac shuddered involuntarily at these revelations, realizing that he had never really desired to know the details of cadaver procurement, even though he would be working even more closely with the demonstrator over the coming months as junior demonstrator in anatomy.

Looking at Isaac with mild humor mixed with real sympathy as he observed his discomfort with this revelation, Moses Gunn said, "As you can readily see, in the cause of medical progress, we have made some moral compromises. You must determine for yourself, if the good that has been achieved outweighs the evil means."

The next evening, as Isaac stared at paper and pen with the painful awareness that he had long owed his sister a letter, he thought about his recent activities and realized that he had few safe topics about which to write.

"Perhaps I'll think of something pleasant to write tomorrow," he mused, as his mind wandered toward images of the many volunteers who had contributed so much to his medical education.

Horton Newby mopped the sweat from his brow in the heat of the noonday sun on an early day in September 1859 as his wagon was being loaded with produce, other foodstuffs, and discreet amounts of firearms and ammunition outside Ferguson's General Store in Shelbyville, Kentucky. During his trip south from Canada, he had consulted with the abolitionist John Fairfield. He felt quite fortunate to have made contact in Cincinnati with the elusive Fairfield, who had a reputation for being in perpetual motion from one daring deed to another. Horton's interest in seeking Fairfield's advice was centered in the abolitionist's legendary use of deception as well as his willingness to arm slaves so that they could defend themselves during some of his riskier schemes. When they had met together for dinner in one of Cincinnati's more unsavory taverns in early May, Horton had even tried to recruit Fairfield to assume the role of overseer on his plantation and assist in the removal of his slaves from Kentucky to Ohio. Fairfield had flatly refused the request and generous financial offer that came with it. Horton vividly remembered his response.

"Mr. Newby, my mission in life is to liberate the 'human property' of people like you and escort them to freedom. You're already planning to free your slaves. What challenge is there for me in that?"

Horton tried to point out the challenge of transporting such a large number of slaves north, especially when his nephew would likely object in more than word alone to the project.

Fairfield replied to his plea for help by saying, "Mr. Newby, you don't need me if you've got the trust of your negroes. What I'd recommend is that you gradually accumulate enough weapons that you can arm your most trusted men and train them in how to use the firearms but keep that fact hidden from your white neighbors. I always tell the slaves I help escape that they may have to fight for their freedom. In fact, I'll tell 'em that if they ain't willin' to fight, I won't give 'em a second thought. You may want to use some kind of ruse as you're leavin' the area."

Horton replied, "Yes. I'm planning to tell the community that I'm selling the plantation and moving to Texas with my slaves."

"That lie should work real fine, at least for a while," Fairfield had commented.

With regular visits to Ferguson's General Store, by September, Horton had gradually collected a nice cache of small arms, mostly revolvers, and ammunition. He also had added some additional rifled muskets so that between the firearms he already owned and the recent purchases he could potentially arm twenty of his male slaves. Old Judge Ferguson, who had acquired the title during a brief stint as a local justice of the peace many years before, had flirted with the world of business over the years and might have been quite successful but for his love of conversation. It was not unusual for him to discourage his more hurried customers with his chatter, while the town gossips kept his business afloat by their faithful patronage.

Horton found that Ferguson was a wonderful conduit through which he could inform the entire county of his plans for a new life in Texas after the death of his wife. Although the old judge always enjoyed adding a bit of his own commentary to the gossip he shared with the world, he managed to convey the basic information accurately, as Horton confirmed when various members of the community who showed interest in purchasing the plantation approached him. Of course, Ferguson couldn't resist offering some additional thoughts about Horton's proclivity for "nigger wenches," speculating as to how this might affect Horton's potential interest in remarriage, since he still was a good prospect for some energetic and ambitious young woman to tame. Ferguson never questioned the purchases of firearms and ammunition after Horton explained to him that he had heard there was a shortage of such material on the frontier and it seemed the better part of valor to be prepared for every possibility, including hostile Indians.

Although a general sense of relief was felt in the slave quarters on the Newby plantation with the dismissal and departure of Thomas Blavey, the natural curiosity that attended the return of their master from his long sojourn in the north was also accompanied by considerable suspicion, especially among those slaves who had developed a certain understanding with their former overseer. Two of Blavey's favorites, Cassius and Pliny, who had served as drivers, had been quickly demoted to the status of regular field hands. Resenting their loss of power and the necessity of laboring side-by-side with those whom they had so recently dominated with the whip, they could only foresee evil coming from this abrupt change in their fortunes. Others who had lived for some time on the plantation and knew its history couldn't help but speculate about their master's latest "noshuns." Even the blacksmith Caesar, who with Horton's support had assumed a more formal leadership role, struggled to understand the apparent radical change in his master's attitudes toward slavery.

Shortly after Horton's return, he met clandestinely one evening with Jenny to gain more insight into the thoughts of his master. Jenny, who was a wellspring of hope, tried to relieve his anxieties about the real intentions of his master.

"Seezer, ah tell ya dat Massa Newby's a new man."

"But Jenny, I see'd what he did wif Tib. How kin ye be so sartin dat he be a new man?"

"But Seezer, we ain't see'd what he did dese las' sevrul year in Canuhduh. 'Sides, tink 'bout de good he dun since he come back. Dat wicked oberseer ain't here no mo' and no mo' dribers. Cashush and Plinee de only folks dat don't like dat."

"Kin we trust 'im, doe? Mebbe, he jes' habbin sum fun wif us befo' he drop de hammer, like he did wif Tib's mammy."

"Fair 'nuff, Seezer. Tain't smaht to not be at least a bit suspishush. Jes' keep a close eye on 'im an' we'll see. But I knows in mah bones dat de good Lawd's bin makin' a new man outta 'im."

"Jenny, ah hopes so. But, if'n he try to sell any mo' ob' our peepul down de ribber, I'll slit his throat faster den you kin cry hallelujah!"

Several months had passed since Caesar and Jenny had discussed their master's intentions in such stark terms. As Caesar was loading the last supplies onto the wagon under Horton's direction, he reflected on the evolution that his perceptions of his master had undergone during that time. The consistent earnestness and respect that Horton had demonstrated in his relations with his human property had gradually won the trust of most of the slaves on the plantation, including that of Caesar. Later, as Horton took great pains to personally train twenty slaves chosen by Caesar in the use of the firearms he had been collecting, Caesar realized that his master was serious about his intent to free his slaves, since arming slaves was illegal in the Commonwealth of Kentucky. Not only did he appear to be quite serious in his stated goal of freeing his slaves, but also, he was clearly willing to risk his own life in accomplishing the task. When Caesar recently warned Horton that he thought Cassius and Pliny might betray him, he was startled by his master's response.

"Caesar, how can I blame them or any of you for not trusting me? Cassius and Pliny have learned to love power from the bad example that white people like me have taught them. It is especially difficult for them to conceive of a society where the color of one's skin does not set one apart but only one's accomplishments. They still yearn for the few crumbs of power that Blavey gave them in exchange for collaborating with him as he caused their own people to suffer. I want to not only free their bodies but also their minds from enslavement. They will only begin to understand what real freedom is when they can see and experience it for themselves."

"But Massa Newby, dey's wicked niggers. Dey ain't worth nuttin'. Dey's only trubbel."

"The same could be said for me for most of my existence. I still hope to be of some real value as a human being and I mean to give them a chance as well. But I must add that at this point it would only be prudent to not let them know of our plans other than in vague terms, and we will definitely not allow them to use the weapons we have been collecting. Have you continued to keep them working in the far field when the training with the firearms has been going on?"

"Yes'm, Massa Newby. Ah don't tink dey suspec' much 'bout de noise. We bin tellin' dem dat you bin shootin' a lot dese days."

As they rode back together to the plantation with Horton's horse following behind the wagon, Caesar gradually became quite agitated and began to speak quickly in hushed tones to Horton.

"Massa Newby, remember when ah tole you dat Cashush an' Plinee cain't be trusted? Dey bin goin' off de plantashun at nite. Ah follered 'em las' nite. Dey bin meetin' wif de ol' oberseer, Blabee. Ah heared 'em talkin' 'bout a posse dat would git Massa Faircloff's niggers back fo' 'im an' den tings would be jes' like dey was befo'."

Horton listened with interest and with a smile replied, "Caesar, it looks like our friends Cassius and Pliny will need to provide some more information to my nephew and Mr. Blavey for us. Did they mention anything about the firearms?"

"No, Massa."

"Before meeting you at Judge Ferguson's store, I had an appointment with my attorney in Shelbyville to complete the sale of the plantation. I am pleased to say that it has fetched a pretty price, which should help all of you as you establish yourselves as free negroes in the North or Canada."

"Massa Newby, I don't unnerstan'. How de sale o' de plantashun gonna he'p us po' negroes?"

"Who made the plantation so profitable? Isn't it only fair that you should enjoy the fruit of your labor? I intend to give all of you, including those members of my family who were once my slaves, equal portions of the proceeds coming from the sale of the Newby plantation."

Caesar looked at his master for a long moment and then in a confidential tone tinged with emotion said, "Jenny allez tole me dat you a diffrunt man now. Forgib me, Massa Newby, but she only know'd de half ob it. You not only a new man but you also a crazy one!"

And with a look of utter bewilderment in his eyes, Caesar waved his hand resignedly as if in benediction over his deluded master. Grinning broadly, Horton enthusiastically grasped the hand in motion, squeezing it tightly, which gave the surprised slave a start.

"Caesar, with the help of the telegraph, I have arranged with my bank here in Shelbyville for the transfer of the money on ahead to a bank in Cincinnati. Please let it be known in the quarters that we will be leaving for Louisville and the Ohio River in one week. We shall actually leave in five days, however, so that we can obtain a head start over my nephew and his friends. Cassius and Pliny will be the only slaves in our entourage who will be handcuffed. Have you ever been outside of Shelby County?"

"No, Massa."

"That could pose a problem. Can any of the slaves read?"

"De only slave I ebber knowed dat could read was Tib, Massa."

Horton winced, nodded sadly, and replied, "Of course, you're correct, Caesar. And fortunately for him he is a long way from here. I am concerned that I am the only member of our pilgrimage who can read the road signs or a map. In case I become indisposed, you may have to make use of my compass to head north to the Ohio River during the day. Do you know how to find the north during the night time?"

"I kin find de drinkin' gourd."

"Good. I will write passes for each of you to travel to Cincinnati, either overland or preferably by steamboat. If for any reason I am unable to complete the journey with you, I have also prepared manumission documents, your free papers, that you must protect at all hazards. Ask among the colored people in Cincinnati for Mr. Levi Coffin. He is a friend to the negro and will help you register the free papers in Ohio. He will also find guides to take you all to Canada where Tib and Cicero live, if you choose to live there. That is the only place where you will be treated as full citizens and can live without the fear of being kidnapped back into slavery.

"Finally, I have written a new will, which is safely in the hands of my attorney, Mr. Ambrose Stone of Shelbyville. He is an honorable man who will make sure that it is executed faithfully should I die in the attempt to leave Kentucky with you. In the will, I state explicitly that I have emancipated my slaves, that it is my intention to remove them to a free state, that the wealth from the sale of the plantation is to be equitably distributed to each of them, and that the prior will, naming my nephew as heir of my estate is null and void. In addition to the copy that is in Mr. Stone's possession, a copy of the will has been sent by mail today to Mr. Coffin in Cincinnati and the last copy I am carrying on my person."

Then pointing to a satchel on the seat beside him, he added, "In this bag are the manumission documents that have been officially witnessed and registered with the help of Mr. Stone. Although he has made a separate record of these documents, it is essential that you protect these papers, for in them lies your future until you reach the safety of Canada. Do you have any questions or concerns? Do you know what you must do?"

"Yes'm, Massa Newby. I gotta keep you alive!"

Chapter Forty-Six

"Yes'm, Massa Blabee, dats what dey plans to do. Seezer bin talkin' 'bout us leabin fo' de ribber soon so's Massa Newby kin take us to Texus wif 'im. We leabin in seben day," Cassius dutifully reported.

"Pliny, what's all this you were sayin' about takin' you niggers north?" Thomas Blavey asked his other informant and then spat on the ground.

"Oh, Massa Blabee, don't you take nuthin he say serious," Cassius interrupted. "Why Plinee, he jes' a fool; tinkin' dat Massa Newby would free his niggers."

Cassius shook his head and rolled his eyes to confirm the sheer and utter foolishness of such an idea.

"Shut up, Cassius! Well, Pliny, out with it. Tell me what you've been hearin' around the plantation."

Pliny gave Blavey a furtive glance and shot a smirk toward Cassius before replying, "I oberhear some o' de niggers talkin' all excited like 'bout how de massa would free dem when dey git to Ohio."

"Do they really think they're goin' north then?"

"All's I kin say, dey awful happy fo' bein' takin' down de ribber."

Blavey held up his lantern and scrutinized the faces of his two former drivers and thought to himself, *I wonder who's lyin' to me. But, maybe there's truth in what both of 'em say. That rascal Newby's been around those abolitionists for so long, they've addled his brain with all their unnatural notions. They may be his property to dispose of as he wishes, but it ain't natural for them to be free. If they ain't gonna be his no more, they still gotta be somebody's!*

Blavey came closer to his conspirators and whispered, "Both of you keep a close eye on all of them, especially your master Newby and that good-for-nothing Caesar, and let me know right away about any changes in their plans."

He was thoroughly disgusted that Newby would entrust the critical responsibilities of an overseer to a slave, which only heightened his suspicions that something *unnatural* like manumission was being planned for the negroes. As Blavey departed in

an opposite direction from the clandestine meeting on the edge of the Newby plantation near the old Louisville and Shelbyville Turnpike, another unseen observer also
made his way back to report on the proceedings to Horton Newby.

"Caesar, it seems as though Mr. Blavey is out of sorts over the fact that he has been
replaced by a colored man," Horton said with a smile, after he heard Caesar's report.
"Don't be concerned about Pliny discovering the actual destination of our imminent
journey. It is almost impossible for a small family to keep a secret, let alone sixty persons. I am convinced that Mr. Blavey and my nephew mean to seize possession of all
of you, regardless of your destination and regardless of Kentucky law for that matter.
No, my friend, I'm afraid you'll have to fight for the freedom that I would give you."

It was Caesar's turn to smile, which he did slowly and with a hint of grim determination. "Let dem jes' come an' try to take mah freedom away fum me!"

The intoxicating aroma of mint and bourbon rising from the frosted silver cup tickled
his nostrils, while the three-quarter time of the waltz wafting through the windows
onto the piazza created a sense of continuous languid motion that had its own inebri-
ating qualities. Something vaguely unpleasant began to penetrate the otherwise pleasant fog that had enveloped him. Was it a noise that was out of tempo with the music?
Yes, that was it, a seemingly incessant cacophonous chatter coming from close by.

"Why Mr. Newby, I declare, you haven't heard a word I've said."

Coming to himself, Horton blushed a deep crimson, greatly to the satisfaction of
his interrogator.

"Please forgive me, Mrs. Avery, the combination of the pleasant night air, fine
music, and a perfect mint julep had for a moment taken me to another place and time."

Looking at the graying but still handsome Horton, Lucinda Avery, having been
recently widowed herself and somewhat past the bloom of youth, saw opportunity.
For with three children between the ages of six and ten and only a few domestics as
their collective inheritance, she was greatly in need of an *opportunity*. It wasn't that
she was without charms. Indeed, she had had many beaus when she finally said yes
at age sixteen to Mr. Avery. But now, twelve years later, through the combination of
childbearing and constant worry over the disaster wrought upon their finances by
her husband's predilection for gaming, she had become more than pleasingly plump,
garrulous, and at times even shrill in her attempts to charm the opposite sex. Having
learned of Horton's imminent departure for a new life in Texas through the extensive
chain of communication that the good citizens of Shelbyville quite willingly provided,
she had determined to insert herself into that new life on the Southern frontier.

"Mr. Newby, you haven't commented on my dress at all this evening. Is there
nothing unusual about my attire, sir?"

"Mrs. Avery, it is a lovely dress, quite colorful."

"Indeed, sir! My year of mourning has ended this week just passed."

"Oh. I see. Well, I thought you looked quite handsome in black."

Normally, such a response might deter some, but not Lucinda Avery. Horton's gentle attempts to distance himself from her were like a flame to a moth. She only hovered more closely in her enthusiasm for the chase. Horton had felt it necessary to reengage with the local community, partly to assist his efforts to find a buyer for his plantation but also to further cloud the issue of his real intentions regarding his slave property. Mrs. Avery moved in the same social circles and would not willingly miss any soiree that the now-eligible plantation owner attended. Horton cheerfully engaged in light conversation with her, which usually meant giving brief responses, in the form of a nod of the head or a grunt of assent to the occasional pauses in her almost uninterrupted monologues. As she began to assume greater familiarity in her address to Horton, he realized that he should pay more attention to the content of her speech, as her designs for their future together were not entirely obscured by her verbosity.

In a brief pause in Lucinda's speech created by an untimely sneeze, Horton said, "Bless you, Mrs. Avery. I have been the beneficiary of your remarkable conversational skills, but I must now bid you my adieu. My duties at home are calling. There are many preparations still to be made prior to my departure. Thus, as an early riser these days, I must also be early to bed."

"Please, dear Mr. Newby, must you be so formal? Will you not call me by my Christian name, Lucinda? Surely, a bond has been forming between us that even a thousand miles will not sunder."

"Mrs. Avery, I trust that our friendship, like the many other friendships I have enjoyed here in Kentucky, will continue regardless of any distance separating us."

Bowing slightly to the disappointed Mrs. Avery, Horton turned on his heel and departed at the early hour of ten o'clock from the evening's festivities that were being hosted on a neighboring plantation about two miles' distance from his plantation. As he thanked his host prior to entering his carriage, his attention was drawn by some raucous laughter coming from the piazza behind him. Recognizing a familiar voice, he turned to see his nephew Gordon Fairclough staggering down the steps, supported by two compatriots. Young Fairclough, although quite intoxicated, was still able, in turn, to recognize his uncle, and shouted in a drunken slur,

"Why it's Uncle Horton! You should come join us Uncle. We'll show you some real fun. It's too tame here for the likes of us."

Tipping his hat in farewell, Horton did not answer his nephew but promptly left in his carriage. Lucinda Avery, who had witnessed Gordon Fairclough's drunken outburst, looked wistfully after Horton and declared, "Now that's how a real gentleman deals with disagreeable family members!"

Any remnants of the languid torpor that had engulfed Horton while he sipped his mint julep and listened to the droning of Lucinda Avery had fully dissipated by the time he arrived a half hour later at his plantation. Jumping down from the carriage, he was met by Caesar and Jenny, who were in a high state of agitation.

"De hour ob deliberance almost at hand!" Jenny virtually shouted, as she could no longer repress herself. Horton gave them both an anxious look, to which they responded, "Yes'm, Massa Newby. Ol' Plinee an' Cashush han'cuff'd in de barn."

Horton discussed additional details of their security with Caesar and the others who had been trained to use firearms for another half hour and then yawning, said, "Friends, now let's try to get some rest. We'll leave promptly at five in the morning."

The almost machine-like chirping coming from some crickets nearby and the rustle of leaves in the trees overhead added a sense of continuity as Horton's lantern cast its light over the headstones of his wife and daughter in the family plot. Unable to sleep beyond four that morning, he had risen quickly and had come once more to commune with the dead.

"Julia, I must say farewell to you and your mother as I complete the journey that you initiated so many years ago." Turning to his wife's grave, he added, "Malvina, I hope you are finally at peace and can understand the actions I am taking. I feel confident of Julia's blessing, for how could she have foreseen where ultimately the plea of a dying daughter would lead?" Hesitating a moment before leaving the graves, he almost said something more to Julia but then thought better of it, only muttering to himself, "Of course, she is proud of them," and departed to join the others gathering quietly in the yard.

Horton was struck by the solemnity of the occasion as he surveyed most of the sixty faces reflected in the light of several torches that were held aloft by some of the slaves. He was moved by the evident joy and exultation already apparent in some, especially that of Caesar and Jenny, but was also struck by the dull, sullen stares of others who did not yet know their true destination. The handcuffed forms of Pliny and Cassius were sitting in one of the many wagons assembled for the exodus, their faces bearing a mixture of fear and sullen anger. Motioning for as many as possible to come closer as he stood on the highest step leading to the piazza of the mansion, Horton began to address his human property, in tones many of them had never heard before coming from a white man.

"Friends, for the sake of your safety and the success of this endeavor, I made a decision to deceive many of you regarding the real future to which I am taking you. I hope that you will forgive me for the deception. Now, the time has come to inform you of the full truth as we make this journey together. It is my intention not to take you to Texas but to escort you to the free state of Ohio, and once there, to record the manumission papers, the free papers, for each one of you. My only regret is that I didn't do this earlier so that many of you would have been spared the loss of family members. Once in Ohio, you will also receive your portion of the money coming from the sale of this plantation. If you choose to stay in Ohio, you will go with my blessing. If you would like to go on to Canada with me, to a country that will give you full citizenship, where you will be free of the threat of kidnappers who would rob you of your freedom, I would be honored by your company."

As Horton spoke, Caesar, Jenny, and the twenty other slaves who already knew of the plan watched the expressions on the faces of their fellow slaves undergo a dramatic transformation. One of the younger women, cried out, "Did I hear free papuhs, Massa Newby? You mean to gib us our freedom?"

"I mean to do just that."

"Gloree, hallelujah!" came from a host of mouths, while Pliny and Cassius stared sullenly ahead.

Caesar now spoke up and said to the crowd, "Massa Newby mean to gib us our freedum, but we gonna hab to fight fo' it, also. Dese yere niggers, Cashush and Plinee, bin plannin' to betray us to de ol' oberseer Blabee and Massa Faircloff. Dey miss de joy ob dribin' us po' slaves."

Someone cried out, "Let's kill 'em. Dey ain't fit to lib!"

Looks of terror now replaced the sullen expressions on the faces of the former slave drivers.

Horton raised his right hand in the air and shouted, "Please, let us calm down. There must be no more killing or torture of negroes. Pliny, Cassius, and I share a common history. We have all caused you to suffer. I beg you all to please forgive them and me. Once they have tasted real freedom, I am convinced they will become new men, people whom you would willingly call your friends. After we set foot on the free soil of Ohio, their handcuffs will be removed, and they will be free to choose their future.

"Caesar is right," he continued. "You may have to fight for the freedom that I would willingly give you. Cassius and Pliny know that my nephew and your old overseer cannot bear to see so much valuable *property* slip away from them. We will all be in great danger until we reach Ohio, and even then, not fully safe until we are in Canada. Thankfully, through a little more deception and my nephew's drunkenness, we will have an early advantage. Initially, we will travel openly toward Louisville along the Shelbyville Branch but eventually leave it for a road that will take us to Portland at the eastern end of the Louisville and Portland Canal, where hopefully we will board a steamboat for Cincinnati. If we encounter any slave patrols along the way, I may need to continue with the deception about moving to Texas."

A rather peculiar scene would have met the eyes of any traveler on the Shelbyville Branch the next morning, especially when considering the standards of decorum set by the peculiar institution. Several wagons filled with negroes had formed a long file, moving at the fine pace of five miles an hour, which was accompanied by nearly twenty negro men on horseback with one solitary white man riding along in the group. No iron collars or chains of any kind were to be seen, except for the handcuffs on two of the slaves riding in one of the wagons, which could only be appreciated on closer inspection. Another peculiarity was the almost festive character of the group as they traveled along the road. With the light of day, many of the women had begun to sing hymns to the point that Caesar who had been riding up and down the line felt impelled to remind them that their rejoicing was a bit premature and would give slave patrollers the wrong idea. Try as they might, they had a difficult time assuming the stolid indifference so characteristic of the enslaved when being transported and a fleeting smile could be seen creeping across many a face.

Riding up to one of the wagons, Caesar remonstrated with a young woman, "Now Alice, wipe dat silly grin off yo' face. You ain't got nuthin to be happy 'bout yet!"

Caesar's many remonstrances were not a futile exercise, for shortly after speaking to Alice, a white man could be seen ahead approaching rapidly on horseback, holding a rifle in one hand. As he came closer, it was evident that he was quite young. While he attempted to assume an air of authority, he was clearly anxious, being somewhat intimidated by the large number of slaves. When Horton saw him approaching, he rode on ahead to intercept him.

"Is that you Mr. Newby? I guess the rumors 'bout you leavin' Shelby County are true after all," the youth said, eyeing the train of wagons filled with negroes and the accompanying colored horsemen with growing trepidation.

"Yes, I am Horton Newby, and as you can see, I am indeed leaving my native county, but not without some reluctance."

Approaching Horton so that he could address him quietly from his horse, the youth, looking first at the large group of slaves and then at their master, said in a low whisper, "Mr. Newby, do you feel safe alone with so many niggers?"

Horton smiled benevolently at the youth, and turning in his saddle, made a sweeping gesture that embraced all of the negroes behind him and said, "These are my people. Why should I be concerned about them? Their loyalty is unquestioned. Unfortunately, I'm afraid I can't express the same degree of confidence about some of my white acquaintances."

With a puzzled expression on his face, the youthful patroller lowered his rifle and motioned for the group to proceed.

Nearly five hours later they turned off the Shelbyville Branch and entered the road to Portland that was unfortunately smaller and poorly maintained, a mere track through the forest. Horton was pleased with the rapidity with which they had made the journey thus far. It was not quite noon and they only had another six to seven miles to go. He knew these would be the most challenging miles of the journey though, because the poor quality of the road would barely admit the width of a wagon, slowing their pace to no more than two to three miles an hour. Any mishap here in this heavily forested area could also make them more vulnerable to an attack from those unsympathetic to their mission. He urged them forward as quickly as possible while at the same time urging caution to avoid ruts in the road that might break an axle on one of the wagons.

They made good progress for the first half hour, only having to stop briefly on two occasions to remove fallen tree branches from the road. But his hopes for a quick trip through the forest were dashed when he heard Caesar calling him from the back of the train to inform him that an axle had broken on one of the wagons. By the time he worked his way back to the damaged wagon, efforts were already underway to repair the broken axle. Caesar, who was ever resourceful, had planned for this contingency and had brought some spare axles and wagon wheels, which were being retrieved from another wagon up the line. Horton, who was prepared to abandon the wagon to avoid further delay, could only admire the tenacity with which the negroes worked to repair the wagon. Rather than disturb Caesar with his concerns about potential pursuit, he accepted the situation and watched the men work methodically.

One of them, looking up at Horton, said, "Massa Newby, dis wagon real valubul. Don't worree, we fix it good."

After nearly an hour's delay, the group was again in motion toward the town of Portland. Horton would only feel safe once they were back out in the open. However, the forest track ended only a quarter of a mile from the town.

Thomas Blavey was in a foul humor that morning. Because his spies had not kept their appointment with him the night before, he had grown suspicious, wondering if he had been duped by his former employer who, after all, might have been feeding him false information through Pliny and Cassius. After waiting for an hour beyond the appointed time for their meeting, he debated with himself about what to do. Growing tired, he decided that he had overreacted and went back to his lodgings on a nearby farm. It wasn't the first time his spies had failed to appear for one of their late-night meetings. He would give them hell when he saw them again the next night.

Meanwhile, he was awful tired and knew he needed some rest. However, sleep eluded him for more than an hour and when it finally came, it was fitful. About half past four, he awoke with a start from an intense nightmare, in which it seemed as if the whole slave population of the Newby plantation were examining and prodding the corpse of a white man, some with slight expressions of pity but most with derisive laughter. As he drew near to identify the subject of the slaves' interest, something about the features of the man seemed vaguely familiar to him. It was at the very moment when he recognized himself as the corpse that he awakened. He was so agitated by the nightmare that he could no longer sleep. As he ruminated over its possible meaning, he resolved to go and spy out the Newby plantation for himself.

After first returning to his usual meeting place with the former slave drivers, with the greatest stealth he could muster, he crept further on to the plantation. Being attracted by the sound of voices, he headed for the yard near the mansion and to his disgust and alarm was able to hear a portion of Horton Newby's speech to his slaves. He heard enough to divine that Texas was not Newby's real destination but rather Ohio, and that his intention was to free his slaves there. Because some slaves were walking toward his hiding place, he felt constrained to retire to a greater distance and missed the rest of Horton's speech.

Why that rascal Newby has tried to dupe me! He's leaving two days earlier than what he told those fools Cassius and Pliny. Well, he hasn't fooled me, Blavey thought as he hurried back to his horse to rouse Gordon Fairclough and the posse. Three hours later, after a prolonged and exasperating search, he found Gordon and his five stalwart drinking companions, the posse, in one of the more disreputable saloons of Shelbyville. Gordon and only two of the others, who had passed out earlier the previous night, could be roused with some difficulty and were nursing ferocious headaches as they rode away with Blavey on the Shelbyville Branch. Blavey drove them hard and within three and a half hours reached the entrance to the forest road to Portland. He jumped down from his horse and surveyed the Branch as well as the forest road and satisfied himself that the wagon train had turned on to the small track through the forest. With an exultant whoop, he said to Gordon, "Your uncle doesn't know that there is another track through this forest that is narrower still but is a shorter, more direct way to Portland. But I know that path very well, for I grew up in these parts. With any luck we should be waiting for that damn uncle of yours and give him a little surprise before he ever reaches the edge of the forest. Now follow me on the shortcut."

"To think he has the audacity to try and steal my inheritance!" Gordon exclaimed as the outrage of freeing perfectly sound slave property permeated his consciousness. "Clearly, Uncle Horton must have lost his sanity. Otherwise, he can only be viewed as a traitor to his kind. My poor aunt Malvina suffered long with his nigger-lovin' ways. Oh! My head. It feels like it'll explode. Someone must have slipped me some tainted liquor last night. Good Kentucky bourbon just wouldn't do this to a man."

Gordon's other two companions followed in sullen silence, wincing in pain from their own headaches whenever their drinking companion and patron would break the silence by expostulating on the evils of abolition.

Chapter Forty-Seven

While Horton's horse plodded along near the head of the column of wagons, he pondered their situation. *By my calculations we must be close to the end of the forest*, he thought.

Just as some movement ahead on the track caught his attention, a shot rang out and he felt a sharp pain in his upper abdomen accompanied by a force that threw him back in the saddle. A jubilant shout that he recognized as coming from his old overseer was almost immediately followed by another shot. This time it came from behind him and he saw his adversary crumple and fall to the ground.

"Good shot, Jenny!" rose from multiple voices coming from the train of wagons. However, Jenny ignored her accolades and was quickly at Horton's side. With Caesar's help, she gently eased him from the saddle to the ground, supporting him in a sitting position. After the first shock of the gunshot wound, Horton realized that he still had his faculties, although pain was a significant distraction. He looked curiously over at Blavey and his companions, all of whom had been quickly disarmed and surrounded by the armed slaves in the group. Blavey appeared to have the worst of it, not realizing that the best shot in the forest that day was a slight, female, colored domestic.

Blavey was the first to break the silence. "I will die with the satisfaction of knowing that you, Horton Newby, a nigger-lovin' abolitionist, will die a slow, painful death. I only wish I could spit on your grave." A coughing fit, which led to the expectoration of blood, briefly interrupted his speech. "Damned nigger wench! Jenny, whoever let you handle a rifle?"

"Tom Blabee, in de time you got left, you oughta be a prayin' hard for de salvashun ob yo' mizrabul soul!" Jenny retorted. "I thought I did you a kindness by aimin' fo' yo' chest but you de one dat need mo' time fo' repentin.'"

"Don't you talk to me about salvation, nigger! I know where I'm goin' and I'll be waitin' for you in the flames, Horton Newby!"

More coughing and expectoration of blood followed this last exclamation. Within five minutes, Thomas Blavey had breathed his last.

Wincing as he spoke, Horton smiled wryly and said, "Mr. Blavey hardly gave me a chance to respond to his greeting. I hope I can make good use of the additional time he has so kindly given me, since I would rather keep him waiting indefinitely and forestall any future meeting between the two of us."

"Massa Newby, what should we do wif dis trash?" Caesar asked as he tightened his grip on Gordon Fairclough, who whimpered as he begged, "Please Uncle Horton, tell them to let me go."

Gordon's plea for mercy was interrupted by a protest from Jenny directed at Caesar. "Caesar, how kin dis yere man be white trash? Don't he come fum a fine Kaintuck fambly? White trash be po' folk who wanna be like dere bettahs but nebbah can becuz dey's trash thru an' thru."

"Jenny, he ain't po' but he still white trash. Look at dat rascal careful-like, an' you'll see."

Jenny then proceeded to inspect Gordon Fairclough slowly from head to toe, insisting that he open his mouth wide and turn around slowly, not unlike a slave at auction, much to his discomfort.

"Please, Uncle Horton, make her stop. She is wounding my dignity as a Fairclough! What would people think, if they ever learned of the indignities to which I have been subjected by your niggers?"

One of his companions who was also being restrained, sniggered and said, "Well ain't that an interesting question now?"

"Oh no!" Gordon moaned. "Now these friends will extort all sorts of things from me to keep silent."

"Hush! I's 'bout to make mah judgment ober you. Caesar, you right as always. He's white trash thru an' thru, jes' as you say. He ain't no genelman an' dat mean he ain't no Faircloff eder. Dis yere white trash gotta be a basterd!"

This pronouncement was followed by uproarious laughter from the whole company. Horton, who was wincing in pain from all the laughing, finally responded to his nephew by saying, "Gordon, I have learned over many years that the truest, most honest judgments often come from the seemingly simple and unlettered among us. I would strongly urge you to hear and understand her words as if they came to you from one of the prophets of old. Now that you have received your diagnosis, may I suggest a heavy dose of humility as just the right prescription for your ailment?"

Horton then proceeded to explain that even if he died, Gordon would inherit nothing from him in the new will, which was already recorded in the Shelby County courthouse.

"For all your fine talk of respect for Southern property rights, you and your companions were prepared to murder me to subvert those rights. There has always been a right of manumission. To complete this act, which is my sacred right as a citizen of Kentucky, I must relocate my slaves to a free state and record their freedom there. Mr. Blavey did do me a favor by his choice of wound. For, I believe I shall survive long enough to fulfill that task. I suspect my companions, with good reason, might have violent plans for each of you.

"You have a choice, I can ignore your pleas for protection and let them promptly decide your fate, or if you will cooperate fully with my instructions, perhaps my sable friends will allow me to plead on your behalf. What will it be?"

In unison, Gordon and his two companions begged for Horton's intercession on their behalf. Horton then conferred with Caesar, Jenny, and some of the other leaders in the group.

After a few tense minutes of waiting on the part of Gordon and his compatriots, Horton spoke up and declared, "My negro friends have agreed to allow you to live as long as you follow our instructions explicitly. If you so much as deviate an inch from what is expected of you, you will perish. Do we have an understanding?"

"Yes!" they cried out in unison.

"Caesar, could you please bring me the inkwell, pen, and paper that are in my saddle bag? Thank you. Now each of you will sit down in the wagon and carefully write what I dictate. It will vary in style but not in substance to reflect the different perspectives of three observers."

Gordon and his companions were now given the opportunity to prepare a written and signed statement to the effect that they were accompanying Mr. Newby as witnesses to the transfer of his human property for manumission in the state of Ohio when Mr. Blavey, a disgruntled former employee of Mr. Newby's, was shot and killed after wounding Mr. Newby in an unprovoked attack. In the confusion, all three had discharged their weapons in the direction of the assailant but were uncertain as to whose bullet hit its mark. After pocketing their written attestations, Horton instructed them to lay Blavey's body on his horse for transport to Portland.

When Gordon began to whine and say, "Can't you make your niggers do that, Uncle?," Horton gave him a whithering look and replied, "Have you already forgotten our agreement? You must follow my directions explicitly or I cannot answer for the outcome. Also, I would appreciate it very much if you no longer referred to my negro friends as 'niggers.'"

Several black faces that were framing his uncle's head smiled grimly down at Gordon, who promptly rose from the wagon and asked his companions to help him pick up Blavey's body.

As they entered Portland, the local sheriff came out to greet the group. Gordon and his companions, as instructed, described the attack in the forest. Horton, who was weakened by pain and blood loss, confirmed the report provided by his nephew and companions and then explained his longheld desire to bring his slaves to Ohio for their manumission, which Gordon and the others reluctantly confirmed.

"Sheriff, I have to assume that my wound is fatal. However, I feel well enough at present to travel and my nephew has been kind enough to agree to accompany me on the remainder of my journey."

Perceiving the perplexity on the face of the sheriff, who had not seen that many negroes traveling with one master before, Horton added, "Sir, you needn't be concerned about my people. They are the most docile, peaceful negroes you will ever meet." Pointing out his nephew's companions to the sheriff, while at the same time giving each of them a meaningful look as he brushed his hand over the pocket in which he had deposited their attestations, Horton added, "Sheriff, these young gentlemen can stay behind to provide you with sworn affidavits and other details of the unfortunate incident should you need them to complete your investigation."

After quickly reviewing the manumission papers Horton had already prepared with Mr. Stone's help back in Shelbyville, the sheriff sighed and said, "Well, Mr. Newby, it appears that everything is in order. Please allow me to escort you to the dock. The next steamboat for Cincinnati should be leaving within the hour. I have sent for our local physician, who should arrive soon, to attend to your wound."

Doctor Adams acquired a grave expression as he examined his patient. Looking more closely at the wound in the upper abdomen that was to the left of center and just below the ribs, he asked, "Did you say it was a pistol shot?"

"Yes, I believe so; but it all happened very fast." Horton replied.

Gordon, who was watching the physician's examination with morbid fascination, volunteered, "Yes, Doctor. It was a small-caliber pistol. Tom . . . I mean Blavey, the assailant, prided himself on being a very good shot, even with a pistol."

In Doctor Adams's limited experience, a penetrating gunshot wound to the abdomen was a death sentence. But he was perplexed in this particular situation. His patient, who was now resting in a stateroom on board the steamboat, was clearly in considerable pain, but in the two hours since the injury he had not vomited, there was minimal to no external bleeding from the wound, and he had even imbibed some water that he had requested without any ill effect.

Horton interrupted his meditation by asking quite cheerfully, "Well, Doctor, what is your prognosis?"

Grimacing, as if he was the wounded man and not his physician, the doctor responded, "The depth to which the bullet has penetrated the abdominal wall is unclear, sir. Under most circumstances, such a wound would be fatal, but I must add that I am perplexed at how well you have tolerated the water, which you just drank. There is no external bleeding or drainage of any kind from the wound, which are favorable signs with regard to completing your travel to Ohio. Frankly, I can only recommend gentle daily cleansing of the wound and the use of laudanum, which I will provide, to address the pain. Hope that the bullet has not fully penetrated into the abdominal cavity but prepare for the worst, which may come in the next few days with the onset of delirium. Ultimately, your fate is in God's hands."

Horton smiled at the physician and replied, "Thank you, sir, for your forthright assessment and confirmation of my situation. I had come to much the same conclusion."

Shortly after the physician had left, Caesar came and reported on the progress of loading the Newby plantation's passengers and their cargo on to the deck of the steamboat. "Dey all on de boat now, Massa Newby."

"Do you have sufficient funds to pay for all of the fares and fees for the cargo?"

"Yes'm. Dat's all done paid for, Massa."

Looking at Gordon, the burly blacksmith asked, "What should I do wif 'im? I could thro 'im ober de side o' de boat tonite," he said with evident pleasure. The slight form of Horton's nephew was now trembling with fear.

"No, Caesar. I don't want to deprive Mr. Fairclough of the opportunity to witness the formal process of your becoming a free man. If you would be so kind as to inform the steward that the two of us will be dining in our cabin this evening, I would appreciate that very much. But, please do take the precaution of placing a guard outside the door until we reach Cincinnati in the morning. If you have the slightest reason for suspicion, do not hesitate to come in and check on us at any time. Thank you, my friend."

"I'll send Jenny in to inspect yo' wound a bit latuh, Massa."

"Oh, Caesar, I nearly forgot a very important thing. As soon as we dock in the morning in Cincinnati, could you please have this letter delivered directly to Mr. Levi Coffin? His address is on the envelope. He will help us with recording the manumissions at the Hamilton County courthouse and with the next phase of our transportation."

An evening alone with Gordon Fairclough, with his continual chatter and constant litany of complaints, was more than Horton could forbear, especially as the pain in his wound increased. After Jenny came to check on him, he decided his only recourse was to take a dose of laudanum to achieve some peace and quiet. He had resolved to endure the pain as much as possible to maintain a clear head, at least until his slaves were safely on free soil and properly manumitted. As the medication took effect, he drifted off into a fitful slumber troubled by multiple dreams, some of which were frightening in their vivid character. Jenny blessedly awakened him in the morning upon their arrival at Cincinnati from one particularly terrifying dream in which he was literally being physically dragged to the altar by the amorous Lucinda Avery, who had kidnapped him, but was talking so much that the minister was having great difficulty administering the marriage vows.

"Oh, is that you Jenny? Thank God! You have rescued me from a fate worse than death."

"Massa Newby, dats jes' de laudanum makin' some mitey pow'ful dreams. We in Sinsinnatee now. Why, Massa, you feels hot! You mus' hab a feber."

Horton groaned in pain as he tried to stand up. "The pain is definitely getting worse," he said with some anxiety. "If I move slowly, I think I can bear it without more of that damnable medication. Gordon and Jenny, please help me dress. We don't want to keep Mr. Coffin waiting."

A few minutes later, there was a knock at the door of their cabin and Horton, replied, "Please enter." A man of middle height with dark hair, wearing the plain dress of the Society of Friends entered. "Ah, Mr. Coffin, it is a great pleasure to see you again," Horton said, wincing involuntarily in pain, as he moved forward to shake Levi's hand.

"Mr. Newby, thou art wounded, sir, and I fear seriously!" Levi exclaimed with concern.

"Yes, unfortunately our band of pilgrims encountered a bit of unpleasantness before leaving Kentucky," Horton replied ruefully. "However, my people have arrived safe and sound, for which, I am deeply grateful to Providence. With your indulgence, shall we proceed as quickly as possible to the Hamilton County courthouse, so that I may complete the manumission of my people?"

Realizing that he had failed to introduce his nephew to Levi, Horton said, "Please forgive my lack of manners. Mr. Levi Coffin, this is my nephew, Mr. Gordon Fairclough of Shelby County Kentucky, who has been kind enough to accompany me to Cincinnati to witness this important occasion."

Not seeing the smirk form on Jenny's face when she heard the introduction, Levi gave Gordon's limp hand a hearty shake and enthusiastically said, "Why it is especially heartening to me when a young Southern gentleman comes to see the light and recognize the evils of slavery. Wouldst thou be interested in purchasing some stock in the Underground Railroad? It is proving to be a grand investment these days."

Gordon's only response was a dull look of incomprehension, which floated back and forth between his uncle and Levi.

Horton intervened by saying, "Levi, my nephew is a bit short on cash these days, which is a pity, for he has always been particularly interested in investments that might yield a great profit."

The dull expression on Gordon's face was quickly replaced with an excited look of anticipation.

"Mr. Coffin, I would be very much interested in hearing more from you about any profitable investment opportunities." Then addressing an aside to his uncle in a whisper, Gordon said, "Uncle would you be willing to loan some money to me for this investment? I will split the profits with you on an equal basis and, of course, pay back the original value of the loan."

Horton smiled and replied, "You couldn't make a better investment than the Railroad of which Mr. Coffin speaks; however, my finances are quite constrained now."

Gordon's flush of pecuniary excitement faded quickly and was replaced with the more durable dull expression so well suited to his physiognomy.

"In the interests of thy health, Mr. Newby, shall we then proceed directly to the Hamilton County courthouse without further delay?" Levi asked.

"What do you tink o' de Massa, now dat you free?" Jenny interrogated Pliny and Cassius after they had just received their free papers. Both former slave drivers were at a loss for words and focused their eyes on the floor in front of them.

Caesar, who by his choice was the last to receive his free papers, came up to them and giving both a sound slap on the back, said, "Bof' o' you niggers kin now find some decent kind o' work. No mo' whips!"

Horton, whose pain was increasing, summoned up his energy to address his former slaves in the foyer of the courthouse. "Friends, I hope with your permission that I can truly call you friends, you are now free persons of color standing on free soil, with papers in your hands, which are proof of that freedom. You are also free to make your own decisions. Mr. Coffin will assist you in receiving your share from the sale of the plantation that until now has been your home. For those of you who would like to go on to Canada with me, I can only restate that it would be an honor for me if you choose to join me in building up the community that already exists there. You will be given an education and every opportunity to enjoy the fruits of your labor. If some of you wish to remain in the United States, Mr. Coffin will assist you in finding the safest communities and the best opportunities that exist on this side of the Canadian border. From this time forth you have no masters except yourselves. Be far wiser masters than I have been."

After his brief speech, Horton collapsed in a nearby chair. Levi brought him some water and feeling his pulse at the wrist said, "It is quite rapid, it must be over one hundred beats a minute and thou art very warm. I fear thy fever is a sign that some putrefaction may be developing in the wound."

Jenny and Caesar approached Horton and announced that only ten of the sixty former slaves wanted to stay behind in the United States while the rest of the group had decided to go on to Canada with Horton. Of those remaining behind, most were hoping to find family members who had earlier escaped to the north from slavery. Levi Coffin had promised he would try to help them find their loved ones.

Caesar leaned down toward Horton and added, "Massa Newby, I wanna read an' write so you cain't die cuz you gotta learn me mah lettahs."

Horton smiled weakly up at Caesar and said, "Caesar, please call me Horton or Mister Newby from now on. I am no longer your master. My fervent hope is that I might be your friend and, God willing, it would be a joy to be your teacher."

Turning to Levi, Horton asked, "My friend, what would be the fastest means of transportation to Canada? They now have their free papers, so we should all be able to travel together on the 'Above-Ground' Railroad."

"The quickest route to follow would be by rail from Cincinnati to Sandusky where thou canst take a steamboat to Windsor. Thou shouldst be able to make the journey in about three days."

"Would you be so kind as to help Caesar make the arrangements? I feel I really must lie down; the pain is quite intense, and I am so fatigued."

Chapter Forty-Eight

Images of faces, intermingled with voices that seemed familiar and yet also strange, moved through his consciousness. Sometimes he felt an overwhelming sense of dread, but of what he could not say. Nevertheless, he could only cry out as the fear crept through every fiber of his being.

This is absurd, he thought. *Why should I be afraid?*

And yet, the same sense of dread would again creep over him, suffocating him with its embrace. At other times, he would all but forget the fear and a delicious warmth would engulf him. The warmth persisted and he remembered long-forgotten caresses received from his negro mammy as a young child and how safe he felt in her arms. A lovely voice began to sing. Oh, if only he could make out the words of the song! But what was this? Someone had interrupted the song.

Please don't stop singing. If you do, the terror, that terrible gnawing fear, will return! he cried in his thought.

Someone was speaking. He had heard that voice once before. Oh, where had he heard it? It was a young man's voice, but this time it was speaking with the authority usually reserved for age and experience.

"This may be quite painful, please steady his arms."

And so, Horton awoke from his delirium with a scream of pain as Isaac Burgess incised the abscess that had formed at the site of his gunshot wound.

"Ah, there is much pus coming from the wound. I am very hopeful this will help," Isaac said as he suddenly realized that his patient had opened his eyes and was staring in amazement at him. "Oh Mr. Newby, I hope thou canst remember me. I am Isaac Burgess, the medical student friend of your son Tib. We met a few months ago here in Canada."

"Here in Canada! Where am I?"

"Well, to be more precise, we are in Windsor, Canada West," said another familiar voice to his right.

"Father, we thought we had lost you!" Tib exclaimed after he could no longer repress his emotion. Looking to his left, Horton recognized his other son, Cicero, who was trying valiantly to hold back his tears. But his attention was quickly drawn to those maternal hands and lovely voice that had been caressing him out of his confusion.

"Oh, my darling, brave, and good man, you have returned to us!" Liddie said as her tears fell on his forehead and she leaned over and kissed him. At the foot of the bed were Eliza and Livia, both looking on with shining eyes.

Later that day, Tib explained to Horton how frustrated and desperate they had been after his arrival in Windsor two days earlier when, upon examining him, the local physician said there was nothing more to do but wait for death. That was when they had sent word to Isaac Burgess, who was working in Detroit that summer, to come. After Isaac had arrived in Windsor, even though he protested vociferously that he had not yet completed his training, Tib and the whole family had insisted that he follow his best judgment in the matter. At this point in the narrative, Isaac reentered the convalescent's room and realizing that he was the subject of the conversation, blushed. Although he was quite weak, Horton did not fail to notice and insisted on hearing Isaac's assessment of his condition.

"Mr. Newby, when I first examined thee, I became deeply concerned that there was progressive putrefaction with an accumulation of pus in thy wound, which must drain. It is possible that in a few more days, it might have found its way to the surface and drained spontaneously. However, the fact that it had been festering for so long made me fear that any further delay in its drainage might result in your death from persistent fever and delirium. Thou mayest still have episodes of confusion over the next day or so, depending on how much more pus remains undrained. I am also concerned that the bullet did not appear with the drainage. To be frank, sir, there is a real possibility that it might erode into a vital structure. . ."

"You mean I may still die of the wound," Horton finished the thought.

"Yes, unfortunately. However, there have been rare but extraordinary cases of gunshot wounds to the upper abdomen with survival for many years."

"Regardless of my ultimate fate, I want to thank you for your ministrations on my behalf. The pain now is much less intense than before I drifted off into delirium."

Within another two days, Horton was up and about, walking short distances in their lodging. By the end of a week, he had ventured outside and was regaining a hearty appetite. There were occasional twinges of intense pain that seemed to come randomly and were at times associated with mild nausea, but otherwise he felt well enough to return to Buxton, where his former slaves and students greeted him with joy. He was deeply moved when Tib insisted on lodging him in his home and was secretly delighted to be so close to Liddie. Cicero was gracious in accepting the new arrangement and gratified to see that his brother's coolness toward their father had vanished.

One fine autumn afternoon nearly a month later, while Horton was resting on the front porch of Tib's home after having taken a walk around the neighborhood, he was quite pleased to see Jenny coming up the road and waved to her. She seemed to be in high spirits as she approached the porch.

"Jenny, you can't hide the fact from me that something good has happened to you recently. Am I not correct?" Horton asked with some amusement.

Jenny paused and slowly responded in measured tones, "Yes—indeed—Mr.—Newby. I—am—very—pleased—to—tell—you—that—I—have—sur–passed—Cae-sar—in—my—studies."

After finishing her laborious but grammatically correct statement, she flashed a big grin at Horton. For some strange inexplicable reason, Horton was moved to tears, which he tried unsuccessfully to hide from the ever-observant Jenny. She quietly approached and trapped him before he could beat a hasty retreat into the safety of the house. Holding his arm, she gently said, "Mr. Newby, I never stopped prayin' for you. You'll make it to the bosom of Abraham yet. That ol' Blavey is gonna be mighty lonesome down there in the flame, if he's still waitin' for you."

Horton retired early that night to his small room after only eating a minimal portion of food. He did not admit to Liddie and the others that his sudden loss of appetite had been accompanied by a resurgence of the intermittent abdominal pain and nausea that continued to plague him at times. He felt a little better as he lay down upon his bed and reflected on the brief conversation that he had had with Jenny. His thoughts turned to Blavey and he involuntarily shuddered at the hate the man had expressed in his dying moments. As he pondered the fate of the unhappy overseer, he could only feel pity for him.

"Who were the most enslaved on my plantation? It certainly wasn't the negroes."

The answer in all its pristine clarity had come to him as if it had been spoken out loud. As his thoughts drifted in space and time, he found himself in a place he had often visited before. At first, he did not recognize it in the darkness, but the howling of the ceaseless wind, the sense of deep isolation without being alone, and the utter despair engendered by the atmosphere, identified it as the second circle of hell. Yes, he knew it well, for long had it been the home that haunted his dreams. But there was something very different about this visit, his sense of utter isolation had gradually lifted.

He sensed a presence. A hand reached out of the darkness and, grasping his, began to pull him toward a very faint but distant light. The roar of the wind had ceased, and he was now surrounded by silence, but a silence so full that it was palpable. It was as if he was being borne on an ocean of silence toward a light that was growing brighter by the second. As his vision acclimated to the growing light, he looked around him and was surprised to see that he was moving at an ever-increasing speed upward and parallel to a vast mountain that was directed toward the same faint light he had first seen upon entering the silence. It seemed to him that there was movement on the mountain, a ponderous, methodical movement in concentric circles, directed slowly upward toward that same light. Had he seen this image before? It seemed vaguely familiar and then it struck him: of course, he was no longer in hell. By some miracle, a guide had been sent to show him, like the poet Dante, the vision of repentance, healing, and could it be possible, even paradise?

The light was becoming brighter now. When he looked down, he was frightened by the height to which he had attained, and a strengthening of the grip exerted by the hand of the unseen guide signaled to him that he should look only upward. The fate of Lot's wife no longer seemed a mere fable to him there. Swifter and swifter, he rose, being pulled through and supported by the silence. The light became more intense as he approached the summit of the mountain and he realized without understanding why, that the silence and the light were of the same substance. It was only *thicker* near the summit of the mountain. There was a paradox unfolding within the silence as well. With its increasing thickness and brightness, something beyond sound became audible to him. It was as if he felt sounds in the silence. His ears were superfluous in that place, for out of the silence ineffably beautiful music filled his entire being. He no longer needed to cry out, "Hallelujah!," he had *become* hallelujah.

His attention was drawn from the sound that he felt to a presence that spoke without words and yet the message gained greater clarity for it was no longer fettered to speech. Like the music that was felt rather than heard, a sympathy extended from the presence, which transcended all barriers. Surrendering to it, he gazed into the brightness, the almost unbearable brightness, and in beholding it, felt a beauty that at the same moment embraced every pain and every joy. It seemed to him that the glory was too much for him to bear and for a moment his vision seemed blurred with emotion. But, out of the glory emerged a figure beckoning to him. It was the figure of a beautiful woman, a shining and resplendent black woman, not the Florentine Beatrice of Dante but his own African Beatrice! Reaching forth her hand she touched his wound while wordlessly saying to his deepest self, "You are healed, dear one."

Awakened by an intense wave of pain and nausea, Horton was barely able to find the chamber pot in time to collect a large forceful emesis. To his surprise, the clink of a bullet in the chamber pot punctuated the painful episode.

To his great relief, the pain and nausea did not return. He felt awe and even some fear as he contemplated the vision of the previous night. With some trepidation, he shared his story with Tib and showed him the bullet. Tib listened quietly without comment until Horton finished giving the account of his dream and the extraordinary event awakening him from it.

"Father, what do you make of it? That was quite a powerful experience; certainly, no ordinary dream. And then to be linked so closely to vomiting the bullet; it is truly remarkable."

"The most extraordinary aspect of it for me was to receive healing from the black Beatrice."

"You mean from mother, don't you?"

"Of course. But I can't begin to express in words how beautiful she was in the vision. The beauty that for a brief moment was revealed to me was her *entire* beauty, a luminous beauty of both body and soul."

Placing his hand on his father's shoulder, Tib said, "Why did you tell me about this first and not tell mother?"

Horton hesitated and then replied, "I guess, I wanted to receive your permission to tell her, son."

Tib looked Horton squarely in the face, smiled, and said, "There was always an ember of love for you hidden deep within my being, father. It has sputtered and grown at times over the past few years but has always in the end waxed stronger. The risks you willingly accepted and the suffering you have endured on behalf of *your people* have truly made them your people. I am deeply honored to be your son and I would be thrilled if you legitimized my status by marrying my mother."

Later that day, Horton with a shyness, uncharacteristic of the once self-assured master of many lives, approached Liddie and asked for the honor of her company for a stroll to view the autumn colors. As he cautiously unfolded for her the details of his dream and ended by reporting the extraordinary manner in which he had been relieved of his pain and nausea, she listened with growing interest while clasping his arm more tightly. Finally, he looked down into her eyes and confessed that he had asked for Tib's blessing and permission before approaching her.

"Oh Liddie, you have always been my Beatrice! Can you ever forgive me for all the sorrow and pain I have caused you and our children?"

"Oh, my dear one, you should know by now that it is a particular weakness, or perhaps it is a strength, in those of African descent that we are so prone to forgive easily and freely. I forgave you long ago and have never stopped loving you. But I am so glad that you have won back the trust and love of our children, for I know that Livia shares Tib's renewed feelings for you as well."

To their great joy and that of the entire community, one week later, the Reverend William King declared Horton and Liddie Newby to be united in the state of holy matrimony before both God and man, with these words, "What God has joined together let no man put asunder!"

Rays of sunlight breaking through the clouds highlighted the delicate, silky green of new leaves emerging from the long dormancy of winter. Bees were buzzing around the large lilac bushes that had begun to fill the air with their intoxicating scent. These images and sensations beckoned to Isaac as his eyes strayed from the sterile whitewashed interior to the vision of paradise framed by the large window near him in the meetinghouse. A disquieting aura permeated the ususally peaceful atmosphere that attended most silent meetings at the Friends' Meetinghouse in Newport, Indiana on April 21, 1861. He looked toward the Elders' bench and could see his former school teacher, Mrs. Way, who had been such a rock of stability for the community, fidgeting uncomfortably in her seat. When their eyes met briefly, he could sense her inner distress. It was as if she could do nothing to prevent the ripples and waves caused by terrible external events, so foreign to the Quaker way of life, from disturbing the calm and tranquility of her community.

As he contemplated her evident distress, he looked at her husband, Dr. Henry Way, who, from the relaxed expression on his face, seemed to retain the calm which at that moment his wife so desperately craved. To be sure, the good doctor felt no need to make sense of the chaos exploding in the world outside the confines of the Quaker meeting. That, however, was the responsibility, or so it seemed, of the ministers of the front bench in the meeting, including Hannah Way.

As the uneasy silence continued, his mind wandered beyond the four walls and this particular spring day. So much had happened both in his own life and in the life of his country in the past several months that he felt as if he were caught in a perpetual whirlwind. Mostly pleasant memories of his time as a medical student in Ann Arbor were mixed with increasingly strident elements. Certainly he could see the discord coming even as he helped teach anatomy to the other students in the fall of 1859. After John Brown's failed attempt to initiate a slave uprising at Harper's Ferry, followed by his trial and execution, there seemed to be no more middle ground where one could meet and engage in civilized discourse. He looked at his Uncle Levi Coffin, who was visiting from Cincinnati that First Day, and remembered sadly how his uncle had so confidently made a case for gentle persuasion based upon reason and charity for the emancipation of slaves. After all, if John Woolman in an earlier generation could persuade his brethren in the Society of Friends, who were no less vulnerable to the selfish rationalizations justifying slavery, to free their slaves, could not the same peaceful transformation occur on a much larger scale?

And yet, he remembered with pain, the verbal and sometimes even physical altercations that occurred not infrequently among the students in Ann Arbor over the slavery issue. It was as if the olive branch had snapped. Where attempts at reasonable persuasion failed, the political process, with its divisive character, had accelerated, polarizing the country. People in the Northern states who may have had limited or no interest in the question of abolition even a few months earlier rallied to the free-soil politics of the Republican party to thwart the Southern "slavocracy." Southerners, assuming that John Brown's radical vision was a commonly held view in the North, demanded even more protections of their *rights.*

Isaac marveled that the election of a moderate like Lincoln, who certainly had no credentials as an abolitionist, could lead to secession in the Deep South. And now only a week earlier, the Southern Confederacy had attacked the federal fortress in Charleston Harbor. President Lincoln had promptly called for seventy-five thousand three-month volunteers to put down the rebellion and restore the union. He knew, as did all these gentle, peace-loving Friends sitting with him, fidgeting in silence, that this rebellion was ultimately about slavery. This was the dilemma tearing at the heart of Hannah Way and so many other gentle souls. Could those for whom slavery had been an abomination ignore the conflict, especially when the fate of nearly four million slaves was at stake?

As Isaac pondered the dilemma facing the Society of Friends, other memories competed for his attention in the silence. He was still gratified by the opportunity to join Dr. Gunn in his general practice in Detroit after his graduation from medical school the previous April. He had reveled in the additional clinical experience gained in his practice with his former professor, but did not hesitate when he received a telegram in December informing him that his old mentor and friend, Dr. Way, had been injured in a fall from a horse. Could he come and take his practice for several months while he recuperated? Dr. Gunn had been very kind and understanding, telling Isaac to take good care of his mentor, but to please contact him as soon as possible, when he might be able return to Detroit and rejoin the practice. It had been a unique pleasure for Isaac to have the opportunity to at least partially repay Dr. Way for his many kindnesses and patient teaching over the years. His old mentor was now fully recovered and had been urging Isaac to contact Dr. Gunn. But now, after the attack on Fort Sumter, how could he return to his own private ambitions?

His thoughts then drifted to his sister, Rebecca, who, having received her bachelor's degree from Oberlin the previous summer, was now teaching at Mrs. Haviland's

Raisin Institute in Adrian, Michigan. He rejoiced at her single-minded commitment to help those in need, both colored and white. Her beauty, poise, and calm radiated a stability that was in short supply in the current situation. He wondered how she would respond to the crisis.

As an older woman rose to break the silence, he was drawn back from his reverie into the meeting. Although she was bent forward and unable to stand fully upright, the infirmity did not inhibit her speech. Extending her neck to the fullest extent possible, she rotated her diminutive form, nearly completing a circle as she quoted the Scripture: "Render to Caesar the things that are Caesar's, and to God the things that are God's."

She said no more, but slowly repeated the rotary movement of her crippled body in the reverse direction as she smiled innocently at the faithful gathered in the meetinghouse. Isaac's gaze instinctively was drawn back to Hannah and he thought he perceived a brief look of painful resignation form on her face which was obscured as she drew her hands to her head, ostensibly to rearrange her bonnet. Once she had completed this maneuver, her face resumed its characteristic placid expression.

The elderly woman had chosen her Scripture quote with care, for it struck a raw nerve in the hearts of those who were present. The silent meeting was no longer silent that day. First one and then others, most often young men, rose and responded to that troublesome passage of Scripture.

"Dear Friends, I apologize for my youth and inexperience, for I am only nineteen years old," one young man began. "My earliest memories are of fugitives from slavery being provided food, shelter, and assistance in their journey to freedom by members of this community. Many have risked fines and imprisonment under the Fugitive Slave Act of 1850 in their conscientious efforts to end this evil institution. Faithful, God-fearing Christians have been willing to risk offending 'Caesar' to follow the higher law of love for one's neighbor.

"But the Lord clearly says in the passage that our sister has quoted that we are to also 'render to Caesar the things that are Caesars.' We all know that this war has come because of the evil of slavery. Indeed, it may be a judgment of God imposed on this nation for this terrible sin. Are we to stand by, refusing to answer President Lincoln's call for volunteers, when we know that if the Southern states are permitted to leave the union, this evil will persist? Whereas, if our nation's arms prevail in the struggle, it will mark the demise of this evil that we have devoted our lives to end? It is not my desire to harm or kill anyone, but I am not certain that in good conscience I can stand by and allow my fellow countrymen to offer up their lives in obedience to both Caesar and God without being willing to offer up mine as well."

Levi Coffin rose to speak, and Isaac could not help but notice the look of gratitude on Hannah's face as she saw him rise.

"Dear Friends, it has been too long since Catherine and I have last visited this dear community, which holds such a large place in our hearts. I felt impelled to rise and respond to our young brother who has spoken so eloquently regarding the dilemma that has been presented to conscientious members of the Society of Friends by the advent of war.

"We cannot, we must not, stand aside from the present conflict. I agree with every fiber of my being that this war is about slavery. None of us would have prayed for the plague of war to come, but now it is upon us. This saying of the Lord challenges us. How are we to respond? To faithfully 'render unto Caesar the things that are Caesars,' must we take up arms in this conflict? There are better ways to resist the common enemy of Caesar and God than to wear a military uniform and bear arms. Have we not already been fighting this war for many years, but in our own peaceful way?"

Another young man rose and interrupted Levi, saying with some emotion, "But sir, the peaceful resistance of Friends and other abolitionists has brought on the conflict. The war that now confronts us is the inexorable and horrible outcome of Southern intransigence in the face of every effort to persuade through gentler means."

Becoming quite agitated, Levi responded, "But, are we to overthrow our peace testimony, which is so central to our identity as Friends, because of Southern intransigence? Surely we can redouble our efforts in aiding the escape of slaves to the North in the chaos that will ensue. This will indirectly but effectively undermine the Southern war effort, since they will depend even more heavily on slave labor. I can only foresee increasing misery to be addressed, as there will likely be many refugees from the conflict that will need succor and aid. Must we resort to arms?"

Another voice contributed to the growing tension by quickly adding, "So are we then to enshroud our cowardice in a veil of piety, allowing others to take all the risks and bear all the losses?"

In exasperation, Levi turned to his nephew, and said, "Isaac Burgess, thou art a learned man, trained in the healing art, what response canst thou give to our brothers in their honest distress over this dilemma?"

Not expecting to be pulled into the debate, Isaac groaned inwardly as he blushed outwardly. Rising to his feet, he tried to make peace in his own way.

"Dear Friends, I am not certain that I can provide any additional light to guide our paths through this extremely challenging dilemma that threatens to divide us. I would first say that I have heard nothing in the discussion with which I would disagree. Herein lies our dilemma as I see it. Conscientious members of the Society have been forced by events that are beyond our control to weigh the call of duty to country against our duty to God. My uncle and I are in full agreement that we would never want to be placed in a position to shed another man's blood, but I also agree with our Friend who feels that he cannot stand aside and allow others to suffer and die in a conflict that will determine the fate of this great evil we have fought against for so long. Far be it from me to judge any of you who choose to wear the uniform of thy country and bear arms. I am in a somewhat unique position as a physician with the potential to care for the wounded in a noncombatant role."

"Art thou implying that thou wouldst serve as a medical officer in the army?" Levi interrupted in an anxious tone. "Medical officers may still have to bear arms to protect their wounded patients."

Isaac paused to clear his throat and then replied to his uncle in a calm voice, "Yes. Uncle Levi, thou art correct. Medical officers in rare circumstances may be required to bear arms. I gave that possibility serious and careful deliberation before I wrote to the governor asking for a commission as an assistant surgeon."

Chapter One

The small village of Newport was located in the midst of a large settlement of Quakers about ten miles north of Richmond, Indiana that was the seat for Wayne County. There were many communities of former slaves and their descendents in the area coming primarily from North Carolina who were settled in the free territory of Indiana by their former owners. The other major portion of the population that had come to settle this part of Indiana was made up of white settlers from the Southern states who often exhibited pro-slavery sympathies. Thus, there was a potent mix of pro-slavery and abolitionist sentiments spread throughout the same county and sometimes even in the same town. For this reason, it was of critical importance for active conductors on the Underground Railroad to exercise due caution in speaking about their activities in support of fugitives. In the second half of the nineteenth century, Newport, Indiana was renamed Fountain City in recognition of the many natural springs present in the area.

The Quaker meeting house in Newport, Indiana in 1847 was like so many other meeting houses of the Society of Friends, notable only in its utter simplicity and plainness. For other than the two neatly arranged parallel rows of benches that separately accommodated male and female worshippers and the facing benches at the front where the elders and ministers sat, large windows placed on each side of the rectangular building were the only décor that broke the monotonous simplicity of the white-washed interior. Perhaps it may be more accurate to say that the Friends who attended meetings were the real decoration of a Quaker meetinghouse. In their plain appearance—the typically gray or black dresses, simple black bonnets, and lack of cosmetic adornment or jewelry of Quaker women and girls, as well as the equally somber garb of Quaker men and boys with their broad-brimmed hats—one might question how much the interior décor was enhanced by the human presence. And yet, it was precisely this fellowship of the devout that breathed life into a Quaker meeting, transforming it, even if for only a brief period of time, into a vital organism. The silence of the worshipers in a Quaker meeting was its life's blood. For it was from the silence that the spiritual creature born of the meeting acquired its vitality. The practice of removing one's bonnet (for women) or hat (for men) prior to rising to speak during a silent meeting is described in the history of Cane Creek Monthly Meeting (Bobbie T. Teague, *Cane Creek: Mother of Meetings*, 84 [Snow Camp, NC: Cane Creek Monthly Meeting of Friends, 1995]).

There was an earnest, even *fierce* peacefulness about Quakers, perhaps especially in this frontier region of America. Friends believed fervently in the great value and dignity of each person and urged their fellow countrymen to recognize the inherent equality of all before God, even those who were enslaved. A few generations earlier, with the leadership of such men as John Woolman, the Society of Friends was the only religious denomination in the American colonies to renounce slavery and emancipate their slaves. Although all Friends eschewed slavery, they were not all in agreement as to the proper means to oppose it. There was a hope that current slaveholders might through peaceful persuasion be moved as the earlier Quakers had been to voluntarily free their bondsmen. But when those bondsmen fled slavery to the Northern states the conflicts in the Quaker mind regarding the proper means of opposition to evil became manifest. For some it was not enough to passively stand aside and wish the fugitive well. Rather some felt impelled to offer support and comfort to the hunted as they pursued freedom, even if this might mean opposition to the laws of the land. The more cautious among Friends were also concerned about the temptations to dishonesty inherent in the harboring of fugitives, for honesty in all encounters was a virtue highly prized among Quakers from the earliest foundations of the Society.

This dilemma also centered on another distinctive testimony of Friends and that was regarding peace. The Quakers had very early renounced violence as a means of resolving differences among persons and nations. It seemed to many Friends that more direct involvement in activities targeting the abolition of slavery could only end in some form of violence. Other Quakers could only respond that love for their fellow man would not allow them to turn away any person in need. This fierce peacefulness led to a separation in the Indiana Yearly Meeting of Friends into two groups in 1843: the larger Indiana Yearly Meeting and the smaller Anti-Slavery Yearly Meeting of Friends.

For an excellent introduction and overview of the history, faith, and practice of the Society of Friends in America see Thomas D. Hamm, *The Quakers in America* (New York: Columbia University Press, 2003).

A fine resource for those who would like to explore Quaker spirituality in greater depth is *Quaker Spirituality: Selected Writings*, edited by Douglas Van Steere (Ramsey, NJ: Paulist, 1984).

Chapter Two

For more information on the Levi Coffin House see:

http://www.indianamuseum.org/levi-coffin-state-historic-site.

Levi Coffin, *Reminiscences of Levi Coffin, The Reputed President of the Underground Railroad* (Cincinnati: Robert Clarke, 1880) (see 108, 118, 119, and 192 for a description of his approach to fugitive slaves and slave catchers).

Antislavery medallion created by Josiah Wedgwood in 1787. For more information about the medallion, see http://www.britishmuseum.org/explore/highlights/highlight_objects/pe_mla/a/anti-slavery_medallion,_by_jos.aspx.

Chapter Five

The Reverend John Rankin was one of the best-known conductors on the Underground Railroad in Ohio. He left a lamp lit in the front window of his home on a bluff overlooking the town of Ripley, Ohio on the northern side of the Ohio River to light the way for freedom seekers. In his letters to his brother Thomas, a slaveowner in Virginia, he presented some of the early vigorous arguments against slavery (see http://medicolegal.tripod.com/rankin1823.htm).

Chapter Eight

Levi Coffin was proud of his innovation of a built-in wardrobe or early closet in his home in Newport (now Fountain City), Indiana. His home can now be toured without obtaining a writ from a judge; please see http://www.indianamuseum.org/levi-coffin-state-historic-site for more details.

See Coffin, *Reminiscences of Levi Coffin*, 363 for an example of a letter written in Cincinnati for slaves hidden there but then posted from Canada to fool their master.

Chapter Ten

Curse of Canaan: The patriarch Noah cursed the children of Ham who exposed his nakedness in Genesis 9:25–27 (KJV): ". . .Cursed be Canaan; a servant of servants shall he be unto his brethren. . .Blessed be the Lord God of Shem; and Canaan shall be his servant. God shall enlarge Japheth, and he shall dwell in the tents of Shem, and Canaan shall be his servant." "Canaan" became synonymous with people of African ancestry in the minds of Southern theologians who used this passage of Scripture as a basis for enslavement of Africans.

"Love one another as I have loved you" (John 13:34).

For reference to Rahab, please see Joshua 2:1–10 and Hebrews 11:31.

Part Two

Josiah Wedgwood antislavery medallion—see notes for chapter two.

Chapters Thirteen & Fourteen

For excellent discussions of the Fugitive Slave Act of 1850 and how it was applied in the state of Indiana see the following:

Charles H. Money, "The Fugitive Slave Law of 1850 in Indiana," *Indiana Magazine of History* 17.2 (1921) 159–98.

Charles H. Money, "The Fugitive Slave Law of 1850 in Indiana (Concluded)," *Indiana Magazine of History* 17.3 (1921) 257–97.

Emma Lou Thornbrough, "Indiana and Fugitive Slave Legislation," *Indiana Magazine of History* 50.3 (1954) 201–28.

Chapter Fifteen

See Coffin, *Reminiscences of Levi Coffin*, 267 for quote at beginning of this chapter.

For "commission merchant and dealer in free-labor cotton goods and groceries" see Coffin, *Reminiscences of Levi Coffin*, 280.

For the source of Levi Coffin's arguments for free-labor cotton and merchandise see Coffin, *Reminiscences of Levi Coffin*, 279 and 281.

"Although I have always been opposed to slavery, it is no part of my business, in the South, to interfere with southern laws or its slaves" (Coffin, *Reminiscences of Levi Coffin*, 279).

For reference to assisting with relocation of mulatto children and slave mistresses of white masters in Ohio, see Coffin, *Reminiscences of Levi Coffin*, 282.

Chapter Sixteen

For more information about the National Road, see http://thisisindiana.angelfire.com/nationalroadi40washington.htm.

For a detailed description of the case of a slave who had been captured by slave catchers and was being transported through Indianapolis back to slavery, which inspired the description of events in this chapter, please see Money, "Fugitive Slave Law of 1850 (Concluded)," 257–97. In the real account, a posse of forty men, paid for at the expense of the US government, were necessary to transport the captured slave by train from Indianapolis on his journey back to slavery.

Chapter Eighteen

For a discussion of Nat Turner and the fears of white slave owners regarding slave rebellions see Kenneth Milton Stampp, *The Peculiar Institution: Slavery in the Antebellum South*, 132–40(New York: Vintage, 1956).

For a discussion of the process and challenges of obtaining the obedience of slaves see Stampp, *Peculiar Institution*, 145–48.

The insoluble paradox of attempting to treat slaves as persons as well as property is stated most powerfully in Frederick Law Olmsted, *The Cotton Kingdom: A Traveller's Observations on Cotton and Slavery in the American Slave States* (The Modern Library. New York: Random House, 1984): "It is difficult to handle simply as property, a creature possessing human passions and human feelings, however debased and torpid the condition of that creature may be; while on the other hand, the absolute necessity of dealing with property as a thing, greatly embarrassed a man in any attempt to treat it as a person" (444).

For the quote from Thomas Jefferson, see Library of Congress. "Letter from Thomas Jefferson to John Holmes." http://www.loc.gov/exhibits/jefferson/159.html.

Regarding the divisions of Christian denominations into Northern and Southern branches over slavery, please see Albert J. Raboteau, *Slave Religion: The "Invisible Institution" in the Antebellum South*, 160–62. (New York: Oxford University Press, 1978).

For a detailed discussion of the innovation and use of the "buckskin cracker" in the punishment and intimidation of slaves, see K. M. Stampp's quotes from Joseph Holt Ingraham, *South-West by a Yankee in Two Volumes*, 2:287–88 (New York: Harper and Brothers, 1835), and Demijohn, "Practical Hints," *Southern Cultivator* 7 (Sep 1849) 135.

Regarding conversion to Christianity making better slaves, see Raboteau, *Slave Religion*, 103–4.

Chapter Nineteen

For a good overview of slave worship, see chapter 5: "Religious Life in the Slave Community" of Raboteau, *Slave Religion*.

"I believe that these poor ignorant and degraded sons and daughters of Africa, who are not able to read the precious words of the Savior, are blessed with a clearer, plainer manifestation of the Holy Spirit than many of us who have had better opportunities of cultivation." The preceding quote was adapted from Coffin, *Reminiscences of Levi Coffin*, 250.

Chapter Twenty

Matthew Garrison was an actual slave trader of the period in Louisville, and the corner of Main and Second Streets was the location of his slave pen. See http://explorekyhistory.ky.gov/items/show/276?tour=9&index=38#.U4dsTsa53wI and http://www.waymarking.com/waymarks/WM8E00_Slave_Trading_in_Louisville_Garrison_Slave_Pen_Site.

For the inspiration for the events described in this chapter, see Coffin, *Reminiscences of Levi Coffin*, 214–15, and 213–14 for the sale price of a captured runaway.

Chapter Twenty-One

George Noel is identified with Nathan Bedford Forrest as one of several prominent slave traders in antebellum Memphis in Saul S. Friedman, *Jews and the American Slave Trade*, 196 (New Brunswick, NJ: Transaction, 1998).

Chapter Twenty-Two

Nathan Bedford Forrest, who later acquired lasting notoriety as a Confederate general during the Civil War, was a successful businessman in Memphis prior to the war, eventually making a large fortune from trading in livestock and slaves.

Chapter Twenty-Three

Drs. Merrill and Cartwright were historical figures. Professor Cartwright published his theories of negro inferiority in the medical literature of the day. For more information about the attitudes of the Southern medical profession toward slaves and their medical care, please see: John S. Haller Jr., "The Negro and the Southern Physician: A Study of Medical and Racial Attitudes 1800–1860," *Medical History* 16.3 (1972) 238–53; Fredric Law Olmstead, *A Journey in the Back Country* (New York: Mason Brothers, 1861), 64; Ariela Gross, "Pandora's Box: Slave Character on Trial in the Antebellum Deep South," *Yale Journal of Law & the Humanities*, 7.2 (1995) 267–316; Samuel A. Cartwright, "Report on the Diseases and Peculiarities of the Negro Race," *The New Orleans Medical and Surgical Journal*, (May 1851) 691–715 (quoted extensively in this chapter), and A. A. Rene et al., "Mortality in the Slave and White Populations of Natchitoches Parish Louisiana 1850," *Journal of the National Medical Association* 84 (1992) 805–11.

[EPI]We are not ourselves when nature, being oppressed, commands the mind to suffer with the body.

—William Shakespeare; King Lear in Act 2, Scene 4[/EPI]

Chapter Twenty-Four

For more information on antebellum slave hospitals see Stephen C. Kenney, "A Dictate of Both Interest and Mercy?: Slave Hospitals in the Antebellum South," *Journal of the History of Medicine* 65 (2010) 1–47. Professor A. P. Merrill's interest in the subject of slave health is reflected in his publication, "Plantation Hygiene" (*Southern Agriculturist* [1853] 1). Please note that a common venue for publication of ideas and advice regarding the health of slaves was in the antebellum agricultural literature of the South.

Also, for a discussion of the use of blacks for medical experimentation and anatomic dissection, please see Todd L. Savitt, "The Use of Blacks for Medical Experimentation and Demonstration in the Old South," *The Journal of Southern History* 48.3 (1982) 331–48.

The most famous instance of a female patient singing hymns to cope with intense pain during an abdominal operation was the first successful removal of an ovarian tumor by Ephraim McDowell in 1809. For more information, please see Leora Horn and David H. Johnson, "Ephraim McDowell, the First Ovariotomy, and the Birth of Abdominal Surgery," *Journal of Clinical Oncology* 28.7 (2010) 1262–68.

Chapter Twenty-Five

"The Father of Waters" = The Mississippi River

For examples of manumission documents, see http://www.teachingushistory.org/documents/JehuJone.htm and http://finding-aids.lib.unc.edu/01294/#d1e56.

Chapter Twenty-Six

". . .jump'd ober de broom." Since slave marriages were not legally binding and could be dissolved at the whim of the slaves' master, they were often solemnized with no more than a simple ritual of the couple jumping over a broom. For a description of the broom ritual and slave marriage in general, see Raboteau, *Slave Religion*, 228–30.

For a description of ". . .dancin' all ober. . ." see Stampp, *Peculiar Institution*, 366.

Chapter Twenty-Seven

For a discussion of the common problem of miscegenation or amalgamation, largely through abuse of slave women by white men on Southern antebellum plantations, see Stampp, *Peculiar Institution*, 350–61. A particularly bitter lament by the white mistress of a plantation regarding the hypocrisy associated with the practice is quoted on 356: "Like the patriarchs of old, our men live all in one house with their wives and their concubines; and the mulattoes one sees in every family partly resemble the white children. Any lady is ready to tell you who is the father of all the mulatto children in everybody's household but her own. These, she seems to think, drop from the clouds. My disgust sometimes is boiling over."

For a discussion of the different branches of Presbyterianism in antebellum America please see Sydney E. Ahlstrom, *A Religious History of the American People,* 1:551–70. 2 vols (Garden City, NY: Image, 1975).

Chapter Twenty-Nine

For a detailed discussion of revivalism and the attitudes of the various Protestant denominations to the camp meeting phenomenon on the western frontier in early nineteenth century America see Ahlstrom, *A Religious History of the American People,* 1:521–50. 2 vols (Garden City, NY: Image, 1975).

Chapter Thirty

The second circle of hell is a reference to the great medieval Italian poet Dante Alighieri's *Divine Comedy* and his description of hell in the *Inferno.* Those damned, who were condemned for the sin of lust, were consigned to the second circle to be buffeted about by its continuous howling winds.

'*Absens haeres non erit!* See http://wordinfo.info/unit/3055/page:4/s:abest.

Chapter Thirty-One

'Be still and know dat I'm God,' is a quote from Psalm 46:10.

Chapter Thirty-Two

Thy people will be my people. Whither thou goest, I will go. Paraphrase from the Old Testament story of Ruth (Ruth 1:16).

"Am I not a man and a brother?" Please see the note in reference to the Wedgwood antislavery medallion from chapter 2.

Chapter Thirty-Three

For a history of George DeBaptiste's and other Detroit citizens' activities on the Underground Railroad providing a basis for the events related in this chapter, see Carol E. Mull, *The Underground Railroad in Michigan,* 78 (Jefferson, NC: McFarland & Co., 2010).

Chapter Thirty-Four

For additional background information regarding the formation and structure of the Underground Railroad in Michigan see Mull, *Underground Railroad in Michigan*, 56–68.

For more history regarding the Second Baptist Church on Fort Street, Detroit, see Mull, *Underground Railroad in Michigan*, 89.

For a fuller discussion of the designation of Detroit as *Midnight,* the last stop of the Underground Railroad in the US, and *Dawn* as a community of free blacks in Canada West starting with page x, see Jacqueline L. Tobin and Hettie Jones, *From Midnight to Dawn: The Last Tracks of the Underground Railroad* (New York: Doubleday, 2007).

Like William Lambert and George DeBaptiste, the hotel owner Seymour Finney played a prominent role in Detroit's Underground Railroad, often entertaining slave-catchers in his hotel while hiding fugitive slaves in his nearby barn prior to transporting them across the Detroit River to freedom in Canada (see Mull, *Underground Railroad in Michigan*, 88, 90, and 91).

Chapter Thirty-Six

With the passage of the Fugitive Slave Act of 1850, what had been a steady migration of freedom seekers from the slave states to Canada over the nearly twenty years since the abolition of slavery within the Queen's dominions became a flood. Not only were slaves seeking the safety provided by Canada's borders, but also many free persons of color sought refuge in Canada from the increasing danger of being kidnapped into slavery that had been facilitated by the legislation. Also, other currents were influencing the emigration of slaves and freemen from the United States. Many black leaders in the abolitionist movement were chafing at the slow pace of change, especially regarding the persistent lack of basic rights of citizenship that were rarely afforded free persons of color. Even in New England, for example, where freemen had enjoyed greater respect and male suffrage, prejudicial efforts by Martin Van Buren and his political allies led to restrictions on black male suffrage in New York as early as 1821, which limited access to the ballot box only to freemen who held property worth at least $250, while similar restrictions did not apply to white men but instead were reduced.

With the advent of so many refugees, Canada West became a vast experiment in which conflicting visions of the nature of humanity clashed. Some leaders in the black community, whose families had been free for several generations, often held radically different views from those leaders with a fresh memory of their own enslavement of how best to assist the destitute fugitive, newly arrived from slavery in the South. The more vitriolic of these debates centered on the question of "begging" or asking for assistance and monies through charitable organizations versus advocating an ideal of total self-reliance on the part of the newly freed. Henry Bibb, a self-educated refugee from slavery, in his newspaper, *Voice of the Fugitive*, advocated strongly for aid to the newly arrived refugees, while Mary Ann Shadd, from a family that had been free for several generations, in her newspaper, *Provincial Freeman*, emphasized the need for self-reliance and attacked Henry Bibb for seeking aid from outside donors. Shadd's anger and frustration were also inflamed by the fact that aid organizations were providing land exclusively to former slaves and not to newly arrived free persons of color from the United States. Even the names of their newspapers reflected the cultural divide within the black community that had immigrated to Canada. Another aspect of the debate centered on the nature of the education that should be offered to the refugees. Most of the projects that were supported by charitable organizations, including that of Josiah Henson in the Dawn settlement and Henry Bibb's efforts in collaboration with the Michigan abolitionist Laura Haviland near Windsor, emphasized the development of basic literacy and acquisition of manual skills in a trade. Some leaders were concerned that such an approach, if applied exclusively, would destine former slaves to become tradesmen and farmers only, while limiting their potential access to the learned professions.

William King had planted himself firmly in the middle of the debates over education and self-reliance among former slaves. He had found his way through a circuitous path that included teaching in the South, marriage to the daughter of a plantation owner, and ultimately ownership of fifteen slaves. Educated at the University of Glasgow, at the time of Sir Thomas Buxton's passage of the legislation abolishing slavery in 1833 he emigrated with his family from Ireland. Although the rest of his family settled in Ohio, he migrated south, looking for work as a teacher, eventually settling in Louisiana. Despite a strong personal repugnance for slavery, he found himself acquiring some slaves as part of his wife's dowry. No longer able to ignore his vocation to become a Presbyterian minister, he finally returned to Scotland from Louisiana for seminary training in 1843 after having achieved considerable educational success as rector of an academy. He kept his history of slave ownership a secret during his seminary training, as the Free Church of Scotland strongly disapproved of slavery. Under the influence of one of his professors, Dr. Thomas Chalmers, he helped develop a program, envisioned by Chalmers as the "City of God," in the slums of Edinburgh, combining education with religion to raise poor Irish refugees from the potato famine out of their misery. His mentor provided him with introductions to many of the leading abolitionists of the day, but he was stung deeply by a public rebuke given by Frederick Douglass who, during a tour of Britain in 1845 after escaping slave catchers in the United States, spoke out against a certain unnamed candidate for the ministry in the Free Church who was a slaveholder from the South. After this he resolved to not only free his slaves but to also provide them with the education and skills to live and thrive as free persons.

Having lost his wife and son to illness and subsequently, in an ironic twist of fate, inheriting more slaves from his father-in-law, he returned to Louisiana after completing his training in Edinburgh with a vision of developing another "City of God" for freed slaves in Canada. Leaving his slaves on his plantation in Louisiana temporarily, he spent a period of time in Canada West where he served as a Presbyterian minister in Chatham, Dawn, and other communities, which gave him an excellent knowledge of the black settlements and a better understanding of their needs. When in 1847 he revealed the fact of his slave ownership to the Presbyterian synod he was fired from the ministry for the deception. Not discouraged, he put into action his plan. Without chains or the other usual accoutrements associated with slave transport, he escorted his fifteen slaves north by water and after landing in Cincinnati he emancipated them. With their consent he left them with his family in Ohio to learn basic literacy and farming skills while he worked in Canada to help establish an association named for Lord Elgin for the purpose of obtaining subscriptions to buy land in Canada West for a settlement to accommodate not only his former slaves but also other fugitives from slavery. The same synod that had fired him earlier now embraced his proposal and helped him make the project one that received broad support within Canada.

King was able to find a tract of 9,000 acres in Raleigh Township near Lake Erie for the settlement. It was a heavily forested area about fifteen miles west of Chatham. Playing on local prejudices among white Canadians against negroes, a local politician and newspaper editor in Chatham, Edwin Larwill, created many challenges for King as he pressed ahead in his attempts to purchase the land and develop the settlement. In addition to purchase of the land by the Elgin Association, the Presbyterian Church of Canada supported the establishment of a school and church as part of the settlement, known as the Buxton Mission. By 1849, he was able to bring his former slaves to the settlement, where they set a standard for hard work, religious commitment, and learning. Fifty-acre lots were provided at very reasonable rates that would be paid back over ten years with modest interest. Only blacks were to be allowed to purchase land during the first ten years of the settlement. Houses in the settlement were required to meet certain standards of size and quality. King's goal was to establish a self-governing and self-reliant community that did not depend on additional outside support beyond the initial assistance in purchasing land. It was to be a demonstration that negroes could succeed through hard work and commitment to the same extent as their white neighbors, when allowed to fully develop their gifts.

To this end, William King made a radical departure from the educational programs developed in the other refugee settlements. He was firmly convinced that colored children, if given the same exposure to a classical education, would be fully capable of becoming scholars of the highest order. He modeled the schools in the settlement on this principle and already, three years later, some of the very same white settlers who had been alarmed at the presence of so many people of African ancestry, now wanted their children to attend the Buxton School. The quality of the education being provided in the Buxton School had overcome prejudice within the white community and had peacefully brought about the full integration of children's education in the area. Not only was it not uncommon to see parents and their children learning basic skills together, but some of those children had already leapt forward academically and were studying the classics. King insisted that it would be just as important to assist in the development of black scholars and academics as it would be to train competent mechanics, farmers, and tradesmen. He refused every offer by the community to serve on the governing body of the settlement, insisting that the success of the community depended on demonstrating their own successful self-governance. However, there was no risk that he would not leave his mark on the culture of the community. Between his efforts in education, his preaching, and his strong advocacy for temperance, Buxton very much bore the stamp of his philosophy. Through his connections, major investments by black Canadian businessmen began to bear fruit in the form of a thriving sawmill, grist mill, and general store under the aegis of the Canada Mill and Mercantile Association, which in turn provided employment for many of the newly arrived refugees.

For additional details concerning the life of the Reverend William King and of the Elgin settlement see Tobin and Jones, *From Midnight to Dawn*, 115–47.

For an account of the partial disenfranchisement of free negroes in antebellum New York in 1821 by Martin Van Buren, see Christopher Malone, *Between Freedom and Bondage: Race, Party, and Voting Rights in the Antebellum North*, 26 (New York: Routledge, 2008).

For a description of William Parker and the Christiana incident and its aftermath see Tobin and Jones, *From Midnight to Dawn*, 135–46.

Tiberius Claudius Nero was the full name of the second Roman emperor for whom the slave Tib was named.

Fortune favors the bold. *Audentes fortuna juvat* Latin aphorism: http://www.merriam-webster.com/dictionary/audentes%20fortuna%20juvat.

". . . another more ancient *motto*, one recommended most heartily by a penitent murderer and adulterer: *Have mercy upon me O God . . .*" is a reference to King David and his repentance and confession recorded in Psalm 51.

Chapter Thirty-Seven

For the descriptions of the early history of Oberlin College and the many interesting ancedotes of student life that have been incorporated into this story I am indebted to Robert Samuel Fletcher, *The Gospel Truth: A History of Oberlin College from its Foundation Through the Civil War*, which can be accessed at http://www.gospeltruth.net/oberlinhistory.htm#35.

". . . promiscuous gatherings . . ." were public gatherings attended by both men and women.

The radical abolitionist John Brown's father, John Brown, Sr., served as an early trustee of Oberlin College and another family member received a bachelor's degree from the institution.

"Eye for an eye, and tooth for a tooth . . ." from Exodus 21:24.

The Preparatory Department of the early Oberlin College, as the name implies, functioned to assist students coming from diverse educational backgrounds in correcting any deficiencies in their education prior to formal matriculation in the collegiate program of the college.

Chapter Thirty-Eight

For more information about Dr. Martin Delany, Negro physician and prominent abolitionist, see Tobin and Jones, From *Midnight to Dawn*, 134, 135.

For more information regarding the historic march to Chatham, Canada West, and voting by newly enfranchised former slaves, see Tobin and Jones, From *Midnight to Dawn*, 126 and 127.

Chapter Thirty-Nine

"Natural philosophy" was an early term for what came to be known as the scientific field of physics.

I am indebted to Nat Brandt *The Town that Started the Civil War* (New York: Dell, 1990) for most of the details of the incident described in this chapter and subsequent events regarding the Oberlin-Wellington rescue.

The Lincoln-Douglas debates can be found online at http://www.nps.gov/liho/historyculture/debates.htm.

Chapter Forty

Laura Haviland was one of the leading female abolitionists of the antebellum period. On more than one occasion, she exposed herself to great personal risk in her efforts to assist fugitives from slavery. She founded the first co-educational institution in the state of Michigan—the Raisin Institute, in Adrian—that admitted persons of any race.

The following references provide background information for the events described in this chapter: Laura S. Haviland, *A Woman's Life-Work, Labors, and Experiences*. 1881. Reprint. (Miami: HardPress, 2016); Mull, *Underground Railroad in Michigan*; Horace W. Davenport, *Not Just Any Medical School: The Science, Practice, and Teaching of Medicine at the University of Michigan*, 1850–1941 (Ann Arbor: University of Michigan Press, 1999); and Wilford Byron Shaw, ed., *The University of Michigan: An Encyclopedic Survey*, Parts I–VII, from Part V (Ann Arbor: University of Michigan Press, 1951).

For Captain Lowry and his sign that portrayed the images of a male and female slave with the caption: "liberty to the fugitive captive and the oppressed over all the earth, both male and female of all colors," see Mull, *Underground Railroad in Michigan*, 94.

Hicksite Quakers—Elias Hicks and his teachings are described in Hamm, *Quakers in America*.

Dr. Alonzo Palmer's *Memorial of Alonzo Benjamin Palmer*, a memoir of his journey to Europe, is a fascinating insight into medicine in the antebellum era, as well as the character of one of the early faculty members of the University of Michigan Medical School. The memoir can be found online at https://archive.org/stream/memorialalonzoboofriegoog#page/n136/mode/2up.

A photograph of Dr. Palmer's home, which still stands on Division Street in Ann Arbor, Michigan, can be seen at http://www.aadl.org/buildings_205ndivisionst.

Chapter Forty-One

Today, shalt thou be with me in Paradise.

—Luke 23:43

For descriptions of one of the most colorful characters involved with the Underground Railroad, John Fairfield, please see Mull, *Underground Railroad in Michigan*, 129–32, and Coffin, *Reminiscences of Levi Coffin*, 428–46.

Chapter Forty-Two

The exchange between Arabella Philips and Rev. Charles Finney has been documented in Brandt, *Town that Started the Civil War*, 39.

"Every man, woman, and child in Ohio, of whatever birth, descent, parentage, complexion, or conformation, is presumed in law to be free." He went on to say that when ". . .the slave. . .crosses our boundary, he is baptized in the air of freedom; and that baptism is irrevocable" (Brandt, *Town that Started the Civil War*, 139).

"Black men have no rights which white men are bound to respect!" This is a bitter and ironic reference to Chief Justice Roger Taney's opinion in the Dred Scott case.

The Langston brothers, the other defendants in the trial of the Oberlin rescuers, and their persecutors were historical figures. The words attributed to them are their own. For an excellent and more detailed presentation of the trial of the Oberlin rescuers and the powerful speech given by Charles Mercer Langston, see Brandt, *Town that Started the Civil War*, 186–90.

Chapter Forty-Four

Dr. Moses Gunn was the first professor of surgery and anatomy at the University of Michigan Medical School. By the time of Isaac Burgess' medical school experience in the late 1850s, Dr. Gunn had a burgeoning general practice in Detroit, three hours away from Ann Arbor by train at that time, where he would travel weekly to fulfill his duties at the medical school. By this time, his friend, Dr. Corydon Ford, had assumed the duties of professor of anatomy, while he retained his professorship of surgery. For additional biographical information, see http://surgery.med.umich.edu/portal/research/mosesgunn/2018/about_moses_gunn.shtml and http://umhistory.dc.umich.edu/history/Faculty_History/G/Gunn,_Moses_.html.

One of the graduating medical students from the class of 1860 at the University of Michigan wrote his required thesis on the subject of amputations. It is available for review on microfilm at the Bentley Historical Library of the University of Michigan.

For more information about the history of hospitals in Michigan and St. Mary's hospital in Detroit, please see http://www.elderweb.com/book/appendix/1809–1930-history-hospitals-michigan, and for confirmation of Sister Mary de Sales' role as superior of St. Mary's Hospital, see *The Metropolitan Catholic Almanac and Laity's Directory for the United States, 1859*, 101, which can be accessed at https://babel.hathitrust.org/cgi/pt?id=wu.89064466717;view=1up;seq=107.

Please see the note for chapter thirty-four regarding Seymour Finney and his role in the Detroit Underground Railroad.

"Resurrectionists"—derisive nineteenth-century term for grave robbers who clandestinely acquired corpses to sell to medical schools for anatomic dissection. For more information about the challenges of obtaining anatomic "material" for medical education in nineteenth-century America, and specifically at the University of Michigan, please see Shaw, *University of Michigan*, 809, and Davenport, *Not Just Any Medical School*, 10.

Chapter Forty-Five

Regarding John Fairfield, see note for chapter forty-one.

For more information about the early telegraphic transfer of money in antebellum America and its development and application during the internal slave trade, see Calvin Schermerhorn, *Money Over Mastery, Family Over Freedom: Slavery in the Antebellum Upper South*, 179–80 (Baltimore: Johns Hopkins University Press, 2011).

Chapter Forty-Six

The Louisville and Portland Canal was created to allow shipping traffic to bypass the falls of the Ohio River and has been in operation since 1830. For more information about the canal, please see https://familysearch.org/learn/wiki/en/ Louisville_and_Portland_Canal.

Chapter Forty-Eight

The fate of Lot's wife no longer seemed a mere fable to him there. Reference to Genesis 19:26 in which Lot and his family, who were fleeing the destruction of Sodom, were instructed to not look back. Lot's wife disobeyed and was turned into a pillar of salt.

For the imagery of Horton's dream, see note for chapter thirty. In Dante's *Divine Comedy*, purgatory is described as a great mountain which penitent souls slowly ascend toward paradise. Dante's guide to paradise was Beatrice.

Occasional victims of gunshot wounds to the upper abdomen have survived without major operative intervention as local tissues wall off the foreign body (i.e., bullet and fragments of clothing driven into the wound) with a powerful inflammatory response. The inflammatory process, including pus that fills the associated abscess cavity may "necessitate" or migrate toward the surface of the skin or also to an adjacent hollow organ (in Horton Newby's case the stomach) and drain spontaneously, clearing the infection and inflammation, allowing eventual healing to occur.